Pulling him up towards her, Hallie was momentarily reminded of the huge difference in their heights – by the time she could reach down to undo his jeans, she was nuzzling his chest, running her tongue over his sweat-slicked ribs, each one standing out under his skin like a railway sleeper under moss. Impatient now, she scrabbled at the buttons at his fly, tugging off his trouser legs – remembering to pull in her stomach as she did so, conscious that he could now see her entire nakedness in the unflattering contortions necessary to get his trousers and socks off. Above her, he was helping her now, yanking down his boxers with equal haste, feet scrambling to kick them off, arms pulling her back up to kiss her.

Again, the difference in their heights meant that they still weren't joined so Hallie went to get a sneak preview with her hand. Trailing her fingers down his heaving chest, she teased them round his belly button until he gasped and pushed her hand down hard. Smiling against his lips, Hallie murmured indistinctly, 'Patience, sweetie, patience.'

Her hand slid down further, further still until—

Hallie froze. Now this couldn't be right.

By the same author

Out of My Head

About the author

Born in Yorkshire in 1968, Susannah Jowitt has worked at the House of Commons as a researcher and spent eighteen months as a political lobbyist, during which her natural idealism and enthusiasm for higher causes were firmly quashed in the bud. She now writes full-time. Her travel-writing and features appear regularly in newspapers including *The Times, Daily Mail* and *Evening Standard.* Her first novel, *Out of My Head* was published by Hodder and Stoughton in 1996.

In the Red

Susannah Jowitt

CORONET BOOKS
Hodder and Stoughton

Copyright © 1998 by Susannah Jowitt

The right of Susannah Jowitt to be identified as the Author of
the Work has been asserted by her in accordance with the
Copyright, Designs and Patents Act 1988.

First published in Great Britain in 1998 by Hodder and Stoughton
A Division of Hodder Headline PLC
First published in paperback in 1998 by Hodder and Stoughton
A Coronet Paperback

10 9 8 7 6 5 4 3 2 1

A CIP catalogue record for this title is available
from the British Library

ISBN 0 340 68057 1

Printed and bound in Great Britain by
Mackays of Chatham PLC, Chatham, Kent

Hodder and Stoughton
A division of Hodder Headline PLC
338 Euston Road
London NW1 3BH

For all the angels who inspired me –
and for the demons that I'm exorcising here

Acknowledgements

To Tilly Sampson and Orla Doherty for providing both characteristic inspiration and constant support; to Daisy Sampson of *The House Magazine* for more of the same and for her political insights; to Dr Keith Hampson, formerly MP for Leeds North West, who employed me, thought I was funny and set me on the road to writing in the first place; to Rory Pilkington, Alex and Mary Creswell, for providing artistic retreats; to Jules, patient flatmate; to the Big Guy for arranging the worst weather on record so that I could meet my deadline instead of getting a suntan; to Ewan Thomson, for being madder than I ever could be and for staving off any despair with the *Reservoir Dogs* mantra; to Doug Sager for being both e-mail buddy par excellence and on-line editor; to my real editor, Kate Lyall Grant; to Victoria Scott, with regret that she has given up agenting; to Sally Shalam of the *Evening Standard*, Cathy Wood of the *Daily Mail* and now Cath Urquhart of *The Times* for keeping me off the street and on those planes travel-writing – and most of all, to my family, for keeping well out of the firing line.

PART ONE

1

Was she never going to leave America? Cass chewed her nails and prepared to do battle.

But – 'What is the problem here?' demanded Carter quietly. 'You're telling me you went ahead and merged two planes without even thinking that some people might just be left behind?'

'Sir, I am so sorry, but if Miss Herbert hadn't have been so late—' ventured the check-in woman nervously.

That did it for Cass. Before Carter had turned up and breezed in, this same trembling bint had been more like the Great Wall of China, inexorably blocking Cass's path back home. Now, with one lousy intervention from Carter, the bricks were crumbling. Even at JFK Airport, sexism was alive and batting its eyelashes. Cass was not a damsel in distress and had no intention of letting any man be her knight in shining armour, especially not the man she was trying to get away from.

'Carter!' she said bluntly. 'Butt out. I can handle this.' She turned back to the bell-hop dressed airline woman. 'I *am* getting on that plane,' she squinted at her nametag, 'Gabby. So why don't you just take the path of least resistance, check my luggage in, give me my ticket and then I'll go fight with the people at the boarding gate. That way, you get rid of me now and I become someone else's problem. How about that?'

Gabby wavered some more, looking from the mulish face of

the tall English girl, to the obvious money, power and charm of the older American man with her. The latter decided her.

'OK, go. Gate 57. Your best hope is to try for an upgrade because Economy is busting out at the seams, and it's more likely you'll get a no-show in Business or First Class.'

'Thank you.' Cass turned round triumphantly to Carter. 'Hah! The Herbert Harrier flies again!'

Carter looked sorrowful and, suddenly, old. 'Babe, I don't want you to go. Why are you doing this? This country has been your home for five years. You can finish your goddamn dissertation where you started it – right here in New York – or you know I can swing you any job in Washington. So why? How am I going to cope with this whole mess?' He tried to take her hand in his, but she bent to pick up her hand luggage instead. 'You're breaking my heart here.'

'If you would lay off the emotional blackmail for one cotton-pickin' minute, you'd realise that all my answers lie in what you've just said.' It was Cass at her most mercilessly analytical – in her mind, she was already long gone on the plane. 'This is all way too complicated. I can't do any work amongst all this mess – and it isn't even my mess – she's your wife, Carter, and I'm not the one who should be trying to get her back on track. Getting involved with you was absolutely not part of my gameplan – this is just my way of gathering up the reins again.'

Cass knew she was resorting to cliché but it always seemed an inescapable part of Breaking Up Conversations. 'Dammit, I didn't want to make a speech – and I'm bored of repeating myself.'

'You know, it's an omen, you not being able to get on this plane,' Carter smiled, his eyes twinkling, 'you're obviously not meant to go – why fly in the face of Destiny?'

'As it were,' they said together, and grinned complicitly. Inside, Cass felt the first dangerous weakenings. Would she ever find anyone again who could push her buttons like Carter could? Someone unmarried, someone without the full 64-piece set of Louis Vuitton emotional baggage, someone young enough to laugh at *Friends* – pick from the list above for a start, warned a firm little voice.

'Stay, little Cass – we'll sort something out, I promise.' Carter took off his kid leather glove to stroke her hair away from her face.

'Bollocks,' said Cass brutally. 'Don't you dare say such meaningless crap. And anyway, have I ever said I wanted to sort anything out? Don't decide things for me, you arrogant shitbag.'

It was water off a duck's back. 'Honey – shitbag?' he raised an eyebrow. 'Another charming piece of slang picked up from those lowlifes you insist on hobnobbing with? High-flying academics and politicians, beware, Cass Herbert *is* the new Dr Johnson.'

Cass just felt tired. 'Oh, try this word for size, Carter,' she started walking towards Departures. 'Goodbye.'

'I won't believe you've left until I see you get on that plane myself, so I'm coming with you to the gate,' retorted a dogged Carter.

'Christ alive. Fine. Keep up.' And she speeded up into the long, swinging stride that had propelled her round Manhattan for the last five years.

Hallie peeked a look at the unfamiliar alarm clock. Shit. Only five o'clock. Well, that was her sleep ration – from now on it was just a freewheel down the Insomnia Highway. No, she couldn't face that. Time to go. Trouble was – how? She was trapped on the wall side of the bed, in the spoon position, with his arm clamped uncompromisingly around her shoulders . . . now was not the moment to start regretting what she'd done. Again.

When she'd come over here last night, she'd promised that, for once, she wouldn't end up in bed. She was going to prove to herself that she too could hold out, could chatter away without getting those paralysing flashes of stomach-lurching lust that reddened her cheeks, shortened her breath, dilated her eyes and as good as put a sign above her head saying, 'Take Me Now'. Just a friendly fumble at the most, to show that she was a woman of the world.

She didn't want to be a girl who *could* say no – how dull – but she hankered to be a girl who didn't have to say yes every time. The trouble was, as far as she could see, that sex was like eating

Pringles – once you pop, you just can't stop. Well, as soon as he had popped her new front-loading bra she just couldn't stop – it was as simple as that.

That was why she was so glad that Cass was returning to the fold. Many had been the time they had compared sex drives and, based on their straw poll of two, had concluded firmly that women definitely had a higher sex drive than men. From there it was a short, logical leap to the principle that women could not be sluts, they were just closer to satisfying their natural, godgiven urges than the sad losers who *didn't* sleep with people on first dates. They'd gleefully presented their findings to Nina, whose noncommittal reaction reminded Hallie and Cass that they had surprisingly little idea about her own natural urges. But then again Nina had been going out with Jerry since the dawn of time – so asking her about first night tactics would probably have to involve some sort of re-birthing hypnosis.

Especially now that Nina and Jerry had got married, Hallie felt that their magic circle of three – forged when they were ten and at primary school – had been compromised when it came to talking about their lovelives. Nina was married and therefore beyond lovelife gossip, and, since her boyfriend John's death the previous October, Cass herself had been rather an unknown quantity to her friends. Hallie and Nina knew that Cass and John had split up before the accident but on whose side, involving what emotional fallout – was anyone's guess.

The last time they had all seen each other had been on New Year's Eve, five months ago, when Hallie and Cass had been to stay with the newly married couple at their cottage in Wiltshire. Hallie, Jerry and Nina had tacitly steered clear of the whole subject of John's death – Hallie had been too shell-shocked about her own break-up with Reuben to broach the subject with her usual blithe inquisitiveness. But from the sound of it, Cass's return from America had more than a little to do with her wish to get away from anything to do with John.

And Hallie knew just how to distract her. They were going to hit the town and hit on some men. Floating onto the singles' parade hadn't been much fun so far – on her own – but she and Cass had always been a dynamite combination and Hallie, for one, knew that she was going to enjoy blowing a few potential Mr Rights. Or even just Mr Meanwhiles.

Meanwhile, this didn't change the fact that she was still pinioned underneath his arm, his duvet and his morning breath – all of which were hot and noisome. Holding her breath, she gently lifted both arm and duvet and wriggled snakelike down the bed. Once out, she started the usual braille-like Pelmanism of which of her clothes were scattered where. Then she started to get dressed, hopping as silently as possible as she tried to get each foot into the corresponding tights leg.

'Whatcher doing?' came a grumbling voice from the bed. 'Another midnight flit?'

Curses. Why did men always wake up when she was just at the bent-over, knickers up crack, finger-in-socket post-coital hairstyle, spare tyres on full Michelin display stage? Life was so unfair. '*I have many miles to go before I sleep,*' she quipped weakly. 'Just call me Paul Revere.'

'And just call me Rip van Winkle, I'm afraid—' he yawned noisily. 'You don't mind if I don't see you to the door like a true gent? I'm on call for the rest of the weekend.'

Little did he know that all Hallie wanted to do was scarper the scene of the crime, leaving as little forensic evidence behind as possible. That way, when she got home to her cosy Islington flat and snuggled into her own bed, she could wake at noon, and imagine that she'd never left it, that the whole night before had been nothing more than a consequence-free dirty dream. Then she could meet Cass off the plane with a clear conscience and an unsullied vigour for the fun and games she had in store for the two of them over the weekend.

Such are the justifications of the self-administered, orally given, Morning After Preach.

'No problemmo. See ya,' she added, with her best nonchalance, savagely tamping down the sudden urge to leap straight back into bed and curl up in his arms like a puppy. Grow up, Hallie, and get home, she tutted to herself.

'Mmmnnngh,' was his parting serenade.

*   *   *

There it was – her nirvana, her Holy Grail, her stairway to heaven – the spiral staircase to First Class. Cass had tired eyes from using them to their best pleading advantage, an aching hand from being clutched by a persistent Carter, and a stain on her jeans where she'd jerked away from him before remembering that she had a cup of coffee in her other hand. She wasn't feeling first class, but, after a battle royal, she had the boarding pass to get her there. Halfway up the stairs, Cass finally relaxed. She'd made it.

'Excuse me – I'm afraid you can't go up there.' The voice below her was polite but firm.

Cass's matched it. 'Oh yes, I can. Look—' she thrust the boarding card into the flight attendant's face. 'Seat 3A. Clear as a bell.'

The flight attendant looked shifty and supplemented her voice with a polite but firm hand on Cass's elbow. 'Could you please come with me?'

In her total amazement, Cass found herself following as meekly as a lamb.

Just outside the plane, the attendant finally let go of Cass. 'I am so sorry, Miss Herbert, but you have been misinformed. Seat 3A doesn't exist on this model of airplane – that's where the emergency exit from First Class is situated.'

'Wh-what?' breathed Cass, feeling a red mist come down over her eyes (dimly conscious of Carter still waiting at the gate – 'I'm not going till this baby leaves the ground, honey!'). 'You have got to be kidding me!'

'I'm afraid not. If you would like to return to the gate, I am sure that the attendants there will be able to sort you out.'

It was the strangest sensation but Cass could swear that she actually had smoke coming out of her ears. 'No fucking way. Now you listen to me – I was given a boarding pass for this plane – I don't care whether it's in First Class or the fucking hold, but I am getting on this plane.'

Why, oh why didn't she possess Hallie's ability to burst into tears at will? Then she had a brainwave.

'What you simpletons don't realise is that it is a matter of national fucking importance that I get back to England on this flight – I am about to start working for a British Member of Parliament, who is forming a new Department under the new Government on the basis of these papers,' – she brandished her tatty black rucksack at them, praying that her M&Ms and new sci-fi novel wouldn't fall out – 'which I have to get to him. So put me on this bloody plane, or there'll be, um, Big Trouble!'

One of the cabin crew who had come to his colleague's assistance, looked askance at Cass and planted himself firmly in front of the plane door. 'Don't threaten us, ma'am, you'll find you won't get very far like that.'

While Cass jumped up and down, screamed some more and did everything short of bounce off the walls of the jetway, she was dimly aware of the steward whispering things down a wall telephone and of a smartly-dressed, middle-aged man, cashmere overcoat and briefcase looped over his arm, coming down to the door of the plane, handing over his boarding pass to another stewardess and saying 'Is 3A on the port or starboard side? I'd like to see Manhattan as we leave.'

Cass broke off from her tantrum and stared at her usurper – then looked down at herself – stained jeans, biker boots and an old shrunken T-shirt. When was she going to learn about power-dressing? A fine consultant she was going to be if she couldn't even make the grade sartorially for First Class, never mind financially.

Suddenly, a small flood of people came rushing off the plane – waving their boarding passes in 'Pick me!' gestures and tripping over their hand luggage in their eagerness to speak to the steward who had been on the phone. Calmly, he lifted one boarding pass at random and gave it to Cass, saying, 'I suggest you join your seat now, ma'am.'

Now completely bemused, Cass did as he said, not believing her luck as she stowed her rucksack away, sat down and stared out of the window.

'Why didn't you take their offer?'

'Excuse me?'

The man sitting next to her gave her a speculative look and repeated his question. 'I'm guessing you are "the obstreperous passenger" they were talking about over the tannoy, that was demanding to be let on the plane?'

'Well, yes, but—'

'A night at the Intercontinental, the Broadway show of your choice, Business Class return tomorrow and four hundred quid in airline vouchers – now that doesn't sound half bad to me.'

'What?!' Hence the flood of people, Cass thought bitterly, realising she'd been suckered on a grand scale. Mind you, it would only have prolonged the agony with Carter. 'Well, you know, things not to do, people to avoid, places to miss. All that.'

'You daft eejit.' His gaze turned warmer as he took in the cloud of dark brunette locks, the skin as pale and smooth as milk, the wide, almost cat-like greygreen eyes with their heavy eyebrows, the determined chin and the long, long legs folded awkwardly into the small seat. 'Still, your loss is my gain. The bloke sitting here before was a right ugly bugger. I couldn't have spent the next eight hours chatting him up, could I now?' Devlin, my boy, you have struck gold here, he rejoiced inwardly. She's a cracker.

Cass looked back at him properly for the first time and her heart sank. He was her age and looked her height, if not taller; dirty blond hair framed a rogue's face in which bright blue eyes sparkled away, and a widelipped smile stretched from ear to ear. Cass, my girl, you have struck out here, she sighed inwardly. He's gorgeous. And knows it. And is going to pester you for the rest of the flight.

Was she ever going to get away from horny men?

'Well, here goes,' he smiled, and stuck out a graceful hand with nails as badly chewed as Cass's. 'Devlin Gray – and knock me down if I'm not happy to meet you.'

'Gladly,' said Cass, tight-lipped, ostentatiously getting out her job offer from Alun Blythe, her lifeline pulling her away from Carter. Only eight hours until her new life began. A new life without pushy guys like the poncey-named Devlin Gray.

Nina came awake to the sensation of having her toes licked. Funny how she didn't even imagine that it could be Jerry any more, even in the mists of recent sleep. 'Babaji, you kinky hound,' she murmured, 'lay off,' and she tucked her feet more firmly underneath her. 'No! Piss off!' as he transferred his attentions to her nose, the only part of her that was now sticking out of the duvet.

Disgruntled to have such an unappreciative audience, the little dog jumped off the bed as noisily as possible and grumbled his way downstairs. But he needed feeding, so she had to get up. When Jerry had given her the irresistible cross between a miniature poodle and a dachshund for her birthday present, had either of them imagined how completely he would take over both their lives? Reluctantly, Nina continued surfacing.

A whole weekend with Jerry. Now this was what being married was all about. None of those boy-girl shenanigans that Hallie whinged about – not knowing how long you should stay if you were at their place, not knowing how soon you could get rid of them if you had planned a Saturday lying in front of a black and white movie, with Galaxy and Cool Blue Doritos Emergency Rations on hand. Not that that had ever been a problem with her and Jerry. On the rare weekends when he wasn't running around issuing meaningless orders to his 'lads', he could slob out with the best of them. Before they got all married and respectable, sex had more often than not involved sweaty crumbs and carpet fluff, with Bette Davis's clipped tones admonishing them from the screen behind. Nina lifted the duvet now to peer at her navel – slightly missing the decadent detritus that used to assemble there – then shut it quickly before the cold whistled in. Now, of course, sex in front of the TV would be more likely to involve hot water bottles and athletic manoeuvres to avoid the bare spots in the rug onto the stone flags beneath.

Poking out one foot, Nina flicked on the blower with her toe, making it almost warm enough for her to get out and put some more layers on, if she did it at speed. How could it still be so cold in May? It couldn't be just her Indian blood that was freezing in her very veins. The cottage had never seemed this arctic when Jerry threw it open for weekend parties, but that was before he left the Army and had to worry about things like heating bills. Maybe it was just being here day in, day out that was seeping into Nina's bones? In more ways than one.

Nina had longed for Jerry to leave the Army for so long, despising all the plummy bonhomie, lingo and insularity of regimental life with all the superiority of the fast-living, town-hitting, body-abusing media chick she used to be. The fact that Jerry himself stayed so irresistible throughout confirmed to Nina that he was the man for her, worth leaving London for, and worth giving up her fledgling travel-writing career for. Not that she'd given up, she reminded herself, it was just that now she was out of the swing of things, being a freelancer was going to take a leetle more application. Not a problem.

The trouble was, now that Jerry *had* left the Army, the usual adjustment to married life was starker for them both. Having snatched what moments together they could, they now spent twenty-four hours a day together, warts and all. Weirdly, it was the little things that grated: discovering that he loved Australian soaps while she despised them; that she had to have music on while she was working, while he could just about cope with the odd Gregorian chant cooing at volume two; that he spoke at double his normal speaking volume when he was on the telephone, while she, used to the gymnastic ears of newsrooms, hissed and giggled conspiratorially into the receiver. All part of the rich tapestry of married life, she told herself now, as she walked into the sitting room and suppressed a sigh at the sight of Jerry hunched in front of his new computer. So much for a cosy Saturday together.

'Morning. I'm just getting a cuppa before going back to bed to watch *Live and Kicking*. It's the only warm place I can find – do you want to join me?'

Jerry flicked the mouse around, then stretched. 'Nah, I'm just taking advantage of cheap phoning time to poke around the Site a bit.'

'Wicked!' said Nina. 'So this is a good time for you to show me round the Internet. The *Standard*'s system was so antiquated that only about three people there had machines capable of surfing. Oh go on!' as Jerry's head swivelled frowningly towards her, 'I don't even know the password – how am I supposed to navigate my own way through, if I fall at the first hurdle?'

'OK, the Twelve Labours of Hercules – coming right up. You just park your little tushie down here and we'll start at the beginning . . .'

Five minutes later, Nina's fingers were twitching on the

mouse, willing it into an elephant to stamp on her husband's big, fat head.

'Stop!' she said suddenly. 'Enough. I'm not a complete moron, you know, despite all evidence to the contrary, you don't have to treat me like a fucking child.'

'A child would wipe the floor with both of us when it came to computers,' said Jerry imperturbably.

'Oh!' Nina clenched her fists. Sadly, one of them was still on the mouse, leading her to click unwisely and none too well.

'You dipstick!' Jerry swore and dived for the mouse. 'You've downloaded that picture – which will take hours – quick, give me the mouse!'

'Bugger off! I can see CANCEL as well as anyone. Jerry! For Christ's sake!' Nina was unceremoniously turfed out of her chair while Jerry took over.

'There! Saved the day.'

'Oh, beat your chest and call me Jane, why don't you, you big lug,' Nina grumbled.

'It's not a toy, you know, my little Nin-compoop.' Call her humourless, but she really hated this new nickname he had coined. 'So please don't mess around with it. I am trying to set up a business on it, remember.'

This was one of those times when Nina had to remind herself very firmly that both she and Jerry were as over-educated and arrogant as each other and that he often had to put up with worse from her than a little condescension.

'Come on, Babaji, let's leave He-Man here clashing with his Cyber-Titans. Zoe Ball needs us.'

'No, come on, calm down – I'll make us both a cup of tea.' Jerry padded into the tiny kitchen, shirt-tails flapping loose over his jeans. How he could wear only a shirt, when Nina was bundled in four layers of wool, was beyond her.

Only slightly mollified, Nina sat down at the console and started flipping back through previous screens, hoping to see Jerry's precious site, where he was setting up a virtual shopping mall for prescription drugs that could be bought over the counter in America, and therefore, effectively, on the Net. Something like that, anyway. Suddenly she stopped, and frowned.

'CHATLINE 36-26-36?' she read out loud. 'What the – this is unreal!'

> houston hotlips@fkg.com: It may be early in the morning for you freezing your butt off over there in England, but here in Texas it's a hot and sweaty night and I'm feeling as horny as a rattler's ass. So c'mon, BIG1, tell me how you'd cool me down. Ice cubes? Or something a little kinkier?

Over there in England? Comprehension was dawning, and she read on with a shiver of growing distaste to see what BIG1's reply was.

> big1@jkenterprises: well, Houston Hotlips, I was always taught that the air is cooler nearer the ground so let's get horizontal – taking our clothes off will help as well – and get some heat-relieving sweat going. Plus, seeing what I have to offer you will shock you down a few degrees . . . then again, who *wants* to cool down? There are bits of you that I want to stroke that should be *hot*hot*hot*–

Nina couldn't read any more of this turgid rubbish. 'Jerry!' she called abruptly, as he came back in with two cups of tea. 'What the fuck is going on, Jerry?' She gestured at the screen. 'Or should I call you BIG1?'

There goes the tea, was her next thought.

2

Hallie should have known that with Cass, she was never going to get your average joyful reunion of lifelong friends. She was expecting the usual Cass, with her clouds of dark hair, floaty skirts and abstracted expression, to drift through from Customs. What she got was a scowling stranger, all tight T-shirt and attitude, who walked up to Hallie, hissing,

'Quick! Throw your arms round me and pretend you're totally excited to see me!'

Obediently, Hallie gave her a huge hug. 'Of course I'm excited, you moron. Do you think I would get up on a Saturday morning to meet just any old lifelong friend?'

'Shut up and kiss me.'

'Cass, have you been over-doing the duty-free?' Hallie leant back in Cass's clutching embrace, eyebrows raised. 'Muah, muah, muah, muah. There! Will that do you?'

Cass's eyes darted over Hallie's shoulder, and finally she relaxed. 'Oh, thank God he's gone. Hi, honeychile.' And this time, she gave Hallie a proper hug.

Hallie looked round at where Cass had glanced, just in time to catch the eye of a devastatingly good-looking man as he turned round one last time before the exit. He tipped an imaginary that in her direction, gave her a rueful smile then disappeared through the sliding doors into the outside air.

'Wow! Who was that? Can I have him? And what was that

performance in aid of?' Hallie started to push Cass's trolley in the direction of the car park.

'He's just this total pest of a guy I was sitting next to on the flight, who wouldn't get the message that I wasn't remotely interested in him, so eventually I told him that I was a lesbian and that my girlfriend was meeting me at the airport.'

'Cass!'

Cass scowled again. 'I know, I know. Anyway, he still didn't believe me. Said something outrageously Irish, like he knew what lesbians smelt like.'

'Irish, huh? Gorgeous and Irish. Oh yes, I would have definitely pretended that I was a lesbian.' Hallie rolled her eyes. 'Although the new dressing style is a touch designer dyke – if you had the short hair as well, perhaps you could have persuaded me.'

'Who said I was pretending?' Cass tossed over her shoulder, striding into the car park. 'Give me a woman over a man any day – so much less complicated.'

'Tell me something I don't know,' sighed Hallie, fumbling in her handbag for her keys. Then she stopped and looked nervously at her friend. 'You are joking, aren't you? You're not . . . well . . . really . . .'

'Christ, Hallie, gullible as ever – would it be so bad if I were?' Cass looked aghast at Hallie as she stopped beside her car. 'What the hell is this? Not a company car?'

'Welcome back to the real world, Cass Herbert, this is indeed my new company car,' Hallie said, unlocking it with one bleep from her keyring.

'You're shitting me! What is it?'

'A Seat Cordoba – we handle the Seat account. Why? Is being interested in cars part of the dyke image?' added Hallie with a touch of acid.

'Whoa there, Ms Sharp, back in the knife drawer. Hey, I'm just looking at the whole Hallie package,' Cass looked her over appraisingly. 'Very grown-up, I must say, company car, cellular phone, neat little slacks suit even on a Saturday. Major groom-up, I'm thinking.'

Hallie felt an unusual stab of irritation, but smiled determinedly as she got into the driving seat, automatically flicking on the Routemaster and programming the CD player. 'It's called getting a decent job, sweetie, with halfway decent pay. Besides, you know perfectly well that I just don't look good in jeans and a sloppy T-shirt – so it's vanity, nothing more complicated. Comes to us all, you know.'

Cass looked thoughtfully down at her own frayed 501s. 'Whatever you say – it's still frighteningly mature.'

There was a small pause.

'So,' Hallie rushed to fill the gap. 'Where to, guv?' Before Cass had a chance to answer, she bulldozered on. 'I thought a quick run back to Trudie's to dump your luggage and have a cuppa, then round to my place so that I can show it off, then we can get ready for tonight.'

Cass gave her a weary stare. 'Tonight?'

'Dum, dam, dum, dam, dum, dam,' Hallie gave up on the *Jaws* theme. 'Sharking. You and me, kid. Tonight. Caspers. Raving is the only way to beat jet-lag – you know it makes sense – and what better way than by distracting yourself with a couple of luscious lambs to our slaughter?'

'Oh, Hallie,' wailed Cass. 'Don't you get it? I'm not into men at the moment – I'm too busy, I'm too fucked-up and I've got better things to think about. Anyway, I like being on my own. Unlike you, I don't want a relationship. Strange but true. Alert the media. Didn't I explain all this when I was over here at New Year? I guess you were too busy mooning over whatshisname to listen. *Just Say No to Men*, that's my motto. Got it?'

Hallie, concentrating on getting onto the M4, just gave her a wounded, why-pick-on-me? look. It was a Hallie special. Was it her imagination or had Cass – always forthright – got even bolshier since she'd last seen her? So much for a hunting partner on the singles' scene. Cass would probably not stop at chasing a man, she'd go the whole hog and savage him to death as well. Perhaps that evening's entertainment wasn't such a good idea. That made two bad ideas, two nights running. Inadvertently, memories of the night before flared up like a livid mosquito bite.

Cass sighed, and changed the subject. 'Talking of New Year, how's Nina? I feel kinda guilty that I haven't spoken to her much since we went down to stay with her. I can hardly believe it's been nearly six months since our little gathering at New Year.'

'Nina's still buried in domestic rural bliss, as far as I know. We haven't talked much either, actually, except when she rang to ask me to send her some pages of PiMS – one of the media directories,' she added in response to Cass's questioning look, 'so it looks like she's trying to get back on track with the journalism. About time, if you ask me. But overall, she sounded boringly content, full of stories about Babaji's latest learning-how-to-lift-a-leg exploits.'

'Yeah, well, that's marriage for you – the mental equivalent of *Slimfast* – "get married and just watch those braincells melt away". How can we stand by and let our two best friends lobotomise each other like this?'

'Still on that rant, then?' sighed Hallie. 'Ever thought they might be happy? I know in your present frame of mind, it's hard to imagine, but one day you'll be happily married and you'll eat your words.'

'No way, José,' said Cass violently. 'I'll eat my way through an Ascot selection of hats before I consign myself to married braindeath. Euthanasia was still illegal, last time I looked. I know it's your stated intention to extort a marriage proposal out of one of the living dead before the year is out, but I'm not going to let my one remaining friend consign herself to an early grave that easily.'

'OK, OK, I get the message.' Was there going to be any safe conversational topic? wondered Hallie.

'Mind you, at least Nina's got the best of a bad lot – if I was going to get comatose with anyone, I would choose Jerry,' Cass mused, still on the same track. 'He may be a tiny bit pompous sometimes but he just about gives me faith in the male sex – unlike Devlin bloody Gray.'

'Devlin Gray? Is that the name of Mr Irish back there?'

'Yeah, the schmuck from the plane, with all his fancy blarney and wild protestations.'

'You had wild protestations after only a few hours? And from a bloke who's a deadringer for that *Babybird* lead singer?'

Why does that always have to happen to Cass? Hallie wailed inwardly, not caring that she sounded like a spoilt child even to herself. Why not me? It's just not bloody fair. Sometimes I hate her.

'Yeah, I can't stand that Big Mac-style sincerity – served up instantly but just leaves you with a bad taste in your mouth later. Jerry, you see, wouldn't know sweet-talking if it slapped him in the face with an oily glove.' Cass laughed a little bitterly. 'Why did Nina have to get the only genuine man around?'

At that moment, Nina would gladly have given her man up, genuine or not. The worst thing was that she didn't know what to be angriest about – the fact that her husband apparently saw nothing wrong with cruising for sextalk on the Internet – or that he did it so badly. Years of sweating over a hot sub-editor's desk had given Nina a hatred for ugly language, blighted further by carelessly scattered punctuation and hideous media-speak mutations. Granted, she was often in danger of being over-pedantic about this, but – really – 'BIG1'?

'Nina, sweetheart,' wheedled Jerry, fair hair flopping over his forehead in that way that always went some way to melting her defences, 'how many times do I have to tell you, I was just doing some research – seeing how involved people can get on the Web, how much their usual inhibitions can be lowered – to see how far we can go with our On-Web advertising.'

'Research?' Nina blustered. 'That's like the undercover cop explaining that he really needed to get stoned, beat someone up and sleep with that prostitute, all in the name of research.'

'Easy, treasure,' Jerry still tried to look repentant, but a smile was creeping in, 'not quite the same. After all, I only tried to sleep with the prostitute, and even then only virtually – with no drugs or violence involved – and as you can see from my poor technique I was hardly on the road to a thousand orgasms with Houston Hotlips.'

Against her will, Nina felt the chuckles bubbling up. 'Oh Jez, how could you choose Houston Hotlips? Have you no taste at all? Surely there was a nice Chatanooga Choo-Choo to get steamy with? And yes, your technique was fucking terrible – try those lines on me, buster, and you're dead meat. Call me old-fashioned, but I prefer more direct methods of communication.'

'Like this?' Jerry pulled her towards him and leant her over into an exaggerated polka dip, then kissed her soundly. 'That direct enough for you?'

Nina was too glad he had kissed her to do more than grimace at the sudden pain in her back. 'It's a start,' she managed before he kissed her again, this time pulling her down onto the sitting-room sofa and dislodging a yelping Babaji.

'Sorry, sweetheart,' gasped Nina.

'Hey, don't apologise—'

'Not you, you berk. Babaji.' Nina collapsed onto him in giggles, planting kisses into his neck, hands going greedily under his shirt, stomach contracting in the pleasurable anticipation of at last making love.

The telephone rang.

'Fuck a duck,' grumbled Jerry, 'I'll get it.'

He stood up, leaving Nina stranded and unkempt, wishing that she could just yell at him to let the answering machine pick it up.

'Hello? No, I'll just get her,' he waved the receiver at her. 'It's for you.'

'No kidding, Einstein,' Nina heaved herself up, pulling her cardigan back around her. 'Hello?'

'What is *with* Jerry? Grumpy or what – he wouldn't even stop to say hi—'

'Who is this?' interrupted Nina bad-temperedly.

'Jeez, you're just as bad! Guess, you harridan!'

'Look, I haven't got time for—'

'Nina, it's Cass, you moron. Hello? Remember me? Bridesmaid? Best friend? Any bells yet?'

'Cass!' gasped Nina. 'Shit! Sorry! Shit – you flew in today, didn't you? We completely forgot!' She pulled an agonised face at Jerry.

'Thanks a whole lot. Well, you can make amends by coming up here tonight. Hallie seems hell-bent on dragging me to some dumb-sounding singles' club, and the only way it's going to be fun is if all three of us go.'

'Cass – I'm not single, in case you hadn't noticed.'

'Dur – no, really? Anyway, single-schmingle – I have about as much interest in scoring as you do, Mrs Kellman – I just thought it would be neat to have a girly night out, just like old times. You can leave old Jezza alone for just one night, can't you? Tell him I'll give him a Cass-special massage the next time I see him, in recompense. C'mon now, let's party.' Cass was beginning to sound pissed-off.

Nina looked at Jerry now lying in front of the fireplace, snuffling into Babaji's fur. She hated this pull on her loyalties. Once, she would have dropped everything to spice girl it up with Cass and Hallie. But if she went now, she could wave goodbye to her cosy weekend with her husband. Hmmm.

'Look, Cass, welcome home. I can't wait to see you, but I can't just drop everything and come up to London at a moment's notice. Jerry needs the car early tomorrow and, you know—'

'Fine,' Cass's voice was cold, 'whenever. Love to Jerry.'

The line went dead.

'Bugger it,' Nina said into it, 'she's hardly back in the country and she's hacked off with me.'

Jerry stretched and looked at his watch. 'I hope you weren't turning anything down on my account, Nin, because I should probably get back to the Net. Cheap phone times, remember? Call me when lunch is ready, won't you? Tell you what, we can probably let this little varmint run rampage here for half an hour tonight and slip into the Nag and Stag for a quick half. Something to look forward to, eh?'

Nina could have throttled him. Instead, she shrugged and opened the paper she once wrote for. But this just reminded her of what her life used to be, before going to the pub to hurl back a glass of sour beer was something to look forward to. She threw it to one side, and gazed wistfully at the phone. Please ring back, she prayed. Persuade me.

Cass looked down at the receiver in disbelief, then stared at Hallie. 'See?' she challenged. 'I told you – marriage pickles the brain! She's blown us off!'

Hallie took the receiver from her, and put it down. 'Thought she might. You have just got to lose these Americanisms, sweetie. Look, we'll leave her to mull it over and try her again later when she's had time to think about it. You know Nina, never one to take a decision lightly.'

'Good idea. She'll come up. You'll see. And I agree with Hallie,' said Trudie amicably, tucking into a cheese toastie. 'Those are terrible phrases you're coming out with, darling. Now come on, aren't either of you going to eat something?'

Cass glared at her grandmother. 'Trudie, how I speak is my goddamn business and no, thank you, nothing for me.'

'God, don't tempt me, Trudie,' Hallie crossed two fingers to ward her off. 'Unless it's red meat or oranges, I'm not allowed it.'

'Not another crazy diet?'

''Fraid so. I've lost half a stone in a week, so at least it's working.'

Cass looked glum. 'Oh, great night we're going to have: I'm sleep-starved and you're sex-starved *and* food-starved.'

In the face of Cass's unremitting bad temper, Hallie couldn't resist it. 'Not exactly sex-starved, actually.'

'Really?' Trudie's ears pricked up at potential gossip. 'New man, Hallie?'

'New, old, second-hand, take your pick,' Hallie boasted. Anything was better than the bald truth. 'Admittedly, Sean wasn't long for this world, but at least I'm getting my oats.'

'Is oat-getting so important, then?' commented Trudie shrewdly.

'Hang on one cotton-pickin' minute,' interrupted Cass. 'Back up! Back up! Who's Sean?'

'Forget him,' dismissed Hallie, 'Sean was someone I was going out with for about two seconds flat. As per usual, it was going absolutely brilliantly when suddenly he dumped me.'

'Oh Hal, what are we going to do with you?' Cass's tone was sorrowful.

'Me? Me? I was doing nothing wrong – I was being so cool you wouldn't have recognised me. It was Sean who first brought up the where-are-we-going conversation! It must have been because that was the second time I'd seen him that week, big wows, but he started going on about how he didn't want me thinking that because we were seeing so much of each other, that we were going out, because he wasn't in a place right now where he could have a relationship.'

'Honestly,' said Trudie, 'you lot can't even go out to dinner these days without having to sit down and analyse it. Why can't you just have an affair and have fun while you're about it?'

Both Cass and Hallie groaned dramatically. 'If only we could,' wailed Hallie, 'but it's not that easy!'

'It's because we're nearly thirty,' explained Cass, 'men assume that it's marriage or nothing that we have in mind—'

'True, in my case, let's face it,' interrupted Hallie, 'even if I don't tell them.'

'Well, you both know it's the very last thing on the agenda for me. The only way I can convince men otherwise is by dating them a couple of times then dumping them myself.' But even as Cass said it, she thought of her inability to break it off with Carter and her heart twisted inside her. 'I can't even be bothered to do that any more – no, it's so much simpler just to give men the finger.'

'I'm not even going to ask what that means,' Trudie grimaced. 'I just think it's sad that you girls never seem to go out on proper dates any more.'

'Ah, but that's where you're about to be wrong, Trudie-baby,' grinned Hallie. 'Since the nineties is all about cocooning, honesty, self-awareness and safe sex, Cass and I are about to practise the opposite – we are going out to hit the singles' scene, lie through our back teeth, kid ourselves that this is what we want and take whatever we can get.'

Cass rolled her eyes at her grandmother. 'And this is what I came back from the States for. But first things first. Before you drag me anywhere, Hallie, I need a haircut. I'm so bored with American "big hair", that this,' she pointed to her cloud of hair, 'has got to go. Look, I even ripped a picture out of the in-flight magazine to show the hairstylist. Pretty clever, huh?'

Trudie and Hallie looked at the picture in silence and exchanged glances.

'No,' said Hallie decidedly. 'I can't let you. Dyke City.'

'Exactly,' Cass retorted. 'It's no-nonsense and professional, low-maintenance, cool for the summer and it'll stop men like Devlin Gray chatting me up.'

'Oh, hark at her,' said Trudie dryly. 'Tough being irresistible, is it, darling?'

Cass shrugged. 'You know what I mean.'

Hallie felt sick. 'I wish I could have a haircut which would *start* men like Devlin Gray chatting me up.'

'Darling, you look gorgeous as you are,' said Trudie firmly. 'Your hair is perfect, you've got such a pretty face, a figure to melt hearts and you're so much smarter-dressed than Miss Raggle-Taggle here.'

'So if I'm so gorgeous, why do you feel the need to reassure me?' Hallie asked sadly. 'Makes me feel like I've phoned you at the Samaritans.'

Trudie whistled. 'If you second-guess every compliment like that, I'm beginning to understand your man problems, Hallie dearest. Take it from a withered old crone like me that self-love transforms someone so much more beautifully than a new hairstyle or a different shade of lipstick.'

Hallie smiled ruefully. 'Ah, so you did notice my new lipstick, then?'

'Come on, enough wallowing.' Cass's tone was brisk. 'Hallie, let's go. Trudie – can I borrow some cash? I haven't sorted out my English bank account yet.'

'And when you have, I'm going to get paid back?' Trudie smiled at Cass's indignant face. 'Don't worry about it – look upon it as a welcome home present.'

'Thanks, Granda,' Cass used her old nickname for her grandmother, banned years ago when Trudie had decided that one thing she had never been was 'grand', leaning over to give her a hug. 'I'll see you later.'

'I'm on duty at the Crisis Centre tonight and then there's some party over at Robbo's so don't wait up for me,' Trudie twinkled.

'Trudie, I despair,' Hallie said heavily, 'you're in your seventies and you have a better social life than me.'

'Mutton dressed as astrakhan, that's me. Shocking, isn't it? Now, be off with you – leave an old woman in peace.'

'How lucky are you, Cass?' Hallie asked once they were back in the car. 'Trudie is the coolest grandmother I have ever met. I'll take her as a flatmate over bloody Beth any day.'

'Well, she's had to be, what with Mum and Poppa being scattered to the four winds. Ricky and I have taught her well over the years. It does feel kinda weird though, moving back in after five years' independence. It's one thing lodging with your grandmother because your parents are too fucked-up and globetrotting to take care of you themselves, but when you're twenty-nine years old? That's sad. I'm just praying that she's eased up on the personal guidance stuff. You remember how she was when we were at Godolphin?'

'Not much stricter than my mother, if I remember rightly, although the Samaritans and stuff came later didn't it?'

'Yeah, even though she retired from running the hotel when we came to live with her, by the time Ricky and I went off to university, she was bored stupid and decided we weren't going to be the only students, so she started her counselling courses soon after.'

Ricky – there was another scalp pinned unwisely to Hallie's bed-head. 'Well, I still think any grandmother who is not only a fully-trained confidante but a ready supply of cash – yes, I noticed the instant freeloading there,' Hallie retorted in answer to Cass's sidelong look, 'is a pretty good bet. It didn't take long, did it?'

'Look, don't start in on me. I'm still a poor student, remember. Not all of us have huge corporate salaries and company cars.'

'Which I work fourteen hours a day for, if you remember, much as I would love to leave the rat race and become a burden on the state. Talking of which, how *is* Ricky?' Hallie asked noncommittally.

Cass shot her a look. 'Hal, he's still too good for you.'

'I asked how he was, not for this old lecture!' said Hallie, stung.

'Well, he's just as wonderful as ever,' sighed Cass. 'Still up at Findhorn, still saving the world.'

'Still unemployed, then?' Hallie couldn't resist it.

'Miaaow! Still on your slaves to the workplace theme, then? Although I guess being at Findhorn is a full-time job in itself. He works in the kitchen, I think, when he's not running the tree-planting weeks.'

Findhorn was a thriving New Age community in Scotland, dedicated to organic, ecologically-safe agriculture, industry, architecture and holistic therapy. Five years before, Cass's brother had spent a week there, but had never left, abandoning his job as an ad-man. The trouble was, he had also abandoned Hallie, who after ten years, had finally just coaxed him into bed.

She was still trying not to feel either guilty that she might have pushed him into the twentieth century equivalent of a monkish retreat or just plain pissed-off about the timing and her rotten luck.

'Jeez Louise, the traffic in London is terrible, isn't it?' yawned Cass, looking out of the car window, as they crawled along the South Bank.

Hallie welcomed the change of subject. 'Well, at least this way we shorten the odds on Beth being out when we get back. With any luck, she'll have left for her Saturday afternoon tennis.'

'Damn, I was kinda looking forward to putting a face to the cursings.'

'Not worth it. Pig City, in character as well as appearance, although she has an annoyingly good body. I should know, she parades it around enough. I swear she bought that flat only because of the full-length mirror in the hall – every morning, scout's honour, every morning, she's preening herself in front of it, starkers. Not a particularly good ego boost, let me tell you. I'm so paranoid about my spare tyres at that time of day that I'm busy trying to wriggle into my control pants while she's asking my opinion about whether it's healthy for her stomach to be quite so concave.'

'Just remind me why you still live there.'

Hallie shrugged. 'Well, it's a gorgeous flat – wasted on her – and at first I was so busy trying to find a job I never got round to doing anything about moving out. Then when I started at Bandwick's I looked into buying, but the housing market has gone so bananas, I couldn't even raise the deposit on a rabbit hutch. And since then – busy, busy, busy. Anyway, there's a strange sort of pleasure in hanging around her to haunt her with my bad behaviour.'

'What do you mean?'

'I delight in dragging my hapless victims back to Theberton Street – especially the long-haired, unshaven artistic types – so that I can shock Beth and her nightmare of a boyfriend and confirm that I am a slapper of the worst order. Hey, gives them something to talk about other than sport, I suppose.'

'Oh, a jock, huh? What's his name?'

Hallie pulled a face. 'Slammer. Sporting accolade, apparently, rather than tequila-related. Need I say more?'

Cass whistled. 'Can't wait to meet them – they sound a little like some roommates I had last year—'

'Cass, I'm so sorry! I've hardly let you get a word in edgeways,' Hallie interrupted, 'what's been going on with you since New Year? And tell me again why you've come back?'

'Gee, to see all my friends who have missed me sooo much,' said Cass sarcastically.

'Belt up, Lucasta, you know what I mean. How's it been hangin'?' Hallie put on a heavily bad American accent, as they crossed the river.

'Wid ma homies, do you mean?' Cass abandoned the *Boyz 'n' the Hood* impression and stared out of the window. 'Oh, you know, the usual stuff – ice hockey games, blading in the park, shopping in Tiffany's, watching pay-per-view, eating knishes from the hot-dog guy at the corner of 5th and Madison.'

'Cass,' warned Hallie.

'Honestly?' asked Cass, preparing to be anything but honest. 'Working my ass off and still failing to make headway on my dissertation. Failing to persuade Poppa to put me back on the family pay-roll since I junked that Fellowship job, so trying to make ends meet by dog-walking some borzois that I had to go and bond with before I was given the job. I had quite a break in March, when my roommate's boss's girlfriend let me run a workshop at an empowerment weekend she was running upstate. But then she got really ticked-off with me because my stuff wasn't feminist enough to fully empowerise her ladies, as she so feministly described them, so she refused to pay me the full rate we'd agreed. All stuff like that.'

'Snog anyone?'

'At that weekend? You really do think I'm a lesbian, don't you?'

'Ho, ho, ho. No, you idiot, how many pillows are at this moment being wept on by broken-hearted men?'

'Given that about one in five men I met was actually straight, I'd say that cuts down on the cull ratio,' Cass retorted. 'Nope, no time. Too busy, too broke, too bolshy for American men.'

Lies, all lies, she thought, involuntarily remembering that time only a month ago, when she had spent a whole weekend holed up with Carter in the George Inn in Washington, afraid to come up for air, gorging guiltily on domestic champagne and bacon waffles. Oh God, how could she have done it?

'Hey, that reminds me. I've got something for you, Hal.' Cass started rummaging around in her rucksack. 'The answer to your prayers.'

'You have Mr Right *and* his large country estate packed away in that bag?' grinned Hallie.

'Close.' Cass held up a slim book. *'The Rules – Time-tested Secrets for Capturing the Heart of Mr Right,'* she read out proudly. 'Basically, it's how to get your man to marry you.'

Hallie stopped at the traffic lights. 'Gimme that!' She grabbed it from Cass.

'It's unbelievable,' Cass warned her. 'Talk about a backlash to girl power – this is the full flogging. Listen to this— "Don't be a loud, knee-slapping, hysterically funny girl. Be quiet and mysterious, act ladylike, cross your legs and smile. Don't talk so much. Wear black sheer pantyhose and hike up your skirt!" Unreal. Can you imagine me doing that?'

'What about this?' Hallie flipped through the slim volume. ' "If you don't get jewelery or some other romantic gift on your birthday, you might as well call it quits." This is classic stuff.'

'Yeah, basically it's saying lie, cheat, and practically steal – but never let them have the smallest glimpse of your real personality until you get that wedding ring on your finger.'

'Sounds good,' said Hallie wryly, moving off again. 'I'd been stumbling towards the same conclusion myself, ever since I broke up with Reuben.'

Cass couldn't help but yawn. 'OK, I'm afraid. Explain please.'

'It's simple. I want lovely shags, but what I'm really aiming for is for the bonking to be followed by the full church-wedding-riproaring-reception deal. You see I'm not prepared to sell out to your man-hating theory. I'm just sick of all this pussy-footing around, pretending that we're all cool and relaxed about commitment. I want to get married! I want to have kids! And I want to get the ball rolling before I'm thirty.

'But men just want the lovely shags. No,' she corrected herself, 'men just want *a* shag. It's like binary for them, more than one shag tips you into the next zero bracket of commitment. Marriage for them is a necessary evil. If they want to carry on shagging you – or perhaps they've even fallen in love with you – then marriage is the required trade-off.'

'And I thought I was cynical,' whistled Cass.

'But I'm not slagging off men *per se*, or romance – it's just that, as I see it, marriage is where men and women really part ways.'

'Nicely put.'

'Men have been brought up to think that getting married is something they have to do at some point, i.e. they have control, so there's no terror involved. Women don't have that control – and have probably been brought up, since kneehigh, to regard marriage as the be-all, where men see it as the end-all – so for women there is that terror that you might not be picked, like the netball team at school, and that – aaargh, Shelfland awaits you.' Hallie stopped the car and started backing into a parking space.

'No terror for me,' said Cass firmly. 'I'm not even going to play netball and I've picked out a really great condo in Shelfland. Book early to avoid disappointment, that's what I say. No sirree bob, no weddings for this wabbit.'

'Oh, you fool, it's good to have you back,' Hallie leant over to clasp Cass's hand. Then she sat up straighter and struck a dramatic pose, arm in the air. 'But I don't care what you think – I'm going to get off my little pedestal of idleness and I'm going to get out there and find Mr Right, instead of just sitting back, letting arrogant creeps like Dr Reuben Cathcart walk all over me and compounding the error by carrying a blasted torch for them. From now on the only torch I'm carrying is for me, and I'll be shining it into every corner to find that man. Just call me the Statue of Libido!' She sat back with a triumphant air.

Cass whooped. 'Go, girl! Look out world, Hallie is coming to shag you!'

Hallie grinned wickedly. 'I say we make tonight a real occasion – drag Nina up here by her hair, dress up, slap on the warpaint, blow some cash and go crazy. What do you think?'

'Fine and dandy. But first, a haircut.'

Hallie gestured across the street at the hairdressers opposite. 'Ask and you shall receive.'

'Bless you, my child.'

'To us!' cried Hallie. 'Friends for twenty years, friends for twenty more!'

'Hallie!' hissed Nina. 'Are you actually trying to attract the attention of every fucking person in this room?'

'Well, that is the point of this godawful place,' laughed Cass. 'Aren't we meant to get their attention so that they call us up?' She gestured at the flashy bakelite phone on their table. 'But who's meant to call us? I can't see any guys here!'

'Oh, they don't arrive til much later,' dismissed Hallie, 'according to my assistant, Karenza, who comes here all the time. Now look, are we going to drink this champagne or what?'

'I think the last time I had champagne was on my wedding day.' Nina regarded her glass dispassionately.

'The last time I got wrecked was on your wedding day,' said Hallie.

'Well, given that the only thing you drink is champagne, that would probably be the last time you had it as well,' reasoned Cass.

Hallie and Nina were silent as they remembered why Cass had missed Nina's wedding nine months beforehand. Cass noticed and, in her jet-lagged state, was irritated.

'Not much call for me to drink champagne at the time,' she said brutally.

'Oh, Cass.' Nina didn't know what else to say.

'Yeah, inconvenient of John to fall to his death two days before my best friend's wedding. He might almost have planned it that way.' Cass glared at them.

'Do you miss him?' Hallie asked simply.

'Do you miss Reuben?' Cass countered. 'Sorry, that was out of line. Oh, God, ignore me. It's been a rough few days.'

'Well, we're bloody glad you're here, that's all I can say,' said Nina stoutly, lighting a cigarette. 'We've missed you, haven't we, Hal? It's good to have the old Bikeshed Blasters back together. All for a fag, and fags for all, eh?'

'Except I've given up smoking,' said Cass ruefully. The other two turned to her in horror. 'I know, I know. But you have no idea what a pain in the ass it is to smoke in New York. Most restaurants, you can only smoke in the bar now, so if you wanted inter-course smokes, you had to get up between each course and push your way through to the bar and back again and then all over again. Anyway, Cart—' she paused, 'a friend of mine persuaded me that since I always promised myself I would give up when I was thirty, I may as well give up a year early. But don't worry, I'm not your typical reformed smoker – I still love the smell, so go ahead, puff away!'

'Well, this is a strange turn of events,' teased Hallie. 'What other insidious changes have crept upon you during your years in the States? Changes that we're only going to see in their full horror now that you are back for good? What secrets lie behind this one-inch hairdo?'

'Jeez, who pulled your word chain?' Cass grumbled, taking a slug of her champagne. 'This new job sounds like it's going to your head, Templeton.'

'And how about your new job?' asked Nina. 'Tell us the latest on the Cass Herbert World Domination Gameplan?'

'Researcher for Alun Blythe, new Minister for the City. Poach all his contacts and use them as my own. Meanwhile, complete my dissertation, supporting myself with the pay from Blythe. Then launch my consultancy and conquer the world. Easy. By that time you'll both hate me for being such a Superwoman and wonder why you ever wanted me to come back.'

'But Cass,' Hallie said, 'we already hate you for being such a Superwoman. We always have.'

Cass threw her head back and laughed. Huck, huck, huck. The other clientele at Caspers had never heard such a laugh. 'Oh boy, I walked into that one, didn't I?'

She looked at her friends as if for the first time. 'You know, I really am glad to be back home.' She raised her glass. 'To us. To the Bikeshed Blasters. We're back!'

'We're back!' echoed the other two.

Every time Nina closed her eyes, she could see the digits of the clock radio dancing in front of her eyelids. 3.42 am, 3.42 am,

3.42 am. She'd read somewhere that sleeping next to clock radios could microwave your head, so she moved it further away on the bedside table, inadvertently knocking off her contact lens case with a little crash. She held her breath.

Next to her, Jerry stirred, mumbled. Then went on snoring. It would take more than a poxy lens case to stop that. 3.43 am, 3.43 am. Would he ever stop?

When Nina had married Jerry, she had congratulated herself on avoiding the pitfalls that lurk unseen in other people's relationships. She'd known him since she was seventeen, had gone out with him for a year then and had fallen in love with him again when she was twenty-two – a total of eight years of relationship. They both knew and loved every last wart about each other, had discussed and agreed every possible scenario for their lives, liked each other's friends, enjoyed each other in public and private. On her wedding day, she had walked up the aisle towards him, had seen his beloved fair face turn towards her and had been assailed by an almost physical wave of certainty. This was right, this was her destiny. He wasn't just her lover, her husband, he was her best friend and right there, amongst all the pomp and circumstance, she knew that she could depend on him to have a laugh with her later about the whole day.

But since then . . . since then, there had been times when Nina hadn't dared stop to have similar moments of introspection, for fear of what she might find out. She had never been able to discuss it with Cass or Hallie. If she couldn't admit things were wrong to herself, how could she ever embark on the rough seas of talking it through with two people who thought that Jerry was the best thing since sliced onions, and that she and he were the steadiest couple since Mary and Joseph?

And with the best will in the world, no-one could have predicted the confluence of three elements – a damp home, Jerry's hitherto occasional snoring, and her equally occasional insomnia. These had come together into long, long nights – the damp of the cottage making Jerry's snoring a more or less permanent fixture and her resultant insomnia a constant thorn in her side. At times like this, in the graveyard shift of the night, she hated him. Really hated him. And would have to remind herself that it wasn't his fault, that it was only snoring, for God's sake.

Each morning, Jerry was mortified. Together they had explored every *Innovations* catalogue – buying nose clips, nostril expanding plasters, mini-electric-shockers a-plenty – but the longer they stayed in the cottage, the more Jerry snored and the more twitchy Nina became. Now they were both waiting with bated breath for the summer, hoping (and in Nina's case, praying) that the dampness would recede and his snoring would magically dry up.

Summer was taking a long time to arrive, thought Nina blackly. Oh, fuck this for a game of soldiers, she was getting up. Taking care to creep past a flaked-out Babaji in his basket, she avoided all the creaky floorboards like a pro and went to make herself a cup of tea. Having flicked on the telly to find and spurn a Chinese war movie, then leafed idly through an old *Hello!* and sorted out the herb rack, she had exhausted all entertainment choices. Perhaps they should get a new sofa: one she could sleep on, she thought, looking across at the unsprung horror Jerry had inherited from his grandmother. With her bad back, there was no way she could crash out on that one, that was for sure.

Putting on Jerry's overcoat as a vain V-sign against the cold, she wandered over to the computer and switched it on. She watched it chuntering through all the starting motions, then out of idle interest clicked on the Internet globe to see what happened next. ENTER USER PASSWORD flashed up. How dare he? she thought furiously. Who else except me is going to play with his bloody toy? That did it. A vague idea of playing a computer game crystallised into a determination to beat Jerry at his own game. Busting his password would be easy.

NINA, she typed.

INCORRECT PASSWORD, the computer retorted. PLEASE ENTER USER PASSWORD.

BABAJI, she tried. Nothing. SNORINGWANKER. Just to see if he knew himself. No joy.

After a couple more abortive goes, the computer warned her she only had one try left. Nina thought hard, tried to be Jerry, thinking hard of a lateral, rib-tickling word. Then she had a brainwave.

ARMADILLO. Only someone who watched as much telly as Jerry did, who had his adulation for Harry Enfield, and whose definition of lateral ideas was less de Bono than de Bonehead could have come up with this one. Now that she thought of it, she remembered that when Jerry had first got the computer he had been obsessed with the Dime Bar ad and would, rather irritatingly, go round the whole bloody time, playing the country bumpkin and shouting, 'Armadillo!' at any given opportunity.

PASSWORD CONFIRMED. Suddenly the screen started flashing colourful pictures at her, beeping happily as it connected up with the world wide web, ending up with the same page that she and Jerry had started from earlier in the day, cursor blinking in the 'Search' box.

For the next few minutes, Nina just played around, typing in things like SNORING REMEDIES/JUSTIFIABLE HOMICIDE ON SNORERS and the like, constantly amazing herself. How could there be nearly 2,000 entries on NOSEPICKING ANECDOTES?

Then she noticed an icon marked FAVOURITES and clicked idly on that. Sure enough, there was the CHATLINE 36-26-36 on which she had caught Jerry and Houston Hotlips. Equally obvious was another, more simply-monikered site: www.adultchat.com. Jerry had clearly been researching beyond the call of duty. Well, she decided suddenly, two could play at that game. Quickly, she double-clicked on the URL before she could change her mind.

WELCOME TO ADULT CHAT. PLEASE CHOOSE YOUR DESIRED ROOM.

Nina read down the list from the Adult Room – 'When you want to get down and dirty. Must Be 18 to Enter' – down to the Darkside Room – 'filtered for your hacking pleasure' – whatever that meant. She decided she might as well start simple and head straight for the Adult Room.

Taking a deep breath, she started typing in the required details. Finally, she was in.

> nk@jkenterprises: Hello there, bad people. I'm a stranger in these rude parts. Would anyone like to show me around?

> badboy@beinemannproud: welcome! *come* in and look around. first thing we have to do is get friendly on our sign-ons – what sort of a handle is 'nk'?

Shit, thought Nina, only amateurs log on with their initials.
How can I carry this one off?

> nk@jkenterprises: Just trying to be a coy girlie
there for a minute, Badboy, 'nk' stands for 'no
knickers', of course.

> badboy@beinemann proud: 'knickers'? 'knickers'?
so, i'm guessing you're english, then? english
people make me hot! i'd love to say that i'd like to
get into your 'knickers' but i guess there wouldn't
be much point in that since you're not wearing any
. . . alright, grrrl! let's get down! do you go down
on first dates?

Nina stared at the screen in horror. What was she getting into?
Quickly she logged out, and turned the computer off, her mind
churning. She was as bad as Jerry. Was this what the future
held for both of them? Logging onto sad git chatlines like the
computer nerds they had always laughed at?

Suddenly she needed to talk to someone. She grabbed the
phone and dialled Hallie's number, then glanced at her watch.
Christ, what was she thinking of? It was four o'clock in
the morning! Before it even had time to ring, she slammed
the receiver down again. Losing the plot. That's what she
was doing.

Hallie woke up with a start, reaching out for the phone. But it
stopped ringing as abruptly as it had started. This was getting
ridiculous. It was four o'clock in the morning – who else would
be trying to get through at this time of the night? Much more
of this and she was going to lose the plot, like Nina was always
accusing her of doing. It had been a miracle she had got to sleep
in the first place, given her racing thoughts ever since she'd come
back to the flat.

And it had all started so well. Thank you, God, Hallie had
thought as she unlocked the second lock on the front door and
let herself in. Beth and Slammer must be spending a rare night in

his jockstrap-infested bolthole in Ealing. So the perfect Saturday night was better late than never. It was only midnight – she knew that there was an old Bette Davis film on Nickelodeon, she had fags, she had chocolate, she had solitude, she was sorted. Oh, the bliss of shedding her gauzy turquoise overshirt, shrugging out of those skintight satin trousers, those five inch wedge boots and the almost surgical tightness of her bodystocking. It was the price she had to pay for looking good, she knew, but why did fashion have to draw her own attention to the worst parts of her body by planting weals there like signs saying 'Too Tight Here'? Letting out her stomach for the first time all evening, she had clambered into her brushed cotton pyjamas and slippersox, carefully unfolded her tartan rug, nicked from British Airways Club World for her by Nina, and settled into the comforting depths of the sofa.

Then she had seen the answering machine light blinking.

Before she could control herself, her heart had leapt with hope. She knew it wasn't going to be him but even after six months, still couldn't stop herself thinking it would be. Shuffling along to the end of the sofa, trying not to dislodge the ashtray she had placed so deliberately on the arm, she had pressed 'Play' on the machine.

'You have four messages', the machine had intoned solemnly. Surely, one of them could be the one she wanted.

But all she got was the sound of someone dropping the receiver back on the hook. Four times. Now that had annoyed her. Why did people bother listening all the way to the end of the message, just to put the phone down? Still, with that little flicker of anticipation, she dialled 1471 to trace the caller. Nothing doing. 'You were called yesterday at eleven fifty three pm,' said the message, 'we do not have a record of the number'. 11.53? That had been mere seconds before she came in, which had prompted much teeth-gnashing. Now the mysterious caller was trying his luck at four o'clock in the morning. Hallie wondered how long the phone had been ringing before she woke up.

Sod it, now she was wide awake again.

Cass opened the door of the refrigerator to see if there was anything even remotely tempting. What was it about English refrigerators, she wondered, that there never seemed to be anything in them that you actually wanted to eat? Although she and her roommates had seldom cooked for themselves, there always seemed to be some jumbo nibbles in the closet-sized refrigerator – Pepperidge Farm cookies, the odd jar of salsa, some left-over Chinese cartons – that were perfect for those nocturnal munchies, or in this case, the jet-lag jaw-ache.

'Got the munchies, eh?' said a soft voice.

Cass whipped round in shock. There was Trudie, sitting at the kitchen table in her most shockingly pink peignoir, feet wedged into fluffy pink mules.

'How long have you been sitting there?'

'Long enough to see you almost fall asleep into the fridge. Go to bed, darling.'

'No, my mind won't stop racing. Anyway, what are you doing up?'

Trudie smiled tiredly. 'The same – can't stop thinking about this poor girl I had to deal with tonight.'

'Tell me about it – at least you didn't have to deal with Hallie on heat!' grimaced Cass, sitting down. 'We went to Caspers, which must be a close runner-up to Hell on Earth, where each table has a telephone on it and you're supposed to ring the man of your dreams and chat him up without him knowing which table is calling. Of course, at this dump, desperate women outnumbered the geekiest looking guys I have ever seen by about ten to one. Nina and I didn't want anything to do with it – although watching these guys puffing themselves up as their phone never stopped ringing was cute in a sad sort of way – but Hallie got into it big-time. That girl really should have gone to acting school as planned, you should have heard the range of identities she got through tonight: French Europopster, Liverpudlian *Brookside* extra, American trophy wife—' Cass broke off as she saw a wave of tiredness wash over Trudie's face. 'Christ, Granda, I'm sorry – I'm totally going on, aren't I? And I interrupted you – what were you saying?'

Trudie shook her head indulgently. 'It's not important, darling. I'd much rather listen to you prattle. Just don't call me Granda, you'll make me feel as old as I undoubtedly am. I see you went through with your threatened hairstyle, by the way.'

Cass rubbed her head self-consciously from back to front, feeling the slick shortness of her once abundant locks. 'It's great, isn't it?' she said determinedly. 'Just what I wanted.'

'So it would seem,' said Trudie dryly and gestured at her to carry on.

Cass finished telling her about the Caspers fiasco but while she was doing so, noticed for the first time, just how much older her grandmother was looking. For a woman who had always looked like an Amazonian Honor Blackman, big-boned but timelessly elegant, Trudie was suddenly beginning to show her age. Deep lines were etching shadows either side of her mouth and her miraculously unlined face was sagging with strain. Cass, who had been looking forward to crying on her grandmother's shoulder about Carter, realised that she couldn't add to that strain with her own pathetic worries and wrongdoings.

'So, do you want to talk about John yet?' Trudie's voice was soft.

Cass started, and shook her head violently, that familiar sense of guilt stabbing her yet again. Trudie, like everyone else over here, had no idea of what was going on inside Cass's head. They all thought she was doing a good job of hiding her grief for John. No-one had the faintest clue about Carter. How could she even begin to talk about Carter when the whole spectre of John was still un-laid?

Inadvertently, her thoughts flickered back to that night before Christmas when she had gone to Meredith's apartment, she and Carter united once again in their nursemaiding of his wife. Him walking her home through the Village. Kissing like teenagers in the street, clinging onto each other – sailors lashed to masts in a storm-tumbled sea. She was meant to be the strong one, the morally punctilious one of the three – how could she admit to Trudie, Hallie or Nina that since she had last seen them, she had been sleeping with a married man, let alone confess the full horrors of her behaviour?

So who the hell *was* she going to confide in? Any of her other friends would be too surprised to hear from her after all this time to serve any purpose as sounding-boards. Cass was beginning to wonder why she had left America: no-one here sure as hell had time for her.

I came back here to re-establish control of my own life, she reminded herself. I came back here to re-focus. Get away from Carter and clear my mind of dysfunctionalism. Concentrate on my career. Twelve steps to launching my consultancy. The first is to finish my PhD. The second is to build a database of contacts through the House of Commons job. Oh, and earn some cash – she reminded herself, fingering the paltry leavings from Trudie's welcome home present – must get some cash together.

Hey, it was a programme of sorts.

3

Twelve steps, Cass reminded herself, as she gazed up at the entrance to 3 Dean's Yard. There were only eight up to the door, but they seemed a lot more daunting than any of her grand consultancy plans. She was meant to have started her new job twenty minutes ago, and so far had only made mistakes, the first of which was going to the House of Commons.

'But this is where I'm working,' she had insisted to the obdurate policeman at the St Stephen's door, feeling uncomfortable in her long skirt and sensible jacket. 'I'm Alun Blythe's new Researcher.'

'At his ministerial or private office?'

'Er, at his secretary's office?' Cass had hazarded, only half-remembering Alun's brief instructions over the phone.

'Ministerial secretary, or constituency secretary?'

'Jeez, I have no idea,' she had retorted. The bastard was enjoying this. 'Mags someone or other?' Why am I asking the goddamn policeman this, she wondered savagely, he's not going to know.

'Oh, Miss O'Sullivan,' the policeman widened his eyes, 'why didn't you say so before? You'll be wanting to go over to Dean's Yard. Number three. That's where her office is.'

Five minutes of intricate directions, one attempted shortcut through Westminster Abbey and a short argument with the man at the security barrier into Dean's Yard later, Cass was finally here, hesitating on the steps. Which button should she press?

'Are you comin' in or what?' barked an amused voice from the grille on her left. 'You've been standing there so long, I thought you might be more interested in the schoolboys three doors up!'

'What?' asked Cass, as the door was buzzed open. Inside, she was met by a round-faced smiling individual, who introduced himself as Paul the Attendant.

'Westminster School is three doors up,' he explained, 'just my little joke. Now, who can we get for you?'

Cass explained who she was and a minute or two later was shown into a khaki-painted, scuffed carpeted office, where amongst a bank of computers, printers, and filing cabinets she could see six women sitting at cramped desks, all studiously avoiding her eye.

'You must be the new researcher,' boomed a big-boned woman almost as tall as Cass, coming into the office behind her, with a huge handbag clanking suspiciously on her shoulder. 'I'm Mags O'Sullivan, Alun's secretary, firefighter and general nose-wiper. Surprise, surprise, the great man himself isn't here yet. Passed out in some gutter, I shouldn't wonder, but you can stumble around the Blythe empire, such as it is, with me. Fat lot of good he would be at showing you round anyway, bloke doesn't know his arse from his elbow most days.'

'Shut up, you bitch,' said a voice behind Cass. She spun round, horror-struck, recognising Alun Blythe from his newspaper picture. 'That is no way to speak about an elected member of parliament behind his arse or his elbow. Mags, you're fired.'

'Oh sod off,' said Mags imperturbably. 'Don't fool around in front of the hired help. He couldn't live without me,' she explained to Cass, who was having difficulty keeping her jaw off the floor. 'Besides, I know too much.'

'You mean, you've forgotten too much, you senile old bag of bones.' Alun perched himself on the edge of her desk, feet on her chair, hitching up a pair of already badly creased suit trousers. These, the crumpled-looking tie, and the straining white shirt hardly made him the picture of statesmanlike sartorial elegance. 'So, you must be Cass.'

'Oh, that's her name,' exclaimed Mags, 'I can never remember, they all come and go so quickly.'

'My point exactly, Mags you monster,' Alun grimaced. 'Do try to be more welcoming. Was she giving you a very hard time?' he asked Cass.

Cass felt it was about time she asserted herself, half-suspecting that this routine was a well-practised one to intimidate new blood like herself. 'Well, she hadn't quite got round to showing me the graves of past researchers – we were still on the scrubbing and swabbing part of the job,' she joked weakly. 'Cass Herbert,' she stuck out her hand, 'and I'm pleased to meet you, Mr Blythe, and you, Miss O'Sullivan.'

For a split-second, there was a flicker of interest in Alun's world-weary eyes. 'I'll fire you if you call me Mr Blythe.'

'Does "sir" suit you better, then?' Cass was beginning to find her level.

Finally, he smiled. ' "Sir" will do just fine. We've got a live one here,' he said to Mags. 'This could be fun.'

'So it would seem,' sighed Mags, but just for a moment she smiled at Cass.

A mere ten minutes later, Cass was settled in Alun's own office, which was two floors above Mags's, and just as scruffy. It had taken five minutes for him to explain her job.

'At first you'll just be dealing with the post, which is a full-time job in itself,' he explained, looking at his watch. 'If you get in before Mags, you collect it from the post office in the House and bring it over here, sorting it into ministerial stuff, constituency, invitations, and general hate- or fan-mail. Chuck all junk-mail, unless you think it's something I really should see. Mags sends on any ministerial bumf, and still does the diary. You sort the constituency mail into ongoing surgery cases, issue-based letters – these generally follow a clear trend, what's going through the House, what's in the papers, that sort of thing – and then the inevitable rogues in the woodpile, which can't be categorised. You'll soon pick up on the trends – and Mags will show you the various stock answers we have to the issue-based letters – but often all that is required is to pass on the letter to the relevant Minister, so you write to them telling them that's what you've done. Mags generally handles the surgery cases but if you get any new ones, it might be good experience for you to start the ball rolling. Then, when you've drafted replies, I come along and look them over, sign them off if possible and that's that. There you go,' and he handed her a huge pile of papers. 'Mags has already sorted this lot, so you've just got the constituents' letters this morning.'

Cass gulped. 'No problem,' she assured him with bravado.

'Make yourself at home in my office upstairs, by the way,' Alun twinkled at her. 'I've just had to move from a single to a double, so excuse the mess. We've taken over some Conservatives' offices since the election – which at least gives me a view of the outside world rather than just a wall – and it's all a bit chaotic up there.'

'Telling me,' grumbled Mags, lighting up a fag. Cass gasped. She couldn't help it. After five years in the States, where smoking was banned everywhere except in the privacy of your own ash-tray, she couldn't believe that cigarettes were allowed in the Mother of all Parliaments.

'Right, let's take you up through the labyrinth,' Alun finished briskly, hopping off the desk, 'what am I late for, Mags?'

Cass gaped again, as Mags plucked a small, panting dog from underneath her desk and, cuddling it close, looked casually at the large, open diary, itself a maze of heavy pencilled crossings-out and squiggles. 'Nine o'clock, meeting Ken in Central Lobby. Uncle Alun's going to be very, very late, isn't he, Gillie?' she crooned to the dog. 'And Spotty Neil rang to say that if you didn't go over there this morning, he would ring the Truancy Officer.' She looked thoughtful. 'I'm not sure he was joking either – do you think they have such things in the Department?'

'My esteemed Private Secretary over in my ministerial office,' Alun explained to a now totally mystified Cass. 'After eighteen years as a happy Opposition backbencher, I'm finding it a little hard to adjust to my new position.'

Mags snorted. 'A little?! You'd need a map to find that bloody office.'

Alun looked defensive. 'I can perfectly well do that job on the run.' His jacket splayed open to reveal pockets, inner and outer, stuffed to the gills with scraps of paper. 'And you're still handling my diary, so the only thing that's changed is the ministerial post, which they will hardly let me get my hands on. Anyway, from what I can see, so far the whole job is just backslapping.' He glanced wryly at Cass. 'You didn't hear me say that.'

'Say what?' said Cass brightly.

'Good girl. Now, enough of this chat. Let's get you moved in upstairs.'

So here she was. On her left, a pile of totally incomprehensible, mostly illegible, handwritten letters from constituents who seemed to have a dizzying array of opinions on subjects Cass knew nothing about. On her right, the various forms she was to fill out to get her coveted pass for the House (never again was she to refer to it as 'the House of Commons', that much, at least, she had picked up) and for the Fees Office.

All around her were boxes, packed and half-unpacked, some in drunken Pisa-like piles, some on their side, spilling an Amazonian rainforest's worth of papers. Dust hung in the air, and the only sound was the creak of the chair as she tried to tuck her long legs under the desk. Cass felt like she'd wandered into some long-forgotten archive, not the office of a governing MP. Nor could she remember the way back to Mags's office, let alone down to the exit. She had understood about one word in ten downstairs, had no idea when she was supposed to break for lunch, or where she was supposed to go. For someone who was halfway through a PhD on the business of gender, who had more letters after her name than any old 'MP' and who never let a little ignorance get in her way, Cass was feeling remarkably clueless and damsel-in-distressish.

If in doubt, she thought, avoid the issue. She picked up the phone and dialled.

'Hallie? Hi, it's me.'

'Me, being our new parliamentary expert? How's it going?'

'Hal, this place is mental, a total nuthouse,' Cass hissed surreptitiously. 'Alun Blythe is in some quasi-dominatrix symbiosis with his secretary, who has a voice like Mr T, probably because she smokes like a chimney – and has not one but three dogs sitting under her desk. No-one else seems to talk to each other, Alun seems to hate his job and God knows what I'm supposed to be doing – I might as well be working in a mailroom, that's what this place looks like anyway. You won't believe how tacky this place is – everything looks like it's about to fall apart and the whole building is painted in various shades of regulation olive. And last but not least, I am totally lost in this warren of offices that seem about as close to Parliament as your offices are. What am I doing here?'

'Don't panic, sweetie,' laughed Hallie. 'You haven't had a job for so long that you've probably forgotten those first-day-terrors. It sounds rather fun to me – better to have chaos than try to fit into some streamlined machine. Seen our Tony yet?'

'I haven't seen anyone who doesn't look or act pre-Jurassic,' Cass wailed, failing to notice the door opening behind her. 'This whole place is stuck in a time-warp – some of the secretaries downstairs are using typewriters, I kid you not. New Labour, New Schlabour – that's what I'm thinking. Blair wouldn't be seen dead here!'

'Hear, bloody hear,' came a voice from behind her.

Cass whipped round to look into the full-bearded face of a merry-eyed total stranger.

'Hallie, gotta go,' she whispered, putting the phone down.

'Alun's researchers are getting better looking by the minute,' boomed the stranger. 'Breath of bloody fresh air, that's what we dinosaurs need. I'm Frank Blackthorn, by the way, and you are—?'

Cass was furious with herself. Was she going to make a fool of herself all day? 'Getting out of here,' she said quickly. 'I'm leaving before I get done for treason.'

Blackthorn laughed heartily, colour going immediately to his red-veined cheeks. 'You're all right, lass, you know that? I shouldn't worry, love,' his voice sank to a conspiratorial whisper, 'you can say what you like here: Alun and I are cut from the same cloth and it's no fancy New Labour tailoring, I can tell you.'

Cass felt like she was getting way out of her depth. 'I'm Cass Herbert – Alun's new researcher,' she added redundantly. 'I'm sorry, this is obviously your office as well, would you like me to leave?'

'Not a chance! I'm not going to pass up the opportunity to be shut up in the same room as a pretty girl. Who knows what we might get up to!' Blackthorn sat down at his desk, on the other side of the room. 'Now you look far too attractive and grown-up to be one of Alun's cannon-fodder researchers. Leave all that crap, and tell me all about yourself.'

If she was working in the States, Cass reflected, she would be getting rich on sexual harrassment compensation from his first few comments alone. Uncomfortably, she put aside the untouched piles of letters and stumbled through a heavily edited life history.

'The psychology of gender?' Blackthorn interrupted at one point. 'What the bloody hell's that when it's at home?'

'It's not as scary as it sounds,' Cass started.

'Sounds scary enough, thank you,' Blackthorn cut her off. 'I'll have to warn Alun that he's got a psychobabbler on his hands. That's what comes of being educated in America, I suppose.' He noticed her glaring at him. 'Oh, don't mind me, lass, I've always been one to call a spade a spade.'

And that makes it all right? thought Cass savagely. Does he even realise that that's a racist comment?

'Well, we'll have to get you introduced to a few of the young folk round here,' he went on, smiling. 'Us dinosaurs can't hog you to ourselves. Tell you what, I'll give our Ted a ring. He used to be my researcher,' he explained, 'and is now a right big noise over at Medios. He'll show you round the place.'

Cass nodded knowledgeably, as if she knew what Medios was, and cringed. Being set up with some sex-starved fearsome political heavyweight was the last thing she needed. She opened her mouth to put Blackthorn off, but he was already dialling.

'Ted? Frank here. Look, are you busy today? Well, shelve all that – I want you to take Alun's new researcher to lunch in the House. Yes, today. Oh belt up your complaining, you need the break. What's your name again?' he asked Cass.

'Cass,' she replied, dying inside.

'The name's Cass and you can meet in Central Lobby at one o'clock. No, Cass is a girl's name, you daft bugger.' He paused, then grinned. 'Don't worry, she's a stunner. She'll blow your socks off, my boy.'

'Hey!' Cass said involuntarily. This wasn't funny.

Blackthorn took no notice whatsoever. 'No pushover, though,

lad – I can feel the daggers from here. Yes, good luck. Right, bye for now – let me know when you have those gambling stats, won't you?' He put the phone down and smiled blithely at Cass.

'Mr Blackthorn,' Cass said heatedly, 'I appreciate you're trying to help but I can assure you—'

'Oh, no need to thank me, love, it's all part of the service. You'll find out it's much more fun round this place if you've got someone to muck about with. Take Alun and me – partners in crime since we both won our seats: him in 1971, me in 1974. It's the only way to keep sane in what you clearly realise is a nuthouse. And now,' he said pointedly, 'if you'll excuse me, I have to do some dictating. I hope I don't disturb you.'

Cass gave up. 'No problem – I've got loads to do here as well.' She pulled the letters towards her in as businesslike a way as possible, but actually just stared into the middle distance in amazement. It wasn't that she had expected MPs to be mini-Churchills of statesmanship and gravitas but she certainly hadn't anticipated two longstanding Labour members to be quite so flippant, irreverent and, well, sexist. She was obviously going to have to lose some of her Stateside edginess.

One thing was for certain, there was no way that she was going to turn up to meet this Ted guy. No way on earth.

Hallie looked up from her latest Giuseppe brief, to see Karenza, her assistant, tripping towards her, loaded down with doughnuts.

'Here you go, Hallie, mid-morning supplies.'

'Karenza, you are a cow,' Hallie said fondly. 'You know I'm meant to be on a diet.' She picked up one of the dough-nuts and bit deeply into it. 'Just because you're size two and a half and need to take your tights in to make them fit.'

'You must be joking!' cried Karenza, pinching a non-existent millimetre of flab from her sunbedded midriff. 'Look at this – I binged so much over the weekend, I was starting to go cold turkey without some chocolate, so I got these reduced-fat doughnuts as a substitute.'

Hallie looked at the doughnut in horror. 'Reduced-fat? What will they think of next?'

'It's great, innit?' said Karenza blithely. 'They're launching them up in Food Fashions tomorrow – "Sin and stay thin" is the strapline, I think.'

'What would I do without you, sweetie? Always got your finger on the pulse, haven't you?'

Karenza waved at the pile of papers on Hallie's desk. 'Hey, anything's better than working – is that still the Giuseppe brief?' Giuseppe was Hallie's last remaining fashion client – an off-the-peg designer range of shops that was struggling to maintain its hitherto unassailed ability to cross over to a High Street clientele, yet with prices closer to Katherine Hamnett than Dorothy Perkins.

Hallie sighed. 'Yup. What do you think of this? When we launch the summer sales, we offer a book of 12 coupons – say, £500 worth will buy £700 of clothes in the sale, then after the sales can be put towards full-price clothes – at perhaps seventy per cent of their real value, and limited to one item a month. That way we offer an extra incentive during summer sales, making them more like real sales, and pull the punters in at other times of the year.'

'Hallie, you're brilliant.' Karenza beamed at her. 'I don't understand a word of it, but it sounds brilliant to me.'

Hallie sighed and shook her head, wondering why it was her curse to have an assistant who was simultaneously so gifted and so AbFab all at once, when one of the desk lines burbled gently.

Karenza picked it up. 'Hallie Templeton's line. This is her executive assistant Karenza speaking. Can I help you?' she trilled. 'I'll just see if she's available. It's someone called Linda Bellman,' she hissed at Hallie, forgetting, as she always did, to put the phone on hold.

'Linda Bellman?' frowned Hallie. 'Oh, I know – yes, put her through,' she said, chuckling. 'Hello, Nina Kellman.'

Nina sounded affronted. 'Linda Bellman! For fuck's sake, when are you going to get an assistant that can get my name right?'

'Isn't Linda Bellman an actress?' asked Hallie mildly. 'Or is it Bellingham? And there I was, thinking that I was about to speak to someone famous.'

'No, just someone who's famously bored, hacked-off and miserable, not to mention dying.'

'Why? What's wrong?'

'I think I've broken my toe.'

Hallie was about to exclaim with shock and sympathy when she remembered this was Nina she was speaking to. 'What makes you think it's actually broken? How did you do it?'

'Stubbed it against Jerry's fucking hard disk and now I can hardly walk. Not that I can walk anyway because my back's been giving me so much gyp. I tell you, I'm in agony.'

'Poor Babaji.'

'Poor Babaji! What about me?'

'I mean, poor Babaji not being able to go walkies – and of course, poor you, you nincompoop.'

'Why does everyone keep calling me a nincompoop?' Nina raged on. 'I am not a nincompoop, never have been a nincompoop and never will be a nincompoop. What sort of a stupid, bloody word is nincompoop anyway?'

Hallie sighed. 'Nina, much as I love you, why did you call? Because if it was just to yell at me, I have enough people to fill that role here.'

'Oh, Hal, I'm sorry – I'm taking my frustrations out on you, yet again. It's just that all morning I've been trying to get up the nerve to call up and ask all my old contacts for some features work – and when I finally do, it turns out that half of them have moved on to other jobs and the other half can hardly remember me and are just being fucking snotty.'

'How many calls have you made?' Hallie asked sympathetically.

Nina made shifty noises. 'Well, only one where I actually got through to the right person—' Hallie laughed. '—but I've left loads of voicemail messages and *none* of the fuckers have got back to me!'

'You left these messages this morning?'

'Yes.'

'Nina, it's twelve o'clock,' Hallie was beginning to feel positively Methusalean in her role as wisdom-dispenser, 'give them a chance. Talk about Captain Paranoia – you're just being your typical freelancer, imagining that no-one has got anything better to do than return your messages – fold up your cape, sweetie, and simmer down.'

There was a large sigh down the telephone line. 'You're right, you're right. If only I didn't feel so shitty, it would be easier to get on with things. Anyway, how are you?'

'Single,' said Hallie flatly.

'No change there then,' laughed Nina. 'At least you don't have to put up with men's annoying little ways.'

Hallie couldn't believe her ears. 'Yes, go on, laugh, why don't you? "Enough of me, back to me" – is that it? How on earth would I know about men's annoying little ways, when the longest I've ever lived with anyone is about three minutes? Do you know, Cass is right, you can be so smug sometimes.'

'What?! What did you say? What do you mean, "Cass is right"?'

Hallie felt her peacemaking urges smoothing over her righteous indignation. 'Nothing. Forget it. The long and short of it is that I still have a sign above my head saying, "Available" like some fallen-down old house in a buyer's market and the most interest I'm getting is the odd bonk.'

'So, more a "short let" situation than the full freehold, then?'

Hallie laughed hollowly. 'Yes, many surveyors' reports, a few exchanges of contracts but not a whisper of a completion, let alone being gazumped.'

'Darling Hallie, never one to let a dead horse go un-flogged,' Nina said, with a residue of sharpness in her voice. 'So tell me about the latest disaster.'

'Imagine the scene. Tesco's on a Tuesday night. Didn't you write about that once for the *Evening Standard*?'

'Yes! Christ, is that still going on?'

'Oh yes, and the lines haven't improved since you went. "You have eggs, I have butter, let's go get scrambled" – that sort of thing.'

'I never went, actually, just vox-popped a few people then wrote about it,' Nina admitted carelessly.

'Typical features journalist,' grumbled Hallie, having suffered at the hands of glibly promising writers many times in the course of her PR career. 'Well, Cass and I are running down the list of singles' options, in the interests of research as much as anything else – I mean, you constantly read articles like yours in the mags and papers – but who actually does these things and do they work?'

'And do they?'

'Well, Caspers was a bit of farce, wasn't it? Although we had a laugh.'

'I suppose you could call it a laugh. If I remember rightly – Cass and I were holding back the giggles all night, while you re-invented yourself as many times as Elton John.'

'Ah, but I have better hair, never forget that. Anyway, Tesco's started off swimmingly – the good thing is that there is remarkably little self-consciousness about it – and I was chatting away quite happily to this relatively hunky bloke, leaving Cass dying of shame in Baking Goods, when I caught sight of what was in his basket.'

'What – a terrible giveaway of his character and secret vices? Prunes for his constipation? Captain Matey bubblebath? Tripe-flavoured scotch eggs?'

'No, nothing like that. Jammy dodgers and cream in a can. That was it.' As Nina did her best mystified silence, Hallie went on. 'Do you remember me telling you about Reuben and me getting all saucy with canned cream, and how he was meant to be whipping me into a frenzy—'

'Very funny.'

'—when the aerosol jammed and he was staring into the nozzle and pressing hard and suddenly it came out, all over his face?'

'I knew it,' Nina crowed, 'you *are* missing Reuben!'

'No, I am not,' said Hallie through gritted teeth. 'But it occurred to me – why else *would* you have canned cream in your basket if you weren't already going home to have foodie sex, or at least planning to, with whoever you were hoping to pick up at Tesco's?'

'Yes, I see, a bit grim,' said Nina thoughtfully. 'And what was the significance of the jammy dodgers.'

'Oh, I have no idea, but I'm sure a psychologist could have a field day.'

' "The red hole leads to sweet pleasures"?' suggested Nina.

'That sort of thing, thank you, Doctor Ruth. Anyway Cass kiboshed it for good at that moment.'

'How?'

'Well, you remember her new haircut? Think old-style Sinead O'Connor, add half an inch? Well, she's obviously fed up with the whole Tesco's thing because she comes butching up to me, holding a butternut squash, which has to be the most phallic vegetable ever grown, and says, "Honeybun, does this work best if it is firm, or just a little squishy?" at which point I get the awful giggles and Blokey sidles off with his jammy dodgers intact, cream can as yet unsquirted.'

Nina finally stopped chuckling to ask, 'Cass isn't going through the lipstick lesbian phase, is she? Because I wrote about that too, ages ago, and it is so five minutes ago.'

'Don't be silly,' dismissed Hallie, conveniently forgetting that Cass had fooled her into thinking exactly that. 'She's still breaking hearts as soon as look at a man. Bitch.'

'Bitch,' agreed Nina good-temperedly.

Goddess, thought Ted, as a scowling girl strode into Central Lobby. She's a total goddess. So tall, what legs, with that pale, pale face and the *Les Mis* haircut. Hardly daring to look further, he buried himself in his copy of *The House Magazine*.

Wimp, Cass cursed herself as she approached the green-shaded desk. Total wimp. Couldn't resist it, could you? Why couldn't you have lunch on your own, huh?

'I'm meeting Ted— Ted—' Shit, what was his name? The attendant, impressive in his white tie and tails, looked impassively back at her. For once, Cass wiped the scowl off her face and looked imploring. 'Young guy? Works at Medios?'

The attendant stared at her, then his whole face split in half like a walnut, and he smiled from ear to ear. 'Mr Austin has good taste, miss.'

'Austin! That's it! Ted Austin!'

'No wonder you couldn't see him, miss. He's over there with his head stuffed in *The House Magazine*.' Beyond the stock phrases of courtesy, the porter reverted to his native Sarf Lunnon accent. 'Have a good lunch, miss.'

Cass sighed. Matchmaking MPs, Cupid porters – was the Palace of Westminster one big dating agency? As she walked across the Lobby, she chuckled to herself. She should bring Hallie here. That would scare the living daylights out of them.

'Ted Austin?' she asked the magazine-clad head. As his face lifted from its pages, his eyes closed briefly, and his lips moved as if in prayer. But it was a nice face, so she didn't hold it against him. A weakish face perhaps; big, apprehensive eyes not quite balanced by a pointy little chin, framed by longish, chestnuttish, wavyish hair. Definitely an -ish face, not too good-looking, not threatening. She breathed a sigh of relief.

'You must be Cass,' Ted stood up, his tone light. 'According to what Frank Blackthorn says, the girl of my dreams.' He had the faintest tinge of an ironed-out Northern accent.

Cass laughed. 'I pity you.'

'You pity me?'

'Those dreams of yours, they can't be much fun. Now *I* have James Bond dreams – they're fun, chasing the bad guys, exploding buildings, great gadgets, no-one gets hurt.'

'One person I am not,' Ted admitted ruefully, 'is James Bond. Hate heights. Can't stomach martinis. Don't have Pussy Galore. Or not even so Galore, come to think of it.'

'Hey, who offered you the part? I'm the one who's always James Bond.' He looked at her askance. 'Well, Jemima Bond perhaps.'

'Well, Jemima, now that we've got the important issues out of the way, would you like some lunch – the best that the Palace of Westminster has to offer us mere mortals?'

'You betcha. I only came because I was starving,' Cass said succinctly. 'Otherwise I would have blown you off.'

'I should be so lucky,' said Ted, deliberately misconstruing.

'Hey, watch it, mister,' Cass warned. 'I'm dangerous when I'm angry.'

'I can well believe it,' he told her seriously, shepherding her out of Central Lobby.

'I'll give you your first tour of the House between here and Strangers' – much easier to take this place in, little gobbets at a time. There's the Medical Room on the left – Members who are also doctors attend there on rota, in theory. In practice, the best you get is a sort of "snap out of it" school of medicine. Mind you, that's better than the old days when David Owen – you remember, old Doctor Death? – used to be the main bloke on call, funnily enough, no-one used to go. On the other side is the Families' Room – like a bleak old station waiting room where MPs' wives and kids hang out if they want – big excitements because MPs' husbands are now grudgingly allowed.'

Cass grinned. This guy was good.

'Equality is slowly limping its way through these revered portals. Even my mate Ben Bradshaw's boyfriend has been allowed a spouse's pass, which has shaken up the old fogies something chronic,' Ted went on. 'But no crèche yet – babies are still politically unacceptable. The laugh is that they're considering turning the Members' Rifle Range into childcare facilities, which would be too ironic.' He led her down the red-carpeted stairs into the bowels of the House and turned left. 'This is the Dining Corridor and through that door,' he gestured at a door leading to sunlight, 'is the Terrace. We'll go there for tea a few thousand times before long. John Prescott even jumped into the Thames from there last year.'

Cass laughed. 'Was he drunk?'

'No, doing it for charity. In a wetsuit. I reckon they could have raised the money just from seeing him in the wetsuit. Diving into the Thames was just an added extra. Right, that'll do for now. Let's get our dinner in.'

He led her into the queue for Strangers' Cafeteria. After a few minutes they were sitting down, Cass staring in disgust at her food, a tough-looking quiche and some sorry-for-themselves chips.

'This is the best?' she demanded.

''Fraid so,' Ted grimaced. 'Well, it's a toss-up between here and Plod's. Believe me, this place has improved out of all recognition since it was done up. It has slightly more variation, but fry-ups are better over at Plod's. That's the Policemen's Café over by the Great Hall. We'll go there next time.'

Cass raised one thick straight eyebrow. Presumptuous.

'Presumptuous, eh?' Ted grinned. 'Don't take this the wrong

way, but I wouldn't mind seeing more of you. This place is only fun when you've got someone to muck around with. Most of my mates from Medios have been sucked into government since the election, a couple have become MPs and are rushing around like headless chickens and the rest are humourless gits, so I need a new playmate.'

'Not totally flattering,' Cass said, then relented. 'Although Frank Blackthorn said almost exactly the same thing. One question: what is this Medios place?'

'A think-tank – nominally independent but basically Blairite – one of my mates is helping set up No. 10's Policy Unit. Quite a newcomer so it hasn't the sort of baggage that something like the Fabian Society has; we pride ourselves on sound, practical schemes, not ideological dogma.' Ted's eyes were shining. 'I never thought I'd say this about a think-tank, but it's a laugh working there.'

'And how come you can get in here?' Cass gestured round her. 'I thought you needed a pass to get around this place?'

'Yeah well, because we're non-profit-making, they're a little more lenient about us bending the rules – I've just kept my pass from the days when I worked as Frank's researcher.'

'And when was that?'

'About four years ago.'

'You've been working for Medios for four years?' Cass whistled. 'Impressive. I've never kept a job for more than two. What keeps the interest?'

'I love this place, for all its weird little ways,' Ted said simply. 'I love politics. It has cast its spell on me, I am bewitched, bothered and bewildered. More the last two after this election.'

'How come?'

'Hang on, what happened to "one question"?' he joked. 'Look, I stood for a Labour seat and missed getting it by 200-odd votes, so I was just a little pissed off. Granted, it was more of a safe Tory seat than anything else and I was put onto it to cut my teeth, but to be so close – and when half of my friends got in – was, well, galling.' He looked down at his plate.

'I sense understatement,' Cass said softly.

'Yes well, next time. Roll on the millennium. Then I shall be one of those four horsemen!' he smiled easily at her. 'Now, enough interrogation – what about you, who is Cass? So far, the only CV I got from Frank was "stunner" and "no pushover".'

Cass twinkled at him. 'All the salient information is there. Yes, I will stun you if you ask too many questions, but it's a painful blow because I do it with blunt objects. And "no pushover" sums the rest of me right up. Now. Coffee? Or is that disgusting as well? It cannot be as bad as institutional coffee in the States.'

With a start, she realised that for the first time since getting back to England she was enjoying herself. Hallie would kill her if she said this to her, but it was so refreshing not having a man hit on her for once.

The feeling of mild euphoria lasted until she got back to Dean's Yard. Hardly had she sat down, than her phone rang. She looked round nervously but Blackthorn had gone. It must be for Alun – no-one could possibly know that she was here – and if so, what was she going to say?

'Hello? Alun Blythe's office,' she said as bumptiously as possible.

There was a pause and then—

'Well, well, well – Cass Herbert. Right first time, so I am. I don't believe it. Well, that'll be the luck of the Irish, won't it?'

The husky voice was distantly familiar.

'Who is this?'

'Ah, Cass, you're after breaking me heart. Don't you remember me? And after all this trouble I've gone to, to track you down, with all I had to go on, a lousy piece of headed paper that I saw you holding on the plane. Do you not think I deserve some recognition for my skills of observation and sleuthing brilliance?'

Cass's heart sank.

Devlin Gray. It was bloody Devlin Gray.

'And you can stuff your fucking freelance policy up your tight little bum!'

If only she had the nerve to say it when they were still on the line, thought Nina mournfully, replacing the receiver. She was too cold to cry, too cold to do anything but un-pry her fingers from the telephone and slump her head into her arms, feet burrowing deeper into Jerry's shooting socks. Everyone and everything was ganging up against her. She couldn't get work for love nor money, had been abandoned by her supposedly devoted husband who had gone off for a day's networking in London, and she couldn't imagine ever being warm ever again. Fuck it, she didn't care if it was now June, this place was still Arctic – she was bloody well going to put on the heating. Just as long as she remembered to turn if off before Mr Bloody Bracing came back.

Once she'd flicked on the wheezing boiler, plucked a warming bar of Galaxy from the larder and put yet another cardigan over the three she had on already, she shuffled back to the desk. It couldn't be right that she was still so cold – she just had to be ill. Maybe she had some deadly strain of summer flu, or glandular fever or, God forbid, ME. ME! That's what it had to be – she felt permanently tired, listless, depressed, shivery, and those were surely the symptoms of ME! What were the others? If only someone had given them the Black's Medical Dictionary she'd put on her wedding list, rather than yet another *bain-marie*, she could have swotted up on it and other fascinating diseases.

Then she had a brainwave. This was what the Internet was for, wasn't it? She could cruise the information superhighway and become the world's greatest expert on ME in ten minutes flat. And, said a little voice inside her, put off doing any work for a few more minutes. Ignoring that little voice, she logged on, typing ME YUPPIE FLU. SYMPTOMS. ALTERNATIVE into the search engine. There, that should cover it.

For the next hour and a half, Nina was in hypochondriacs' heaven. There were no less than 100,000 entries in all, some fantastically random, some lurid, some so despairing they brought sympathetic tears to her eyes. Finally, she had information overload and logged out to the Demon Internet menu page, leaning back in her chair and rubbing her eyes; back and toe problems forgotten, shoved aside by these new exciting symptoms. There, winking temptingly at her, was the menu of Jerry's favourite options, including that Adult Chatline again. She glanced at her watch. Only three o'clock. Jerry wouldn't be back for ages. Oh, what the hell.

She logged in and registered her presence in the chat room.

> badboy@beinemann proud: welcome back, little miss
no-panties. glad to have you back on line. :-)
thought you'd shot through. now that ur here ru in the
mood to play with badboy?

Despite herself, Nina's stomach gave a little lurch of excitement.
Oh, sod it. Why not? She had dared to put on the heating, she
probably didn't have long to live, what with her ME and Jerry's
fury when he returned to a warm house, so she could dare to
do this, couldn't she?

> nk@jkenterprises: what did you have in mind,
badboy? I feel I should tell you that I'm not just not
wearing knickers today. How does nudity grab you?

She looked ruefully at the four cardigans wrapped round her,
the blanket over her legs and the heavy wool socks pulled up
over her fleecy leggings. If Badboy could see her now. Oh, the
power of the imagination.

'Come on, use your imagination!' Hallie urged Cass. 'It's a
well-known fact that women really go for the idea of a special
night out, even if the men end up paying for it—'
    'Hey that's sexist!' Cass interjected.
    'Hark at you, Miss PC. Although for this sort of thing, I may
be wrong – this might be the sort of treat that women do pay
for,' Hallie scribbled a few notes in her notebook. 'Where was
I? Oh yes, so we offer them a special weeknight rate, set aside
one dining room for early romantic dinners; they're tucked up
with all their toys upstairs by ten o'clock, plenty of time for
some healthy midweek sex and a good night's sleep, then it's up
bright and early the next morning for a pre-work massage, facial,
pedicure, whatever. Bingo! The Cosmopole Care-Package!'
    Cass looked round the breakfast room of the Cosmopole
Hotel. 'You're not really going to call it that, are you?' she
wrinkled her nose. 'It sounds more like something kids get
sent at summer camp.'
    'Working title, darling, I'm a PR girl – can't resist a bit of
alliteration. If you think of a better one, just let me know. Pass

me another brioche, would you? If I eat enough here, I won't have to buy myself lunch.' She grimaced at her friend. 'This week, I'm on a broke week, not a dieting week. Dieting is so expensive and at the moment I cannot afford it, so I'm reduced to stocking up on free food when I can and starving myself the rest of the time.'

'Good idea,' agreed Cass, 'but you should taste the food at the House.'

'The house? Whose house?'

'House of Commons, dumbo. The food may be subsidised but it's so gross it's a diet in itself.'

'Well, if it was any good, lobbyists wouldn't be able to persuade any of the MPs to come out to lunch, would they?'

'Guess so. I wonder if Alun is a lobbyist-friendly Member? I can't really see him being that way but with this new City job he must be getting mobbed,' Cass chewed thoughtfully.

'What's he actually like?'

Cass perked up. 'He's great, just great. He takes a bit of getting used to, I suppose because I was expecting some lofty politician – the ones I met in the States were such arrogant pricks – but Alun couldn't be more,' Cass's tone turned ironic, 'of a "man of the people". You should see him with his secretary, Mags – they're such a double act, it's totally hysterical. I have no idea what I'm doing most of the time, and, to be honest, I'm not really sure the job is going to be what I wanted. For the sort of contacts I wanted to make, I should have got a job in his Private Office over at the Ministry. Then again, if I worked there, he would hardly know who I am he goes there so seldom. But I'm having a total blast and—' Cass looked over and saw that she had lost her friend's attention completely, as Hallie gazed round the breakfast room and scribbled down notes. 'And the best moment was when Alun took me round the Chamber, bent me backwards over the Speaker's Chair and fucked me senseless, with Ken Livingstone looking on and taking notes for his next performance there.'

'Ken Livingstone, eh?' murmured Hallie. 'Good.' Then her head shot up. 'Hang on, what did you say? Alun did what?!'

'Got your attention anyway,' smirked Cass.

'Pig.'

'Swine.'

'Same as pig.'

They smiled at each other, their childhood ritual completed.

'Talking of shagging,' Hallie grinned, 'any gossip? Have you been giving Pamella Bordes a run for her money? Caught out any MPs doing what they shouldn't?'

'Hardly. It's a positive hotbed of respectability so far. The only people I see are Ted, Alun, Mags and the other secretaries in her office and this other MP called Frank Blackthorn. He's happily married, I think, and Mags and all the secretaries are totally worthy women in tweed skirts and sensible shoes – although I have a suspicion that Mags might drink: she's got this huge purse that clinks when she comes in, and which looks much lighter when she goes home again. But Alun, even though he is divorced and so is fair game for any hankypanky, seems as straight as a die.'

'Very disappointing,' said Hallie briskly, rummaging in her bag and bringing out a camera. 'Who's Ted?'

Cass looked proud. 'He's my new friend. I met him on the first day and we clicked, just like that. For a few moments I was actually being nice.'

'So you don't fancy him,' Hallie nodded knowingly. 'What's he like?'

'He's lovely. Really sweet, funny, clever. A little puppy-dog.'

'You definitely don't fancy him then.' But from the sound of it, he's fallen for you, as they always do, thought Hallie uncharitably. She stood up, camera in hand. 'Now you keep sitting there, sweetie – I'm just going to run round and take some pictures.'

'What of?'

'Oh, you know, the breakfast room – the sort of people who are here and the potential it has for possible breakfast events – like presentations, informal demonstrations etc. Back in a sec.'

The Cosmopole was the new hotel of the moment. With its starker-than-Starck decor, impossibly crowded bar and viciously expensive Yen sushi restaurant, it was currently top of the pops in the media. The trouble was, that no-one was actually staying there: above the baying of the bar and the ringing of cash-tills in the restaurant, were echoing, silent rooms by the dozen. Bandwick & Parker were pitching for the opportunity to fill those rooms and Hallie had come up with an idea to achieve this without overburdening the already saturated evening catering. Part of her research was to check the Cosmopole out in the mornings, hence why Cass and she were gorging themselves on a Cosmopole continental breakfast.

After a few minutes, Hallie came back and sat down again. 'You know, snooping round with a camera like this has given me an idea. Wouldn't it be a wonderful gossipy morning TV programme if you had cameramen hidden in the dining rooms of a few of London's poshest hotels and almost as a live feed, were able to bust the rich and famous couples who were noshing on their Crunchy Nut Cornflakes after a hot night of getting up to no good? It would be like *Hello!* but live and on the telly!'

Cass thought for a moment. 'There's a fatal flaw – anyone rich and famous and up to no good wouldn't be breakfasting down here, they'd be romping through a room service smorgasbord.'

Hallie sighed. 'You're right. Of course you're right. But it is funny watching people and speculating on what they're up to. Take that couple behind you, I got a picture of them virtually snogging over their sausages: if they're married, then that gives me real hope.'

Cass twisted round to see the back of a middle-aged man in a crumpled suit with his head close to that of a thirtysomething woman with still lustrous black hair and a perfectly oval face.

'Cass! Be a little more subtle!'

Cass turned back quickly. 'No way are they married. They're far too into each other. If they were married they wouldn't be speaking. No, I'm surprised you haven't gone on the manhunt here yet, Hal, there's a couple of really dishy guys over there.'

Hallie followed her glance. 'Cass darling, they're gay.'

'No!'

''Fraid so.'

'Christ,' said Cass ruefully. 'My gaydar is letting me down. I was such a faghag in New York, you'd have thought I would be able to tell at first glance but I suppose my friends there were so obviously gay that I stopped having to try to work it out.'

'Gaydar? Oh, I get it. Yeah, well, take it from someone who has finely tuned antennae, those blokes are off-limits as far as we're concerned,' Hallie assured her. 'Talking of which, are you ready for tomorrow's extravaganza?'

Cass frowned. 'Tomorrow?'

'Fulham Funsters? The singles' club? Oh, don't say you've forgotten!' Hallie wailed. 'You promised! I can't go on my own.'

'No, that's fine!' Cass assured her. 'It'll give me the perfect excuse to curtail my drink with Devlin bloody Gray – you know, the jerk from the airplane?'

Hallie nodded.

'The creep tracked me down right to Alun's office, just from seeing me re-reading my job offer letter from Alun when I was on the plane, and would not take no for an answer. So I finally gave in and said I would have a short drink with him tomorrow. This way I can get out of it real quick and easy.' Cass looked satisfied.

'I wish I were in a position to "finally give in" to a date,' Hallie said morosely.

Devlin was not going to give in and concede defeat; his Celtic ancestors would be spinning in their graves if he let a mere colleen walk all over him. In all his twenty-six years, Devlin's easy Irish charm had cracked even the hardest nut within two dates at the most. Numerous bets taken out when he was at Trinity College, Dublin, that he wouldn't be able to sweet-talk this or that nice Catholic girl into doing unholy things on him with their rosary beads had netted a sweet little extra-curricular income. But he had to admit that he had met his match in Cass.

At first glance on that plane, she had fallen neatly into Dev's generous bracket of women he found attractive. Nearly as tall as he was, with an irresistibly Black Irish combination of a cloud of black hair, cat-like palest green-grey eyes and pale skin, and a feisty outlook, she had seemed a worthy adversary. Even the fact that she had been hostile and had resorted to faking lesbianism had spurred him on. If she's running that hard, he had patted himself on the back, she must be keen.

But a man of Devlin's ego, laid-back and easygoing as he was, could not take the sort of sustained scorn that Cass was dishing out. Outright aggression he could counter; being ignored left him nowhere to go. Not to mention that the gorgeous if badtempered temptress he had chatted up on the plane had been transformed into a crop-haired virago who looked more Sinead O'Connor than Maureen O'Sullivan.

'So why won't you have dinner with me?' he pressed on.

Cass looked up from the newspaper she was apparently absorbed in, thick eyebrows still so tightly knitted together that Dev couldn't even see into the green eyes that had initially bewitched him.

'What? Oh, dinner. I'm bored of restaurants. And I'm broke.'

'Well, that's no problem,' said Devlin happily.

'Do you really think I would let you pay for me?' Cass said with politically correct vitriol.

'Not at all!' he said, outraged. 'You'd be paying for yourself every step of the way, so you would. No, but first I need to reimburse you.'

'Huh?'

'Because I promised myself that for every full sentence I got out of you tonight, I would pay you a fiver. Now, by my calculations,' Devlin started counting out notes with exaggerated aplomb, 'so far that means I owe you forty quid. Put half aside for your savings account and we've still got enough for a halfway decent dinner!'

Cass tried to maintain her sternness. 'Here's a full sentence for you. Go directly to jail, do not pass go, do not pick up two hundred pounds – and no, I will not have dinner with you. Is that clear enough for you?' she smiled at him triumphantly.

Progress! exulted Devlin. A smile! From little acorns grow stonking great oaks. I'll have you in my bed yet, you prickly pear. 'Didn't quite catch the last part,' he said, beaming at her with all the little-boy-lost charm he had, 'but I'm an old hand at spending the night in jail. It's all part of being a glamorous rock star, you know.'

'Yes, the Blazing Sadlads,' said Cass dryly. 'Hey, U2, watch your back, the Sadlads are poised to steal your thunder. So, have you reached the glamorous heights of trashing hotel rooms yet?'

'Not quite – it would surely be a case of coals to Newcastle if we were to trash the fleapits we usually stay in,' Dev said ruefully, 'but I have a great story. I'm told that one of the boys from Marillion or AC/DC made a right old mess of his hotel room when he was staying in the penthouse suite of some ritzy high-rise hotel but when he came to check out, he was an amiable soul indeed, standing there like a lamb while the concierge totted up the bill in its thousands. Eventually the concierge plucked up the courage to ask him why he hadn't thrown the telly out of the window. "I've always wanted to throw a telly out of a window," sighs the concierge. The rockstar looks at him, looks at the bill and smiles. "Tell you what," he says, "add a thousand to the bill – and you go and throw that TV out – go nutty!" Isn't that grand?'

Now Cass couldn't help but laugh. 'And this is the peak of your ambition, is it? Throwing TVs from a great height? Question is – who are you going to end up as? The rockstar or the concierge?'

But she had long lost Devlin's attention. Sweet Jesus, he was thinking dazedly, she laughs just like Yogi Bear – huck, huck, huck. By all the saints, I love this girl. I have to have her. Suddenly he had a plan – a cheeky plan but, as they said on the *Enterprise* every time, 'it might just work, Captain'.

'Forget about the Sadlads just for a moment,' he urged her, 'and let's talk about us—'

Cass snorted derisively. 'Us? There is no "us"!'

Dev pounced. 'Yes, but there could be, couldn't there? I mean, it's nearly nine o'clock so you're as good as having dinner with me now. Then, once you've had dinner with me, what's to stop us heading off to find the real craic – in Dublin? I'm not an unreasonable man, I'll give you a month before you have to come, but in the end, you'll have to – you'll know it makes sense. If you don't, you'll know you've been a coward, a lowdown, yellow-bellied coward. So come on, I dare you!'

Cass was looking at him in horror. 'What time did you say it was? Nearly nine o'clock? Shit squared, Hallie's going to kill me. I have to go!' She leapt up from the table, grabbing her leather jacket, then paused. 'And as for me coming to Dublin – dream on, buster, dream on.'

And with that damning parting line, she left the pub.

Don't you worry, Cass, thought Devlin broodingly, I'm good at dreaming . . . you after a day's carousing round Temple Bar, relaxed and tiddly; me having just come off stage, the screams of a hundred groupies ringing in our ears. You'll hardly be able to resist me, but I'll hold back until we're in our suite at the Clarence, soaking away the day in our rooftop Jacuzzi. Then and only then, will I touch you like a lover. I'll pull you gently towards me, positioning you right over one of the more powerful jets, so you'll gasp and blush as sensations you have never known before flood through you. Meanwhile I will be stroking you gently with sandalwood oil – every last delectable inch of you – until you're a quivering slick bundle of desire and then—

'Look, have you finished with these glasses?'

Devlin opened his eyes to see the barmaid leaning over him, her tired, sweaty face looming uncomfortably close, that harsh voice still echoing in his ears.

Mary, Mother of God, but I hate London, he thought, standing up abruptly and pulling his jacket over his erection. I just have to get her to Dublin.

I am going to have to do this on my own, thought Hallie savagely, mentally loading an arsenal of guns to use later on Cass. I can't believe I am going to have to do this on my own. She looked again at all the Fulham Funsters literature she had been sent. 'Enter by the King's Club door on Park Walk,' the invitation instructed her, 'and follow the signs.' Sounded simple enough. She drained her Diet Pepsi and stood up to leave the Goat in Boots, the pub underneath the King's Club. Leaving by a side entrance, she found herself on the right street, just next to a vividly painted, bright red door leading up a flight of intensely blue steps. At the top of these, she paused. Ahead of her were two blokes, both good-looking, lounging in a magnificent, but untidy, dimly-lit room, and having a fag. Perhaps these were her and Cass's dates, gulped Hallie nervously.

Taking her courage in all limbs, she tottered into the room. 'Er, excuse me,' she waved the Fulham Funsters brochure vaguely at them, 'do you know if, well, where, I mean, you know—'

One of them took pity on her. 'Not here, I'm afraid, we're just getting this room ready for a party tomorrow.' He looked at her consideringly. 'I think you need the top floor. Don't bother knocking. The door will be open – just go in.'

'Top floor. Great. Thanks.'

Embarrassed? thought Hallie furiously as she stumped up the stairs. No, no. I am just going to kill Cass.

She finally reached the top floor and there, sure enough, was one door, slightly ajar. Pushing it open with a creak, Hallie stepped gingerly in. There was a long dark corridor with the soft sound of muted voices coming from a room at the end. Bingo! she thought, I've made it. She negotiated her way down the corridor and pushed the door open. As she did so, the voices stopped.

Inside were five people, clustered round a shiny lino table covered in maps and papers, holding what looked like glasses of orange squash. One of them, an officious-looking woman with a bun and Nana Mouskouri glasses, picked up a clipboard and crossed the room to confront a frozen Hallie.

She looked Hallie up and down, without saying a word, checking something on her clipboard. Then, 'So they sent you did they? Turn round, please.'

A bemused Hallie did so.

'Hmmmm, yes, well I suppose you will have to do. Please change next door, then join us.'

This could not be right. Hallie finally found her voice. 'I'm sorry,' she started tentatively, 'is this not the Fulham Funsters?'

All five of them stopped what they were doing, and stared at her.

'No, obviously not,' stumbled Hallie, 'sorry to bother you, must have gone one floor too far, my mistake, carry on, please.' As she spoke, she was backing towards the door, spun round into the corridor and legged it, out of the flat, down the stairs and into the street, crashing straight into an astonished Cass.

'Hallie! What the—?'

Hallie hardly knew whether to laugh or cry. 'Cass, it was unbelievable – I think I just avoided getting sucked into some sort of sect, or terrorist cell, or something deeply spooky anyway.'

'The Fulham Funsters are a sect?!'

'No, well, I don't think so – oh Cass, it was so weird.'

Cass looked at her watch. 'Well, we still have time to grab a drink in this godforsaken town, so let's do it, and you can tell me all about it.'

'OK,' said Hallie meekly.

4

Hallie was going to have to leave without her knickers.
Why oh why hadn't she got up when he'd left for the hospital? That way she would have had time to compose herself, find all her scattered clothes and have time to go home before work. Instead she had lain in a post-morning-glory daze, glorying in the warm scents and squelches of lovemaking, gradually falling into a deliciously recreative nap, until it was well past 8.30. Now she'd only had time for a 30-second shower, her hair was still tangled at the back in that telltale pillow friction giveaway, and she was going to have to head into the office in these obvious date clothes, without being mentally prepared for the inevitable ribbing. Oh, and she still couldn't find her knickers, despite tearing the bed apart, firtling down the back of every sofa and armchair and even checking the overhead lampshade, remembering one past embarrassment, when some bloke's mother had guessed that Hallie was hiding in her son's bed because of the bra still swinging from the chandelier light.

She might have suspected him of taking them to work with him as some sort of trophy but why would he suddenly start doing that now? So, no knickers anywhere – leaving Hallie to do her Sharon Stone impression all day. She would just have to pray that her lightning speed shower had taken care of any rogue juices – this was not the day to be cooped up in an airlessly hot office trying to impress the whole of the Labour Millbank team that she was the right person to join the B&P team, if she was going to smell like she'd just left an orgy.

Worse was yet to come, as she crept past Josh's room, only to be caught red-handed as she wrestled with the front door latch.

'Hallie!' Josh came out of his room, rubbing his eyes. 'This is a surprise! You weren't here when I came back last night were you?'

'Er, no,' confessed Hallie, 'I arrived quite late. About midnight.'

'Now, that's what I call a midnight feast for my dear brother!' he grinned. 'Has he left for the hospital already? Are you not staying for a cup of coffee? We haven't had a gossip for ages.'

There's one simple reason for that, Hallie thought savagely. 'No, sorry, Josh, I have to go – late for work.'

'Yeah, how is the new job? I couldn't believe it when Bro told me that you'd joined the ranks of the taxpayers and had a proper job. You traitor!'

'When are you going to change agents, Josh? You must have realised that JDN are scumbags and pompous weasels by now, if the best auditions they can get you are on *Crimewatch* re-constructions. And how is the cartooning going?'

Too late, Hallie realised that she was being drawn back into her bad old habits, of being too involved with this fascinating, mercurial, ultimately destructive family. 'On second thoughts, I really must go – I have the biggest meeting of my career today. Bye Josh.'

'Hallie! Just one more thing!'

Hallie paused at the door. 'What?'

'That fetching little see-through number you have on,' grinned Josh, 'it's buttoned up wrong. Just a thought, if you're going to,' he mugged, '*the biggest meeting of your career.*'

'Ohhhhh,' growled Hallie, slamming the door behind her and re-buttoning her top. This was positively the last time she was going to do this, just turning up unannounced, jumping into bed with him and, worst of all, staying the whole night.

It was all the fault of that, that *berk* she had made the mistake of going out with last night.

'Hallie, you'll love him,' Karenza had assured her. Even then she should have seen the danger signs – what was she doing allowing herself to be set up by her assistant? 'He's called Saul, he's my friend Tiffany's boss, he's loaded, dishy, split up with his girlfriend last year and has been single ever since. What more could you ask for?'

Hallie, buried in political briefs, fending off a posse of client calls and dealing with a shrewish Beth demanding to know when she was going to pay the gas bill, hadn't felt able to answer at the time. Now, however, she could sit down and give Karenza an A-Z of what more she *should* have asked for, before allowing herself to be subjected to Saul's company for longer than it took her to swig down her first Diet Pepsi.

Drinks at the Criterion, dinner at Quo Vadis, drinks afterwards at his club, Soho House. It was any girl's dream date. But the danger signs were there from the beginning. Five minutes after they had introduced themselves, Saul had leant forward conspiratorially and said something which made Hallie's blood run cold.

'You know, I thought the girls had to be exaggerating when they described you as being as pretty as Anthea Turner, myself being rather a fan of Anthea, as well as an old, old friend. But I'm sure Anthea wouldn't mind me saying that you are, if anything, even prettier than her. That's not bad, is it, being prettier than a media icon? And it's not bad for me, either, if you catch my drift, heh, heh, heh.'

Despite this unpromising beginning, Hallie hadn't given up without a struggle. Karenza and Tiffany had promised that Saul was a lovely man, an eligible dream come true. He was certainly good-looking, with his three-piece, high waistcoated suit, shiny cobalt-blue shirt and razor-sharp haircut, waxed into little peaks at the front – a little too Jason Orange for her personal taste, but beggars couldn't be choosers. After all, he'd had a long-term girlfriend until last year – he couldn't be that bad. She must try harder.

Sadly, after only a few minutes, Hallie had to face facts. She was stuck with a namedropping, media-obsessed, humourless git who thought that being on first name terms with the Spice Girls gave him the sexual allure of Brad Pitt; that in the post-Cold War period, fashion was the new idiom of revolution and should be taken as seriously; and that Damien Hirst's formaldehyded animals in Quo Vadis were 'an ironic contemplation of the origins of food – where the savagery of the exhibits is seen through a glass darkly in the sophistication of Marco's food'. Hallie had to nip to the loo to write that last piece of bombast down, knowing that she would have to have proof for herself later that this was not a prospect worth pursuing and convinced that otherwise Karenza wouldn't believe her. Every time she had opened her mouth, she had been uncomfortably aware that Saul was just waiting for her to finish what she was saying before launching into another 'famous-people-I-have-met' anecdote.

Even Hallie's natural eagerness to please had been stretched by Saul's post-prandial tirade of semi-fascistic drivel of how men did men's things and women did women's things and that was just the natural order of things. Then the bill arrived. After ten minutes of watching it sit in the no-man's-land between them, Hallie had surprised herself by throwing politeness (and political correctness) to the winds.

'So, isn't paying for dinner a man's thing?' she heard herself saying, watching her hand pushing the bill towards him.

But Saul had the nerve to push it back, saying, 'Oh, I'm sure Bandwick & Parker could cover this, couldn't they? Hey, what can I say – I'm a pirate. Take from the rich and live life to the max: that's my motto – and one you', he pointed at her with both index fingers, 'should remember in your line of work. After all, B&P would kill to get my', now he was gesturing back at himself with his thumbs, 'company as a client. You know it's true, sweetheart.'

The fact that he was probably right didn't make Hallie like him any more, but she had gritted her teeth and paid the bill. Then when they stood up to go, she had been unable to resist jogging her hip at precisely the right angle to tip her carefully re-filled coffee cup all over his cream linen trousers. 'Oh, I'm so clumsy!' she had exclaimed, as he leapt up swearing and cursing, then added sweetly, 'but then I suppose clumsiness is just a woman's thing, isn't it, Saul? I'd never make a good pirate, would I?'

Even then her pride wouldn't allow her to duck the final hurdle at Soho House, a decision she regretted when they got there. Watching Saul, semi-hunched to hide his coffee stain, waving at everyone and anyone at the incongruously shiny steel bar and making phoning gestures at them with little finger and thumb while saying, 'Call me on the mobile tomorrow!' made her want to slide unobtrusively between the wooden floorboards. Talk about the Hunchback of Wotcher!Smarm – well, she may be desperate but no way was she going to be his Esmerelda. At the earliest opportunity she had pleaded tiredness, rejecting his immediate offer of a 'few lines of Charlie – total rocket fuel, sweetheart' and had dived into the night. Avoiding the carousing crowds on the pavement as she walked down Shaftesbury Avenue, Hallie realised that this was yet another night she was coming home alone after a date. It couldn't be coincidence. It couldn't be the fact that Saul was a creep; it must be more that she was somehow deficient, had kiboshed the date herself. Who was she fooling, being so picky?

It had now been over a month since Cass had come back and together they had plumbed the depths of singles' hell. Cass had done her best to humour Hallie but obviously couldn't understand why Hallie was so deadset on finding a man; nor could Hallie confide in Cass her real reasons, fearful as she was of condemnation from her morally-didactic friend. At the same time, Hallie had not dared bring up John's name with Cass, not wanting to open old wounds, so their old frankness was sadly curtailed.

I will tell her, Hallie had thought as she looked for a taxi in Piccadilly Circus, but just not yet. Once a taxi pulled up, the thought of going back to Beth and the damp-shirt-smelling Slammer had depressed her so much, that, without thinking through the consequences of her action, she had asked the cabbie to go to Primrose Hill instead, phoning him quickly from her mobile to warn him that she was on her way.

When he opened the door, to find a mulish-looking Hallie in her battered finery, he had said nothing at first, just ushering her in with a raised eyebrow and an exploratory hand on her waist.

'Don't read anything into this,' Hallie had said defensively. 'I've just had a terrible evening and felt like a bit of a pick-me-up.'

He had laughed. 'I'm a pick-me-up now, am I? So who failed to pick you up tonight?'

As per usual Hallie found herself telling him everything, deliberately making the whole nightmarish evening funnier than it had been and casting herself in her habitual Lois Lane-like role of deprecating feistiness and wit. All through, he had listened with his usual attention, interspersing the odd dry comment and stroking her gently from face to hip as they cuddled closer on the sofa.

'My poor little Hallie,' he had said finally, 'you have to stop beating yourself up about today's creep, yesterday's creep, tomorrow's creep.'

'Thanks a lot,' she had retorted. 'They're not all creeps. Saul was apparently so irresistible that none of his exes have since found boyfriends, remember, because "once you've had the best, you won't want the rest" so most women obviously don't think he's such a moron.' She shook her head. 'I'm just conducting a thorough survey of all demographic types. After all, I would hate to go for one stereotype of man—' she pulled a face at him.

He ignored this. 'But when are we going to find you a decent man, who's going to appreciate you for the funny, quick-thinking, talented little thing you really are?'

As ever, Hallie felt like a sunflower turning its face to a huge, golden sun. Feeling herself about to say something she would regret, she bit her lip and opted for lightness. 'I'd settle for an indecent man just at this moment, believe me.'

'I can do indecent,' he murmured, dipping his lips to nibble softly at her earring.

'I said settle for, you idiot, not shoot myself in the foot with,' she gasped, her hands going up by Pavlovian reflex to rake gently at his back.

'Mmm, quite right, very sensible,' he had agreed, carrying on regardless.

And that had been that, thought Hallie now, as she emerged from Tottenham Court Road tube, feeling the morning breeze whip at her sleep-deprived skin. Another grope, another guiltfest. Another day of trying to ignore the fact that every step she took forward in her career was mirrored by yet another step backwards in her personal life. Take the last month as a little petri-dish demonstration. The great coup of her Giuseppe idea, which the client had loved and had then instantly leaked to the media –

resulting in days of coverage – had happened in the same week as she had finally chosen which man to go out with from Elite Introductions.

She had chosen well – he had been good-looking, interesting, good for a banter and a flirt, and the only reason she could work out why he'd gone through the Elite treatment was because he was a thirty-eight-year-old divorcé whose friends were all married. The trouble was that he obviously thought that he had *not* chosen well. Towards the end of the dinner, he had suddenly stopped being able to look her in the eye, had started looking at his watch, murmuring about how he needed his sleep and she'd never heard from him again. How galling was that? To descend to the depths of dating agencies and then to be rejected?

Maybe she would have to give up the proactive search for a man and depend on fate and happenstance stepping in to provide, if not Mr Right, then at least Mr Meanwhile. Anyway, given her current cycle of job success/life failure, today was not the day to hang out for the man of her dreams. Because today was the day she was moving up the ladder from PR fashion and consumer guru to public affairs spin doctress. Today was the day she was pitching for *herself*: to be taken on by the Public Affairs side of B&P as their PR liaison to the Labour Party account. If all went well, she would retain her independence and remain Account Director on her favourite accounts, while being attached to the Public Affairs team and all their political shenanigans. It was not the day to fuss about her continuing sexual independence.

Watch out world, she thought irrepressibly, here I come. From fallen woman to rising star in one easy movement.

'Today is the day I make all your dreams come true!' Cass said triumphantly, as she and Hallie sat in Bellamy's, the Parliament Street bar for the Bright Young Things of Westminster.

'Great views from up here,' Hallie replied absently, looking over the sun-soaked, almost sleepy traffic of Parliament Square. 'I've given up dreams-which-come-true, by the way, after last night's fiasco.' She had given Cass an edited and dramatised version of events with Saul, missing out the last part. Playing an imaginary violin for herself, she had told her friend that she had sloped sadly home to Islington after the Worst Date of All Time.

'Ah, but that was a blind date. This isn't, this is just an opportunity to meet new – and by all accounts, gorgeous – people, one of whom I know and can vouch for. Just like you've been saying you wanted – fresh meat which comes from a butcher you know, rather than sending off for mail order steaks, where you don't know what you're getting.'

'Charming analogy, Cass,' said Hallie dryly.

'Since when did you start using words like "analogy" in casual conversation?' Cass teased her. 'Oh, I know, since you became,' she deepened her voice, 'The Most Powerful Woman in Politics!'

'Belt up, you cow. Just tell me what you're wittering on about, so that I can tell you "no", finish my Coke and get home in time for ER.'

Cass looked long and hard at her friend. It was not like Hallie to be so irritable.

'Do you remember Devlin Gray, the guy I sat next to on the plane, coming back from the States?'

'Yup. The prat.'

'Well, it turns out that he isn't a prat. He's actually a nice guy,' Cass said carefully, remembering that she was going to have to tread carefully if Hallie was going to fall for this one, 'who's in a band called the Blazing Sadlads.'

'My favourite film!' Hallie perked up. '*Blazing Saddles* is, anyway.'

'Exactly – that was the first thing I thought of,' Cass lied. 'Anyway, I've been seeing a bit of him this past month, and he invited me – along with a load of other people,' – careful, Cass, you're overdoing this, 'to watch him and the Lads play at some music festival in Dublin this weekend.'

'What – and you want me to come with you?' No thank you very much, thought Hallie sourly – yet another weekend of trailing in your wake as every male with a pulse throws himself at you. Oh yes, just what my ego needs.

'No, I need you to go instead of me,' Cass said quickly. 'I've totally double-booked myself, and I'm going to have to go on this gender workshop weekend down in Tunbridge Wells, so I'll have to blow Devlin & Co off. And it just seems such a waste, having bought the plane tickets already.' She brought them out of her rucksack to wave at Hallie, 'So I suddenly thought you should go instead of me, hang out with Devlin and the Lads, mooch around Dublin, listen to some great music and generally hang loose for a change.'

Hallie was looking unconvinced. But not hostile to the idea.

'And I hope you don't mind,' Cass went on, 'but I've already told Dev that I can't make it and that you're coming in my place and he actually said, "Oh *Hallie* – is that the blonde babe you were with that day at the airport?" so I guess you could say it isn't a blind date at all – because you've both seen each other before and you obviously both liked what you saw.'

Hallie looked impressed. 'Mr Memory, if he can remember a split-second impression from that far back.'

'What can I say? He's Irish!'

'And therefore pissed as a fart from dawn onwards no doubt,' Hallie was suddenly gloomy again. 'Not much fun for me being as good as teetotal.'

Cass crossed her fingers. 'The incredible thing is he hardly drinks – at least, not when he's about to play,' she added swiftly, in response to Hallie's disbelieving look.

'And what about the tickets? You can't transfer tickets from person to person.'

'Yeah well, this is where having a friend who used to be a travel journalist comes in mighty handy,' Cass crowed. 'Nina says that if you fly from Stansted or Luton, you don't have to show your passport – which means you can fly on anyone's ticket, as long as they're the same sex, because no-one checks your ID.'

'You've been discussing all this with Nina?' said an outraged Hallie. 'I can just hear how that goes: "Oh, what are we going to do about poor, desperate, little Hallie – she can't find herself a man" – well, thanks a lot!'

Cass was beginning to wonder if she wasn't getting in over her head here. 'We're not trying to find you a man – far from it, I wouldn't wish Devlin on anyone as a serious prospect. No, but you're always complaining that you never meet new people and I guess I thought this was the perfect opportunity. And of course I talked to Nina about it – she is our best friend, you know, and is beginning to feel kind of left out of our lives, by the way – and she says that if you don't go, she will, because apparently Jerry is being boring at the moment, and she fancies a weekend on the razzle.'

As Cass had hoped, Hallie rose to the bait. 'Hey! No way! Give me those tickets! Nina's already got a man – I'm not going to let her hog this occasion. What the heck, Dublin is fab, apparently. Yes, I'll go!'

Thank God for that, thought Cass wearily, I convinced her. Now Cass just had to convince herself that she was doing the right thing, setting Hallie up like this. After the first shock, she was sure that Dev would be fine – he was Irish, after all, and totally easy-going – he would see the joke. And she would pay him back for the tickets. Hallie need never know that Devlin had sent them to her, already paid for. He could afford it, with his rich stud-farm-owning father, and certainly wouldn't hold it against Hallie. Yes, she was definitely doing the right thing.

'Go, girl!' she said in her best Harlemese. 'You gonna have a good time wid dese boyz!'

'Whatever,' said Hallie, her mind already planning what she was going to wear.

Like so many other nights since she had married Jerry, Nina was lying rigid beside him, as he began the long, snuffling journey into a full-blown snoring session. Even with her eyes open in the darkness, she could picture the mucus gathering into the back of his throat, the phlegm settling flatly in his lungs, could feel the slight shifts into position as he rooted further down the bed, off the pillow and stretched onto his back, could hear the timid whistles and flutings that were like little air raid sirens for the blitz about to follow.

The difference this time was that Nina wanted him to start. She was, in fact, tense with impatience for the nocturnal rock'n'roll to get rumbling. That way she would know that she had no chance of sleeping for a while and that Jerry was deeply asleep enough for her to get up and out of bed without disturbing him.

At last, she felt him take in a huge lungful of air through his nose. Sure enough, what came out was the usual road-hammer cannonade. He was off. Gently, she pulled back the duvet, extricated herself from his protective arm and slid out of bed, groping in the dark for her bedsocks and fleecy sweatshirt, to go over her pyjamas.

Having cocooned herself in the usual shell of blankets, Nina was soon logged on. She looked at her watch. Nearly two in the morning. She was almost exactly on time. So this was what it felt like to be unfaithful, she mused, making secret rendezvous with your lover, sneaking away from your husband. Because she and BadBoy were lovers now. Over the past few weeks, Nina had logged on nearly every day, soon going into a private on-line chat-room with BadBoy, and together they had gone straight to the heart of things. Moving on from the smutty, arch banter of their first few exchanges, they had become more serious and intent. Swapping sexual fantasies had just been the start, yet all the time they had preserved their anonymity by not revealing their names or anything pertinent about themselves. Now, tonight, they were crossing another line in their relationship . . .

>badboy@beinemann proud: nk ru there?

>nk@jkenterprises: I'm here, BadBoy, ready and waiting. Ready and nervous, actually.

>badboy@beinemann proud: actually? gahd i love your english accent. don't be nervous hon, i'll be here to hold your hand.

>nk@jkenterprises: isn't that what I am meant to be doing?;)

>badboy@beinemann proud: nice use of emoticons darl, you're a fast learner. ok here's how we're gonna do this. i'm gonna tell you what i'm doing then you're gonna tell me your reaction, then its your turn and i tell you how i'm feeling - turn and turnabout. geddit?

>nk@jkenterprises: my English reserve is holding me back here a bit, BadBoy, but underneath it all I'm willing and eager. I love the thought of the resurrection of the written word – that it can have the power to make you and me feel turned on, illicit, naughty and, OK, yes, a little bit foolish. Do you remember that bit in Lawnmower Man where Joel and some computer goddess make virtual love – and what we saw was two shiny, Terminator 2-like beings getting all swirly and cosmic? Well, for me that was just plain silly. But this, this is like going back in time to our ancestors writing each other love letters and leaving them in their secret old oak tree for each other to find. There is an old-fashioned romance to this medium that thrills me so, go ahead, woo me, bring me flowers made of bits and bytes, bring me chocolates of emoticons and sweet-talk me with acronyms!

>badboy@beinemann proud: nk, you just crack me up. almost as much as you turn me on. i've already got a hard-on which is straining at my jeans, so i'm just going to take it out and give the poor guy some breathing space. i'm sitting here staring at the screen, wishing that i could see you there, feel you here, and here and here. instead i am having to imagine the person behind your words – this blue-eyed, petite little miss thang – naked before me, her tiny breasts peaking from underneath a wave of golden hair, that sassy, foxy look i know you have when you type those words to me, the little pink tip of your tongue squirming its way out from behind your teeth in concentration. aaah, if i could just be that little pink tip, nudging myself into your wet, little mouth –

There was a pause. Nina stared at the blinking cursor on the screen, half-horrified, half-wanting to laugh. So much for Victorian romance! And how could she have told all those lies about her appearance? For BadBoy's purposes, wouldn't her real-life brown hair, brown eyes, brown skin have served just as well? Was this now her cue to come on board and talk BadBoy through her reactions, then start some action herself?

>badboy@beinemann proud: sorry about that, nk, things got kinda out of control there for a second. howya doing at that end?

Fuck me, thought Nina appositely, my turn now. Oh well, here goes nothing.

>nk@jkenterprises: I like to feel that you are here with me, BadBoy, your curly black hair and green eyes boring into mine, as I peel off my clothes. I watch them widen as I take off the lingerie I have worn especially for the occasion and you can see right to the heart of me. Then I take your hand and pull it towards me so that for the first time you can feel the smooth curves between hip and breast, into the hollows of my neck and up round my chin, trail your fingers over my lips, plumped with desire now, igniting anew the fires in my cheeks. My breath is coming faster now as your fingers send vapour trails of lust down every vein to the centre of me, my--

Nina paused, hitting the 'Enter' key by mistake. She was pleased with herself for getting so carried away but stumped for an acceptable word for – down there. Wasn't fanny something different in American, like bum? BadBoy would think her very strange if she started talking about lustful sensations in her bum. Perhaps she should just move on—

>badboy@beinemann proud: nk, can you just cut to the chase? i don't know if i can hold on much longer here.

Nina stared again at the screen. 'Cut to the chase'?– What the fuck was that supposed to mean? Oh, this was just ridiculous;

as bad as, if not worse than, Jerry and his Houston Hotlips. Who was she kidding, that this was romantic, or provocative, or sexy or anything but a sad waste of her sleeping hours? She thought for a moment then typed quickly.

```
>nk@jkenterprises: so you want me to cut to the chase,
do you? Well, here's the chase, BadBoy - I'm Diana,
you're Actaeon, my hounds are coming over the hill. If
you don't get it, go and look it up. Rough translation
is as follows: call me old-fashioned, but you blew
it, NotGoodEnoughBoy - so this is bye-bye. Signing
off now.
```

Cass looked at her watch. It wasn't too late to phone Hallie on her mobile and call the whole Devlin thing off; she'd just be checking in at Stansted. What had she been thinking of? She went to pick up the phone, but Trudie was yattering away to one of her cronies. Well, that was that. She would be late for this party, if she was to wait for her grandmother to stop gossiping. Hallie would live.

Jamming her open-face helmet on her head, Cass ran down the stairs of the flat.

'Bye, Trudie! I'm taking the scooter – hope that's OK!'

'Lucasta, wait!' came the answering yell, then Trudie's face appeared over the banisters. 'Where are you going?'

'Oh Trudie, you know! That lobbying party – Westminster Thinking, or Planning, or something like that – in the Reform Club.'

'Dressed like that?'

Cass looked down at her kneehigh heeled boots, black jodhpurs and close-fitting little black and blue Diesel jacket that she was so proud of. 'Yes – what's wrong with it?'

Trudie's tone was dubious. 'Makes you look like a jockey who's lost his horse. But there's no accounting for taste amongst those politician-types, so maybe it's just the ticket. And how come you think you're taking my scooter? It is *my* scooter, you know, not *the* scooter.'

'Oh cool your fruits,' said Cass cheerfully, 'you don't mind really, do you? It'll take me hours to get there by public transport now.'

Her grandmother sighed indulgently. 'Just go, child. Go and make a nuisance of yourself with someone else.'

'Not a nuisance, Granda, I'm making contacts tonight. I'm,' Cass crossed her eyes, 'networking, hacking, backslapping, you name it.'

'Get out of my house, you primordial slime,' laughed Trudie.

'OK, and you get back to your phone call. If someone called Ted rings, can you say I'm on my way?'

'Is he one of your contacts?'

Cass laughed. 'Ted? No, he's just a friend. A sweet, sweet friend.'

She reminded herself of this five minutes later when she zipped up to Ted's flat only to be told by his flatmate that he was running late and would meet her at the party. Stony-faced, Cass climbed back on the pistachio green Vespa that was her grandmother's pride and joy, and revved crossly towards Westminster. That bastard. He knew that she would know virtually no-one at this party – it was highly unlikely that Alun or Frank Blackthorn would go – and he had promised to get her over the hurdle of walking through the door into a sea of blank faces. Once over this first barrier, Cass would be fine – she knew from a long experience of business school, consultancy and Columbia faculty parties that she only needed to be introduced to one person, for the social ball to start rolling.

Goddamn it, she thought defiantly, I'll be fine anyway. Who needs a sap like Ted?

In the month since Cass had started working for Alun, her expectations about politics and her job had changed beyond any sort of recognition. Hot on the heels of her realisation that, as private researcher to a working Minister, she was out of the power stream, came the recognition that she was having fun, real fun. It was like being an undergraduate again, but this time with some cash. Not a treasure trove, admittedly, but the House itself was so cheap, and Ted's expense account so bountiful, that they seemed to get a lot of bang for their buck. It never occurred to her to feel guilty of taking advantage of Ted's obvious crush on her.

In the euphoria of the Labour victory and with Blair's tradition-trashing little changes, there was a giddiness afoot in the corridors of power, not just amongst the mandarins and ministers, but right down to the porters and postmen, that hadn't been felt for years. Accustomed to being a team of one in her academic world, for the first time since she'd left management consultancy six years before, Cass felt part of this communal whirl and boy, was she going to enjoy it while it lasted. By staring into the bright sun of her new world, she could blind herself to the shadows and confusions she had left behind her in the States, and that was fine by her.

She had arrived at the Reform Club by now, its torches flickering feebly in the still bright daylight. Hearing the buzz of voices above her, she handed her invitation to the jaded-looking porter, took a deep breath and put on her most indomitable face, which to anyone who didn't know her looked more like a black scowl. Striding up the stairs and admiring the rococo overabundance of decor, Cass's face lightened as she saw a waiter carrying out a bottle of champagne, lifting it to his lips and draining it.

'Hey, save some for me!' she called softly.

The waiter whipped round in horror, then saw her smiling, and grimaced guiltily back. 'Oops. Fair cop, guv,' he joked unsteadily.

Cass was still grinning as she entered the huge salon, already crammed with laughing, heckling, red-faced men in suits – a monochrome carpet of greys and blues, studded with the occasional dart of fuchsia pink or red of women who still thought that power-dressing involved shoulder pads and bright, short, tight suits. Today, her gaydar was working well, so without pausing – thereby demonstrating that yes, she knew nobody – she launched herself straight up to a couple of exquisite peacocks, cuffs immaculately starched, white collars sitting stiffly atop bright, one-coloured shirts, trusting to her experience that gay men were much more approachable in these situations.

'Hi, I'm Cass, and I don't know a living soul here,' she stuck out her hand boldly.

One of the peacocks chuckled, and shook it heartily. 'Never admit to that, darling, we're all meant to be Westminster's players here. It wouldn't do to openly display ignorance. What you have to do is depend on politicians' belief that they have a good memory for faces – which they don't – then you just waltz up to them, remind them where you've met before, making it up of course, then they have to pretend that they remember you, and you're off and away!'

Cass threw her head back and laughed – an honest-to-goodness Cass bellow – which caused several people round her to stare curiously. 'I love it!' she cried delightedly. 'A crash course in politics. Thanks—?'

'Julian Albarn – no relation to Damon.'

Cass smiled knowledgeably, not having a clue who Damon Albarn was supposed to be, but learning fast to pretend that she did.

'I handle public affairs for the Pools Promoters Association,' he went on, 'with the assistance of the lovely people who are paying for all this.' He waved his glass of champagne. 'And this is Tim Stourton, formerly adviser to Michael Portillo and now—? How shall I describe you now, Timmy?'

'Retired, you bitch. Please excuse me,' his friend addressed Cass, then turned on his heel and stalked off.

Julian kissed Cass enthusiastically. 'Thank you, darling. You don't know this but you just rescued me from about twenty long minutes of listening to that bitter little queen rail against all sorts of slings and arrows.' He sighed with relief, flagging down a waiter for a champagne refill. 'Now, how do you fit in here? You're far too good-looking for politics, did anyone ever tell you that – you'll be fair game before you know it.'

'Not a chance,' Cass assured him cheerfully, 'I'm far too ornery to be Pamela Bordes. I'm researcher to Alun Blythe.'

'Oh, Alun, he's a lamb, isn't he? Drinks far too much, but still manages to be one of the sharpest MPs around. He's the new Minister for the City, isn't he? Now that must be a thankless job, especially with all this pensions business looming.'

'I guess,' Cass said. 'Does he drink that much – I mean, I've never noticed.'

'You obviously haven't been hanging out in the Marquis, my sweet—' Julian's attention suddenly switched sharply to something over Cass's shoulder. 'Oh my God, Tim's marching up to Stephen Twigg with a look I know well. Silly old goose. There's going to be a godalmighty scene unless I head him off at the pass. Sorry, darling, I'll catch up with you – it's Mother Poof to the rescue.' And he darted off.

Alone again, Cass looked round for another friendly face. In the nearest corner, now weaving slightly, was her waiter friend. She walked up to him, promising herself that she would start networking in a minute, and tapped him on the shoulder.

'Any champagne left for me?' He recognised her and blushed. 'Don't worry,' Cass assured him, 'I won't tell.'

'I don't really work here,' he said nervously, 'I'm actually a junior account executive at Westminster Planning; our boss thought it would be a good way for us to meet the bigwigs if we were pouring them their drinks, but it's hard to resist having a few on the way. Mind you, he looks as if he's had more than a few,' he pointed behind one of the pillars at the end of the salon.

Cass followed his finger, and laughed again. Leaning up against the pillar, in the dimness there, looking from behind as if he was busy talking to someone, was a man, fast-asleep on his feet. Just then, a knot of people moved away from the end window, so that a shaft of evening sunlight fell on his face. 'Wow,' Cass said involuntarily, her heart bucking crazily, 'he's gorgeous.'

'Who's gorgeous?' said a peeved voice from behind her. 'Honestly, I can't let you out of my sight for ten minutes and you're picking someone up!'

'Ted!' Cass turned to greet him, blushing.

Ted looked at her narrowly. 'Someone who can make the impregnable Cass blush.' His tone was light. 'Now this I have to see.' He looked beyond her, at the sleeping man, and his face fell. 'Oh Christ, not him. I know him – you haven't got a chance of breaking his heart – he's even tougher than you are. And he's not gorgeous – except in a really obvious, eyelashy way. He's got bags under his eyes even a backpacker would balk at carrying, and he's going really grey. Anyway, he's ancient, at least thirty-five, and he's far too nice for you.' He broke off and stared into his drink, frowning.

But Cass couldn't stop looking at the man. I feel like I know him, she thought dazedly, and he's beautiful and I want him and I want him now and how am I going to get him? Wake up, she told him silently, and notice me, fall for me, then fall in love with me so that I can go off you. I don't need you. I don't need any man.

'You know him?' she said finally, casually, unable to resist asking. 'Well?'

Ted was staring at her through narrowed eyes.

'Well enough. He's an American TV reporter, with some sort of roving brief, trying to make British life interesting to the Yanks. We worked together quite a bit before the election. Why?' he went on bitterly. 'Do you want me to introduce you? Fancy him, do you?'

Cass shook her head violently. 'Christ, no, don't you dare introduce me! I mean, he's obviously beautiful, but I have a major problem with men I'm attracted to – I can't talk to them.' She smiled broadly at Ted. 'Useless, aren't I?'

He stared at her for a minute.

'Come on,' he said finally. 'I thought we were here for you to graduate into hackdom.'

Cass tore her eyes away with determination. 'You'd better believe it, buster. Let's get backslapping! I'm not here to be distracted by a pretty face.' She frowned at him intently.

Never had Ted wanted so much to be a pretty face.

'Ladies and Gentlemen, we will shortly be landing at Dublin's Shannon Airport. Thank you for flying with Ryanair and we hope to see you again soon.'

Hallie had only just got her breath back. She was meant to be a high-flying PR exec – how could she have gone to the wrong airport? She could have sworn Cass had said Luton Airport – she could distinctly remember having a bit of a Lorraine Chase moment when Cass had mentioned it, so how come it flew from Stansted? And it would have been far too easy if there had been a Coachlink between the two airports, wouldn't it? So she had squandered nearly seventy quid getting a taxi to hare between the two, and had then run without stopping to breathe, from check-in, through baggage control, and along an endless walkway to reach her departure gate, yelling 'Excuse me! Plane to catch!' as she puffed past other people. She would never forget the noise that man's head had made against the side of the walkway as she had barged past him, just as he bent to get something out of his carry-on bag.

Now she was arriving, thoroughly out of sorts and out of pocket, for a trip that she was getting more and more dubious about. What had she been thinking of when she agreed to this? Surely she gave up picking up Cass's leftovers when they were each about sixteen? At least Cass had warned this Devlin Gray that she was coming – but did that make her look desperate or what?

But the worst was yet to come. Her heart sank into her insoles as she came through the arrival doors, to see Devlin holding up a huge sign emblazoned with 'YOU CAME, YOU BEAUTY!'

Hallie stopped stockstill in horror. He clearly still thought that Cass was coming. That was it, Herbert was dead, she would kill her. How could she have fallen for such an obvious con? There was obviously more to this Devlin situation than Cass had admitted, so she had sent her to do her dirty work. What a cow. What a stinking, BSE-ridden, parasite-laden cow.

Hallie would have given her lilac, Ghost-clad right arm to have walked straight past Devlin and straight over to Departures to get on the first plane back, to a murder scene with Cass, but he was staring at her now, obviously half-recognising her. As she stared back, mind churning, Hallie decided that she wasn't going to take this lying down. She was here now, for goodness' sake. Dublin was at her feet for her to discover; she might as well salvage something from the situation.

Lifting her chin in the air, Hallie tossed back her blonde curls and walked over to a suspicious-looking Devlin. 'Hello!' she smiled, 'I'm the Beauty. You must be Devlin.'

Devlin looked at her in horror, but Hallie's smile didn't crack. 'But where's Cass?' he said furiously.

'She's blown you out,' Hallie said maliciously. Closer up, he was even better-looking than she had remembered, dirty blond hair falling over a thin, Models-One sort of face. Much better looking than the guy from *Babybird*. 'And gave me the tickets. Sorry to disappoint you, but it was nice to meet you, albeit briefly.' No point in letting him know that she had been duped as well, she thought stonily, as she started to walk away from him. Now, where the dickens was she going to stay? Everywhere was bound to be booked up with this music festival.

She turned back to him reluctantly, but still gripped by the same proud demon that had carried her this far. 'Had you booked Cass a hotel room?' she demanded.

'Yes,' replied a still-dazed Devlin. 'At the Clarence.'

Hallie gulped. Even she had heard of the Clarence, that Bono-owned shrine of modern luxury that cost about two hundred quid a night. She was going to be well and truly bankrupt after this weekend. 'Any chance I can buy the booking off you?' she said as airily as she could manage.

Devlin blinked and visibly pulled himself together, looking at Hallie properly for the first time. 'Sure, and wouldn't I be a bastard if I were to throw you out onto the streets? I'm sure we can come to some sort of arrangement. Tell you what, how about I forget I ever invited Cass, and we can pretend it was you all along.' He even managed a weak smile.

Hallie tried not to notice how his hands were shredding the cardboard notice to pulp.

Pride struggled with practicality. She didn't want to feel like the shrimp cocktail when he wanted the Dish of the Day, but it was nice of him to cover up his disappointment. He didn't have to make such a kind offer, he could've just let her walk into the sunset. He really was a gorgeous bloke – so why was Cass being so casually cruel?

Simultaneously, Hallie's heart softened towards Devlin and hardened towards Cass, as she thought of a plan. She knew her friend so well, and knew that even if Cass didn't want Devlin, she probably didn't want anyone else to have him either. So Hallie would seduce him, infuriate Cass and get a shag-filled weekend with a gorgeous man into the bargain. All bases would be covered – how hard could it be?

'Deal,' she smiled, holding out her hand. 'I'm Hallie.' And you'd better get ready to rumble, she added silently.

Cass was persevering with her networking. Now she was talking to her host. 'In a nutshell, what I will be trying to show women is that we don't need to act like men in order to succeed, or even more importantly, that we don't need to act as men expect us to. Our femininity, if you like, has its uses not its disadvantages.'

'Oh yes,' laughed the man, jollily, 'I'm a sucker for feminine wiles myself.'

Cass swallowed hard. 'As a matter of fact, that's what I'm trying to avoid. We should be able to empower ourselves without having to resort to such psychological devices. Nowadays, getting on in your life, your career – it's as important to be able to compete with other women as it is with men, so "wiles", as you call them, are not only unnatural but are outmoded. It's all about finding your own psychological level in the welter of gender confusion and stereotyping. I'm just trying to facilitate that process, much like I hear that Lynne Franks is doing – but without her spiritual mumbo-jumbo,' she added, in a weak attempt to lighten herself up.

'Oh yes, girl power. Rather. So which is your favourite Spice Girl, eh? Heh heh heh. Absolutely fabulous,' he winked. 'I do hope you do well, my dear.' And he moved on.

'Condescending bastard,' Cass spat silently after him. 'I hope your rotten bloody consultancy folds tomorrow.' Then she heard muffled snorts of amusement behind her and swung around to find Ted there with another man, who was just turning to help himself to a passing tray of canapes.

'Just one suggestion, Cass,' Ted chuckled. 'This is a drinks party, sweetheart, not a seminar. Ease up on the jargon – with these fat cats, it just ruffles their fur the wrong way.'

In her disappointment, Cass flipped. 'And what the fuck do you know, Mister Election Loser? Perhaps those two hundred missing voters were looking for some jargon from you? You are supposed to be from a think-tank after all!'

'And you can't lose your temper so easily, if you're ever going to make a go of what sounds like a great idea,' drawled his companion, turning back from his deep-fried cheese balls, looking her up and down with a wide smile.

'And who the hell are you to tell me what to do?' Cass stormed. Then she did such an obvious double-take that Ted choked on his champagne. It was the man she'd last seen asleep next to a pillar, looking, if possible, even more dropdead gorgeous when he was awake. What was more, he was looking at her with a narrow-eyed appraisal that she knew well. Cass suddenly felt short of breath. 'Wha—?'

Ted almost enjoyed her discomfort. Almost. He prayed that this was a good idea. Bearding the lion in his den had always worked for him before, and hopefully, this way she would see that the guy was the sort of obvious charmer that he already knew she detested.

'Cass Herbert, this is Wilbur Coolidge, a mate of mine who's working over at CNN. Wilbur, I forgot to tell you that Cass has just come back from five years on your turf – you were doing a PhD at – was it Columbia, Cass?' Ted stopped abruptly. Why had they both gone so pale?

'C-Coolidge?' Cass stammered. 'Wilbur Coolidge? B-but you're—'

'John's brother,' said Wilbur brutally. 'And you're *the* Cass Herbert. Didn't we meet at the funeral? Oh no, I'm sorry,' his tone was pure acid, 'you couldn't come, could you? Too busy with your gender studies, huh? Ted, don't waste your time with this one – she's the kind of cold-hearted bitch that *does* give women a bad name.' Pausing only to dip a quail's egg into celery salt, he stalked off.

There was a stunned silence.

'Cass?' Ted said softly. 'What's going on?'

To his horror, Cass burst into tears. Then, just as suddenly, she was in control again, her tears drying up as quickly as they'd flooded out, leaving Ted stranded, proffered handkerchief in mid-air.

'Christ,' she said, 'I was not expecting that.'

Neither was I, Ted thought, neither was I.

Hallie was woken up by sunlight shining into her eyes from an unaccustomed angle. She opened them squintingly, cursing herself for not closing the curtains, and looked at her watch. Nine o'clock. Great. Another day in Paradise. She kicked discontentedly at the pure linen sheets and gazed blackly at the minimalist splendour of her room at the Clarence.

Things were not going to plan.

From the moment Hallie had walked into the pub with Devlin

the night before, she had wanted either to go straight home or to metamorphose miraculously into Cass. It was obvious that the rest of the Blazing Sadlads had been listening obediently to Devlin's ravings about Cass and were expecting a tall, rangy cucumber of coolness in biker boots and bare midriff, not a small, curvy butternut squash of blonde perkiness, immaculate in fitted little lilac jacket, pale mauve bootleg slacks and the very latest high-heeled wooden mules.

'So where's the goddess, Devlin?' they ribbed him mercilessly, looking blankly over Hallie's head. 'Lost her already, have you, you daft fucking eejit?'

Devlin, true to his word, had done his best. 'Stop your ballockin' – this is Hallie,' he said, putting a protective arm around her shoulders, 'and we have to show her that Dublin is where all the craic is.'

Hallie tried not to look alarmed. She hardly touched spliff these days – surely she wasn't going to be expected to dive straight into crack? Wasn't crack the instantly addictive stuff? Talk about sex, drugs and rock'n'roll. These boys, in their torn, flowery shirts, worn-looking black jeans and paisley scarves, with their still-pasty faces and the sort of floppy hair no-one would be seen dead with in London, were almost like a caricature of a rock band. Remember the plan, she told herself firmly, and don't forget that it was you that wanted to meet new people . . .

'This is Fiachna – bass guitarist, Alan – fiddler, Aidan on drums, Martin tinkles the ivories,' Devlin nodded to each in turn, Hallie smiled and they waved blearily back. 'Then this is Siobhan and Eithne,' he gestured at two terrifying-looking women, all hennaed black hair and eyeliner, hemmed in together in a deep sofa, 'our backing singers and brass section. Siobhan blows a mean trombone.'

Whatever she blows, I'm sure she does it meanly, thought Hallie nervously, blanching at the malevolence pulsating from them as they took in her strawberry blonde curls, immaculate lilac lipstick and pearlised nail varnish. I can do cool too, she wanted to tell them, it's just that the pastel princess look *is* cool at the moment, back on my planet.

After that she had tried, she really had. Judging that she was on a hiding to nothing with Siobhan and Eithne, she had ignored them completely and had concentrated on flirting outrageously with the boys. Imagining that they were potential new clients, Hallie had pitched herself as the rock chick groupie type, all wide-eyed, breathless gestures and admiration. At first all had gone well; Martin found himself telling her about transposing Elvis Costello with Rachmaninov in his Grade Eight piano exam; Fiachna almost forgot that he was going out with Eithne in his eagerness to light Hallie's cigarettes; Alan had to be restrained from playing her a little riff on his violin.

But the more pubs they went to, the more they all drank and the more sober Hallie felt. She had hoped that the fact that they were playing the following night would make them hold back somewhat, but Cass had lied about that too – they drank like true Irishmen. Seldom had she longed so hard to like the taste of alcohol, so that she could fit in. The whole night seemed to follow a well-known route – no-one ever asked anyone where they were going to next, they all just seemed to know, as they trooped into ever smaller, smokier, noisier pubs, hailing people they knew, swapping gossip from the festival, downing pint after pint of dark, creamy beer. Now Hallie was awash with gallons of ginger ale, her new mules were killing her feet and she was beginning to feel less like a rock chick than a washed-up pebble. Even Eithne and Siobhan became friendly after a few hours – a sure sign that they were no longer feeling threatened by her – with one leaning on each of her arms as they tottered down the pedestrian precinct in Grafton Street.

'You're a great girl, Hilary,' slurred Siobhan, as they waited, shivering, outside Lillie's Bordello. 'What's with you and our Dev then?'

Hallie glanced over at Devlin, talking low and fast to the doorman. 'Well, I think the fact that he's brought us to a brothel doesn't bode well, does it?'

Eithne, Fiachna and Siobhan cracked up, weaving straight into the path of a rickshaw, pulled by an impoverished Trinity student, who yelled at them furiously. 'A brothel? Bejaysus, you're joking, aren't you? This is Lillie's Bordello – a nightclub, you eejit.'

It was obviously too late in the day to get away with sarcasm, Hallie mused dryly.

'Devlin! Get this! Hilary thought you were bringing us to a brothel!'

Devlin looked over his shoulder and smiled noncommittally. And that was the problem, Hallie thought, he was proving to be a tough nut. Initially charming and loquacious, a few beers later, he had turned rapidly morose and silent, talking when spoken to but otherwise staring into the middle distance and drumming his fingers on the nearest surface. Piqued by his increasing withdrawal, Hallie had pulled out the whole bag of tricks – hanging onto his every word (not hard – there weren't many), regaling him with amusing anecdotes, hand on his knee at every opportunity. She had done everything short of taking her clothes off and telling him to get on with it. That was still an option, she thought bad-temperedly, as they pushed their way into Lillie's – a nightclub that looked more like her old grannie's front room with its dim, fringed lamps, flock wallpaper and clustered ancient antimacassared armchairs – and on into the VIP room. No-one would notice nudity in here, it was so dark and crowded, with its dimpled leather sofas and booklined walls, but then neither would Devlin, already sinking into the depths of a single chair in the corner.

Pulled onto a suddenly amorous Aidan's knee, Hallie just wanted to go home and stick pins into a wax doll bearing a strong resemblance to Ms Cass Herbert. Her former friend would be in her element here – tall enough to be noticed wherever she went, loud enough to be heard, dropdead gorgeous enough to break even more hearts and hard-headed enough to match them drink for drink. If Cass were here, Devlin wouldn't be over there pulling books out of the shelves halfheartedly, he would be trying to pull her.

That had decided her. It was time to go. Pouring her drink out onto an already sodden carpet, Hallie waved the empty glass at Aidan, shouting that she was going to get a drink. Wriggling her way through the hotch-potch of furniture and people she finally burst out of the VIP room and into the nightclub proper. She looked around for the exit but hesitated. Out here they were playing some great music and if there was one thing that Hallie loved to do, it was dance. Sod the Sadlads and their drunken ramblings, she wasn't going to let Dublin get her down. She would just slip in a few songs before heading back to her splendidly lonely hotel room.

Underworld, the *Chemical Brothers*, *Faithless* and *Everything But the Girl* all conspired to keep Hallie on the dance floor. Forgetting her misery, her aching feet and her sloshing belly, she swamped herself in the music, eyes closed, hair losing its careful curled-under coiffure as she tossed her head to the beat, arms thrashing like a good'un. Eventually the spell was broken by a slow song, whereupon everyone on the dancefloor went into their partner's arms, leaving Hallie as obvious as Old Maid in the card game. Unabashed, she skipped off the floor and out into the street, welcoming the lick of the cold night-air on her sweat-streamed skin, the sudden airy feeling on her slick-haired scalp, still high from her cavortings.

It was only now, in the harsh light of day, that Hallie remembered the sad failure of Mission Devlin. It was Saturday morning and her flight left for London in just over twenty-four hours. She was on her own all day anyway, because the band were practising for that night's gig, and, after her disappearing act last night, they probably didn't want anything to do with her tonight. Ho-hum, it looked like she'd blown it. So much for the shag-filled weekend, roll on the touristy Dublin Experience. Lucky she'd brought that guide book.

She picked up the phone receiver by the bed. 'Hello, can I order some room service? Oh, he has, has he? Right, yes, er, send it up. Thank you.'

Now that was intriguing. Devlin had already ordered breakfast for her and had left something for her. A tray arrived quickly and, unlike most hotels Hallie had stayed in during her PR career, the food still looked like breakfast. With it was a bulky envelope. She ripped it open impatiently.

'What happened to you last night? Sorry I was being such a berk. Have fun today – here is the programme for the music festival – check out Meetinghouse Square in Temple Bar for the best gigs today – turn left out of the back door of the Clarence, then right – just ask if you get lost. We're practising over at the Basilica all day. If you want to, you can join us there about six, before we go out for sustenance before our gig. Make sure you get a cab – the Basilica is in a rough area. Devlin.'

Hallie melted back into her pillows, clutching Devlin's note like a talisman. What a lamb. All was forgiven. He may not be about to leap into bed with her, but, aah, bless him, what a lamb. It was time to make the best of perhaps not such a bad job.

'Nina? It's Cass.'

'Mnnngh?'

'Nina, it's ten after twelve – how can you still be asleep?'

There was a pause. Then some muffled mumblings. Jerry came on the line. 'Cass? Sorry about that. Nina's dead to the world. She's got terrible insomnia at the moment, so she tries to catch up during the day. She's just gone to stick her head in a bucket of cold water. How are you?'

'Oh, you know, I'm fine. What's up?'

'Er, nothing much – the website is proving a bit of a tricky bastard; Nin's struggling to find some features work, usual stuff. Oh – I completely forgot – some American bloke rang here the other day, saying that he had this number from when you were here at New Year, and that he was trying to get in touch with you, so I gave him your number at Trudie's. You are still staying there, aren't you?'

'Oh, fuck, you didn't? Fuck fuck fuck.'

'Steady on, old girl, no need to bite my head off. What else do you expect me to do? I wasn't aware I had to vet your calls for you nowadays.'

'Try not to be quite so pompous, Jezza, it doesn't suit you.'

'Cass, was there any reason you rang? Or was it just to wake us up, swear at me and insult me?'

'Sorry, bad day. That's all. Just forget I called, will you. I have to go. Don't worry about it.'

'Cass? Don't hang up! What's wrong?'

'Nothing. Nothing. Who was – what – I mean, did he leave a name, this guy?'

'Yes – one of those silly surnames as Christian names. Honestly, Americans, eh? Forester? Something like that. Hang on, I wrote it down.'

'Fuck. Forget it. Bye.'

'Wait, Cass! Here it is – Carter Wylie.'
But the line had gone dead.

Devlin sneaked a look over at the passenger seat as he slowed down for the traffic lights. Something about her intrigued him, almost against his will. When Cass had failed to show up at the airport yesterday, he had been so busy putting a brave face on events, that he hadn't really taken Hallie on board. Then, when they were out and about with the band, he had seen right through her little game, all that flirting and carrying on with the boys just to try and get his attention. She and Cass had obviously cooked this up right from the moment he had dared Cass to come to Dublin – a little tease for naughty Devlin, whereby he would fall for Hallie and then she would turn him down and report back to Cass that, yes, Devlin Gray was a flibbertigibbet libertine. Well, he wasn't going to play ball. Hallie might be attractive enough but she was so obvious, such a little coquette, so not his cup of tea, that Devlin had felt himself withdrawing away from his usual courtesy right into moody Irish bastard mode.

Then, at Lillie's, he had watched her leaving the VIP room and had felt a prick of conscience. So he had followed her. And had seen her on the dance-floor, oblivious to everyone, dancing like a wild thing possessed, her face for once free of that manically cheerful mask, set now into expressionless concentration. Just watching her from the edge of the dance-floor, he had felt like a voyeur, intruding on her private world, eavesdropping on a Hallie she didn't show to the outside world. So he had crept away, waiting for her to come back to the VIP room. But she hadn't, and he had felt almost bereft for her presence, cheated by her unexpected independence.

And today, when she'd finally turned up at the Temple, he had been surprised again. Gone were the pastel colours and demure little city-slickerette suit. Instead, she was wearing tight black trousers over high-heeled boots, cinched in at the waist over a shiny, tight, white body stocking, displaying an impressive cleavage which disappeared tantalisingly when she pulled her white linen shirt across her chest. Far from being pouty and petulant about being left alone all day, she had gobsmacked them all by telling them how she'd managed to strike up a conversation with none other than the Edge just as she was leaving the Clarence, had accompanied him to the Film Centre bar in Meetinghouse Square and in that short five minute walk had extracted a promise from him to come to the Sadlads' gig in the Basilica. Devlin had amazed himself by wanting to kiss that delighted grin from her face, but had found himself waiting in line behind Aidan, Martin and the rest of the crew. 'U2!' they had crowed, picking her up and swinging her around in the empty converted church, 'bloody U2 are coming to see us. You're a marvel, Hallie, a bloody marvel!'

'So come on,' he said now, as they stopped at the lights, 'did you really speak to the Edge, or was it pulling our legs you were?'

Hallie looked at him, offended. 'Of course I did. Do you really think I would make up something like that?'

Devlin was about to apologise when a hand suddenly came through Hallie's window, holding a syringe of what looked like blood.

'Get out the fockin' car,' yelled a high-pitched voice, 'or we stick her full of AIDS!'

Hallie and Devlin looked at each other, horrified, and scrambled out of the car.

There were two of them, no more than lads, in lowslung baggy jeans and dirty plaid shirts, looking nervous and trigger-happy as one of them grabbed Hallie and put the needle to her neck.

'Give us yer fockin' wallet and yer car-keys,' screamed the other one, his eyes as round as saucers as he saw that the car was an Alfa Romeo. 'That blood's got AIDS in it, so don't fock around wi'us, or my pal will stick it in her!'

'I wouldn't bother,' Hallie said sharply. 'I'm already HIV-positive.'

There was silence, as both lads and Devlin gaped at her.

'That means I've already got AIDS,' she added quickly, sounding as upper-crust English as Devlin had yet heard her. 'So, go ahead, stick it in. Maybe then I'll get cured. You know what they say about bad blood curing bad blood.' She made an apologetic face at Devlin. 'I'm sorry, darling, I did mean to tell you, but the timing was never quite right. You don't mind, do you?'

'B-b-but—' spluttered Devlin, before she cut him off, half-turning in the slackened embrace of her captor to address him directly.

'You didn't grab my arm, did you? It's just that I've got rather a nasty lesion on that arm, so I hope you don't have any cuts on your fingers because then you might get infected too. Unless of course, you already are? But you're not, are you? You've just read about syringing in the papers and you thought it was a handy way of ripping someone off. Sorry, boys, you picked on the wrong person. But then you never can trust the bloody Brits, can you?'

The lad dropped his hand from her neck, as if he'd been bitten and backed away. The other boy followed suit. Devlin was still frozen to the spot.

'You're fockin' mad,' one of them said. 'You're a fockin' madwoman. You're fockin' welcome to her, mate,' he shook his head at Devlin. 'C'mon, let's get out of here, Barry.' And the two of them took to their heels and fled, leaving Devlin, car-keys dangling from his lifeless hand, staring at a composed Hallie.

'Whew,' she said mildly, stretching out her hands and looking at the slight tremor there dispassionately, 'I wasn't sure if that would work. I think we should get back in the car, don't you? I don't really like the look of this neighbourhood.'

In a daze, Devlin got back into the driver's seat. He started the engine, but didn't drive off. 'That was the most incredible thing I've ever seen in my whole entire life,' he said softly. 'How on earth did you think of that so quickly?' He turned to her, recovering fast and a huge smile plastered itself across his face. 'You little beauty! You just saved my life!' As best as he could in the confined spaces of the car, he threw his arms around her, feeling, as he gathered her into a hug, that she really was shaking.

'Hardly,' laughed Hallie, pushing him off gently. 'I just saved your wallet and car.'

'Almost the same thing – let me tell you. If I'd lost this car, my Da would have killed me, that's for sure. But seriously, how did you think of saying all that stuff so quickly?' Devlin stopped suddenly. 'Unless, unless—'

'You're not going to believe this, but I'd thought it all up beforehand,' Hallie smiled, 'and no, I'm not HIV. Not that you'd have to worry about that.' Devlin looked sharply at her. 'It's just that I hate exercise so much that on those blue moon days when I do actually go to the gym, the only way I can stave off the boredom is by dreaming up all those scenarios when you wish you'd known what to do. Like if you're raped – how do you react? Or in a bank which is being held up? Or if you see someone being beaten up on the Tube? All those situations where you say afterwards, "What if I'd said this? What if I'd done that?" – well, I sit there on that flipping exercise bike, making the miles go past by planning what I would do. I happened to read an article about syringing a few weeks ago, so that scenario is one I'd thought about quite recently. So, there you go, not so amazing, after all.'

Devlin shook his head. 'I'm afraid I'll have to disagree with you there. Most people just read the newspaper at the gym – but no, not you, you're writing your save the world speech – it's, well, *you* are incredible.' He suddenly burst out laughing. 'The look on that poor eejit's face when you were going on about the lesions on your arm – to be sure I thought he was going to have a heart attack there and then!'

Hallie started laughing too – gusts of nervousness blasting out of her. 'It wasn't as good as your face when I asked you if you minded me infecting you! Now that was a classic!'

'Hey, it would be an honour!' he joked. There was a tiny silence, and a lightning look slid between them. Then he groaned. 'I can't believe I said that – how sick am I? Come on, I'm going to buy you the biggest drink in Dublin. Oh! No, I can't – because you don't drink!'

'Well, I do, actually,' Hallie grinned naughtily. 'I'm just a massive drinking snob. I hate the taste of all alcohol except vintage champagne.'

'Dom Perignon, it is, then!' cried Devlin in relief. 'Dinner at Tosca's, champagne all round, then back here for the gig, then it's time to really play, by God!'

And that's not all we're going to do, he found himself thinking. Cass Herbert, you can go roast your head in a bucket – I think I've just found your replacement. Hallie, get ready to rumble . . .

*   *   *

'Cass, darling, what's the matter?'

Cass heard her but couldn't bear to look her grandmother in the face and continued to sob furiously, head deeply buried in her arms on the table. Next she felt Trudie sit down next to her, pull her arms gently away from her face and gather her into a gentle hug. 'Come on darling, spill the beans. This isn't like you. Who were you speaking to on the phone just now? Is it something to do with that?'

'No. Yes. Sort of.' Cass buried her head in Trudie's shoulder and wailed. 'Oh Granda, what am I going to do? I've fucked up. Really fucked up. How did I manage to screw everything up? I'm not a bad person, I know I'm not. But he called me a cold-hearted bitch and he's right, I have been. And oh, why didn't I go to the funeral? And now *he's* trying to track me down and I came here to get away from him and try and salvage something, but I've just ended up hurting him too. It just seems like I'm hurting everyone from that family – and I never wanted to do that! Never!'

'Cassie, honey, I know you'd never want to hurt anyone,' Trudie soothed her. 'Now why don't you just slow down and tell me everything. It all sounds like a dreadful muddle, but, you know, there's always a beginning and an end to every tangled ball of wool.'

Cass gave a watery chuckle. 'Jeez, you really sounded like a grandmother then – all homespun advice and proverbial wisdom.'

Trudie rolled her eyes. 'God forbid. Now, come on, let's get this all sorted out – then we'll go for a right old burn on the Vespa!' Her eyes twinkled.

But Cass was looking more composed now. 'No, for once I'm not just going to unload everything on someone else. That's what I was trying to do with Nina – I rang her this morning but wimped out of speaking to her – and really, it's something I have to deal with on my own. You probably guessed that it's all to do with John's death – I ran into his brother, well, half-brother, yesterday and he thinks that I'm this totally heartless cow, because I didn't go to John's funeral and . . . like, for lots of reasons. And then there's this . . . other guy, who I got involved with when I shouldn't have – and I ran away from that situation too. It's all just a big mess but, you know, you're totally right – it can be sorted.'

Trudie looked at her long and hard. 'Well, OK, if you don't want to get it off your chest, that's up to you. But just remember, that's what your friends and I are for – Hallie, Nina and me: we're your confessors, that's our job.'

'I'm not sure Hallie and Nina would agree with you on that any more,' said Cass sadly. 'I'm not sure how I would even broach the subject with them these days. I wouldn't know what to say.'

'What is Cass going to say?' gasped Hallie on a last note of conscience, as Devlin peeled off the final layer of her bodystocking.

He looked almost offended at this, and carried on stroking her back. 'Was she not the one who stood me up? I'm thinking that she gave up her rights to say anything when she sent you in her stead! Now, will you just shut up and let me get on with transporting you to a place of sheer pleasure?'

'Oh, sheer pleasure works for me,' Hallie giggled, in a delicious haze of champagne and desire, as his hands slid down to cup her waist.

'Such a tiny waist,' he said in wonder. 'Look at that, will you? I can get both my hands round it with room to spare.'

'Just call me Scarlett,' she murmured, thinking that there was a part of his anatomy she was looking forward to getting both her hands round with room to spare.

But Devlin was way ahead of her, head dipping to between her thighs. 'Now I'm thinking that this is less Scarlett than the most delicious pink.' He kissed her gently right . . . there. 'Like an unfurling rose.' He kissed her again, with the same tender firmness that had reduced her to a spiralling kaleidoscope of lust when he'd kissed her on her lips, from the moment they left the Kitchen nightclub, in the basement of the hotel, all the way up in the lift, to the bemusement of the bellboy, and all along the corridor until at last they had reached her bedroom and then, finally, her bed. 'Aah, but you're lovely down here.' With deft little pulses, he dipped and whirled his tongue like a kestrel diving for prey.

Hallie couldn't speak. Just blushed and squirmed. And came. Before she'd even had a chance to get more than his shirt off him. She had to content herself with running her fingers through his sweat-soaked hair, the memory of him pumping his guitar and ululating into the microphone in front of a hall full of gyrating music-lovers just making her groan and shudder deliciously even more. Pushing herself more frenziedly into his mouth, her hands slipped down to his shoulders, feeling the leaping muscles there, the smooth heat of his skin, the soft down on his shoulder blades. Eventually she could stand it no more, the pleasure she was receiving from his tongue was too intense now, it was almost like she was being electrocuted every time he touched her there: she had to get skin to skin with him.

Pulling him up towards her, Hallie was momentarily reminded of the huge difference in their heights – by the time she could reach down to undo his jeans, she was nuzzling his chest, running her tongue over his sweat-slicked ribs, each one standing out under his skin like a railway sleeper under moss. Impatient now, she scrabbled at the buttons at his fly, tugging off his trouser legs – remembering to pull in her stomach as she did so, conscious that he could now see her entire nakedness in the unflattering contortions necessary to get his trousers and socks off. Above her, he was helping her now, yanking down his boxers with equal haste, feet scrambling to kick them off, arms pulling her back up to kiss her.

Again, the difference in their heights meant that they still weren't joined so Hallie went to get a sneak preview with her hand. Trailing her fingers down his heaving chest, she teased them round his belly button until he gasped and pushed her hand down hard. Smiling against his lips, Hallie murmured indistinctly, 'Patience, sweetie, patience.'

Her hand slid down further, further still until—

Hallie froze. Now this couldn't be right.

5

'Until what?! You have to tell me – the suspense is killing me! What couldn't be right?' Cass was on the edge of her seat.

Hallie pulled an agonised face. 'Needle-dick, pure and simple. I couldn't believe it. Here is the best-looking man I've ever been to bed with, who's charm and kindness personified, who's talented enough to make the Edge himself make him an offer, who's made me come within seconds of jumping into bed with him, who's got muscles to die over and skin to cry over – and when we get to the heart of the action, it's Thimble City.' She held up her little finger and crooked it in half. 'I mean I nearly miss it completely – I'm wandering past, going, "Is this it? Or is this just some firm, funny little bollock?" Pardon my language, but, I mean, disappointed?! I nearly cried!'

Cass was nearly crying with laughter. 'Oh God, that's awful! Poor Devlin! Poor you! Christ, that sucks, that really sucks.'

'You're telling me,' Hallie agreed gloomily. 'And I had to. Suck, that is. Poor lamb, he must know he's Mister Tiny in that department because as soon as I stopped exploring – even for a second, before I recovered and carried on – in that second, he, well, collapsed. What there was to collapse. Then, of course, I felt so bad that I just had to get him up and at 'em again. Oh Cass, it was like sipping at a doll's tea party—'

'Stop! Please! I can't bear any more!' Cass was chewing on her knuckles by this time.

'And then the sex was just embarrassing. Him on top, me on top, whatever, it kept falling out. I mean, I just kept losing it, kept having to say, "Er, Devlin, perhaps if we—". Oh goodness, I just wanted to die. Until finally, we found this position where if I sat on his lap, with both of us sitting up and my legs round his back, and I hardly moved, just used my' – Hallie blushed, 'well, interior muscles, then that was – good. Not great but – good. Good enough for him to come, anyway, which was a load off my mind, let me tell you.'

'And off his, I would imagine,' Cass choked. 'Fuck me, that's the most agonising story I've ever heard. You poor, poor guys. How was he afterwards?'

'Well, he's a lovely cuddler and luckily we both fell asleep soon afterwards. Then in the morning, we overslept and I had to rush about so much that there wasn't time for any embarrassment. I mean, we knew before we even went to bed that there wasn't going to be any more to it than a fling so—'

'Why? How did you know?'

Hallie's look turned steely. 'Because, surprisingly enough, I'm not so desperate that I would take your leavings for anything more than a bonk.' And that's a lie I'm going to stick to, she thought.

Cass looked hurt. 'That's not fair. How could Devlin be my leavings when I never had him to leave in the first place? Anyway, I never intended you to go to bed with him, I only wanted you to—'

'Why, was I not good enough for him? Was I just good for getting you out of your corner, but not good enough to get him into mine?'

'Hallie! Stop twisting everything I say. That's total crap and you know it! Jeez, it was a misguided attempt to sort my life out and give you some fun into the bargain. I don't know why I bothered, since by staying behind, I screwed my life up but good.'

Hallie looked mulish, determined not to pick up the conversational bait, but couldn't resist it. 'OK, how come?'

'You know the lobbying party I was going to, where I

was going to start the ball rolling on getting some good contacts?'

Hallie nodded.

'Well, I saw this guy there who was totally, I mean totally, dropdead gorgeous.'

'Sounds good. No doubt you showed your interest in him by being as rude, offhand and/or silent as you possibly could be,' said Hallie, who knew Cass's chat-up methods – or lack of – from old.

'Didn't even get a chance before, by some total freak of coincidence, it turns out that he's John's sort-of brother, Wilbur Coolidge—'

'Wilbur?! What kind of name is Wilbur? And what do you mean, "sort-of" brother?'

'Oh, Wilbur is a childhood nickname that stuck, can't remember why. And the Coolidge family is such a complicated set-up: step- and half-siblings littered all over the place. He's something like John's ex-stepbrother but adopted half-brother, if that makes any sense.'

'Nope. None whatsoever. But carry on.' Hallie smiled.

'Did you ever see *Clueless*? Well, it's sort of like that – where Wilbur is like the ex-stepbrother because his father got divorced from John's mother – except by that time Pa Coolidge, Wilbur's father, had adopted John, which is why John was called Coolidge—'

'Cass, I meant carry on with your story, not with some genealogical minefield!'

Cass sighed. 'Anyway, the point is that he hates me and I'm bound to run into him all over the place because he's some sort of CNN reporter with a roving Parliamentary brief.'

'And what's so bad about that? Can't your ego take that sort of regular bruising?'

Cass didn't rise. 'No, it's not that – I mean, I could see that before he knew who I was, he fancied me as much as I fancied him – and that's the problem; what is it with me and Coolidge men? I seem to have some sort of fatal fascination with them. What am I going to do?'

As much to her own surprise as to Cass's, Hallie lost her temper. 'Oh please. Spare me. For a start, why do you have to do anything? Why would he hate you anyway? You went out with his brother. You split up with his brother. His brother died in a dreadful accident. What is that to do with you? Why do you think you have to be so intricately involved with everything? The whole universe doesn't revolve around Lucasta Herbert, you know!' She started ticking points off her fingers. 'He doesn't hate you – you just reminded him of John and that gave him a momentary shock – don't dress it up into anything else. And how can you possibly know that he fancied you? Or do you imagine that all Coolidge men – no, no, all men, full stop, are automatically going to throw themselves at your feet?'

Cass tried to interrupt but Hallie was still in full flow.

'Because they're not, you know. You may be amazing-looking but you're not irresistible. You're bolshy and unapproachable to anyone that you might find remotely fanciable so usually it's only the saps and lackeys that try to get anywhere with you. If you ask me, this guy Wilbur doesn't find you half as attractive as you assume he does. Perhaps he's genuinely not impressed by you and you find that rather hard to take on board. In fact, I bet if you were to ring him up and ask him out for a drink, he would refuse to go.

'And that wouldn't be for any trumped-up family politics reason, it would be because – wonders of all wonders – Cass Herbert has come across someone who is genuinely immune to her supposed charms. Now, wouldn't that be a challenge? Care to take me up on it?' she finished. 'And don't you dare come back with any rubbish about sour grapes – this is nothing to do with Devlin, or anyone – these are home truths and I should have said them years ago, before your ego ran away with you.'

Finally, Hallie was done. For a moment, she and Cass stared at each other, Hallie defiant, breathless with her own nerve for stepping outside the role of Hallie the Peacemaker just for a few minutes; Cass stunned, reeling under the unexpected onslaught, surprising herself with the one thought that was running through her head – 'thank God I didn't tell her about Carter, thank God I didn't tell her about Carter' – over and over again.

'I . . . I . . .' she started. Then she swallowed and tried again. 'I never knew you thought such things about me. How could you still be friends with me if you think those things about me?'

Hallie sighed. This was the last response she had been expecting. Cass angry, she could have fought back. Cass defensive, she could have made her see sense. Cass defeated was a new one on her.

She reached out and touched Cass's hand. 'You idiot, it's precisely because I am still your friend that I can think and say these things about you. Friendship isn't some Hallmark card, you know – we're allowed to have evil, stinky thoughts about each other – that's what should make us friends, not just the fact that we've *been* friends since we were ten. Friends don't keep these secret thoughts from each other – otherwise they fester away.'

Inadvertently, Hallie thought of the big secret she still couldn't bring herself to tell Cass and shied away from that Pandora's Box.

'You're right. I suppose.' Cass deliberately turned her thoughts away from the Carter issue and ventured a grin at Hallie, still shaky on the new ground between her and her usually submissive friend. 'Though I still think you're wrong about Wilbur – I could swear that underneath it all, he does fancy me.'

Hallie smiled back. 'Prove it, then.'

'Yes, I'm a freelance features writer at the – no, Babaji. Stay! I said, stay!'

'Ooh, that must be so exciting. Who do you write for? Good boy, Fergus. That's a good boy!'

'Oh, no one paper in particular – I've just started a big assignment with the *Daily* – Babaji, please, *please*, just *sit* there – on the Primrose Path columns in – do you know the Saturday supplement, *Forty Eight*? It's just that I've been feeling so run-down lately and it's hard to – Babaji, please, get *off*! – get excited about it because it's such a load of old—'

'You mustn't plead with them, Mrs Kellman – that won't do the trick at all. He is awfully sweet, your little dog, the way he just won't leave your heels! Yes, *Forty Eight*, I read it every weekend. It's terribly good, isn't it, and I do think it's got the best telly pages. Here, Fergus! A-a-and, SIT! Good boy. Who's Mummy's best boy?'

Except for when she had been snuggled in bed, this was the first time in months Nina could remember being warm. Close to boiling point would have been a more accurate description. She couldn't decide what was worse, the embarrassment of Babaji failing to do anything she told him to or the toe-curling smalltalk she was having with the various other 'mothers'. Whichever, she was now bright red in the face and down to one T-shirt – her sallow, spongy limbs in harsh contrast to the wiry, tanned extremities of all these *country folk*.

Puppy-training was not going well.

'You must get Babaji trained,' Jerry had insisted. 'He's your dog, he's seven months old now and he's going to turn into a right little terror if you don't knock some sense into him – anyway, I hear it's one of the best ways of getting to know the "right sort" of people from round here.'

'You are joking, aren't you?' Nina had asked dangerously, having been quite happily making friends with the postman, the farmer working the next door field and Mrs Amin at the village shop, those being the three people she ever came into contact with.

Jerry smiled. 'Course I am, Nin-compoop, but then again, don't you think it would be nice to have some sort of social life down here? We can't just import our friends from our previous lives for ever, you know, we are *country folk* now.'

So for the last three weeks, Nina and Babaji had both changed to go out: Nina from her usual tracksuit bottoms and slippersox into jeans and Timberlands; Babaji from an adorable rascal into a clingy, deaf little clown.

Sure enough, the right sort of people were trailing around with their paragon labradors and biddable little Norfolk terriers, but Nina was always too busy trying to peel Babaji off her right shin to keep track of the meaningless gibberish that passed for chat. Consequently, she was convinced that they thought she was a mindless junkie who couldn't sustain an ordinary conversation. Added to that the fact that she was a different colour – absolutely the wrong combination of pallidity and Indian skin instead of the rosy, pink faces she saw all around her – and she felt herself to be kept firmly in the box labelled Different. At least that was one step up from the box labelled Weekender.

If she could just get Babaji to do one thing right, that would be a good omen. She dragged him once again to the other end of the village hall. Having never been on a lead before these classes, Babaji regarded this rope around his neck as a wizard new toy to pull against. By this time, Nina was resigned to the humiliation of seeing her little dog grab the lead with his teeth, sit down firmly and happily let himself be pulled along the shiny floor on his backside, two rows of tiny little gnashers grinning naughtily up at her.

'If you do this right, you little bastard,' she hissed quietly into his ear, 'then that means I'm going to be the new Zoe Heller.' Babaji licked her gratefully and wriggled joyfully out of the lead. 'Now SIT.'

He sat. Nina stared at him. He stared back. She turned her back on him and started to walk down the hall, feeling like Orpheus in her desperate temptation to look behind her, staring with frantic concentration at her feet. So far, she couldn't hear the scrabble-scrabble of tiny paws.

She was over halfway when she couldn't resist the tiniest peek behind her. There sat Babaji, butter not even close to melting in his mouth. If he had been human, she could have sworn that he would have been filing his nails, rolling his eyes to heaven and asking her, 'Are you done yet?'

She was nearly at the end, and was already designing her by-line photo for the top of her syndicated column when she heard the door open. As soon as she did, Babaji gave a joyful bark and flew past her, hurling himself at . . . Jerry. There was a ripple of laughter amongst the other dog-owners – and no doubt amongst the other dogs, Nina thought savagely. Jerry looked up winsomely from tickling an ecstatic Babaji, to look at the crowd of faces – Mrs Barber, the trainer, shaking her head, everyone else chuckling, and Nina, contemplating her less-than-Heller-like future with a face like thunder, and realised that his entrance had been less than perfectly timed.

'Oops,' he grinned, that lock of fair hair falling over his forehead.

*   *   *

'Oops,' thought Cass, as she narrowly missed the kerb of the roundabout exit. After five years of living carlessly in New York and after the more recent nippiness of Trudie's Vespa, she was finding it hard to adjust to the controls and dimensions of a car. But she and Alun were driving off to an evening seminar near Guildford that night and he didn't want to take his ministerial car for some reason, so he had lent his car to Cass the night before on the proviso that she drive it into work this morning.

This had suited Cass fine because she had wanted to go and see her old friends Andy and Tamsin, who were impoverished actors living way out in Ealing and this meant she could sleep over there. The only thing she had been surprised about was how crappy Alun's car was: a filthy old rustbucket of a Vauxhall which looked more like a minicab than an MP's car, and which had 'CLEAN ME' scrawled in the dirt on the bonnet.

All the way in from Ealing, Cass had been deliberating whether today was to be the day she plucked up the courage to ring Wilbur Coolidge. Normally she would drown herself and hang herself out to dry rather than make the first move with a man, but the combination of Wilbur's hostility, Hallie's challenge and the spectre of Carter tracking her down had piqued her into contemplating direct action. She had discussed the bare details with Andy and Tamsin the night before but they had been too amazed by her current lifestyle to give her any decent advice.

'You haven't even snogged anyone since you came back to England?' Andy had dropped his cigarette into his vodka in astonishment. 'But that was weeks ago, months even! Cass, what happened to you in the Big Apple? Please – don't tell me you've become all puritanical? Are you not meeting anyone?'

'You're going to qualify for Born Again Virgin status, if you're not careful,' teased Tamsin.

'Will you both just stop?' Cass had demanded. 'It hasn't even been two months yet, and I'm meeting lots of people. It does sometimes seem like all my old friends are now off in couples' – Andy and Tamsin pulled faces at each other, 'but I've got a new job, remember? Thermos flasks full of piping hot talent there, if I so wanted.' Her thoughts flickered momentarily to Wilbur, then away again, 'But I don't. I'm too busy. I don't need men, and, at the moment, I don't want a man. So there.'

'Definite Born Again Virgin material,' Andy grinned at Tamsin. 'Get your matchmaking head on, love, before it's too late. We must know a suitably gorgeous single man. What about Mike?'

'Not good-looking enough – anyway, he's back with Eva again. They've even moved in together this time.'

Cass lobbed a cushion at them. 'Fuck off and die, both of you. If you dare try set me up, you know what will happen, don't you? I'll just be my usual friendly self and—'

'They'll go home feeling castrated and about as thick as two short planks,' Andy finished for her. 'Yup, seen it all before.'

Of course they hadn't let it rest there. Even that morning, as Tamsin left early to go to her photocopying job in the City, she had popped her head back round the door to say, 'I've been giving your Born Again Virgin dilemma some serious thought during the night. First thing you've got to do, is grow your hair a bit longer – you must be scaring men off as soon as look at them – and then—'

'Tamsin!' Cass had felt her sense of humour, always thin in the mornings, begin to evaporate. 'If you want to bug someone, do it somewhere else, OK? I'm not listening.'

Honestly, she thought now, as she pulled into the House of Lords car park – the summer option for MPs' cars – it's as if my friends who are in couples feel threatened by single people like me and feel that they have to get us paired up like them as soon as possible. Perhaps that's why Hallie is so keen to get hitched herself – she's had five more years of brainwashing by these people than I have.

She stopped as a policeman sauntered over from the little black sentry box he shared with another copper.

'This is Mr Blythe's car, isn't it?' he asked.

'Yes, and I'm his researcher, Cass Herbert.' She showed him her pass.

'Okey-dokey.' He started to check it over with his oversized dentist's mirror, then paused as he walked past the bonnet. He read what was scrawled there and looked at Cass, raising an eyebrow.

'I know,' Cass shrugged, remembering the 'CLEAN ME', 'Alun says I must do it today – do you know somewhere I can go to get it done?'

Then she watched in amazement as the policeman's face creased, and he started to laugh like a hyena, stumbling weakly back to share the joke with his mate. Cass frowned, parked the car, wondering what the big amusement was all about, got out, locked it, then froze as she saw the bonnet.

'CLEAN ME' had been scribbled out. Now it said, 'BORN AGAIN VIRGIN NEEDS SEX. ANY TAKERS?'

Cass looked with horror from the two hysterical policemen back to the bonnet – and ran. She was going to kill Tamsin. Slowly.

'Why are we meeting up here?' Ted asked as he came into Alun's office. 'I thought you never came up here – you prefer being downstairs in amongst all the gossip.'

'I do, but unfortunately today the gossip is all about me,' Cass said grimly and told him briefly about the Virgin Incident as it was already being described downstairs. 'If only I hadn't said all that stuff about Alun wanting me to "do it today", it wouldn't have been so bad but now everyone's convinced that Alun and I are having a re-run of Colin Moynihan and Pamella Bordes.'

'So, you need sex, huh?' Ted suddenly looked more bright-eyed and bushy-tailed.

'Fuck off, Ted. In your dreams,' Cass said carelessly.

Ted blushed. There was a tiny pause.

'Well, thank God you don't work for a woman MP or the News of the Screws would be onto you for the New Labour equivalent of the Jerry Hayes–Paul whatshisface story,' he grinned manfully.

'Jeez, you're right,' said Cass thoughtfully. 'I mean, at the end of the day, everyone here knows that it's all a big joke, but it could so easily be misconstrued by the media, couldn't it? It would just take a few more tiny examples – however innocent they were in actuality, like both of us going to this seminar tonight – of something going on between Alun and me and – kablam! – front page news!'

'Why else do you think politicians are such ripe fodder for scandal? It's because so much of what they do is in the public gaze and because they sell newspapers.'

'But it makes you think – that the sort of scandal that sells a few newspapers can be cooked up out of nothing.'

'And yet look how many politicians really do get mired in the most bloody awful messes,' Ted added dryly, 'so it's perhaps a case of "no smoke without fire" after all? Hey, you should ask your mate Wilbur Coolidge about it, he's the one in the media, he should know all the dirt.' Ted looked at her closely. 'So, been in touch with him?'

Cass glared at him forbiddingly. 'So likely, you moron. I'm in constant contact with all the people who call me a cold-hearted bitch. Oh yeah, just hold me back from calling him and asking him out on a hot date.' She ignored the fact that she was considering doing just that and pressed on. 'And the last thing I would do is tempt fate by giving him any little shreds of gossip to try and weave together.'

The phone rang. Saved by the bell. 'Hang on, Ted, let me just get this. Hi, this is Alun Blythe's office.'

'Cass? It's Hallie. You're going to think I'm mad but – do you remember that breakfast we had at the Cosmopole?'

'Uh-huh.' Cass rolled her eyes at Ted.

'Well, tell me I'm wrong,' Hallie went on excitedly, 'but I think I took a photo of your boss!'

'What – Alun? He wasn't there.'

'I'm sure it's him – do you remember you pointed him out to me the other day when I came for lunch – and he was the one, if you remember, who had his back to you that day, so you wouldn't have seen him, but I got a picture of him face on, having breakfast with some bird.'

'Whoooo, having breakfast. Big bupkes deal, Hallie. He's allowed to, you know, he's divorced, and the last I looked, breakfasting with a woman in a public place wasn't a capital crime.'

Hallie sounded deflated. 'Yeah, I know. And to be honest, it all looks pretty innocent. She's probably a PR like me. But I still think it's an amazing coincidence!'

'You're right,' Cass agreed, making winding-up motions with

her hands to a laughing Ted. 'Any other croissanty calumny hot off the press? Because I have to go now.'

'Oh har, har, clever-clogs. Look, I'll courier over the photos and you can see for yourself.'

'Whatever you want to spend your company's money on, pumpkin. Bye now – oh, and don't break too many nails this weekend, y'hear.' Cass put the receiver down and grinned at Ted. 'Now that just proves my point exactly. My girlfriend Hallie thinks that she's taken some pictures of Alun having breakfast with some woman – and suddenly she's all excited about an MP buttering the toast of the Cosmopole's answer to Mata Hari! Instant headlines! The next thing you know she'll be using it to publicise the Cosmopole like the good PR girl she is.'

'I can see it now – "The Cosmopole – affairs of state or affaires on a plate!"'

'That's terrible – I thought you were supposed to work at a think-tank? Anyway,' Cass became brisk. 'I've just got to finish this stuff before we go out to lunch, so let me clear you a space and you can sit down. I swear that Alun never actually bothered to clear this office out when he took it over after the election, there's so much crap in it.' She grabbed a pile of papers and tried to open a drawer in the spare desk next to Alun's. 'I mean, look at this – it's jammed with rubbish.' She plucked one letter out at random. ' "Dear Mr Boyd-Cooper, I am writing to complain"—'

'Hang on – this used to be Mark Boyd-Cooper's office?' asked Ted.

'Yeah, that rings a bell – and there have been a few things of his lying around.' Cass fell silent as she carried on reading. 'You know, this is actually kind of interesting,' she waved the letter at Ted, 'it's from one of his constituents who won the lottery, complaining about Avalon's total invasion of her privacy and their refusal to let her shun publicity.'

'Really? Avalon are all over the papers at the moment about just that sort of thing – and their bonuses and all that. But then again eighty per cent of the big winners don't take the publicity so why should they pick on her?'

'I don't know, but get this – she says that when she threatened Avalon that she was taking it up with Boyd-Cooper as her local

MP, the local Avalon rep – "*he was a bit tipsy at the time because he'd taken me to the pub*" – laughed and said that Boyd-Cooper was so deeply in their pocket that he wouldn't take any notice. She's asking here what Boyd-Cooper has to say to that – and guess what he's scribbled across the bottom?'

'Bloody heck, I dread to think!'

Cass squinted at the scrawly handwriting. ' "*Nothing to do with us*" – I can't read the next bit – then, "*tell the old bag to shut up and enjoy the cash!*".'

'What a charmer—'

'Wait, there's more: "*On that subject, say yes to Avalon's Sandown evening – and ask how the French junket is coming along – and tell Eddie to let me know about those PMQs*".' Cass looked up, wide-eyed, at Ted. 'Shit! Cash for questions!'

'We don't know that,' Ted said dampeningly. 'No, but it's interesting about him apparently being so deep in their pockets. No wonder he was thrown out at the election.'

Cass looked disappointed. 'What, Boyd-Cooper's gone? You mean to say we can't use this for anything?'

'Old news, love – who cares how bent one of the many out-of-work Tories is?'

'Yeah, I guess you're right. Shame, though, think what the paparazzi could have done with it before the election!'

'Well, keep hold of it just in case I'm fighting him for a seat at the next election!' Ted joked wryly. 'Come on, I'm hungry – and I've got a lot to do this afternoon. Can't you leave that stuff?'

'All right, all right, cool your fruits, I'm coming,' Cass said shortly.

Then she suddenly realised that somehow she was going to have to wheedle Wilbur Coolidge's number out of Ted, without appearing to backtrack on her earlier protestations. Perhaps it was time to start being nice to dear, sweet, old Ted.

'Newsroom.'

'Is Wilbur Coolidge there?'

'Sure is – who shall I say is calling?'

'Um. Er. Well, er, Cass. Cass. Herbert. Lucasta Herbert.'

'Lady, make your mind up!'

'Cass Herbert. That'll do.'

'Whatever you say. I'll put you through.'

Instead of putting her on hold, Cass could hear him shouting across the newsroom. 'Coolidge – line 3 – Cass Herbert. Yeah. Cass Herbert! How the heck should I know? Just take it, will you? Line 3.'

She gulped.

'Wilbur Coolidge here.' The tone was, at best, cool.

'Hi, this is Cass Herbert. Do you remember – we met—'

'I know who it is. What can I do for you?'

Cass took a deep breath. 'Would you like – I mean – I know what you think – but—' Oh, for fuck's sake, Herbert, will you just get a grip, she berated herself silently. 'Listen, will you have a drink with me?' It came out sounding a lot more aggressive than it probably should have.

'OK.'

OK? OK? That was all he was going to say?

'OK,' she replied limply. 'Seven-thirty. Jack's Bar, Notting Hill, do you know it?'

'Yeah, I think so.'

'Well, if you get there first, order me the creamiest, most revolting looking cocktail on the menu.' That was supposed to intrigue him.

It didn't. 'Whatever. Make mine a whisky sour.'

'Done. See you.'

'Wait! When are we having this drink? Next week? This week?'

'Oh!' Cass was losing her nerve. 'Well, tomorrow night, I guess. Unless you – I mean, it's Saturday night, you're probably—'

'Tomorrow is fine. Goodbye.'

Cass replaced the receiver with a shaking hand. This chatting-up-men thing was no fun at all. On a syllable by syllable count, Wilbur Coolidge sure was a low scorer. He clearly was not going to live up to his reputation as a charmer with her. The whole conversation – such as it was – had been all too nerve-racking: how the hell was she going to get through a whole evening? She was going to have to create a dinner date, so that she could get away early. She picked up the phone again.

'Ted? Cass here. You're not doing anything tomorrow night,

are you? Oh, you are? Well, do you want to leave that early and pick up a late-ish movie with me? Great. I'll see what's on at the Coronet around nine, nine-thirty. What? OK, no subtitles. That's the Gate, you klutz, and I'm the one who's supposed not to know London any more. OK. I'll call you on the mobile tomorrow afternoon. Uh-huh. Bye. Oh, wait! I don't know how you did it but you left your Psion over here in Alun's office. Yeah, of course I've been snooping. Now I know all your dark little secrets! OK, I'll bring it with me. Later, dude.'

Well, she couldn't exactly admit that she'd lifted his Psion from his jacket pocket when he'd gone to pay the bill at lunchtime, could she? At the time, it had seemed easier than asking him for Wilbur's number. Easier than copping a load of grief and trying to explain her motives for contacting him.

Hallie would be proud of her, Cass comforted herself.

Hallie was proud of herself. If Karenza and Co at Bandwick & Parker could see her now, she thought smugly, they'd be amazed. Gone were the neat, little trouser suits, high-heeled boots and neatly curled hair and eyelashes of Hallie Templeton, PR dynamo. In their place was Hallie the Country Girl; hair tied back in a ponytail, lashes unclogged by mascara. New green jeans were tucked into spotless, steel-capped Caterpillar work boots, topped off by a green gingham shirt and chunky Aran sweater. She had condensed her washbag into an old pencil case by decanting all her lotions and potions into tiny little Body Shop bottles and for the first time in three years, had taken off all her nail varnish. Only briefly, as it turned out, because she couldn't quite bear the thought of breaking her medium-length but carefully nurtured nails but she'd compromised with a couple of coats of hard, clear polish as a deterrent. She had hidden her mobile at the bottom of her backpack, for use as a lifeline in emergencies, and was only going to bring out her portable ashtray if she thought she could get away with it. She had her sleeping bag – borrowed from Slammer so no doubt as noxious as the Ganges – and her lunch-box, a plastic Lion King satchel that was Karenza's pride and joy, and had bought new 'workgloves' as instructed, from a gardening centre outside Camden.

She was the walking embodiment of a Dry Stone Waller.

Landing the British Trust for Conservation Volunteers' account had been Hallie's first pro bono coup for Bandwick & Parker, and the first since they had launched the pro bono initiative. So giddy had she been with her own brilliance, that when Mary-Jane and Fiona, public affairs directors of BTCV and her new best friends, had asked her if she wanted to see what a working weekend was like firsthand, she had agreed without really thinking it through. That had come later – by which time, Karenza and Roland, her new boss on the Public Affairs team, had found out, had stared at her and fallen about laughing.

'Hallie!' Karenza had gasped. 'You can't! You just can't! Dry stone walling! You!'

'Oh, team leader, can I just have a latte and a brioche before we start breaking up large rocks?' mimicked Roland cruelly. 'What do you mean, there's no escalator up to the top of that hill?'

'You can mock, you can tease, you can sneer,' said Hallie calmly, 'I'm actually looking forward to it. When was the last time you put something back into the environment, Karenza? Apart from smoking menthol fags instead of Camels? And Roland – I bet your idea of a good weekend in the country is to climb into your BMW, check into Champneys, and lie by a pool being waited on hand and foot by white-gloved waiters.'

'You bet,' agreed Roland cheerfully. 'What's wrong with that? At least then I get to sleep in a bed. At least then I get to eat something other than lentil lasagne and parsnip wine. But, hey, if you want to hang out with a load of beardy-weirdy, woolly-pully, vegetarian nature crusaders, don't let me stand in your way. Your professional keenness is duly noted.' He smoothed his own neatly-trimmed beard complacently.

'Good to know that you're not falling into exactly the sort of social stereotyping that B&P have been hired to disprove. I'll tell Mary-Jane and Fiona about the beardy-weirdy part,' threatened Hallie. She didn't mind Roland thinking that she was being a pious, eager beaver. Better that than them guessing the real reason for her going on this dry stone walling weekend.

Despite her bravado with Cass, the Devlin set-up had brought Hallie close to the end of her single tether. She had tried Dateline, she had gone to the evening classes, she had let herself be set up by both friends and colleagues, she had given good telephone in Caspers and had sported her melons in Tesco's. She had not sat around on her bum waiting for Mr Right – she had gone out there looking for him. And what had it got her? Zip. Diddly. Just a few phone numbers that had probably been given to her deliberately wrong; a couple of mix'n'match dinners where a couple of lonely scallops always teetered artistically over a sprig of rocket and a dribble of lemon coulis; the heartbreakingly disastrous shag with Devlin and, at the end of the day, an ego that was so bruised and battered that she could keep arnica in business until the millennium.

Then, when she had been gazing in horror at the BTCV brochure sent to her by Mary-Jane, wondering what on earth she had let herself in for, she remembered that Nina had been on some sort of working holiday when she had been doing her travel-writing and had raved about them being fertile breeding grounds for romance. She gave her a ring.

'Oh fuck yes,' Nina had assured her, 'singles heaven, apparently. If you want a good, steady man who's into doing his bit for the environment, then these charitable working holidays are the kipper's knickers. Mind you, you have to choose them fucking carefully – I was on a tree-planting week in the Highlands which was bloody heavy-duty – dreadlocks and Swampy-lookalikes aplenty – and all that bending down and mucking about didn't half do my back in. It's never been the same since. No, something like dry stone walling in the West Country is probably your best bet – they're the Formula One of working holidays. You just have to make sure that the accommodation is marked as being "simple". That way you all sleep together – the alternative is "dormitory" when they separate men and women and put you into bunk-beds, which is no fun.' She paused. 'Are you sure about this, Hallie? I mean I know you're desperate but is this really up your street?'

Hallie had been so annoyed about the 'desperate' tag that she hadn't thought twice before lying through her teeth. 'Gosh, it's not for me. We've just taken them on as a pro bono account and we're thinking of a publicity angle. I noticed in the brochure that they have a policy of discouraging groups of friends, even couples, from booking and it got me thinking of possible singles' promotions: "Romancing the Stone" – that sort of thing.'

Nina laughed. 'That's OK, then. I couldn't really see you lugging flagstones around the countryside in the pursuit of love.'

'No,' said Hallie. 'Obviously not.'

Which was why she was here on Weymouth station platform, all kitted out in her new rural finery, determined to prove everyone wrong and as an added bonus maybe find, if not Mr Right, then at least that equally elusive Mr Meanwhile.

'Hayley?'

Hallie turned round to see Michael Praed staring intently at her. Well, perhaps not Michael Praed himself, but a dead ringer – Robin Hood from hood to foot, BTCV sweatshirt peeping out from under his kagoule.

'It's Hallie, actually. As in Happy.'

'Happy Hallie. I like the sound of that,' he smiled, eyes crinkling very prettily.

Hallie crinkled back. Things were already looking up.

'Cass, there's another man for you here at the door,' sniggered Paul the Attendant, 'but he says, sorry, he's not available for sex. He's just delivering a package from Bandwick & Parker.'

Sometimes it amused Cass how efficient the lines of gossip were between every strand of personnel in the Houses of Parliament. This was not one of those times.

Once she'd collected the package from a courier who was almost as embarrassed as her, Cass fled back to the office to look over the photos of the Cosmopole. Hallie was right, she saw immediately, it *was* Alun in a couple of the photographs, smiling that relaxed, lop-sided grin at a woman she vaguely remembered seeing that morning, a curtain of black hair half-hiding a calm-looking, oval face.

He looked younger somehow, in photographs, than he did in real life, but perhaps that was because it was breakfast-time. By the end of the day, Alun's face seemed to sag, the heavy bags under his eyes leeching all the light away from his other features, deep lines appearing either side of his nose.

At first, Cass had thought it was just disillusionment with a job that was so far more an exercise in damage limitation on rising interest rates and the brewing windfall tax than a real opportunity. But after the Westminster Planning party and Julian's sly comments, she had found herself noticing that Alun did seem to go AWOL for large amounts of the day. Perhaps he was off propping up some bar – the Marquis had a Division Bell, so that explained why he was never actually late for a vote – and whenever he and Cass went out for a drink, they both seemed to put away an unconscionable amount of wine. He was certainly late for everything except Divisions. One day, fending off an irate *Newsnight* producer demanding to know where he was, Cass had made the mistake of barging into Mags's office and, abandoning her usual pussy-footing round Alun's intimidating secretary, had asked where the hell he was. It had been four o'clock in the afternoon and Mags herself was three-quarters of the way through the cans of ready mixed vodka and tonic she carried in her handbag. The tornado that had accompanied Mags's boozy bellows never to be so impertinent again had persuaded Cass to shelve her questions until a better time.

She couldn't really complain, however – her job was a cinch for most of the time, studded by an occasional interesting frenetic rush round with Alun himself. He was fulfilling his part of the bargain admirably, introducing her everywhere as 'my brightest researcher yet' and making sure that everyone knew about her consultancy plans – and Cass found herself liking his cynical but affectionate manner more and more. The trouble was that she felt that she wasn't exactly justifying her position. After three years of combining a ton of PhD work with numerous teaching Fellowships and casual money-earners at the same time as trying to live like a real Noo Yawker – i.e., at eighty miles an hour – Cass was finding that the desultory pace of constituency letters, speech-writing, non-urgent research and the *laissez-faire* attitude of her English PhD supervisor was leaving her too much time to think about other things – like men. And now the same old guilts about John and Carter swirling round her head were being joined by uncomfortable thoughts about Wilbur Coolidge.

'An ECU for your thoughts!'

Cass jumped and dropped all the photographs on the floor.

Frank Blackthorn grinned at her – still-white teeth framed by thick lips and his bushy grey beard.

'Haven't seen much of you up here lately,' he said. 'Alun been keeping you hard at it? Or has that rascal Ted been squiring you round too much for you to do any work? I tell you, love,' before she had a chance to get a word in edgeways, 'people are beginning to talk. Ted's old friends are noticing that he's no longer in Bellamy's so much – he's out and about with this young lass, so they say.'

'I know that you can't bear that your matchmaking failed, Frank,' Cass sighed, picking up the photos, 'but, really – *Ted*? He would be the first to tell you that we are, we really are, Just Good Friends. Anyway, I'm surprised you haven't already heard – I'm a Born Again Virgin.'

'I'm not even going to pretend to know what you mean. Here, do you want a hand?' He bent down to help her, handing her the photos he'd picked up without looking at them, then heading over to his own desk.

After a few minutes, Cass could stand it no longer. Much as she wanted to like Frank Blackthorn, because he was bluff and friendly, red-faced and merry, she couldn't, quite. In such a small office it was impossible not to hear every last sexist word he said while on the phone to his cronies, impossible not to feel hemmed in by his creaking bulk, his terrible wheezing and coughing as he hacked into a motley assemblage of handkerchiefs, toilet roll and on one memorable occasion, a constituent's letter. 'It's all he deserves,' Blackthorn had said that time when he'd caught Cass looking at him aghast, 'bloody nonce.' But above all, it was his claustrophobic appreciation of her that had Cass backing into the corner. He never lost any opportunity to tell her how lovely she was, how Ted was crazy about her, how Alun thought she was the best thing since sliced bread, how she was the pin-up of the porters and attendants. It drove her mad.

'So,' he said now, 'where's Ted taking you tonight? Lovely evening for it, I'll bet, whatever "it" is. Why I'm here on a Friday afternoon and not up in the constituency like I'm meant to be is beyond me. The wife, you know. She wants to stay down here this weekend, so I thought I'd surprise her and stay behind as well, interrupt her shopping and her nail-filing. What, you're not off already?' as Cass stood up abruptly, leaving the pile of photos open on the desk to remind herself to show them to Alun, and grabbing her gym bag.

'I'm going to the gym.'

'Oh yes, much better that you keep up those gorgeous legs than do any work,' he laughed. 'I'd come with you and watch, but I don't think my dodgy ticker could stand the pace.'

Cass ground her teeth and said nothing as she stalked out of the office. Five minutes later, she was striding through the windowless rabbit warren underneath Norman Shaw North, another of the peeling Parliamentarian outbuildings that, like Dean's Yard, were being cast even further into the shade by the shiny new Parliament Street and Bridge Street constructions. Feeling no temptation to visit the solarium – notorious pick-up zone for the Gay Mafia since the sunbed room was one of the few innocently lockable rooms in the Palace of Westminster, leading one pretty male researcher to be asked by his straight boss why he was suntanned only on one side – she changed and went straight into the gym. As was usual on a Friday afternoon, when both MPs and Peers fled London for the country, it was empty, so Cass got straight down to it, losing herself in a punishing treadmill session.

When she came up for air, and headed for the bicycles, she saw she had been joined by two others, including none other than Paddy Ashdown, who was giving it some SAS-style welly on the rowing machines in front of the bikes. After a few minutes of this, Cass was mesmerised by the brute determination and effort being displayed by the LibDem leader. It wasn't a bad effort by a someone who had to be coming up for his bus-pass.

'With all that huffing and puffing,' whispered a voice from the next door bike, 'I'm beginning to feel like one of the little piggies!'

Cass turned and smiled at the fortyish, dark-haired woman next to her. 'I know what you mean.'

Just then, the door opened and in walked Annalisa Smith, the latest sensation to hit the Palace of Westminster. One of the most startling ripple effects of the tidal wave that was the Labour victory was the replacement of the infamous Dragons – Tory secretaries who had been entrenched in the House for decades with one Member or another – by younger, prettier secretaries brought in by the influx of younger, handsomer Labour MPs who had surfed into Parliament on Tony Blair's coat-tails. Forget the loose cannons who might have snuck past the Labour screening procedure to cause trouble for the Labour hierarchy later in the long term, it was some of their secretaries who were most immediately causing red faces and tight collars around Westminster.

Annalisa Smith was already the most notorious. In the two months since the election, Ted had told Cass, it was rumoured that she had slept with no less than four Members and no-one knew how many Peers, let alone her new boss, a frightened-looking twenty-four-year-old Member who still lived with his mother. With her dark, glossy hair, falling neatly from a middle parting to tuck behind her ears, her heart-shaped face and determined pointy chin, not to mention her alarming habit of wearing little icecream-coloured suits, both halves of which always, always rode up to show her tanned, muscley thighs and midriff – it was as if she was custom-designed to make powerful, coherent statesmen drool insensibly over her like schoolboys. Even in her gym kit she looked impossibly good – minuscule turquoise lycra top straining over perfect pert breasts, royal blue thong bisecting two cheeky little buttocks in matching turquoise cycling shorts, silver belly-button ring glinting. Cass was just looking at her admiringly, wishing she could bear to show her own body off like that, when there was a muffled explosion of laughter from beside her.

'Look at Paddy!'

Cass looked and had to gulp back one of her loud shouts of laughter. Far from sweating it out unglamorously on the rowing machine, the onetime Para had dived off at Annalisa's entrance, stripped off his sweat-stained singlet and was now showing off his burly muscled torso by doing one-armed press-ups in the middle of the floor. Annalisa could hardly miss him.

Without batting an eyelid, and ignoring all the other empty exercise mats, the brunette bombshell lay down on the mat right in front of Ashdown's nose and started warming up – lying on her stomach and stretching her arms back to pull her feet towards her head – oh-so-inadvertently giving Paddy the full benefit of her jaunty little cleavage, staring unsmilingly into his contorted face, the small, pink tip of her tongue just escaping from between her Cupid-bow-shaped lips. The temperature in the gym seemed to have gone up by at least ten degrees.

Cass and her companion could stand it no longer. As quietly as they could, they tottered off their exercise bikes and crept out of the gym into the changing room, waiting until the connecting door was closed before venting their laughter.

'Do you reckon she even noticed we were there?' giggled the other woman, her northern accent getting stronger the more she laughed. 'That's not *the* Annalisa, is it?'

'Come on, we're women – no way did she notice us – and yes, it is,' groaned Cass, 'isn't she unbelievably beautiful?'

'She's a cow. And she doesn't half make the rest of us secretaries look like sheep's bums.' The other woman began to fix her appearance in the mirror. Cass looked at her properly for the first time.

'Do I know you?' Cass asked. 'I do know you! You look so familiar!' Suddenly it came to her. 'I've got it! I saw you having breakfast with my boss – you're the one in Hallie's photos!'

'Oh, who's your boss?' The woman carried on brushing her hair unconcernedly. 'You don't work for Frank, do you?'

'Who? No, I work for Alun Blythe. I'm Cass, his researcher.'

There was no pause in the brushing. 'Of course, the remarkable Cass.' The woman smiled in the mirror. 'I'm Gwenny Blackthorn – Frank Blackthorn's wife and secretary – and I've heard all about you from Alun.'

'Oh, that Frank. Wow! I didn't realise Frank's wife worked here!' But you're so gorgeous and he's so . . . not gorgeous, was Cass's immediate, luckily silent, reaction.

'He tries to keep it a secret,' grinned Gwenny, 'given that I was also his secretary when he was married to the first Mrs Blackthorn.' She paused. 'So where did you say you recognised me from?'

'Oh, from breakfast at the Cosmopole, a week or so ago. My friend Hallie is doing the PR there and she was snooping round taking pictures and by this totally weird coincidence, she happened to get one of you and Alun. It's funny actually, because we were saying only this morning that it's pictures like that that give paparazzi their ideas,' Cass added guilelessly.

'Except that Frank was there as well,' Gwenny laughed. 'Unless your paparazzi are looking for a threesome, in which case – hey, it's a fair cop!'

Cass laughed as well. 'If it was two women and an MP, then there could be something in it, but I can't really see two MPs' egos sharing one women in a threesome, can you?' Then she threw her hand to her face. 'Oh my God, I don't believe I said that – I am so sorry – that was so incredibly rude – Jeez, when am I ever going to put my goddamn brain in gear – what can I—'

Gwenny laughed again and patted her on the arm. 'Speak your mind, love, I'm from the North. We're so used to putting our feet in it up there that we have our mouths fitted by Clarke's Rightsize. Oh, I am glad I met you – where have the boys been hiding you all this time? And what are you doing here at this time? Surely Alun doesn't make you work Friday afternoons?'

'No, not usually, but we're driving up to this seminar outside Guildford this evening. It's all very complicated. I'm driving Alun up in his car; then I'm driving back tonight, leaving him there to get the train back tomorrow. Why he doesn't come back with me tonight, don't ask me. Anyway, you're here aren't you?'

'Yes, but I'm staying down here this weekend. I've left Frank to go up to the constituency on his own, poor love.'

'Oh, that's right – he said something about that. Except that he hasn't gone up – he's stayed down as well – to surprise—' Cass broke off. 'Fuck, I've done it again! What is wrong with me?'

This time Gwenny grabbed her arm with some urgency. 'What? Frank's still here?'

'Yeah, I just left him in his office. God, I'm really sorry I blew it.'

The older woman smiled again. 'Don't worry, I'll still act surprised. Oh, he is an old goat – treats at the Cosmopole, unexpected re-appearances. I don't know – married for fifteen years and I still haven't trained him out of surprises! Don't be fooled, love, when they say marriage takes the romance out of a relationship. They just feel like they have to do dafter things to qualify as romantic!'

'I'm not fooled by anything that anyone says about marriage,' Cass said firmly. 'I don't believe in marriage.'

'No wonder Alun likes you so much,' marvelled Gwenny, 'you're both as cynical as each other. I must tell him I've met you. In fact, I need to talk to him anyway – you don't have his mobile number on you, do you? – I'll give him a call while I remember.'

'I have a strange and inexplicable memory for telephone numbers,' Cass said, reciting it.

'0802 756895 – 0802 756 – look, I'll have to run for the payphone down here before I forget it. It was grand to meet you, love, and I'm sure I'll see you again very soon. Oh bugger it, what was the number again?'

'0802 756895,' Cass reminded her, watching her speed out of the changing room. What a great woman. Shame she had to rush off like that, but what a character. And married to Frank Blackthorn. Well, they said strange things happen in politics. Funny, Cass couldn't remember for the life of her seeing anyone who resembled the bushy-bearded Blackthorn in the Cosmopole dining room that morning. Mind you, she hadn't recognised her own boss from a bar of soap. Just goes to show how nondescript politicians are when they're outside their own little milieu, she thought wryly.

It was nearly August, Hallie thought savagely, feeling the rain trickle down her neck. When was summer going to start? She was the wrong person, in the wrong place, at the wrong time. But the most galling thing was that Karenza, Nina and Roland had all been right and she had been wrong: dry stone walling was obviously not for her.

If she was honest with herself, Hallie had expected to feel superior to the sort of people she thought would be going on these working weekends. At first glance, that superiority had been dented. Geoff, the Michael Praed lookalike, might have been wearing a kagoule and might have talked long and earnestly about the shared enterprise they were embarking on but after a few minutes of gazing at him and not listening to a word, Hallie suddenly realised that he was the one feeling superior. To him she was fools' gold: a glittery city slicker, trapped by the drudgery of a deskbound job and the petty dictates of material aspirations, into a moral vacuum devoid of values and decent hopes. Not that he'd said as much, of course, but his clear, untroubled gaze was enough to unearth Hallie's shallowly buried paranoias.

It was the same with the rest of the crew. By the time they had all rolled out their sleeping bags on yoga mats on the floor of the church hall, Hallie thought she had taken their measure. Ned, the divorcé from Chichester with a needy gleam in his eye; Vi, the single librarian of indeterminate thirtysomething age; Alan, the unmarried jigsaw enthusiast whose horny toenails were truly scabrous specimens; Nerdy Loser, Homespun Spinster, Bearded Trainspotter – they were all types Hallie was expecting. What she hadn't anticipated was that, to them, she was just as much of a stereotype: the Snotty Scoffer. It hadn't taken long for her to concede defeat – she just wanted to be liked, after all – and soon she was bending their ears and tickling their fancies with her most sparkling banter over the lasagne. But it was hard work making her accent as streetwise as possible, being comprehensively self-deprecating and steering round all inverted snobbery pitfalls at every turn of the conversation.

It was also taking rather longer to master the dry stone walling. She'd seen pictures of dry stone walls in the brochure and had seen people scramble over them in countless episodes of *Emmerdale* and they had always seemed perfectly simple examples of flat stones laid over each other in your average red-brick herringbone pattern. There was even a pile of lovely flat Portland quarried stone a matter of yards away. But oh no, that was far too simple. Using stone that was lying there was like building the Newbury bypass, Hallie thought rebelliously, easier for everyone all round but expensive and not politically correct. No, they had to dig up all the old stones – lying about from when the wall they were re-building had collapsed and re-assemble it with them before using the expensive, purpose-cut stuff. Trouble was, these old stones were a hundred years old and now more closely resembled funky asteroids than walling flagstones.

'A good stone-waller never puts a stone down without placing it, Hayley,' said Geoff mildly, as Hallie tossed a particularly mutant avocado-shaped specimen away, in a fury. 'You just have to play with all the angles before you can find a way of fitting it in.'

'Give me Tetris anyday,' snapped Hallie, then she blushed. 'I'm sorry.' Luckily, Geoff was looking blank. Despite the fact that he was the same age as Hallie, the Gameboy phenomenon had obviously passed him by. Yet again, Hallie felt shamefully alien. 'I'm not sure I have the patience for this.'

'Tell you what,' he suggested kindly, 'why don't you try smashing the really hopeless rocks into little pieces to go in the centre of the wall. We call it the "hearting".'

'Ooh, you little hearting-breaker!' quipped Hallie.

'Honestly, if I had a fiver for all the times I've heard that joke, I wouldn't be a computer programmer from Chichester for much longer,' snickered Needy Ned, passing. 'I myself find smashing the hearting is a wonderful way of getting all that road rage out of my system. Biff! That'll teach you, Mister Swanky Cosworth driver. Boff! Take that, Miss Blonde Bimbo MX-Fivey. Ker-pow! You'll think twice about overtaking me next time, won't you, Mister Saaby-Waaby?!'

And Ned was her best prospect for romance, thought Hallie bleakly. Last night, in the pub, while she had manfully struggled through a half of Guinness, unwilling to admit yet again that she was a precious urban softie who didn't like the taste of alcohol, Ned had lost no time in paying court. The poor lamb had obviously been reading up on his women's magazines because he'd tried to push all the right buttons. He had talked nicely about his ex-wife, referring to his divorce as his Life Graduation ceremony, from which he had grown into a full and honest person. He had entertained her with tales of derring-do, painting himself as a Milk Tray man of action who thought nothing of hurling himself down muddy tracks on his mountain bike, tackling a C2 wall at the local climbing centre and kayaking on the wild waters of the River Dee, 'safety equipment, helmets, ropes and the like being what they are these days'. He had paid lipservice to her career and aspirations, like any well-trained wooer, and had hit the right balance between desperation and flattery in his compliments. Hallie had felt positively ungrateful to be left cold by all this textbook gallantry, especially given her motives for coming here in the first place.

For Nina was right. Get fifteen people humping rocks together, cooking together, snoring together and packing lunchboxes together and Cupid's arrows were spoilt for choice. Geoff had made more than a wall with his now girlfriend; Vi the only vegetarian turned out not to be a spinster – her fiancé had decided on a hedge-laying weekend on this particular date but they had met on a scrub-clearing week in Cheshire; and even gentle Alan had nearly persuaded a chiropodist fellow-fence-mender out on a date. Shame he hadn't managed, thought Hallie, shuddering again at the sight of his scaly feet.

Outside the noisomely cosy environs of the church hall, even the surroundings were conducive to romance. What with the shingled length of Chesil Beach and the ancient swannery of the Fleet lagoon below and the blurred reminders of medievalism in the terraced slopes all around, they were spoilt for vistas, even if the rain was doing its best to dampen any enthusiasm. I'm just not cut out for this, thought Hallie mournfully. Who was I kidding? I'm a shallow townie strumpet who has the cheek to be looking for someone who's got something more going for them than just their availability. How dare I be so fussy? Who do I think I am?

Into such gloomy introspection broke Geoff's cheery tones. 'Teabreak!'

'Goodie!' cried Ned. 'And I've made some lovely homemade scones!'

Oh crikey, he cooks as well, Hallie sighed – he really is the perfect man. Well, unless they come with clotted cream, strawberry Bonne Maman and a pot of Earl Grey, I'm just not interested, she thought sourly, not sure if she could face another session of meaningful compliments. Just then the rain stopped, the wind dropped and the clouds cleared momentarily. Further up the hill, Hallie could now see the 600-year-old Chapel of St Catherine, built by the monks of Abbotsbury in the windiest spot in the county, Geoff had explained, as a penance for carousing with nuns. They had had the right idea, she giggled to herself, and decided to pop up and have a look around.

Red-faced, puffing and realising that desultory Saturday roller-blading was not the way to get fit, she arrived at the tiny chapel. Inside, it was empty, plain of all decoration except for a plaque on the end wall. I don't believe this, thought Hallie as she read how St Catherine was the patron saint of spinsters, I am being haunted by my singleness. Then she groaned as she read the poem inscribed underneath.

> *Send me a husband, St Catherine*
> *A handsome one, St Catherine*
> *A rich one, St Catherine*
> *A nice one, St Catherine*
> *And soon, St Catherine . . .*

Too bloody right, St Catherine, prayed Hallie.

'Can I help you?' said a male voice behind her.

Hallie spun round to see a man with the sweetest face, manliest chin and kindest eyes she had ever seen. 'Yes, you certainly can,' she blurted, falling instantly in love.

Too late, she saw the dog-collar.

Swirling in and out of consciousness, Nina gasped with pleasure. He was on top of her, all around her, in her, covering her skin with tiny shocks of pleasure in an erotic assault of lips, hands, tongue, teeth. Yes, yes, yes, she thought, her hips arching to meet his. Oh yes, yes, just there. She gasped as he slid into her, her hands clutching convulsively at his back, that familiar shiver of ecstasy creeping up the back of her neck, blood roaring in her ears, explosions of light behind her closed eyelids, pressing herself to him in an urgent attempt to share every inch of skin. Inside her, he bucked and reared involuntarily.

'Slowly, slowly,' she mumbled, still half asleep. 'Ohhhh, BadBoy . . .'

'You're right,' he gasped, 'you're right!' Then he paused. 'Why am I a bad boy?' he asked, sounding amused.

Nina's eyes flew open. There, above her in the gloom, her smiling husband was leaning up on his elbows, hips still pulsing into her, her legs wrapped tenderly around him. 'Jerry!' she yelped, her arms falling away from him.

Inside her, she felt him shrink momentarily. 'Yeah,' he nodded, smile wavering. 'Who else would it be?' He looked at her accusingly and pulled out of her. 'Who did you think it was? You were the one who woke me up to seduce me!'

Desperately clearing the last wisps of sleep from her mind, Nina thought quickly.

'Bruce Willis,' she admitted, biting her lip guiltily.

'Bruce Willis?!'

'I was just having the dirtiest dream ever – and I'm afraid Bruce Willis had the starring role,' she grimaced, gathering Jerry close for a hug. 'So you've got quite a lot to live up to!'

Jerry looked relieved. 'Well, yippee-kye-ay, Mrs Kellman – look out!' he said roughly, turning them both over so that Nina was now on top. 'I'm coming in!'

Later, Nina lay sleepless while a slack-jawed Jerry snored happily beside her. That had been a truly narrow escape. Having dirty dreams about a filthy-minded, puerile Internet boyfriend called BadBoy was just not on. She had obviously reckoned without her subconscious when she had signed off the other day. Even now, after wonderful sex with the man she loved, there was a nagging sense of unfinished business there. Perhaps flouncing off-line like that hadn't been final enough. Perhaps there was some sort of cyber-etiquette she needed to follow before she could erase BadBoy from her system. Or maybe it was just the thrill of having virtual sex with someone she knew nothing about, not even their name, that was still lingering, even though she now knew how tacky on-line sex could be. So far, not knowing anything about BadBoy had been titillating – so perhaps if she found out more about him, the frisson would fade.

This is positively and absolutely the last time I do this, she promised herself, as she snuck downstairs. I'm a happily-married woman who has just made passionate love to my husband. I have a dog, a life in the country, a job and responsibilities – I do not need to enact some clichéd cyberloser's link-up.

> nk@jkenterprises: badboy RU there?

> badboy@beinemann proud: you're back! i knew you wouldn't be able to resist it nk, sorry if i came on kinda strong last time. truce?

Nina did sometimes wonder how it was that every time she went online, BadBoy was always there. Did he never do anything else except loiter on the Information Superhighway?

> nk@jkenterprises: OK. Anyway, I need to talk to you in private, Badboy. Can we go into the private chat room?

> badboy@beinemann proud: no problemmo. i'll set it up.

Two minutes later they were alone.

> badboy@beinemann proud: that's what i like to see – a girl who gets straight down to business. whaddya wanna do sugarpie? <WEG>

> nk@jkenterprises: slow down, badboy. Can we talk?

> badboy@beinemann proud: that's why we're here hon. talk away!

> nk@jkenterprises: I want to know more about you – what's your name, how old are you, what do you do, what do you look like, what music do you like, where do you live, who are beinemann proud – all those things that we promised each other we wouldn't ask.

> badboy@beinemann proud: <frown> why the sudden curiosity?

> nk@jkenterprises: I feel embarrassed saying this <GD&R> but I dreamt about you tonight – then woke up in the middle of having sex with my husband. So I just thought that if I found out some more about you I could get this whole thing into perspective.

There was a pause.

> nk@jkenterprises: Badboy?

>badboy@beinemann proud: i'm here. i just didn't real-
ise you were married. this makes quite a difference.

> nk@jkenterprises: Yes, it does. Are you married?

> badboy@beinemann proud: <hollow laugh> no. you
really hadn't guessed, had you? it was kinda fun
fooling around in the beginning because i knew you
didn't have a clue, but this is getting out of hand
if i'm coming between you and a husband.

> nk@jkenterprises: Didn't have a clue about what?
What haven't I guessed? Badboy, what is going on?

For at least two long minutes, the cursor just blinked at
her.

> nk@jkenterprises: Badboy, are you there? What is
going on?

> badboy@beinemann proud: well here goes nothing.
you wanted to know about me? my name is nancy levine.
i am 24 yrs old. i live in ann arbor, michigan, where
i am a graduate student and part-time para-legal at
a law firm called beinemann proud. i thought it would
be fun to masquerade as a man on the www for a while, as
well as my normal lesbian net relationships. sorry.

Nina stared at the screen, eyes nearly falling out of her head.
After all that, BadBoy was a lesbian?

'Can I get you another daiquiri?'
  'Yeah. No. Whatever. Yeah.'
  'I'll take that as a yes.'
  As Wilbur went to get the drinks, Cass looked after him,
cringing inside. How can I flirt with this man? she thought in

horror, he's a Coolidge. To hit on him is tasteless, ill-timed and cack-handed. When am I going to get that damn family out of my system? She should just go home.

From the moment she had walked into the bar and seen him sitting there, casually chatting to the people on the next door table, she had known that this wasn't right. He was a nice guy, who was naturally going to expect her to talk about John – fondly, grievingly, affectingly – and she couldn't do that. The only way to deal with this ridiculous set-up, which she had got herself into, she had reminded herself shortly, was to fall back on the Hallie Challenge and seduce him. That way, she would get him out of her system, prove herself to Hallie and consign Wilbur Coolidge to the landfill site of Herbert cast-offs.

The trouble was that Cass couldn't seduce her way out of a paper bag when she actually put her mind to it. Just like the *Mastermind* genius who couldn't win a quid out of the pub quiz machine; just like the clothes designer who couldn't sew; just like the astronaut who couldn't mend his son's Buzz Lightyear doll; Cass had never had to do the legwork – there had always been someone else to shoulder the burden of doing the chatting-up. She could bat her eyelashes like a pro if dared to; she could respond and banter with the best of them; she could flirt with anyone she wasn't interested in but when it came to Eve introducing Adam to look at the apple, let alone persuading him to eat it, Cass's Bible would have been a hell of a lot shorter. Vampish archness was so far removed from her usual brutal candour that Cass knew, even as she was hearing herself, how false it sounded so would then subside into mortified monosyllables.

As she saw him coming back, frown as much in evidence as it had been since she'd started her clumsy seduction, she belatedly faced facts: he certainly didn't fancy her, with every crucifying bit of prick-teasing she was just deepening his lousy first impression of her, and that this was all just reminding her why she'd given up men in the first place – she hated being out of control so much. She'd give it five minutes and then she was out of here – off to the flicks with nice, safe Ted. In the meantime, she would just give up on the *femme fatale* attempts.

'There you go,' Wilbur smiled tightly, as he slid across her daiquiri. 'A truly disgusting concoction. How on earth did you ever get it together with John Junior? I thought he was a strictly beers-only kind of party animal.'

He'd done it. Breached the wall of the unspoken between them. Cass stared at him. She'd been dreading this since the beginning of their conversation, but now that it was out there – a direct question floating between them – she was no closer to knowing what she wanted to say.

'Look,' he said gently. 'We both know why you wanted to meet me – it was nothing to do with me, it's all tied up with John Junior. So why don't we just cut straight to the chase? I know you must be missing him like crazy – no-one here must have a clue what you're going through – and if I can be some sort of punching bag for you, then, hey, that's what families are for. I just want to say that I'm truly sorry I was such an asshole at that party the other night. It was kind of a shock to meet you after all this time and I didn't handle it well. There, that's my speech. Now don't feel you have to come back with one yourself – if you don't want to talk about it then that's fine, but I thought we should just stop pussy-footing around the subject and get it out there.' He looked at her expectantly.

To her horror, Cass felt a betraying thickness at the back of her throat. It was even worse than she had expected. He thought her Psycho Siren act was part of her deranged grief. Why did he have to be such a nice guy? Why was she such a bitch? She daren't even respond, fearing that opening up that Pandora's Box would unleash all the vile and ignoble horrors she was trying to bury.

She stared at her cocktail for a moment, then sighed and pushed it away. 'You know, the first real date I had with John was in a cocktail bar – that one at the bottom of Morgan's Hotel. He thought it would impress me because it was so totally "in" at the time. Then he thought he'd spoilt it all by losing his temper with the barman when they didn't have any Murphy's stout. But actually, I was kind of relieved – up till then I was beginning to think that John was like every other man I'd met in New York – either gay, status-obsessed or totally over-confident.'

'He was never any of those things,' Wilbur shook his head,

then grinned. 'Almost a little too far the other way. It was one of the things I missed about those Coolidge Clan round table talks – endless hand-wringing on how to give John Junior some direction, some drive. But I did hear that he improved when you two started dating.'

He looked her up and down, at the way she dressed, almost like a man with her broad-striped, skinny-ribbed T-shirt, her white hipsters and her battered trainers. It sure didn't do justice to her figure.

Cass ignored the gentle probing. Enough talk of 'you two'. Time to divert the subject to him . . . like how was it fair that he should have the longest, thickest eyelashes she'd ever seen outside a drag club? How was it possible that gunmetal-grey hair, cropped savagely close to the skull could look almost better on him than on George Clooney? That dimples could suddenly be so sexy?

'Yeah, how come I never met you at those bloody awful Coolidge get-togethers? I remember John once saying how he hadn't seen you for a long time.'

'Oh, I've been the black sheep of the family for years,' smiled Wilbur ruefully, 'due to career choices not befitting a Coolidge.'

He noticed her raising an eyebrow – where had she learnt that – a Roger Moore film?

'And it was hard, once Meredith and Pa divorced and she re-married. John was only five to my seven when our parents married – then he was adopted by Pa and suddenly became my and my sister's little brother for nine years. Then, when he was fourteen, they split, and John was no longer supposed to be my brother, just my father's ex-wife's son. Pa had to fight to be allowed anything to do with him, because Meredith wanted to cut every link she had made with the Coolidges – it was bad enough that John had taken the Coolidge name – and anyway, by that time I had burned a few boats of my own away from the family.'

'What sort of boats?'

Wilbur looked Cass straight in the eye. 'I became a ballet dancer.'

Cass laughed out loud – huck, huck, huck. 'A ballet dancer?! I should say that wasn't a Coolidge choice! Wow! How cool! John never told me any of this. Was it fun?'

He must be gay, she thought, with a strange sense of relief. No wonder I found him so attractive. Anyway, Ted's right – he has got huge bags under his eyes, and his nose looks broken; he's not so great.

She laughs just like Yogi Bear, Wilbur found himself thinking, and she throws her head so far back that her neck looks three times as thick. Strange girl.

'Yeah, it was terrific while I was at the Academy, even better when I joined the Oklahoma State Ballet *corps de ballet* straight out of college – with all those beautiful women, I was like a kid in a candystore – but after a few years I wanted out.'

Cass put the gay idea into cold storage, to mull over later. He definitely dressed too well to be straight, with his white V-neck T-shirt and battered black leather reefer coat making him look like the inspiration for Tom Cruise's *Mission: Impossible* look.

'Why?'

'Oh, by that time I was about fifth male lead at the Okie – which should have been fine, but it wasn't. I suddenly realised that I wasn't ever going to be good enough to be the lead, even at the Okie, let alone at the Met, or the San Francisco Ballet. It was time to concede defeat. So I started treating it like a job, not an obsession, and began taking evening classes in Media Studies.'

How was it possible to have such transparent skin, he wondered. Except for the dusting of freckles over her nose, you'd think she'd never seen the sun.

'Clever,' said Cass, 'choosing something where you could use your experiences in the dance world to good effect.'

Nice hands, she noted. Tanned, with neatly clipped nails, baby pink with white half-moons, just like they should be.

'That's what I thought. Got a job as Arts Correspondent at a local cable station in Atlanta that was trying to put itself on the map with a cultural angle. That folded, but by that time I'd done a lot of work with a bunch of local Senators, Congressmen and the city mayor covering the fight for funding for a couple of dance schools, so another station up in Baltimore took me on for a roving brief on political-slash-arts issues. Then eventually, after a couple of years at CNN, I was able to shake off the arts tag and concentrate on a total mixed bag of issues. Loved the idea of the English election and no-one else gave a damn so CNN sent me over here to fool around, and now I'm just keeping my head down, hoping they don't send me back to the States. How about you? How is the world of politics treating you?'

At least we're off the subject of John now, Cass thought with relief, launching into the story of her and Ted coming across Mrs Harrison's lottery letter that morning. 'And the ironic thing was,' she concluded, 'I looked her up this afternoon in the electoral register, just for a laugh—'

'Looked who up?'

Did she know that she moved her head slightly from side to side, when she became sincere? It was a mannerism Wilbur hadn't seen since he'd left the States, except on *Friends*, *Frasier* and *Spin City* repeats.

'This lottery winner who refused to take the publicity – and I found out she wasn't from Boyd-Cooper's constituency at all, she was from the next door one, which happens to be Frank Blackthorn's – you know, Ted's old boss and my boss's bosom pal. If she'd known that, she'd never have written to Boyd-Cooper, we'd never have found out about his links to Avalon and the whole thing would've been a total damp squib. Mind you, it was anyway, because we've only just found out about it. Just think how useful that would have been in the election campaign. Not that we exactly needed it, in the end. The thing that got me thinking, though, was if we had found it before the election, how do you go about leaking an exposé? It's one of those things you always hear about – leaks and suchlike – but what is the best way?'

Why was he staring at her like that? wondered Cass crossly. It was almost as if . . . oh no, it was that look a man gives a woman when he thinks that she fancies him. That was the last thing she needed, the cheeky bastard. So that's what he thought, was it? She'd show him.

Wilbur tore his eyes away from Cass's suddenly truculent face. Any minute now and she would think that he found her attractive. That was the last thing he needed. 'It's usually a question of who you know, I guess. In this case,' he smiled charmingly, 'you can push any leaks my way. That's my job, after all!'

Smoothy git, thought Cass. She noticed he was now unable to meet her eyes.

Touchy miss, thought Wilbur. He noticed she'd stopped that nervous jiggling of her foot.

6

'It's useless,' sighed Hallie. 'We are freaks. Every other life-form on this planet just has to snap its fingers and it's paired up. If an animal lives a solitary life, that's because it chooses to. I mean, you don't see David Attenborough saying,' she dropped her voice to a hoarse whisper, 'And here we see the Lesser Spotted Spinster, known by its drab plumage and drooping tail, a species remarkable for its total failure to catch a mate; its habitat a large, empty bed; and its diet a steady stream of Doritos and television.'

The three of them were together for the first time since their evening at Caspers and, to no-one's great surprise, Hallie was already up on her bandwagon. Sitting in Nina and Jerry's kitchen, clearing up after a long Saturday lunch, all Cass and Nina could do was humour her.

'Female animals don't even have to try! Pheasants, tigresses, pea-hens – Drab City! They're so smug and sure of their chances, they don't even bother dressing up – it's blokey that has to tart himself up and dance attendance: "Hey, you want to choose me, I got shot at four times a week last season but I just love the smell of gunsmoke in the morning!" says Mr Pheasant. "Well, I roar louder than anyone else and I do a nice line in petrol ads," boasts Mr Tiger. "Pah! I can dance like Nureyev and my feathers beat his lunch-box anyday," caps the Peacock.' Hallie looked thoughtful.

'Do you know, that gives me an idea for Giuseppe Hombre. Chuck me that pen, will you?' Cass slid the biro across the table, but even as Hallie started scribbling, she hardly drew breath, 'What I mean is, it's so unfair – when was the last time a man did a sales pitch on himself for your benefit?'

Then, as Cass opened her mouth to speak—

'Actually, don't answer that. I don't want to know. Put it this way, I can't remember the last time I was *seduced*, wooed, courted. The sort of man I've been hooking up with seems to consider that his work is done after a few nominal stabs at "You look nice" and "I'd love to see you again, but I really need to work on my pecs at the gym"—'

'Hallie, now you're exaggerating. I don't believe a guy actually said that.'

'That's nothing! I was at a party last week and I was talking to a friend of mine, this man who's been a mate for years but I've half-fancied him nearly all that time. He was asking which girls were single at this party, so I looked around and, surprise, surprise, there was, like, one other single woman apart from me. So I say, "Oh, just me and Nikki," and he says, "Isn't Nikki the one who's juggling about four men on the trot? Well, I suppose I'll have to join the queue." And just for a joke, I say, "Well, thanks a lot, what about me? Am I not even an option?" expecting him to say something about us being friends and all that stuff. And he just looks at me and says, "Look at it this way, Hallie, who wants to make reservations at an empty restaurant?" And this is a friend, for goodness sake!'

'Great line, though,' Cass grinned.

'I know. Why can't I think of lines like that? Then I might stand a chance. Because, at the end of the day, I can't blame men. I agree with them – if what you want is a succession of one-night-stands, glued together by the odd dinner and night out at the opera, why shouldn't you be happy with that? If people like me are so desperate for attention that they'll go for a shag first and hope for commitment later, then we deserve all we get – or don't get, as the case may be. I'm the one who's out of sync here, with all my little dreams of love, marriage and domesticity. No-one else is even trying to help – I mean, Cass, that night last week when we were invited out to dinner, as a couple, for heaven's sake! Three couples and us two! How am I supposed to find the man of my dreams like that!'

'Now you're not making any sense, Hallie,' said Nina, still up to her elbows in the washing up. 'If everyone else is in a couple, as you say, then how can you be the one who's out of sync for wanting to be in a couple?'

'Those women are just better liars than Hallie.'

'Cass!'

'Nina, it's true! I know you're way beyond all the shenanigans of dating but I've studied this. It's the age-old story of honesty being the worst policy. Never say you want commitment, never let on that you're available, never ever betray that you might like them too – then you've got them hooked. Cynical, maybe, but true and you know it. That pheasant doesn't want an easy lay. That tiger needs something to roar about to his tiger-pals. That peacock needs to feel that unless he spreads his tailfeathers and really struts his pea-cock polka stuff, that pea-hen is never going to spread her legs.'

Cass pointed across the table. 'And men are the same, Hallie. You think I have some Svengali effect on men? It's because they know that I am not interested. Their mistake is that they think I'm putting it on to encourage them to strut their stuff. They know they'll have to have a lot more than fancy plumage to get my attention, so that awakens the beast in them and really gets 'em going. It's not just sexual politics – it's older than that, it's primeval anthropological gender signatures.'

'And there endeth the lesson according to Cass,' grumbled Hallie. 'Hallie Templeton, Case Study No. 243 in the great, the unfinished, the revelatory Dr Herbert Dissertation.'

The putative Dr Herbert stuck her tongue out at her.

'Hi, girls,' said Jerry, bustling in from the garden, 'what are you doing inside? It's a cracker of a day.' He paused. 'Ohhhh, I see. Girl-talk, is it? Do we love men, or do we think that all men are bastards? Just so that I know.'

'Knock it off, Jerry,' grinned Cass. 'Anyone would think you really were pompous.'

Nina dropped a mug onto the draining-board.

'Still chained to the sink, my little Nin-compoop?' Jerry went over to give Nina a hug, her arms rigid by her sides. 'Tell these lazy bints to get off their arses and give you a hand.'

'And what about you, Jerry?' Hallie said softly. 'Are you going to help? It's your mates creating most of the mess. They're still watching the cricket, by the way.'

'That's what got this whole conversation started, Jezza.' Cass pointed an accusing finger at him. 'How could you be such a nice guy, yet have such godawful friends? Are they Neanderthal bores, or what?'

Jerry shrugged. 'I'm just the best man, remember? I was given the names for this stag night and told to get on with it. These guys are OK, actually. There are worse ones staying up at the Lodge – they really do give the Army a bad name.'

'And you invited us down – why?' Hallie grinned. 'To set us up? I'm desperate, but not that desperate!'

'Yep, those guys are making that nunnery seem awful attractive,' joked Cass.

'For fuck's sake, *I* invited you down,' Nina snapped. 'Why does everything revolve around men for you two? Is it so impossible that I should have my two best friends down for the weekend, when I've hardly seen you in the two months since you've been back, Cass? I'm not just here to cook for you and clean up after you, you know, I can still talk. For all you've talked to me, I might as well be fucking invisible!'

'Oh, Nina!' chorused Hallie, Cass and Jerry.

'Oh, Nina!' she mimicked. 'Oh, you can all just fuck off.' She ripped off her marigolds. 'Babaji? Walkies! Babaji!'

Babaji sidled in from the sitting room, where he'd been having a fine old time hoovering up crisps and beer, unnoticed by the spellbound cricket-watchers.

'Come on, you little mutt.' Nina scooped him up and hugged him as if her life depended on it. 'We're going for a walk.' And she walked straight out of the door.

Hallie was the first to break the silence left behind her.

'Should I go after her?'

Jerry sighed. 'No, you know Nina and her tantrums. It'll blow over in a bit.'

'Where did that come from?' marvelled Cass. 'One minute Hallie and I were comparing notes on how useless we were with men, the next – boom! Armageddon! I mean, we wouldn't exactly expect Nina to be too involved with that topic – she's married, for chrissakes, she's solved the riddle!'

'To tell you the truth, she's been testy as hell, lately. It's my snoring, you see. We've tried everything but I don't think she's getting any sleep, which makes her work problems all the harder to deal with.'

'Work problems?'

'Oh, she's getting nowhere with the freelancing. She got this assignment from *FortyEight* – something about interviewing celebs for their Primrose Path column?'

Hallie and Cass looked blank.

'Oh, I don't know, it's all to do with who was the person who first put the celeb onto the primrose path to fame and fortune. Sort of a greatest influence without the high moral overtones. Some utter tosh like that. Anyway, Nin came up with this list of topical names – people with things to promote at the moment – and has literally spent the last two weeks glued to the bloody phone, chatting up their agents, publicists, you name it. In fact, we ended up fighting about it, because of course I need the phone to get onto the Net.'

'Yes, but surfing is much easier and cheaper at night, when not so many people are on it,' Hallie pointed out. 'So why don't you share out telephone time or something?'

'Or get another line put in?' added Cass.

Jerry looked boot-faced. 'Thank you, my little egg-suckers, don't you think we've thought of these things? The fact is, I do need to e-mail – and talk to – potential investors during the day and, Cass, you big lanky know-it-all townie, we're in the countryside, you know. Have you seen how far away the nearest junction telephone pole is? Have you the least idea how expensive it would be to put in an extra line?'

'Don't come the superior asshole with me, James Kellman. You never used to be such a tightwad about cash and you know perfectly well that Hallie and I are only trying to help. She's been our best friend since we were ten, remember? A whole seven years before you showed up – and I introduced the two of you so I'm just trying to smooth the way for this couple that I made.' Cass frowned. 'Jesus, if this is how you talk down to Nina, no wonder she's pissed at you.'

'Pissed at me? Honestly, Cass, these Americanisms of yours are enough to try the patience of a saint. Anyway, Nina's not angry with me – she's just, I don't know, tired, frustrated, hormonal. Girls' stuff, probably. Nothing to do with me.'

Cass and Hallie exchanged looks.

'Whatever you say, Jez,' Hallie said briskly, steering him out of the door. 'Now you go back to your mowing, strimming and primping, and leave us to cheer up your wife. What time are you lot off to your stag night?'

'We should be leaving quite soon,' Jerry looked at his watch. 'Probably a capital notion if you take the old thing in hand. Give her a good girly night in, like the bad old days. Do her good to have a giggle. You have no idea how left out she feels from your little threesome these days.' He disappeared up the garden, whistling.

Hallie glared after him. 'So now it's our fault, is it? I don't think so, Mister Dysfunctional.' She turned back to Cass. 'Is it my imagination or has Jerry changed out of all recognition since he and Nina got married? I'm sure he never used to be this . . . well, pontificaty.'

'Pontificating,' corrected Cass absently. 'Yeah, it's weird that he should get through the whole Army thang without changing too much, then suddenly turn into his asshole of a father as soon as he gets out. I'm sure it's just a phase – something to do with finally throwing off the cuffs of an institutional life for the uncertainty of the big wide world. I remember doing a few case-studies at Columbia on the sort of male who buries himself inside institutions as long as possible. Something to do with lack of a strong mother figure, I think—'

'Look, it's Nina who's our prime concern at the mo,' Hallie interrupted. 'I propose we take out a couple of videos, get a really yummy takeaway – Thai, perhaps – and settle in for a right good vid-veg and a gossip.'

'Look around you, Hal, show me the Blockbusters and Thai

restaurant that is going to furnish us with this feast? You klutz. But I agree with you in principle. Let's try and make this an occasion – push the boat out – be silly, like we used to be, instead of all gloomy, like we've been lately.'

'Nice plan, Stan.'

Together they went into the sitting room and crouched in front of the Kellmans' meagre video collection, provoking a predictable barracking from the lads whose view of bored-looking, blue-pyjamaed cricketers was being blocked.

'Oh, cool it, guys,' grinned Cass. She squinted at the cassette she was holding. 'What's this? The sound of—' she looked over at Hallie, a smile spreading from ear to ear. '*The Sound of Music.*'

She sat back on her heels. 'Hallie, I have an idea.'

'Fuck them, I am not going to cry. Nina Parvati does not cry. Nina Parvati does not cry.'

Nina swiped at the undergrowth savagely, then stepped unseeingly into a small patch of nettles. At the sting of the plants on her bare legs, tears sprang irresistibly to her eyes. That did it. She couldn't even go for a walk without reminding herself how out of place she was here. Anyone who stood the smallest fucking chance of being *country folk* would know about not walking bare-legged through shady woods. Strangled sobs broke out of her as she remembered how excited she had been at the thought of moving into the countryside. Those pastoral dreams of long walks, jam-making and a healthy lifestyle.

But that had been back when she still *was* Nina Parvati. She wasn't Nina Parvati any more. She was Nina Kellman and Nina Kellman was a totally different kettle of fish. Nina Kellman was as fractious as a spoilt child, she was as crabby as a withered old crone, she was as hormonal and difficult as a menopausal matron. Forget the healthy lifestyle – Nina Kellman felt ill in the country, either too hot or too cold, deprived of sleep by Jerry's snoring, now being provoked by his hayfever, and left with too much time on her hands to think about her symptoms of headaches, mysterious pains and stiffnesses. Because most of all, Nina Kellman was bored, bored, bored.

She emerged from the copse into a field, lush summer grass

catching at her heels. Ahead of her, Babaji was in seventh heaven, woolly ears flying as he galloped his way through the tall grass, zebedeeing up every few yards to see where he was. Recognising exactly where she was, Nina caught her breath. This was where Jerry had proposed to her last summer.

It had been one of Jerry's rare leaves back from the regiment in Germany, when he'd managed to wangle a week off for a two-day course. The cottage's most recent let had just been wound up and was temporarily empty, so they had sped down here on Nina's motorbike, frantic for the opportunity to spend some time alone with each other. Planning to go for a long walk, they had only made it this far before Nina, whose only exercise was walking up the escalator into Northcliffe House to start her day at the *Evening Standard*, had collapsed, pink-cheeked and laughing, into the grass.

'She just can't make it, Captain!' she giggled, in a terrible Scottish accent. 'Will ye just have some mercy?'

'Och, you're a weak little wazzock, and no mistaking.' Jerry did a creditable impression of a falling oak, right on top of Nina, breaking the fall with his elbows just before crushing her. 'A nice wee rogering should fitten you up, lassie.' He dipped his head to kiss her.

Nina lifted her hand to cradle his face, closing her eyes as she traced the familiar, beloved features; his thick, soft eyebrows, hardly visible to the eye they were so blond, with the small scar when he'd passed out after her eighteenth birthday party; the strong, springy waves of blond hair coming off his forehead in what she always teased him was a McDonald's arch; his left ear with its ragged edge where he'd flicked it with the end of a bull-whip in a moment of regimental horseplay. She knew all the secrets behind this face. This face was her A-Z to the last ten years.

Apart from the three years they had been at their separate universities, they had been together all that time. They had lost their virginity together, travelled together, lived together briefly, had sailed through all their rites of passage together. When Nina had had her big break at the *Standard*, Jerry had been the one waiting in Derry Street with an enormous magnum of champagne and a huge papier-mâché thumbs-up he had spent all day making.

When he had been told he was being posted overseas to Hong Kong, she had sulked for two days, then had wrapped herself in aluminium foil and tied her hair back so tightly that her eyes had gone into slits, topping it off with a large piece of white card. 'I'm a Chinese takeaway,' she had joked tremulously, 'can't you take me away to Hong Kong?'

And after ten years together, having sown their wild oats in what Jerry laughingly called their Wilderness Years, they still couldn't get enough of each other. So they had made love then and there in the long grass, not caring about voyeuristic ramblers or curious hang-gliders and with each re-seduction of each well-known inch of their trembling bodies, they had giddily reiterated their love. This time it hadn't taken long, Nina's yelp as she had felt some creepy-crawly slither over her foot tipping Jerry mistakenly over the edge into instantaneous orgasm. She had laughed inwardly, not minding that she hadn't yet come, and hadn't set him right. It was the tiniest of deceptions.

Lying there, feeling him breathe into the hollow of her neck, gazing up at the cloud-scudded blue sky above, Nina felt she couldn't be happier. She hadn't even minded that he was squashing her. But slowly, she had become aware of a tension creeping through his muscles. Then he had sighed deeply and had sat up, pulling his T-shirt over his head and shrugging his shorts back on.

'Nin, darling, whack some clothes on, will you? Someone might come.'

'I was under the impression they already had,' giggled Nina. Then, as she saw his expression, 'Sorry, serious face, is it?'

'Serious parade face, I'm afraid. Now, look here, you know you said, when I agreed not to stay in the Army, that if you were in my shoes you'd listen to me, if I ever gave you the same sort of career advice?'

'Did I? You must have caught me at a weak moment! Don't scowl at me! Of course I said that, and I meant it, sweetheart. What did you have in mind? I'm very happy travel-writing, you know. Even if it does give us precious little holiday time together, there will be the odd press trip where we can go together, once you're not shackled to that regiment of yours. And I'll try—'

'Nina, belt up!'

Nina frowned. 'Well, get to the point, will you? What do you want to tell me to do?'

'Well,' Jerry looked uncharacteristically flustered, 'I was thinking more in the line of you giving up the travel-writing altogether.'

'What?!' Nina narrowed her eyes. 'Oh no. Don't tell me. You've gone back on your bloody word.'

'Nina, you're—'

'You're not leaving the Army at all. You are going to go to Staff College. After all that. You filthy fucker.'

'Nina! Just—'

'You expect me to chuck in my career just so that I can follow you round the killing fields of the world like some sick-fuck camp follower? Well, fuck that.' Nina was spitting now. 'And fuck you. I won't do it.' Suddenly she lifted her fists and started pummelling him savagely. 'I won't do it.'

'Ow! Darling!' Jerry gathered her fists between his own, rolled her over on her back, put one hand over her mouth and held her down, ignoring the bolts of lightening sparking from her dark eyes. 'I'm not going anywhere! I'm not staying in the Army! If you'd just listen for one bloody minute, I'm not asking you to give up your journalism, just the travel bit of it!'

Nina looked mutinous, but stopped swearing at him through his fingers.

'Better. Now do you promise only to tell our grandchildren the basic gist of this? I mean, I know I'm meant to be on my knees, but lying on top of you, gagging you and holding you down? I'm not so sure.'

Nina started to look confused.

'Just to paraphrase your charming terminology, this filthy fucker wants to be your filthy fucker for the rest of our lives,' he teased her, taking away his hand to reveal her jaw dropping in amazement. 'I'm sorted now. I know what I'm doing, where I'm going to be, which means I can be even more certain who I want to spend the rest of my life with. I want you where I can see you every day, make love to you every day, be sworn at by you every day, not snatching moments between your travel assignments.'

He took a deep breath, suddenly looking heartbreakingly

vulnerable. 'What I'm bumbling towards saying, like the total arse I am, is – Nina, my darling Nina, will you marry me?'

And that had been that. Of course she had said yes. She had been wanting him to propose for years, but had given up hope of ever hearing him ask. Of course she had said yes. She had loved him since she was seventeen years old. She could not imagine ever falling in love with anyone else, let alone someone who was also her best friend, her partner in crime, her comedy sidekick, her sous-chef. Of course she had said yes.

But a mere fourteen months later, here she was again, looking at the same tussock of grass, but this time wanting to kick it into the next field. How could it all go so wrong so quickly? They had been so full of plans about his Internet prescription business, her freelance journalism, living in the cottage—

It was no good. Nina Kellman lay down in the grass and sobbed her heart out. If only it was as simple as things not going according to plan – the Internet business still not up and running, her hating every minute of this freelancing stuff, the cottage more often a torture chamber than an idyllic refuge – but those were just the symptoms. At the heart of it all was the insidious little voice whispering sibilantly that perhaps Jerry and she shouldn't have been so confident that they knew each other well enough to know that they were ideal life partners.

Babaji returned from his adventures, black nose dull with dirt, coat tangled with burrs, tail wagging so hard his whole body oscillated like a moving snake. Seeing Nina lying with her head under her arm, he thought this was some new game of hide and seek and sought out her face, nuzzling impatiently and scrabbling at her arms with sharp little claws.

'Ow! Gerroff, you little bugger!' Nina emerged to gather her dog into her arms. Cuddling him close brought her back to the edge of tears. She loved him so much that sometimes she thought of him as her magic cloak, the only thing sheltering her from the dull rain of her life, but at the same time, she sometimes thought he would smother her as well.

When Jerry had given Babaji to her, Nina had thought that her cup would overflow. It had been at three o'clock in the morning on New Year's Day, nearly at the end of her birthday party, by which time she had given up hope of Jerry having remembered.

She, Hallie and Cass had retreated to her bedroom for a gossip when he'd burst in.

'Ta-daa! Happy Birthday to you, Happy Birthday to you,' he had carolled loudly and tunelessly, swaying in the doorway. 'Happy Birthday, Nin my darling wife, Happy Birthday to you!'

Then he had collapsed onto the bed with the rest of them, taking care not to squash the large box he was carrying. He woozily held up his face for a kiss. 'Love you.'

'Flattered, hon, but no bananas,' said Cass, pushing him away. 'Try the next one along.'

Unabashed, Jerry snuggled up to Nina. 'Love you even more. Do you want a birthday present?'

Nina had looked curiously at the box he was carrying, which seemed to be moving. 'If you've given me a snake, Jerry Kellman, I will kill you, you know that, don't you? I may be Indian—'

'But you're certainly no charmer!' quipped Hallie. 'Just get on and open it, will you?'

'Oh Jerry.' For once, Nina could say no more. She had ripped off the wrapping paper to find an open box underneath. And there, now frozen with fright, was a small black bundle of fluff. Black-eyed girl and black-eyed dog gazed at each other in mutual amazement. Then a tiny, shiny nose sniffed upwards cautiously, and a little pink tongue emerged to lick the hand that Nina was cautiously putting into the box. Carefully, she scooped the ball of wool up into her arms. Far from being alarmed, the puppy instantly relaxed and went to sleep. 'Oh Jerry.' Nina looked up, eyes shining. 'He's—' she checked to make sure, 'he's adorable. You're adorable.'

'He's a doodle,' Jerry said smugly. 'Cross between a dachshund and a poodle. And I know I'm adorable. That's why I'd like you to adore me. Right now. Push off, you two and take the puppy with you. My wife and I are going to have sex now.'

Nina had loved his masterfulness then.

The little puppy had been a wriggling emblem of her new, settled, grown-up life. But it was the walks with him, the puppy-training classes, the endless clearing-up after him that brought home to Nina not only how alien she felt living here, but also how Babaji was tying her to Jerry and the cottage as surely as a baby would have done. She couldn't re-start her travel-writing – Jerry had always made it clear that Babaji was her dog and her responsibility, so going away and leaving him to do his house-husband bit was clearly out of the question – and she couldn't even escape up to London whenever she felt too claustrophobic, for the same reasons.

'Oh my little Sisyphean stone,' she whispered into his neck, 'stick with me while I ride this little storm out, will you? I need you to be my best friend.'

Only a few months ago, she wouldn't have relinquished that spot to anyone but Jerry. Now it was her dog that claimed first rights, not even Hallie or Cass. Well, that sums up my life, she thought wryly.

Hallie stirred the fondue grimly. She was nearly thirty years old. What on earth was she doing? It had seemed like a good idea at the time. A silly idea, perhaps, but there was nothing wrong with silly if they could have fun with it, if they could cheer up Nina.

'Let's watch *The Sound of Music*, dress up like the von Trapps, eat Austrian food and generally make an occasion out of this!' Cass had suggested lightly, and Hallie had agreed enthusiastically, her sense of ceremony rising to the bait. But with the other two slumped in front of *Barrymore* next door, and her slaving away in here, the fun hadn't yet come to fruition.

Nor had the fondue. Never having made one before, Hallie poked at the half-coagulating glop suspiciously and checked trusty Delia for clues.

'Hallie, how's it going?' Cass came into the kitchen, pulling uncomfortably at her improvised lederhosen – a pair of Jerry's moleskin shooting plus-fours, held up by a ratty pair of braces. 'Just remind me why we thought this would be a good idea?' she hissed as she got closer.

'Just what I was thinking,' whispered Hallie. 'It's the sort of thing that would work on blasted *Friends* – Monica would have cooked the fondue perfectly, Phoebe would be strumming Smelly Cat to the tune of "Favourite Things", and Rachel – Rachel—'

'Rachel would be giving good hair,' supplied Cass. 'She'd be singing the strength back in and saying, "Because I'm vurth it" every time Julie gives Christopher Plummer that "why me?" look!'

Hallie groaned. 'Talking of hair, do you realise that we can forget ever being like *Friends* – we're not even like those Wella Experience girls either side of the ad breaks: at least that way we'd have the yummy pizza delivery boy.' She noticed Cass's blank look. 'Oh, I forgot – Miss Posh New Yorker hasn't seen it here, have you? Never mind. But we have to go through with it now. We promised Jerry we'd cheer Nina up, remember?'

But she'd lost Cass's attention. She was now staring in horror at the fondue.

'I know, I know. I'm sure it's not meant to look like that either, but I had to improvise a bit. Nina doesn't seem to have any cornflour, but I reckon gelatine is almost the same thing, don't you? Both thickening thingies.'

'What? Gelatine? You're kidding! No, I was looking at the pot.' Cass frowned. 'Are you sure it's OK to cook fondue in a Pyrex dish?'

'Yeah, why not? The whole point of Pyrex is that it's heatproof, isn't it?'

'Well, I guess so,' Cass started uncertainly, 'I just always thought that it meant heatproof in the oven, not on the hob but if you're sure—'

'Sure as the deodorant,' said Hallie firmly. 'Now can you start cutting some bre—'

Bang! As if in slow motion, they watched the Pyrex pot explode, sending up ribbons of cheese like streamers from a partypopper. Then there was no sound except for the hissing of melted cheese incinerating itself on the hob, and the slow liquid flop of cheese down the walls, off the sideboard, onto the floor.

'What the—?' Nina burst through the door, stopping short at the sight of a stunned Cass and Hallie, liberally spattered with fragrant yellow droplets. 'What happened?' Her eye fell on the pool of cheese, studded with ceramic shards. 'Oh my God. Oh my good God. Oh my God.' One side of her Danish pastry style plaited hairdo slowly unravelled itself as she shook her head.

'I don't think God was within listening range on this particular instance,' said Cass dryly, peeling one long Gruyere rope off her arm. 'More the devil's work, I should say.'

'Cass!'

'Oh Hallie, lighten up will you? This is not the time to be holier-than-thou, this is the time to be—'

'Hungry,' said Nina pointedly.

'And smelly,' added Hallie, biting her lip.

There was a pregnant little silence and then all three of them broke down, Hallie inadvertently putting her hand in a puddle of cheese as she clutched the side for support. The fact that their laughter had a faintly hysterical tinge to it didn't escape Nina, who was the first to recover.

'This is like that scene from *Asterix in Switzerland*,' she grimaced, 'cheese everywhere. Come on, fuck this, let's just have a carpet picnic, like the bad old days.'

'Carpet picnic!' echoed the other two. 'Brilliant!'

'Dips, chips, chocolate and toast,' said Cass dreamily. 'Boy, am I going to have to hit the gym on Monday.'

Hallie and Nina groaned at her, all too conscious of their flabby middles beside her exposed midriff.

'We should clear this up first,' Hallie demurred. 'It'll be even worse if we don't – it's going to be horrible when it sets.'

Nina and Cass crossed knowing looks. Trust Hallie the Peacemaker to come up with the sensible solution.

'Five minutes to clear up,' said Cass firmly. 'Then it's eyes down for the movie, voices up for the choruses, total pig-out, get loaded, and no more moping about men. Who wants them anyway?'

'What do *you* want?'

'Huh?'

'What do you want? A pint or a bottle?'

'Oh, every time a pint, Wilbur. The best British beer doesn't come in a bottle, except perhaps, for Newky Brown. If it's a quality local, you bring it straight from womb to lips with one pump. Bit like the best British women, eh? Have you found that, mate? Eh?'

'Whatever you say. Back in a sec.'

Stop being Mike Tyson, Ted berated himself, and try the Muhammad Ali treatment. Try the dancing bee-sting, not the bulldozer.

He gazed at himself dispassionately in the mirror above the bar. Why was he so bloody average-looking? He didn't stand a chance with Cass, so why put himself through the torture of probing Wilbur's intentions? Wilbur – whose charm was already making him the catch of Westminster, who looked like a dissolute bloody film star with his laughter lines, deep-shadowed eyes and grey-tinged crop of hair. Perhaps he should get a similar haircut instead of his own glossy bob?

'Get your hair cut,' his agent had told him during the election campaign, 'and we get a couple of hundred extra votes from the blue rinse brigade, just like that.'

Ted had scoffed. 'My hair's not even down to my shoulders – getting a couple of inches lopped off isn't going to make any difference.'

Famous last bloody words. He had lost by 222 votes, God's idea of a cruel joke. It would somehow trivialise the tragedy of his defeat if he now got a haircut to win over a woman.

'How far would you go to get a woman?' he asked, as Wilbur set their drinks down on the bar.

'How far would I go? Timbuktu, if she was cute enough. I hear desert girls are total babes.'

'You know what I mean.'

'Yes, I do. And I don't like it.' Wilbur twinkled at Ted. 'Any woman you have to go that far for won't appreciate it. Trust me, I used to be a ballet dancer – I once broke an ankle trying to impress this total primadonna, in all senses of the word, and fell on my ass, again in all senses of the word. So, who's the girl?'

Ted sidestepped the question. 'I reckon it's total bollocks that you used to be a ballet dancer. You've just hit on that as the best way to throw women off balance and straight into your lap, you bastard.'

Wilbur stretched mightily, and grinned. 'What can I say? You're right. I couldn't have planned it better if I'd tried. It's almost worth the years of pain, hardship and humiliation I had to suffer on the way.' He slapped Ted hard on the arm. 'So, c'mon, 'fess up – who's the girl? Anyone I know?'

He's playing with me, the bastard, thought Ted. He knows perfectly well I'm talking about Cass, and he's not giving a bloody thing away.

'No, it's no-one you know. No-one at all, really. Just a theoretical question. I mean, personally I love all women, but especially the tall, ball-breaker type,' Ted said slyly. 'How about you? Do you have a type, or do you just shag anything you fancy?'

Wilbur gave him a quizzical look. 'Well, everyone loves a challenge, don't they?'

Ted stared levelly back. 'I suppose they do.'

'So how's it going with that bloke with the silly name?'

Cass knew perfectly well Hallie remembered Wilbur's name. 'Do you mean Devlin? Because he's finally speaking to me again. He's coming over in a few weeks to play a couple of gigs at some pub up near King's Cross – the King's Crustacean, I think—'

Hallie didn't betray for a moment that she herself had not been rung by Devlin. 'I meant Wilbur. Finding my challenge a little hard to achieve? Not quite the walkover you anticipated?'

Why were they stalking around each other like stiff-legged dogs?

Cass relented. 'Total washout, if you must know. I swear it's because of you daring me but I did actually try hitting on him. It was a total disaster – especially since he thought I was doing it out of some twisted, cathartic grief thing for John – so I soon gave up. You were right, he doesn't fancy me at all. The good thing is that he's actually kinda fun to hang out with – Ted's working really hard at the moment so he's not around so much to jerk around with during the day – but Wilbur seems to do about as much work as I do, so I've seen him a couple of times.'

'But do you fancy him?'

'Well, he is cute in a rumpled sort of way, and he is totally flavour of the month round the House. But, oh my God, does he know it! The other day, I actually heard him—'

'Look, is anyone watching this bloody film except for me?' Nina turned and glared at them. 'Because I'll turn it off, if you two want to gossip.'

Hallie and Cass looked guilty. 'Sorry, Nin. We'll shut up.'

I don't want you to shut up, she screamed inwardly. I want you to include me, stop talking about people I've never even heard of, stop comparing sexual exploits as if you assume I'm no longer interested in sex, stop reminding me of the bad, old life in London. I want you to stop being so polite to me every time I open my mouth, as if I'm some basket case great-aunt you have to humour. They'd known each other for twenty years – since when did they cover up with each other like this?

'No don't shut up,' she said, trying to be more conciliatory. 'Just fill me in on the gossip, so at least I know what you're talking about. Like who was this vicar guy, Hallie, that you mentioned falling for on that dry stone walling weekend? He seemed to come and go even quicker than the average Hallie conquest?'

Hallie stuck her tongue out at Nina. 'Thanks a lot. No, Phil's absolutely sweet and, yes, for a moment or two, I did entertain visions of serving tea at the vicarage and teaching Sunday School to all the little children—'

'Hey, you'd be great at that – PR for God and all that!' Cass joked.

'Shut up, you heathen. No, but I only got as far as having a crush on Phil because he's just too good for me. I've seen him quite a few times since and the man is a walking, talking saint. But even more than that, he's just a lovely guy – funny, self-deprecating, relaxed. He's brilliant – I've never seen anyone so at peace with himself, his mindset is so clear, he just radiates serenity.'

'Mindset?' Nina wrinkled her nose. 'Danger, danger. Incoming PR-speak. All weapons on alert! He sounds like a pious bastard, if you ask me – and how come you've seen him quite a few times? Don't tell me you've been popping down to Dorset whenever the whim takes you?'

'No, he was looking into the possibility of planting a church in that chapel down there. He invited me to go along to the church in London where he's a curate and it all went from there.' Hallie avoided their eyes. 'I've started going to this course there. It's actually really interesting.'

'Whoa, just hang on there one cotton-pickin' minute,' whistled Cass. 'What's "planting a church" when it's at home? You didn't tell me any of this part – course, what course? And since when did you go to church? And all to get a man – now, that's what I call desperate!'

'For the last time, I am not desperate!' Hallie stormed. 'My religion has always been important to me. You probably never realised this because you were living it up in London while I was commuting in to school from Beaconsfield, but I went to church every Sunday until I was about seventeen. The Alpha course is just guiding me back, that's all, and it's nothing to do with any man.'

'Alpha course? Hang on, you're not talking about that charismatic church sect thing, are you? Holy Trinity Brompton? I wrote about that once in the *Standard*.'

'Nina, it's not a sect. Don't be ridiculous, you're being a typically sensationalist hack. It's all about finding your way back to Jesus—'

'Yeah, and giving him a tenth of whatever you earn while you're at it,' scoffed Nina. 'It's all coming back to me now – HTB! A load of Sloanes with no social life, filling their empty nights with God – Monday night, wine and cheese with God, Tuesday night, home bible readings with God, Wednesday night, ceroc with God. Isn't that right?'

Hallie struggled to retain her sense of humour. 'You're talking complete rubbish, Nina. You should really come and see for yourself before subscribing to total ignorance.'

'Doesn't sound so very different to all your other dating agencies,' mused Cass. 'I bet this HTB is a breeding ground for romance, huh? Necking in the nave? This is my Body, given for you, and all that? Sounds great!'

At last Hallie smiled. 'I can't deny it – there are a lot of tongue-hanging-out single blokes. Trouble is, I have yet to be convinced about the Christian approach to sex – OK, so I want to get married, but how do you persuade someone to marry you without sleeping with them? Maybe that'll be in week three of Alpha.'

'Being celibate saves you from getting your heart broken so much, I suppose.'

'Yeah, but I kind of like getting my heart broken,' insisted Hallie, 'at least that way it feels like a muscle is being used.'

Cass snorted scornfully. 'Who needs that sort of exercise? I've got better things to do than work out with men.'

'I'm beginning to think Jerry and I never will work out,' said

Nina gloomily. Then when the other two turned on her with reproachful eyes, 'Just kidding! Don't panic.'

But she wasn't kidding, and she was the one beginning to panic.

'Yes, but you're married,' Cass said, 'so you've already done the hard work. I could never imagine liking anyone enough to inter myself alive with them for the rest of my life. Once you're in a marriage, there's no getting out of it. That's what alarms me.'

You and me both, thought Nina.

'Hello? Divorce, anyone? One in three people these days seem to bounce in and out of marriage without a backwards glance, so I don't think they believe there's no getting out of it,' scorned Hallie.

'Yeah, I read about this hole-in-the-wall machine in Arizona where you can pay thirty bucks and get divorced in your lunch hour,' said Cass wryly, 'but divorce is just a bit of paper. My parents got divorced when I was seven, remember, but they never really got out of the marriage. Poppa still goes apopleptic whenever I mention Mum's name – and every time he gets married to one of his Californian wifelets, Mum goes into her room and doesn't come out for a week. Is that healthy? No sirree bob, you're not going to catch me anywhere near the altar. Relationships are bad enough. The closest I am going to get to anyone can be in cyberspace, for all I care – if I'm ever that desperate.'

Nina shuddered. 'Don't talk to me about cyberspace.'

'Jerry driving you mad with his Internet business, is he?'

'Well, yes, but it's not that. I got myself into this adult chatline and, er,' Nina took a nervous swig of wine, 'well, I sort of had this weird fling-thing.'

'Oh Nina, check you out, girl. Internet affairs are so yesterday,' sighed Cass. 'What was his name?'

'Badboy.'

Hallie snorted. 'No! And was he? Did you talk dirty to each other?'

'Hardly a Christian question, Hallie. Yes, Badboy was bad but more importantly, BadBoy was actually a BadGirl. Yes,' she confirmed in response to their shocked faces, 'trust me to get my cyberkecks off with a fucking lesbian!? Is that not divine fucking justice or what?'

'Have you told Jerry?'

'And have the whole Houston Hotlips thing stuffed down my throat? No way, José.'

Hallie was laughing. Cass, Nina noticed, was not. 'What's up with you, Herbert?'

Cass stood up and started pacing. 'I just think it's tacky – two newly-weds who should have eyes for no-one else, both cruising the Net, making out on the mainframe like a couple of sad highschoolers on their parents' PC. It's pathetic.'

'Hey, tell us how you really feel, Cass!' Nina rose as well, pointing accusingly at Cass. 'For a girl who sets up her best friend with a rejected admirer just to get him off your back, then strings along some poor bloke who's obviously got the hugest crush on you, and is now copping off with your dead boyfriend's brother—'

'I am not!'

'—you really know how to hike up to that moral high ground, don't you?'

Hallie held up a hand from the floor. 'Children, children.'

'Butt out, Hallie,' said Cass, matching Nina glare for glare. 'Yeah, well I'm not married, am I? I only owe it to myself to behave – you and Jerry owe it to each other not to screw around with other people.'

'What is it with you and marriage? Getting married doesn't automatically change the game, you know, it just moves the fucking goalposts! Just because I got married doesn't mean I suddenly became any more confident, any more settled – I'm still just one person, not an anonymous half of a marriage. Show me the sodding marriage vow that says "I promise not to talk dirty on a computer screen!" and then I'll admit I did something wrong!'

'Changed your tune, since you caught Jerry that time, then?' Cass taunted her.

'Fuck you! Yes, I have! Does that make me a serial killer? No! It just makes me inconsistent. Much like your good self, I might add. Who was it that said that Britain was the Stonehenge of the world – a place of amazing knowledge and mystery but where no-one would actually choose to live – and that America was the only place where anyone could get anything done. And suddenly you're back here, in some dead-end job in Parliament, not getting anything done. Is that not bloody inconsistent?'

'C'mon Nina, let's take it down a notch,' reproved Hallie.

'Oh Hallie, bugger off with your fucking jargon.' Nina could feel herself losing control now, unleashing Nina Parvati, wild child and whirlwind, once more. 'Don't do this peacemaker thing now – you're hardly in a position to referee, are you? Hardly scoring highly in the consistency charts, yourself! At least I'm with just the one man – you and your Seans, your Sauls, your Phils, your Devlins – how many men do you need to hoist your own petard, Hallie?'

Leaving Hallie gaping, she turned back to Cass. 'And, Cass, don't give me some shit about John having anything to do with it, because he died in October and you didn't say one bloody word about coming back when you were here at New Year. Doing the griefstricken widow thing nearly nine months later just doesn't wash—'

'Nina!' Hallie gasped.

'Well, I'm sorry, Hallie, but we've been pussyfooting round the bloody subject ever since she came back and I'm sick to the backteeth of having to excuse her for her selfishness, her total lack of interest in anyone else, her obsession with walking all over men wherever she goes. When was the last time she really cared about us? Why do you always have to be the peacemaker? Why do I always have to be the one to say these things? Why does she always have to have the fucking whiphand here?'

'Right, I've had enough,' stormed Cass. 'I'm not going to stand here and let some dog-in-the-manger housewife, with nothing better to do than complain about her life and interfere in other people's, poke her big nose into things she knows nothing about, just because she daren't look into her own backyard. Jerry was right – you are—'

Hallie burst into tears. 'Stop it! Stop it! Both of you! Just listen to yourselves! This is insane!'

Cass and Nina stopped and stared at her, fists clenched by their sides. What was her problem?

7

'So, are you excited?' Cass cradled the phone receiver under her chin as she carried on sorting out Alun's correspondence. If Mags caught her still sitting at her desk, she would be dead meat. First thing in the morning was not the time to mess with Mags's hangover.

'What about?'

'The conference, you dork. The first Labour Party Conference since 1978 when we're in power – and we are both going to be there, forging Labour's way into the next millennium, making history! It's exciting, OK?'

Hallie sighed. 'Whatever you say. I'm not so sure I'll be making history, I'm more likely to be making the tea. Having been director of my own accounts for the last eight months, I'm not sure I like being office junior on the Labour Party account, even if it is,' she mugged, *our most prestigious client.*'

'Office junior? I thought you said you had some cool-sounding title?'

'Well, if you think "PR liaison to the Labour Party" sounds cool, then you're easily impressed. Anyway, when are you going up?'

'Oh, not until the Tuesday and back again on Friday evening. You?'

'Lucky you. I have to be there from Saturday to Saturday. Apart from anything else I have to miss a really crucial Alpha session, which is unbelievably annoying.'

'An Alpha session? Oh right, your God-squadding. Oh, shame. One less saved soul.'

'Father, forgive them; for they know not what they do,' said Hallie airily. 'Luke 23: Verse 34.'

'Wow, you rock!' said Cass admiringly. 'Bible quotes off the top of your head! Bless you, my child. St Paul to the Corinthians, Chapter Twelve Verse Two.'

A reluctant laugh bubbled down the phone line. 'Cass, you're an idiot. Now, have you made it up with Nina yet?'

'No. Is that why you called?'

'Well, it has been three weeks. It's all getting very childish.'

'No kidding! Sending us to Coventry that Sunday – even Jerry, just because he'd come home roaring drunk at five o'clock in the morning: what else did the stuck-up cow expect from a stag night? – was just plain immature. And then when we heard about Princess Diana dying and she just completely lost it? Throwing us out like that? Anyone would think she'd lost a member of her own family! Who would ever have thought that Nina Parvati – onetime media wildchild and iconoclast – would have reacted like that?'

'Oh, come on, Cass. You know how it was after Princess Di's death. Total mob hysteria. No-one expected to react like that, but she was effectively part of our lives since we were children. You must remember her wedding day? Us three, all of thirteen years old, camping out with Trudie on the Mall, and sneaking off to drink that bottle of disgusting Cinzano? It was after I puked up over that policeman that I became teetotal so I've always rather associated Lady Di with that. Anyway, you're about the only person I know who wasn't shocked by how griefstricken they were when she died. The whole agency here were in tears that Monday, and the meetings at HTB have been chock-a-block ever since and incredibly moving.'

'Oh purleeeze, give me a little break. The woman was a basket-case going out with an Arab dirtbag, a media invention with a pretty smile. How could we grieve for someone we didn't even know?'

Hallie's tone was careful. 'Well, unlike you, I've never lost someone close to me so I wouldn't really know. All I can say is that it was a shock and I happen to know that Nina felt really left out of the whole phenomenon. When I took the bull by the horns and rang up to apologise about our fight, I made the mistake of telling her about how crowded the streets were with that weird community of emotion – the heat of the candles, the silence and the scent of the flowers – and I just know that she wished that the three of us were together in that crowd, just like we were in 1981. So just ring her and kiss and make up, OK?'

'Gee, Hallie, this religion stuff sure has made you sentimental, hasn't it? No, I'm sorry, I won't yank your chain any more, I promise. Hey, did you hear Princess Diana was on the radio?'

'What?'

'Yup, and on the dashboard, the steering wheel, the gear stick . . .'

'Cass, you're—'

'I know, I'm one sick puppy. Just one more: did you hear that the Ritz offered Princess Diana a room for the night?' "Naah, that's OK, thanks," she said, "I'm just going to crash with my boyfriend . . .".'

Hallie groaned. 'Cass, stop trying to change the subject. You're making me feel like an old nag.'

'You *are* an old nag, pumpkin. That's why I love you. OK, I'll make it up with Nina – anyway she would be the perfect case study for my emotion-led, dysfunctional, problem-solving hit parade.'

'That's really going to pacify her.'

'Yeah, well, why is she the one that needs pacifying? What about me? She was the one who called me—'

'Cass, you're a twenty-nine year old PhD student. Listen to yourself, grow up, and ring her. Why not? You know she wouldn't have said any of that stuff if she hadn't been really unhappy.'

'I don't get it. What has she got to be unhappy about? OK, sure, her career's not exactly peachy right now but she has a loving husband, rose-trailed cottage and cute little doggie, all those things that the rest of us are supposed to be aiming for – what gives?'

'Cass Herbert – Captain Sensitive. I just hope that you're like a doctor – totally unsympathetic with your nearest and dearest but when it comes to your patients, you've got a great bedside manner, otherwise your career is going to be over before it begins.' Hallie sounded brisk. 'Do you remember that time you got off with Bobby Wallis at the Netball Club disco, when he was going out with Nina? Just ring her before we have a similar feud situation on our hands.'

'Bobby Wallis. Netball Club disco. Nope. Nothing in the memory banks on that one. Are you sure it wasn't Dom Dimmond at the Hendersons' Christmas party?'

'No,' said Hallie dryly, 'that was when Dom was going out with *me* – and you've just admitted something to me that you've been denying for twelve years. How are any of us still friends with you?'

'Search me,' Cass replied blithely. 'Gotta go, Hallie honey, much as I love all this nostalgia – the other line's going.'

'Just ring Nina.'

'Yeah, yeah.' Cass flicked between lines. 'Hello, Alun Blythe's office. Oh, hi Wilbur – what's up? What's this I hear about you and Annalisa Smith? Please tell me the rumour-mill is wrong?'

'Why – would that bother you?'

'Only your lack of discernment. She is the House bike, you know, and I'd hate to think that you were just the latest one to be wearing the yellow jersey on her Tour de Commons. I'm not so sure it's your colour.'

Now she could flirt with him, she realised. Now that she was no longer interested in flirting with him, she was able to. What was she like? How useless was she?

'I have absolutely no idea what you're talking about. And anyway, why are you chatting to me like this – haven't you got work to do?'

'Actually, it's a miracle, but I have. I have a speech to write.'

'Well, good, because it's not you I'm after – it's your boss, and it's urgent. The President has just announced this tax break on private US investment in NATO countries' companies. In percentage terms it's tiny but it's an unbelievable comment on the Clinton–Blair relationship that this could come so soon in the new government's term. Obviously we're onto Blair's office, but we also need Blythe's take on the City reaction. I've been trying to find him through his private office – they're a humourless bunch over there, huh? – but he's not answering his mobile and I thought you could help me out. Where is he?'

'I have no idea. Just for a change. And his secretary, Mags, isn't here at the moment. Let me look in the diary, see if there are any clues. Nope, not a lot. Just GB Ltd, which is usually his joke for ministerial business. And they say they don't know where he is either? Strange. Look, I'll scoop up to his office here in Dean's Yard and have a look around. He sometimes leaves his pocket diary—'

'Wait a minute! Can't we bleep him? He must have one of those pagers that Mandelson was doling out?'

Cass laughed. 'Are you kidding? Don't quote me on this, but Alun loathes the sight of Mandelson. He's certainly not going to carry round a bleeper, like a puppy dog with his master's leash, so that Mandy can call him in at will. You know they're only allowed to have them on "vibrate" when they're in the Chamber?'

'Yes, but Cass—'

'Well, Alun says it's hysterical – when there's going to be a Division and Mandy wants to Whip into shape those that do have the bleeper, you suddenly see 200 MPs sitting up and looking kinda startled, some even titillated, then they're all whipping open their jackets and looking down into their crotches. As Alun says, it's like they've all been given a quick poke up the prostate – which would be right up Mandelson's street – and that the next thing you know, the Whips will be putting the pagers on during Prime Minister's questions, when Blair's about to tell a joke, to jolt them into laughing.'

'All fascinating, Cass,' Wilbur said dryly, 'but it doesn't get us any closer to finding Alun, does it?'

'I'm on the case, Commissioner Gordon. There won't be peace in Gotham City until I find that infernal Joker!'

'Flake. Get back to me when you find out anything.'

'Wilco. Hey, Wilbur, are you still going to that tug-of-war thing this evening?'

'If this has all blown over by then, yes, I am. Baroness Templeman would kill me if I didn't.'

'Yeah, well, David Faber said he would weep for a week if I didn't cheer on his Commons team.'

'Aren't we the little heartbreakers? Looks like we're on opposing sides then. Loser buys the beers.'

'Deal. See ya.'

She tried ringing Alun's office but the phone was on divert. Then she had a brainwave. Punching in a quick extension number, she waited impatiently for the phone to be picked up.

'No. 1 Parliament Street.'

'Oh, is Gwenny not there? Gwenny Blackthorn?'

'I know who Gwenny is, my love. This is the Parliament Street attendant. And no, she's not. She went out about half an hour ago and didn't even remember to put her phone on divert. I had to do that. Honestly, the things I do for these ladies—'

'When she gets back, can you say that Cass is looking for Alun, and does she have any idea if he's with Frank, or if not where he might be?'

'You're talking far too fast for me, my love, but I'll give her the gist. How about that?'

'Perfect. Bye now.'

Putting the phone down, Cass scribbled a message into the book, just in case Alun came in while she was searching for him.

'If anyone sees Alun, can they tell him to ring Wilbur Coolidge at CNN urgently?' she asked the room at large.

'If I see that bloody Blythe,' grumbled Marnie, an ancient and auburn-haired secretary of such longevity at the Palace of Westminster and such devotion to the House, that she was known as the Olympic Flame, because she never went out, 'I'm going to rip his face off. He owes me twenty quid and he nicked off with my favourite pen yesterday. Bloody kleptomaniac.'

Cass sighed. Forget the seat of ancient power and democracy, this place was more like a school playground, Mags and her crony secretaries the school bullies, and Alun the feckless, wayward scalliwag about whom everyone loved to grumble. 'Twenty quid. Favourite pen. No problem. I'll get them back for you – if I ever find him.'

'You're a sweet child, Cass,' smiled Marnie. 'Your useless boss doesn't deserve you.'

Nearly thirty and I'm a sweet child, thought Cass as she took the stairs up to the second floor two at a time. Way to go. She hadn't even been here three months and already she was beginning to feel like part of the family. If only the world that had been reared on *House of Cards* and *Yes, Minister* could peek in and see that politics wasn't just about wheeling and dealing, plotting and feuding.

The magnificent gold leaf and intricate Gothic patterning of Pugin's corridors of power over in the House may have seen some newsworthy scandals over the years, but over here in the shabby nooks and crannies of Dean's Yard, it was hard to imagine headlines being created. Here the scandals were about Mags's ugly Staffordshire dogs, Gillie, Sunny Jim and Smithie, named after Mags's unlikely Labour pin-ups, Arthur Scargill, Jim Callaghan and John Smith, and devoted to crapping everywhere they could. Not so much filth and sleaze, as filth and pees.

As she approached Alun and Frank's office, Cass heard a muffled voice inside and she paused. If it was just Frank inside she didn't want to go in, reluctant to ask him where Alun was and invite offers to help, involving the two of them prowling the quiet corridors of Westminster. She still didn't quite trust him not to harass her. So she put her ear to the door.

'—worry about it. It's just lucky she let the cat out of the bag before you came down to Guildford that weekend. Since then we have been as discreet as anything—'

No, that was Alun's voice. He must be on the telephone. Or perhaps he was with someone. As she put her hand round the doorknob, Cass looked down to see the tacky 'Do Not Disturb – Alien Sex in Progress' card that Alun had picked up on a fact-finding trip to San Diego last year, which had clashed with an *X-Files* Fan Club Convention. She hesitated again, but it did sound like he was just on the phone, and this Clinton announcement sounded like the sort of initiative Alun could really get his teeth into, which could only have a good knock-on effect for her. It was worth disturbing him.

Compromising, she pushed the door open a tiny crack to check for herself whether there was anyone in there with him.

What she saw in the three-inch gap was enough to drive all thoughts of Wilbur's interview from her head and freeze her on the spot – long enough to see Alun lower his hands from Gwenny Blackthorn's face, pull back from the kiss he had just planted on her lips, and gather her into his arms, nuzzling his head into her neck.

'Look, Frank's so tied up with all this Avalon business, he's not going to care what you get up to at Conference. He told me himself that I was to look after you for the last couple of days, because he has to go back up to the constituency straight after the Avalon party. We'll have two whole days together!'

Cass closed the door quietly before Gwenny opened her eyes to reply, and leaned against the doorjamb, mind whirling. So much for the lack of scandal in Dean's Yard.

The Newbury CyberCafé. So it did exist, marvelled Nina, as she pushed open the creaking wooden door and went in. When she'd first surfed into the Local News website a few days ago, she had not been able to believe her eyes when she had seen the crude advertisement for the newest thing to hit Newbury since the Kennet Shopping Centre.

Yet again she needed to get out of the house. Although she and Jerry had been momentarily re-united, after their terrible row following his stag night behaviour, by their mutual shock about the Princess of Wales, the weeks since had seen the rifts re-opening. He had suddenly taken to restricting her to certain times she could use the computer. Nina had stormed off in a fit of pique, sold some ugly but valuable painting his rich Uncle Martin had given them for a wedding present and bought a laptop with the proceeds. Jerry had gone berserk. The painting had been an heirloom and what on earth was she doing buying her own laptop? Why could she possibly need one? He was the one with computer skills. Babaji had watched bemused as they hurled insults across the kitchen at each other, only wagging his tail when Jerry stiffly apologised a few minutes later. In their headier days, they would have spent the rest of the afternoon in bed, making up, but this time they merely made each other enough conciliatory cups of tea to float a WI battleship.

Nor was work going miraculously better now that she had her dinky little computer. She and Jerry still squabbled about their online time, sharing the same telephone line, which meant that she couldn't access the Internet as often as she would have liked, to provide her with some much-needed new ideas. The stuff she was doing had become impossibly stale. That morning she had finally pinned Marco Pierre White down to giving her a Primrose Path interview – after three days of constant flirting with the outrageous Yorkshireman – only to be told by the commissioning editor at *FortyEight* that they had already done him. In vain did Nina protest that she'd asked the editor's bitch of an assistant to send her a list of logged-in Primrose Paths, on which Marco's name had not figured; she had still ended up looking like a bloody idiot. Swearing yet again at the long-suffering phone receiver as she slammed it down, Nina had grabbed Babaji and jumped in the car.

Bored of trawling the Woolworths and sausage shops of Marlborough for things of interest, she had headed for the busy metropolis of Newbury. Only after a happy half hour hurling the car round the sweeping curves of the A4, singing Carpenters' songs at the top of her voice, Babaji joining in occasionally, had Nina recovered. Then she'd remembered the advert for the CyberCafé, decided to see what these things were all about, to see if it might solve her Internet spats with Jerry, had crawled through the interminable traffic of the little town, getting inextricably tangled in the infernal one-way system, and had finally found the café.

Summer had finally arrived, in the form of a September Indian summer, and already Nina was longing for the cool of the preceding months to return. This hot, damp weather always made her feel dizzy, sluggish and fat. Where before she had been able to swaddle her spongy, bulging limbs in layers of tracksuit, jumper and cardigan, now no amount of long, drapy skirts and wafty blouses could disguise the fact that her previously muscular compactness had atrophied into the present blancmange. Perhaps she had a thyroid disorder – didn't that involve serious lethargy, weight gain and hot flushes?

As they went into the café, it was hard to tell who was the more hot and bothered, her or Babaji, both of them blowing black, curly fringes out of their eyes, Nina tempted to pant as pathetically as her little dog. Luckily, the café was shady and cool, not the bastion of techno sterility she had been half-expecting. With its glass-fronted counter of flapjacks and sandwiches and its ancient coffee machine, it was more like the vegetarian bistros she used to work in when she was at Oxford. Nor was she expecting so many people – about ten of them, mostly young and male, all clustered on rickety, wooden chairs around a central speaker, a man of Nina's age.

'Hi there,' he said, 'have you come to join our seminar?'

'Er, no,' said Nina quickly. 'I'm just having a look around. Don't mind me.'

'No problem,' he smiled. 'Will you need help using any of the terminals?'

'I'll work it out,' she assured him. 'Is it OK if I have my dog in here? It's just too hot to leave him in the car.'

'There's a terminal up the other end,' he pointed, 'well away from the food – as long as you keep him there, it should be OK.'

'Thanks. C'mon, Babaji, heel!' To her amazement, Babaji obeyed her.

Ten minutes later she was finally beginning to relax, so engrossed in plumbing the mysteries of the Downing Street website, in preparation for her Primrose Path interview with the Head of the Policy Unit there, that she didn't even notice someone sit down at the terminal next to her.

'God, this is crap,' she muttered. 'This is like a party political broadcast. Don't any of these people know anything about the Net?'

The man next to her looked over at her screen. 'You should have seen it when the Tories were in control, it was chronic.'

She glanced over at him, to see her dog flaked out happily in his lap, pink tongue still hanging out of his mouth, woolly flanks heaving.

'Babaji!' He opened one eye and cocked half an ear, then closed it again. 'Babaji, get down off there!'

'It's OK, really,' Babaji's new friend insisted. 'I don't mind. My name's Steve, by the way.'

'Nina. Come here, you little bugger—' She leant across and

tried to pick Babaji up, inadvertently sticking her hands right into the stranger's crotch.

'Ow!'

Nina promptly dropped Babaji in her embarrassment. Right back into his lap. Sharp claws and all.

'Fuck! Ow!'

'Oh shit. Sorry.' To her dismay, Nina felt herself begin to laugh. This was terrible. She had just poked someone in the gonads – twice – and all she could do was laugh. 'I – I – I'm sorry—' In the blink of an eye, the laughter turned sharp and shrill, an ugly note of hysteria creeping in. 'D-Don't know why I—'

'Hey, don't worry about it. I never wanted children anyway.' He smiled and looked closely at her. 'One of those days?'

Oh God, if only, thought Nina. More like one of those lives. 'One of those days,' she agreed flatly.

Just then, a kerfuffle broke out at the other end. 'But it wasn't fair,' wailed one of the few women there, 'I thought he meant what he said. I left my boyfriend!'

Nina and Steve raised eyebrows at each other.

'Sounds like she's having one of those days too,' said Nina. 'What is going on up there?'

Steve grinned. 'It's a seminar to Resolve Virtual Reality with Real Reality,' he said, straight-faced.

'Real Reality? Oh please, you have to be joking. In Newbury?'

'Well, I'm not sure the good folks of Berkshire have quite got to grips with the fact that Internet relationships aren't the modern equivalents of Victorian courtships, with their love-letters and secret assignations.'

Nina blushed, remembering her naive exchange with BadBoy on that very subject. 'It's a sweet idea, though, don't you think?'

'Yes, but consequently those people up there have had difficulty realising that cyberspace romance isn't real.'

Nina now shuddered. 'Thank God it isn't.' She looked at her watch. 'Talking of reality, my husband will be sending out the marines soon. I'd better go home.'

'Oh, just before you go, do you know anything about e-mail? I signed up to the Net without realising that you had to buy a whole extra package to send and receive e-mails, and now that I have it, I don't really know what to do with it. I have to proposition various American editors for some work via e-mail and I wanted to practise before I made a technological fool of myself.'

'Are you a journalist? Me too.'

'No, I write books really. Crime novels and short stories for magazines, that sort of thing.'

'Well, what I know about e-mailing could be written on a pin-head, but I do have an e-mail address – if you like you can send me a test e-mail to see if it works,' Nina suggested absently, scrabbling in her handbag for the business cards she'd had printed up in Paddington Station the last time she went up to London. 'There you go.'

Steve took it. 'Are you sure that's OK? I mean, we've only just met—'

Nina waved her hand. 'Oh pish-posh. I'm feeling reckless today. If you're a serial killer, you can e-mail me with the gruesome details of your latest murder. No, us writers have to stick together, don't you think?'

Steve laughed. 'You bet – and let's not pretend it's not great displacement therapy, fooling around with the Net, rather than working!'

'Ouch. Busted,' said Nina with feeling.

Cass sat at Mags's desk, staring blankly at the appointments diary. GB Ltd wasn't anything to do with Alun's Ministry, it was Gwenny Blackthorn. She couldn't decide whether she was more galled by the moronic simplicity of the code, or by the fact that she had fallen for it.

'A really great liar always sticks as closely to the truth as possible,' one of her classmates at Columbia had once told her, when Cass had rolled out some tragically complicated excuse for being late with a paper. Well, Alun Blythe and Gwenny Blackthorn were obviously world-class liars. No wonder he'd proved such a tenacious political player. And her! Cool as a cucumber in the gym that day when Cass had let the cat out of the bag about Frank kiboshing her chances for a cosy love-in with Alun down at Guildford.

Now that Cass thought about it, so many things added up – all those times, with their complex arrangements, that she had ended up driving Alun's car for him, dropping him in random spots throughout London, all those cryptic messages she had delivered to him. No wonder he thought she was such a good research assistant – she had practically been his pimp! How could she have fallen for it? Especially given her own involvement with Carter back in America, she should have recognised the signs.

She flicked idly back through the appointments book, clocking for the first time just how many entries there were for GB Ltd. How could he be so blatant about it? Was he insane? He was sleeping with the wife of his best friend. All three of them worked at the frontline of politics. How stupid could he be? Cass suddenly wished there was someone she could talk to about this. But Hallie now worked for the Labour Party – if this somehow got back to Alun's old enemy, Peter Mandelson, Alun would be mincemeat, so she couldn't tell her. Nina was off-limits for obvious reasons. What had happened to their friendship that their loyalties were suddenly so scattered?

'What are you doing?' Mags's voice was sharp.

Cass spun round guiltily, her heart sinking. Alun's secretary was obviously still in the stranglehold of one of her bad hangovers, her eyes slack and bloodshot, her mouth turned down in deep lines.

'I'm trying to find Alun for an interview with CNN.' Cass swallowed. 'And all I can find is this GB Ltd. Does that mean anything to you?' Might as well play the innocent, she thought, that's what everyone round here seems to assume I am.

Mags was too old a political player to be fooled by this for a second. She glared suspiciously at Cass. 'What do you think it means?' Then she relented. 'Here, turf yourself out of my chair, and let me fill you in on a few things.'

Oh shit, thought Cass, this is way too heavy. I might as well wave this job goodbye.

'You see all the people in this office?'

Cass nodded nervously.

'We're the last word in respectability, aren't we? With our sensible clothes, and the fact that we've worked here for about a million years, you must think that we're all dinosaurs, right?'

'No way—'

'Right then, look at Mrs Johnson in the corner. Now she looks like your grandmother, doesn't she, with her blue rinse and pleated skirt?'

'Not mine,' interjected Cass, trying not to let herself be totally steamrollered.

'Did she tell you she only got married last year, having lived with her mother until she was fifty-three? No? Then I reckon she didn't tell you either that until about two years ago, she was having an affair with a Peer, did she? For thirty-five years. Thirty-five years – because he wouldn't leave his wife all that time. Do you know why it finally finished? Because he was eighty-two and hadn't been able to get it up for years, so the whole thing just petered out.'

Cass was longing to know where this was going.

'And look at Geraldine by the door. Did you know that she used to work for a Conservative member? Back in the Seventies, she worked for this right tosser called Nicky Fairbairn, where her job consisted mainly of juggling his mistresses – all four of them. Now each of them had a codename,' Mags's glance fell inadvertently to the GB Ltd in Alun's diary, 'according to where they lived in London and it was Geraldine's job to make sure that none of them found out about each other. Well, one day she got in a right muddle and sent Belgravia and Victoria to meet Nicky at the same time. All hell broke loose, Belgravia ended up trying to hang herself from a lamp-post outside the House of Commons, so Nicky had to marry her and fire Geraldine.'

'Mags, I—'

'Then there's good, old Marnie, the Olympic Flame herself. You'd hardly believe she used to be a right little stunner in her day, would you? Of course, she's had a hard life, bringing Susie up on her own. You know, her daughter Susie?'

'Yes, she came in the other—'

'She's a bastard, poor kid. No-one knows who the father is – not even Marnie, or so she swears. Mind you, she was sleeping with three Conservative Members at the time, so it figures.'

'Marnie was?' gasped Cass. 'Sleeping with Tories? But she's so Socialist!'

'Which is why, when all three of them stepped forward with

offers of child support, she turned them down flat. It was all right to sleep with them, she said, but she was damned if she was going to accept their dirty Tory money and, anyway, it would be unfair since she didn't know which one was the father.'

Cass was speechless by now.

'So you see, Cass my love, you don't have to dig very deep to find the dirt in this place – which is why none of us do. Separated from their wives all week, working these irregular hours, carrying such burdens on their shoulders, how can we possibly know what pressures our MPs have to relieve? We're just the hired help and it's their business not ours, what everyone else gets up to. We all work for our individual members and just happen to share offices with other secretaries. We may even be friends with each other, but that's as far as it goes. It's not like a company office, Cass, you and I owe our loyalties to just one person, and that's Alun. Now do you understand?'

Cass stayed silent. So much for her cosy little school-yard analogies only half an hour before – this place was a total crock of shit.

'Oh yes,' she said slowly, looking Mags squarely in the eye. 'I understand, all right. Loud and clear.'

'Clear as a bell! It was as if someone had struck a tuning fork inside me. There I'd been, half of me sitting back from the whole thing, arms crossed and thinking only about scoffing at the whole thing, half of me getting in a total state, all my worries and paranoias floating up to the surface, like scum on a pool. And I was beginning to feel like a champagne bottle, all these thoughts and attitudes shaking up inside me so that any minute the cork was going to come flying off.'

Hallie sighed deeply, stretching out her feet along the length of the sofa and tucking them under his legs.

'Then Nicky, who runs Alpha, came up to me and asked me if he could pray for me. Pray for me! And I was so embarrassed to be singled out from everyone else that I went bright red in the face, tears welling up, and mumbled something non-specific. And he just puts his hand on my back and suddenly it's as if all the heat from my face is rushing to where his hand is and

I feel this radiating warmth from his touch, so hot it's almost uncomfortable. Then, as he starts to pray out loud, as I said, it was as if that warmth set off this tuning fork, this hum, this sort of singing vibration inside me. I'm half-listening to what he's saying but I'm really listening to this extraordinary sound-sensation, not in my head, but from much deeper within – if I didn't think it sounded ridiculous I would say it came from within my heart.

'This huge peace came over me and I felt so calm, calm like I haven't felt in an age. I just sat, stood and prayed with the others for the rest of the meeting and afterwards, when we were having a drink, one of the other leaders came up to me and asked me how I felt. When I told him, he just nodded and beamed at me and said, "Yes, we all feel that way when the Holy Spirit visits us. You never really get used to it." The Holy Spirit!'

'Hallie, what got you into all this?'

Hallie was uncharacteristically silent.

'OK, do you think it was the Holy Spirit?' he asked reasonably, pulling her feet onto his lap and starting to massage them.

'I don't know. It's very confusing trying to look at these things with a cold logic that is nothing to do with what has been, for over ten years, a rather rusty old faith. What I do know, though, is that it was an overwhelmingly physical sensation – one that I've never known before – and yet it was as if it flooded my body and my mind with this euphoria I could never have imagined before. And it wasn't just that one time, either. I've been going to HTB now for over a month and it's the same nearly every time. Some people even speak in tongues, the Holy Spirit touches them so much. OK, I'm sure that it can be explained away by science but it's hard to see – I mean, you're a doctor, how would you explain it to me?'

'Well, I could get all technical and start talking about hysterical projection where it may be that because you want to believe, that you are able to create this extreme reaction in yourself by subconsciously instructing your brain to release the chemicals and hormones that make up the ingredients for this ecstasy. But if you step back from that, you have to ask yourself, that these are just the signposts – and why are you going this way? Who's telling you? Put less fancifully, if the Holy Spirit were to "visit" you, wouldn't it choose those same signposts, release the same chemicals, because that's the way you feel ecstasy, that's how you recognise that it's there?'

'You've lost me.'

'What I'm saying is that it's all very well for us men of science to start explaining any phenomena away by citing physical, x=y reasons for them – but you just have to allow for faith. I used to see it all the time in Accident and Emergency – that inexplicable spark that can keep a person alive, that moment when you can see them fighting back—' he paused, and laughed. 'Listen to me, you've got me raving now!'

'What fire, though! What fervour! This is great. I never knew you were a Christian?' This could be a way to get him back, thought Hallie quickly. She had forgotten how she could talk to him as she could talk to no-one else – the shorthand of two people who know each other so well. These Oprah chats, where nothing was taboo, but with no audience, so she could be as bald as she never could be with others, having no fear that he would mock her. Where the words travelled from so far within her that they diluted themselves into dispassion by the time they finally emerged.

'Come on, Hallie, use your nouse – would I be Christian with a name like mine? It's a couple of generations back but we did used to be Jewish, so I would feel uncomfortable with any specific faith. I suppose I just believe in some sort of divine order. Any skilled doctor must feel the same.'

' "Any skilled doctor" indeed,' Hallie teased. 'Well, Doctor Divine, if you can exercise your skill in the direction of coffee . . .'

As he stood up, she couldn't help but let her eyes follow the movement, the thick muscles of his shoulder-blades contracting under his T-shirt as he stretched, seeing his thighs strain against the thin cotton of his sarong. No-one who had ever seen him in his usually impeccable three-piece pinstripe suits, Harley Street to the core, could have believed that this was how he dressed off-duty during the summer. 'I started doing it on my internship in Bombay,' he had once told her, showing her how he just wound the strip of cloth round his narrow hips, 'no underwear, no clammy, wrinkly trousers, everything as nature intended me to be, without being arrestable. Along with the poetry of *Bhagavad Gita*, the most useful thing I learned in India.' And then he had sung her a love song – a ghazal – from the long, epic poem.

She had riposted with the entire lyrics of her favourite David Bowie songs, remembered from schooldays when nothing else was deemed important enough to commit to memory. Just when she was up to her fourth Ch-Ch-Ch-Changes, he had grabbed her, whereupon quoting poetry had given way to jiggery-pokery. On this very sofa, she thought, stroking the worn, gold brocade of the enormous sofa, remembering how easy his sarong had been to peel off, and how hard her tights had been, both of them rapidly descending into weak giggles with each desperate tug. How had they ever come from there to here?

'There you go,' he interrupted her reverie, putting the coffee mug down and stroking her arm as he settled down beside her. 'Drink it up, then we can go to bed. I have to be in early in the morning.'

Hallie's eyes flickered once to his, then stared down at her coffee. The part of her that had been listening to her preachers, Phil and Nicky, talk about the sanctity of sex wanted to cavil. The part of her that had been listening to Cass and all her talk of empowerment, wanted to protest at his presumption. They weren't going out with each other so why should he assume that she was going to stay and sleep with him?

But the other half of her knew that if she did demur, then that would prompt the sort of deep and meaningful that he hated and she dreaded – dreaded because she never knew which carelessly callous word or phrase would wrench open the floodgates of her feelings and embarrass them both.

'You're meant to drink it, not stare at it, you fool.' The tone was teasing but there was an underlying impatience.

Hallie did look up then, studying his dark, floppy curls and down-turned dark eyes, one hand going up to her neck to finger the gold cross that she had so recently re-hung there. She waited for the familiar kick of desire to plummet into her guts. Yes, there it was. But this time there was another sensation – the cool scratchiness of the pearls set into the cross.

'Are you OK?' he said then, leaning forward to tuck a stray

lock of blonde hair behind her ear. That was because he knew her so well – he knew that she hated having hair around her face. 'Don't you want to stay?'

It was the tenderness and familiarity that undid Hallie. Yet again.

Her hand fell away from the pendant and pulled him towards her. 'Of course I want to.'

Jesus Christ still can't match up to this, was her last coherent and blasphemous thought.

'So, where's your lapdog?'

'I'm sorry?'

'Is Ted not coming?'

'Not that I'm aware of,' Cass said absently. Then she snapped to attention. 'What did you call him? My lapdog? How dare you? You're meant to be a buddy of his!'

Wilbur clicked finger and thumb in front of Cass's face. 'Just trying to get through here, honey. Where are you? Is it nice there?'

'Just because you can't bear anyone not paying you the full and proper attention you deserve doesn't mean I can be perky on demand,' said Cass flatly. 'God, this is a totally weird event.' She peered out, to where the leaders of the land were falling about, covering themselves in mud and roaring with laughter. 'Can you imagine a bunch of Senators and Congressmen putting aside their political differences and doing a tug-of-war in the pouring rain, when they've got a big vote on just a couple of hours later?'

'I can imagine certain Senators doing anything,' Wilbur commented dryly, noticing that Cass shot him a sharp look as he did so. 'For publicity,' he assured her.

'I guess. But this is an annual event apparently, and the media can hardly be bothered to turn up any more. Perhaps it's because they get politicians rolling around in their own mud the rest of the year, so where's the entertainment value in this? Still, I guess it raises money for charity, which is nice.'

'Yeah, and you haven't seen the Westminster Wobblers, have you?' chuckled Wilbur.

'The Westminster Wobblers? That covers a multitude of evils. Some strange new Euro-faction of the Tories – the ones who can't decide what they believe in? A not-so-humble pie-eating team?'

'Very funny. They're the cross-party soccer team – I did a short film on them for the station, admittedly in their pre-election guise. Wobblers is right – a more laughable, crumbly bunch of oldtimers it would be hard to imagine. They try, though – I went to watch them play this cheesy TV team, the Primetimers, or something like that, in a charity match – and it was hysterical. These grey-haired, balding guys shambling around on their last legs, hardly making contact with the ball – one guy fell over at one point onto his enormous beer gut and just bounced right back up again. My cameraman had to stop filming: he was laughing so hard the camera was shaking like a leaf.'

Cass scowled at him. 'What is your job again? One minute you're just breezing around, doing whatever you want to and having a right old laugh, the next you're doing your Walter Cronkite thing on latest developments from the White House.'

'And what's wrong with that? You know as well as I do that back home no-one gives a damn about British politics. My job is to find things that might spark some interest.' Wilbur shrugged. 'More often than not, my stuff is dumped in favour of some kid being yanked out of a wellshaft in Alabama but, hey, you know, they pay me and it keeps me out of trouble. Anyway, talking of the White House, thanks for finding Alun this morning.'

'I'm sorry?'

Wilbur sighed. 'Cass, I have got other things to do. If you're not going to listen to me, I'm out of here.'

'No, but I didn't find Alun. Is that what he said?'

'Well, he mentioned that he'd got a message from you, through Frank Blackthorn's secretary's office.'

'Yeah, that'd be right,' Cass said savagely.

'What is *with* you? And they say PMS is a media scare story!'

'Shit, I'm sorry.' Cass looked around at the small gathering of MPs, Peers and groupies, huddled from the rain under the specially erected marquee on Abingdon Green, more usually the site for vox-popping political pundits. 'Look, this is dull. Do you want to get out of here and grab a beer? I have a dilemma I need to talk about with someone – and you'll have to do.'

'Gee, thanks. Make me feel special, why don't you?'

'Don't flirt with me, Wilbur, I'm not in the mood. Come on.' Cass started edging her way out of the marquee.

Wilbur shook his head bemusedly and followed her, not quite sure why he allowed her to boss him around like this.

Ten minutes later, they were ensconced in the Marquis pub.

'Can you just forget that you're a reporter for a minute?' Cass asked him, as they propped up the bar.

'Like a shot,' Wilbur confirmed cheerfully.

'OK, off the record, what would you do if you found out your boss – oh, this is stupid, you know exactly who I'm talking about.' Cass glanced around her, and lowered her voice. 'I found out this morning that he's having an affair – with the wife of his best friend, no less. How can he be so stupid? All three of them are in politics – if it comes out it'll be just like Tory sleaze all over again. It'll totally dent the Government's image, just before the Conference and just as all the fuss about the Glasgow mafia and Robin Cook is dying down. It would be a disaster. So what do I do? Hint to him that I know, and that if I stumbled onto it, others are bound to? What would you do?'

'Cass, what are you talking about? Do you mean Alun is having an—'

'Shush, you moron!' Cass hissed.

Wilbur rolled his eyes. 'Watergate lives again. OK, you think your boss is sleeping around. So what? *He's* not married. So who cares? And what can you do? Say anything to him and all that happens is that you look like an idiot. Butt out is what I say, it's none of your business.'

Cass looked mulish. She was obviously formulating some crushing argument, thought Wilbur, smiling inwardly. Obviously not a woman who spoke before she thought. He gave her his best quizzical look, peering ironically at her through a curtain of eyelashes. 'What? Not dramatic enough? Too compromising? Welcome to politics, honey.' He smiled at her lazily, leaning back against the pillar.

The riling worked. 'That totally sucks!' Cass snapped. 'This is meant to be a better Britain, with clean politicians helming the ship for the first time since 1979. I joined the Labour Party to get away from amoral backslappers laughing in the face of the nation they're supposed to be governing. People like Jonathan Aitken and Neil Hamilton who seriously believed that they were in such a position of power that it didn't matter how evil and corrupt they were, because no-one would ever be able to bring them down. They could sleep with whoever they wanted, do as many dodgy deals as they wanted and then just lie, lie, lie their way out of any trouble. Well, I'm still naive enough to think that that's wrong.'

Wilbur refused to let himself get pulled into a debate of morals. 'You can climb down from the People's Platform now. What are you getting so steamed about?' His tone turned ironic. 'Maybe they're in love? Maybe each of them is serving some sort of emotional need in the other one? Had you considered that? I mean, you're the one who doesn't believe in the sanctity of marriage. Al—,' he glanced around exaggeratedly, 'your boss isn't married so maybe he doesn't either.'

'Bollocks,' Cass said brutally. 'I just don't buy that. When you become a politician, you sign up to some sort of moral code—'

'Oh grow up, Cass,' said Wilbur wearily. 'You're – how old? – twenty-nine? You don't seriously believe that crap, do you?'

Cass frowned. 'Well, yes, I do. And it makes me sick that you can be as laid back about this as you are about everything else. As I said, I'm naive, but I refuse just to let my idealism collapse. He's sleeping with another man's wife! Him and his Cabinet pals are the leaders of this country – why shouldn't I expect something more from them than the same lying and cheating that we've had for the last eighteen years? I didn't come back here to work for a party as bad as the one we're replacing! I came here to get away from all that bullshit, the sweet-talking, the empty promises, the—' She stopped suddenly and reddened.

Strangely, she looked almost guilty.

'Come on, Cass, now you're just being pompous. Politicians are still human, under just the same pressures as us ordinary mortals – in fact, greater pressures, since they're hardly ever at home out of temptation's way. Are you telling me you've never slept with someone you shouldn't? Someone unavailable?'

'Wh-what? Wh-what do you m-mean?' Cass stared at him as if she'd seen a ghost. As Wilbur started at her reaction, some shred of memory replayed itself in his head, a half-buried fragment of conversation between his father and his aunt. That, and the lightning look she had given him earlier when he'd mentioned Senators. 'Just a second,' he said slowly, his face concentrating into an accusing look. 'So why did you come back here? Exactly whose bullshit and sweet-talking were you running away from? Did someone in American politics bother you so much?'

Cass was now white, the beer mat she had been playing with shredded into tiny pieces. 'What are you talking about? No-one. Nothing. No-one!'

She couldn't have confirmed her guilt more if she'd tried. Just as had happened the first time he had ever met her, a picture of John Junior, puffy-eyed and miserable that last weekend, streaked through Wilbur's head, followed by a flash of the same white-hot anger. Gone was the lazy mockery of a moment ago.

'So that rumour was true,' he bit out. 'You goddamn little hypocrite. So much for idealist politics, eh? The Student and the Senator – now that's what I call a romantic pairing. You have an affair with my brother's stepfather just a few weeks after his death – and you dare to stand here and preach morals to me? You bitch. You total bitch.'

Cass shrank from him, bowing her head from his hailstone rage.

'How could you? You weren't content with the damage you'd already caused to our family? Not happy with dumping John Junior out of the blue like that? Without even giving him a reason? Making him so fucking miserable that he didn't know what he was doing? Have you never asked yourself why he only had one safety rope out there on that mountain? Because he forgot the other one. And why did he forget it? You tell me, Miss Compassion.' Wilbur knew he was going too far now, but he couldn't stop himself. 'You as good as killed him, you know that, don't you?'

Cass lifted her head, eyes blazing. 'Now you wait a minute, mister! It was a freak freezing spell and an accident and you know it! It had nothing to do with the safety rope – no-one had two safety ropes there that day – it was October, for Chrissakes! I will not be held responsible for John's death! And I didn't—'

'Yeah, but you thought about it, didn't you? You felt guilty – that was why you didn't come to the funeral. And what a fucked-up way you choose to repay his mother for his death – by stealing her husband while her only son's body is hardly cold in its grave. Or maybe it was going on even before John Junior died – maybe that's why you dumped him.'

Cass was as coldly angry as he was now. 'Can it! I didn't steal anyone's husband. If you don't know your facts, I suggest you shut the fuck up. I'm not standing for any more of this.' She started to gather up her belongings.

'No wonder you changed the subject every time I brought up John Junior's name. Can't exactly make you sleep easy at nights, living with that guilt. What is it with you and Coolidge men, anyway? Some sort of fatal attraction? Was that why you were trying to add me to your collection that night in Jack's Bar?'

She froze again in pure shock. Bingo, he'd hit the target again. 'Well,' he added cruelly, 'you'd better work on your seduction techniques, babe, because this is one Coolidge you're not going to get your hooks into.'

Cass visibly pulled herself together, shooting him a look of pure dislike. 'I was dared to get off with you by a friend. I'm glad you noticed how laborious I was finding it. Not even for a dare could I summon up the enthusiasm necessary. Of course, now that I know you're such an easy lay, I know I needn't even have tried. Not that I would want to – you may think you know everything, including about Carter and me, but you obviously don't realise that he is a caring, attractive, genuinely nice guy, whereas you are a self-satisfied, gone-to-seed bully boy, with more connivance than cock, and more wham-bam than wit. Goodbye, Wilbur Coolidge. Have a nice life.' And she stalked off.

Well that, as they say, is that, thought Wilbur.

It was still raining, as Cass peeled herself off the scooter, eyes still screwed up from squinting through the rain, cursing herself for leaving the visored helmet at home that morning.

Just the perfect end to the perfect day, she thought, as she let herself into Trudie's flat. In a way, she was glad that things had come out into the open at last between Wilbur and her, even if he did have most of his facts wrong. At least now she could say goodbye to Coolidge men once and for all. Now she could really begin her fresh start.

On the stairs was a note in her grandmother's writing. Cass waited until she reached the top and had peeled off her sodden clothes before reading it. As she glanced at what it said, she sank down onto the top step.

'A friend from America rang. Says he's planning a trip over here very soon. You must ring him and tell him your plans. Here's the number – 001 312 555 4486. There's the leftovers of a failed River Café recipe in the Belling, if you want it. I'm off to the Crisis Centre – back around midnight. Big kisses, Trudie. PS. Book me into that nursing home – senile me forgot to tell you your friend's name. Carter Wylie. Isn't that the name of one of those yummy *ER* doctors? If so, can I share him?'

Carter. Coming here. So much for that fresh start. Now what was she going to do?

8

Brighton. Wedding cake buildings bespattered and smeared by rain, a picture postcard scene that had fallen in a puddle. Ted stared out of his hotel window onto the sea. It looked about as grey and churning as he felt, with a Big Daddy of a hangover bouncing fatly off the walls of his quivering brain, bulbous fists flying. It was only Wednesday of the 1997 Labour Party Conference and already he wanted to slink home like a mangy cur.

This was meant to be his conference, the one where he arrived in glory, not as a hanger-on but as one of the chosen ones. As they did a hundred times a day, his thoughts went back to that night at the count. For one long dizzying moment, as he watched the battered metal ballot boxes being emptied onto the long lines of trestle tables and sorted into piles, he had thought he was going to win. The cheers of his supporters down the hall, as the national results came flooding in over the radio only reinforced that view. If Stephen was going to rub Michael Portillo's nose in it, then surely he too could swing this safe seat his way?

He had tried his best to concentrate on what his agent and key campaigners had been saying to him, but all the time his jittery mind was skipping forward to the moment when the Mayor, puffed up in her Sunday best and glittery chain, would step up to the mike and start intoning the results. He would straighten his tie and rake back his hair, setting his jaw in manly nonchalance – 'Oh, did I win? Well I never,' – and wait for her to say, '. . . and I therefore declare Edward Albert Austin duly elected Member for Hexham'. Then he would step forward, smiling self-deprecatingly, would shake the defeated Watkinson by the hand, clapping him on the back in hail-fellow-well-defeated camaradarie, and then take the mike himself.

His speech was to be short and modestly untriumphant. 'I am proud to have won this election for the people of Hexham, for Tony Blair and for the new Labour government. Don't go thinking of me as the Member for Hexham. Groucho Marx had it right with that well-known remark, "I don't want to join any club that would have me for a member". Westminster is no longer an exclusive club for the privileged few. Everyone in this constituency, whether you voted for me or not, is now a Member for Hexham. I'm going to London merely as your voice – your voice, your receptionist, your clerk, your foot-soldier. I will speak loudly on your behalf, I will deliver your messages, I will cut my way through bureaucracy for you, I will fight your battles. And I will do all that with the support of the people who have carried me this far – my agent, and the rest of the campaign team.'

He never got to make the speech. Even as the Mayor was reading out the results, Ted was grappling with the need to look impassive, trying not to give away to his supporters that he already knew the result, having been called to one side by the returning officer just before he went up on the platform.

The LibDem candidate was expected to take votes from his rival, as was the Referendum Party. When these had been announced and while votes for the Monster Raving Loonies and Natural Law Parties were being read out, Ted watched his team exchange feverish looks. Anthea and her calculator did some lightning work and she gave him a cautious thumbs up. He grimaced back at her.

'Edward Albert Austin, the Parliamentary Labour Party, twenty-three thousand, five hundred and seventy one,' recited the Mayor solemnly but indistinctly.

'Paul Watkinson, the Conservative Party, twenty-three thousand, seven hundred and ninety three. I therefore declare that—'

There was an agonising pause as the returning officer whispered into the Mayor's ear. In the audience beneath the platform, Ted could sense the shifting whispers and hisses as everyone argued about what they'd heard.

'I shall say again,' said the Mayor testily. 'Edward Albert Austin, the Parliamentary Labour Party, twenty-three thousand, *five* hundred and seventy one.'

For a panic-stricken split-second, Ted's team obviously couldn't remember how many his rival had polled. But only for a split second, as they worked it out and the room erupted, Watkinson's team throwing their blue rosettes into the air, shiny pink faces beaming in relief, ties being loosened from around panting plump necks. By contrast, his supporters were still, silent. They seemed smaller, slighter. He glimpsed Anthea doffing her red Britain Deserves Better cardboard visor and burying her face in it in a moment of mute misery. Through the shouts of the victorious Conservatives and the veil of his own shock, Ted dimly heard the Mayor declaring that Watkinson was the elected Member at the top of her voice.

Thank God the next few minutes were a blur. He had been on automatic pilot, hearing only one thing – his grandad, catching him crying after school one day, saying, 'Best the buggers, Teddy lad, best the buggers. Think you've got a broomstick up your bum, walk straight back out there and ignore them. Then choose another way to beat them. Best the buggers!'

He'd bested those buggers by getting a scholarship to the grammar, gone to Cambridge and had hit politics still running, being elected to Lambeth council at twenty-four, then selected as the candidate for the hopeless seat of Hexham at the tender age of twenty-seven and turning it into a marginal during the previous months of unofficial campaigning and the previous three weeks of the official battle. He would best them now by shoving that broomstick right back up his bum and accepting the narrow defeat with the same nonchalance he had rehearsed for his victory speech.

He had been carrying that same protective veil of nonchalance round with him in the weeks and months since, trying not to let anyone see how much he minded the sight of his victorious ex-colleagues and friends ambling through the House in their shirtsleeves, in contrast to his officebound suit jackets. Their informality and subtle air of belonging had constantly mocked him. When he queued for food with them in Strangers' and then watched them go through to the Members' Dining Room, or chatted with them outside the Whips' Office while not being able to follow them into the Chamber, he hugged the last rags of *sang-froid* more tightly around him, smiling and chatting blithely with all and sundry. Ted's a grand lad, he could hear them thinking, a right doughty player.

He would have to cloak himself particularly effectively, in the next few days, in the self-congratulatory euphoria of the first Labour Government Party Conference since 1978. He might be there as one of the leading lights of Medios, the most innovative think-tank in the country but, dammit, he couldn't help thinking bitterly, I should be here as a Member of Parliament, not as some poxy pundit.

To make matters worse, he was also here as a lovesick fool. For the last couple of weeks, he had been successfully avoiding Cass, damned if he was going to witness the budding flirtation between her and Wilbur Coolidge. It hadn't helped that he had been privy to the usual rumours about Wilbur and various Westminster women. Annalisa Smith, it was reported, had failed to snare him after she'd apparently had a tantrum when he'd refused to buy her a solid silver House of Commons ashtray – 'this is one head that portcullis isn't going to crash down on,' he had apparently drawled to a lobby journalist. But that hadn't stopped his name being connected with good-looking women all over Westminster from that shy Lords' librarian to female MPs of all persuasions.

How did he do it? the men of Westminster wondered. He usually looked half-asleep, he had grey hair, a face full of creases, for an ex-ballet dancer he looked soft and slack, not muscle-bound, and amongst the suits, ties and uniforms of everyone from attendants to Peers, he looked incongruous in his battered leather reefercoat and white V-neck T-shirts. Yet Wilbur didn't just get the women, he got the stories. CNN were reported to be ecstatic with the eclectic mix of gossipy titbits and colourful commentary he was sending in. In the flurry of reportage that had followed Princess Diana's death, Wilbur had stood out for his ability to convey the mob hysteria of the British people without losing his own perspective on the tragedy. He had also been the first American reporter to confirm that the Prime Minister's Press Secretary Alastair Campbell had been the one to coin Blair's mood-capturing 'People's Princess' moniker for Diana, and had secured a short interview with Campbell against the candlelit banks of flowers and supporters surrounding Westminster Abbey the night before the funeral. Such was his ability to make politics watchable that the tattlers were beginning to joke that, one of these days, your average John Doe in an American street might even be able to name the British Prime Minister.

In his heart of hearts, Ted knew that it was this mixture of louche coolness and effortless success that would have attracted Cass, just like he'd read in women's magazines, but it didn't make it any easier to restrain himself from telling her that Wilbur was undoubtedly a bastard. Undoubtedly. Even if he personally liked the bloke, no-one could be that good. Could they?

Cass could, he sighed. Forget the fact that she looked like something you should be able to win in the lottery. It was with her Loonytoon laugh and her inability to suffer fools remotely gladly that she had sent his heart running for cover. And there it had stayed, wounded and cowering in the shadows, as he larked about with her as if he were her brother, for fuck's sake.

Keep it cool, he had counselled himself, she'll never go for you if you give in to the lovesick puppy yelping inside you. Keep it cool, he had reiterated, when he had watched her eat Coolidge up with her eyes. Down boy! he had restrained himself, when she and Wilbur had met and had spat at each other like wildcats, don't get your hopes up.

But Ted knew he never would make a move on her. Not til he could be proud about himself could he be confident enough to tilt at that particular windmill. And since his recce mission in the pub with Wilbur two weeks ago, he no longer dared hope. Coolidge had made it very clear that he knew Cass's every movement, that they were in constant touch and that it was just a matter of time before they were scoring some serious tonsil hockey. Of course, this should have roused Ted to some primeval competitive club-waving and plumage-puffing but he couldn't bear it. So he'd slunk away like the loser he was, and had spent the last two weeks licking his wounds so that he would be toughened up in preparation for the next time he saw Cass Bloody Herbert.

Someone knocked at the door. 'Room Service!'

Ted's heart kicked like a mule. He'd know that faintly transatlantic voice anywhere. He rushed to the mirror and started raking his fingers through his hair. Thank God he was already dressed, she definitely wouldn't approve of his pyjamas. He puffed nervously into cupped hands. Breath-check OK. Fingernails OK. Stubble needed attention. Too fucking bad. Not exactly likely to kiss her. He pointed at himself in the mirror and repeated his mantra. 'You good-looking bastard, go out there and best the buggers!'

There was more knocking. 'Hey! Room Service!'

'C-coming!' he called breathlessly, tucking his shirt into his suit trousers, and running towards the door. Just before opening it, he looked down and groaned. No socks – and he hadn't clipped his toenails for weeks. But if he kept her waiting much longer, she might give up and go away. He'd just have to hope she wouldn't notice.

He opened the door.

Cass swept past, lobbing him half a bacon sandwich. 'There you go, pumpkin, it's a bit cold now, but I couldn't eat all of it.' She threw herself onto his bed. 'Your hotel room's much nicer than mine. Alun and I totally forgot about booking rooms, so I'm marooned back there somewhere in some really weird guesthouse. There are antler heads everywhere, and a massive tiger rug in the tiniest front room you've ever seen. It took me twenty-five minutes to walk here and I am wetter than a redneck in the bayou so can I dry out here for a bit?' She looked expectantly at him, then grimaced. 'Oh Ted, horny toenails or what? Eeeugh. Spare me.'

'Hello Ted. How've you been, Ted? Haven't seen you for a while, Ted. I've missed you *and* your horny toenails, Ted.'

'OK, so we're dealing with a major-league hangover here – right? Well, eat up that bacon sarnie while I hop in the shower – do your radiators work? can I dry out my clothes on them? – and then we'll go out for some serious OJ- and coffee-injections.' Cass looked anxious. 'Brighton does have proper coffee shops, right?

Sure it does, Cass, you snob. Ted, you haven't got anything to go to, have you?'

Ted glanced at his watch, knowing full well that he was meant to be going to a fringe meeting in half an hour. 'Nothing for a couple of hours. But how are you? How did you know where I was staying?'

'Well, I got here last night and Alun took me along to some drinks party. And there was Julian Albarn – you know, that guy who lobbies for—'

'I know Julian. So he told you? How on earth did he know?'

'I get the impression he knows everything. A major pie-fingerer that one, I'm thinking.' Cass started unbuttoning her long Nehru-style jacket, revealing only white skin underneath. In it, she looked like a severe young Maharajah. Out of it, she would look like—

'Cass!' Ted turned his head away violently, blushing, and busied himself with putting on his socks.

'Mister Prude!' teased Cass. 'Looky here, boy,' she put on a southern belle accent, 'I got me a little camisole top to save my honour,' she snapped the strap loudly to confirm this, 'so don't you go gettin' all blushed up for nothing, my little chickadee. Let me jest hang this here jacket over the radiator and I'll be out of y'alls hair now.'

Ted said nothing until she'd gone into the bathroom. So much for him being tough and prepared. What was he like?

'Julian was telling me some good gossip at the party,' she yelled over the sound of the shower. 'Apparently there's a clash tonight between the T&W union-fundraiser and Hallie's B&P New Labour pat-on-backathon. Total split between Old and New Labour. Blair's furious, apparently, although he's agreed to go to both, because he thinks that, of course, everyone will go to the one with the free champagne, not the one where most people have to pay to get in, then New Labour will be blamed for deliberately sabotaging the unions. Did you say something?'

'No,' he shouted back, hoping that his boss either couldn't hear or by now had left his hotel room next door, otherwise he was in for some serious ribbing. 'Carry on!'

'Oh. OK. Well, Hallie's now got to spend the whole day rushing round like a blue-assed fly, trying to persuade old curmudgeons like Frank Blackthorn and Alun that Mandelson isn't trying to undercut the unions. It's a mess. And all over some lousy parties. I think it's just stupid.'

The shower was turned off, and Cass emerged from the bathroom, the usual teatowel-sized hotel towel not managing to cover more than a couple of inches of long leg, rubbing the other one over her growing-out crop. Ted almost managed not to stare.

'Ohmigod, that feels so much better. I was kinda wondering if I was ever going to feel warm again. You don't have a vest I can borrow, instead of shivering all day in this dumb camisole?'

Ted looked pained. 'Do I really look like a vest-wearing bloke? No, don't answer that.' A thought suddenly occurred to him. 'Have you seen Frank yet?'

Cass paused in her towelling, and gave him a sidelong look. 'No. Why? Should I have done?'

'No, it's just that I had to get some gambling facts and figures to him before the Avalon fringe meeting this afternoon and I forgot to check where he was staying.'

'You're always giving him papers on gambling, aren't you? What has Frank Blackthorn got to do with Avalon?'

Ted raised his eyes to the ceiling. 'You're the one with the bee in her bonnet about Avalon! You tell me!'

'No, it's just weird . . .' Cass floated off into one of what Ted called her cud-chewing looks. 'You remember Mrs Harrison?'

Ted glanced at his watch. At this rate, he wasn't even going to make his second fringe meeting. 'No, I don't remember Mrs – oh, hang on a tick, she was the whingeing lottery winner, wasn't she?'

Cass glared at him. 'The lottery winner who had her privacy totally invaded by Avalon even when she refused publicity, you mean. Yeah, well, she wasn't one of Mark Boyd-Cooper's constituents in the end – she was one of Frank's.'

'Yes, they had neighbouring seats,' confirmed Ted. 'So?'

'So don't you think it somewhat strange that Boyd-Cooper was accused of being totally in Avalon's pockets and now Frank is all involved with them? It all seems a little too spooky.'

'You forget that I used to work for Frank,' Ted reminded her.

'He is as straight as a die. In fact, I reckon he's asking me for all this stuff so that he can use it against Avalon at that fringe meeting this afternoon. Come along. You'll see. Of course, then you'll have to give up your little conspiracy theory. Shame! By heck, I reckon you were in America too long, my girl – the next thing, you'll be accusing Frank of having distinguishing marks on his dick!'

Cass didn't laugh at his topical wit. She looked alarmed. 'Why wou—? Oh, I get it. Very funny.' She glowered at him. 'You think sleeping around is confined to American politics? Grow up, Ted. Get with the programme.'

'Days gone by, chuck,' he waved his hand airily. 'Days gone by. A Better Britain with Better Behaviour. That's us.'

'Right. In your dreams.' Cass looked weary. 'Now, you were looking for Frank? Because I know where Gwenny is staying, and I presume that where Gwenny is, you'll find Frank – or someone who knows where Frank is. Like Alun.' She looked searchingly at him.

'Gwenny's down here? Why?'

Cass relaxed her intense gaze and slumped into his pillows. 'How should I know? Anyway, there seem to be quite a few secretaries down here. I bumped into Annalisa Smith last night.'

'That figures,' said Ted. 'She couldn't let all these spouse-less hotel rooms go to waste, could she?' Then he stopped, horrified. What if Cass had heard the rumours about Annalisa and Wilbur? Then his comment would be construed as confirmation of Annalisa's shamelessness.

'I think Annalisa's kinda cool, actually,' said Cass absently. 'She's a party-girl, admittedly, but she's fun to goof off with. I like the way she's shaken up all those stuffy guys in the House and I bet if you ask any MP, they'll say she's the best thing they've seen since Pamella Bordes. Actually, I said we might meet up with her after the B&P party tonight, go get looped with her or something.' She grinned at him. 'Hey, you never know, you might get lucky.'

'How is it that you've been working at the House for about two and a half minutes and you know everyone, get invited everywhere, hear so much gossip? And since when do you organise my social life?' he grumbled. 'I haven't even seen you for two weeks.'

And five days and fourteen hours, he added silently. But at least she doesn't seem to know about Annalisa and Wilbur, even if I am so far down on her own list of romantic options that she's setting me up with the House bike.

Cass looked surprised. 'No way! Jeez, is it that long? Yeah, well, I've had a few things to deal with lately.'

Wilbur, thought Ted morosely. I don't want to hear any more.

'And I was kinda hoping you wouldn't mind me filling up your dancecard for you,' Cass idly knotted one of his ties round her neck, 'because I just realised last night that I have nothing to do at this conference except schmooze some guys that Alun's putting me in touch with, and now that Hallie's gone headless chicken on me, I don't have anyone to play with. I mean, I know you're here to work but Medios are just here for information-gathering, aren't they, not real work?' She looked up at him beguilingly through her eyelashes. It was a look Ted had seen Wilbur do a million times. He couldn't stand it any more.

'What about Loverboy Coolidge?' he demanded abruptly. 'Aren't you going to *play* with him?'

Cass jerked back, face like thunder. 'Wilbur? You have got to be kidding! I wouldn't cross the street to trip up that fucking jerk. The guy has got tickets on himself! How could you even think that? Jeez, give me some credit!'

Oh, be still my beating heart, thought Ted fervently, hangover suddenly gone.

'Nina! How are you, sweetie? Long time, no see. What have you been up to, you sly thing!'

'Oh, you know, getting married, going freelance—'

'That's great! Sooo exciting. I am so jealous. Look, I am sorry, darling, you know how it is round here. Guts for garters if I don't find this picture. Bye, sweetie!'

'Bye.'

'Nina Parvati! A stranger in these parts! Well! Don't you look fat and happy. Bumpkin life suits you!'

'Yes, but it's great to come up to London occasionally—'

'Don't you believe it – it seems to have rained solidly all summer. In fact, we haven't had a summer. I've got permanently prune-like feet from determinedly wearing little strappy sandals through two-foot-deep puddles. Anyway, I have to get these cuttings back to the library before four o'clock or Linda Lee Potter goes on the warpath to get them from me. Keep in touch, won't you, Nina?'

'Yes. Bye.'

'Wotcher, Nina – how're you keepin'?'

'Fine thanks, Barry. How's tricks? Taken any good pics lately?'

'Bloody awful, to tell you the truth. This bloody rain. Plagues my life, I can tell you. Oh well, gotta go. Cheers, Nina.'

'Cheers. Bye.'

'Nina darling, tell me again who you're hanging round to see?'

'Um. Well. Barbara, really, or Vicky. I thought I'd pop in and see them about some features ideas. I rang this morning and they said just to swing by any time.'

'Tom – hasn't Barbara gone to some awards lunch?'

'Yup, won't be back until five. And said she'll be too pissed to do anything constructive after that.'

'And Vicky's gone totally AWOL. Said something about a flood from the upstairs flat. Sorry, Nina, looks like you've had a wasted trip. Why don't you leave a note?'

Wearing her smart new Mary-Janes was possibly the biggest mistake she had made all day, Hallie moaned to herself, as she tottered across the Exhibition Hall, the balls of her feet more like great balls of fire. And on a day when her new crossover into public affairs was rapidly blowing up in her face, that was saying something. She now knew how Oliver North and Henry VIII's whipping boy felt – being the scapegoat for other people's cock-ups was a thankless task. At least if she had been responsible for scheduling the party and its clash with the T&W's fund-raiser, she might have known how to set in train the usual damage limitation. Give her Giuseppe models knocking themselves out while injecting heroin between their toes and she knew how to administer mouth-to-mouth air-kisses. Give her dry stone wallers who refused to smile at a photo shoot and she knew how to get them to say 'trees!' instead of 'cheese!'. But give her the task of plumbing the undercurrents between Old and New Labour and she was barely capable of a feeble doggy paddle.

She didn't even know what the targeted Labour MPs looked like. Roland, his Harry Hill-like face scrunched up in barely averted panic, had grabbed a copy of *The House Magazine*'s Who's Who issue out of his briefcase, whipped a highlighter from his suit jacket and had torn through the magazine, frenziedly circling who he considered to be more Old Labour than Blairite. Given that he seemed to have just gone for the faces that were older and grumpier than the other Labour Members, Hallie was beginning to suspect that he was as out of his depth as she was.

Now all she had to do was match the photos to the faces – out of the 23,000-strong crowd that made this the biggest Labour conference ever – without being caught doing so. Then chat to them casually, being as charming as she knew how and introducing herself as Bandwick & Parker's new bright light. Then gauge from their reaction to B&P's name whether they a) disapproved of B&P's Mandelsonian position *vis-à-vis* the Labour Party and b) knew about the clash in parties that night. If the answer to both a) and b) was yes, then – simple – she had to persuade them that B&P were lovely, benign Labour supporters and that they could easily go to both parties. In fact, B&P would be providing shuttle buses between the two different hotels (that had been Hallie's idea and had earned an almost approving look from Roland), so there didn't need to be a clash. The whole thing was a joke.

Hallie cursed Cass. She was meant to be helping her out, promising last night to enlist all her new buddies to act as sweepers for this stupid Mission:Impossible. Hallie had rung her at her guesthouse this morning, but she'd already left, which had given Hallie false hope that Cass was already on the case but she'd seen neither hide nor hair of her so far. What happened to the support of friends in a crisis? Hallie looked at her watch. It was nearly noon, less than seven hours until the party.

'Oh my Lord God,' she prayed very, very fervently. 'I know I'm not supposed to call on you for help with unworthy tasks but please, please, please – I need your help now. Just let me get through this and I'll see that you get your money's worth back again. I'll finish Alpha, worship with all my voice, and I'll do the whole tithing thing—' She paused, horrified at herself. What was she trying to do – bribe God?

But then her prayers were answered. Over the babble of exhibitors and the general crowd, Hallie heard a distinctive laugh – huck, huck, huck. It could only be Cass. By walking back on her heels, she could avert the worst of the pain from her shoes. Looking like Minnie Mouse, she hobbled swiftly in the direction of the laugh. When she got there it was to find Cass sitting, feet up on a desk at the Pools Promoters' Association stand, obviously just having a good gossip with Julian Albarn.

'Hi Hal! You look knackered, poppet, why don't you have my seat?'

For once in her life, Hallie saw red. 'You know, I don't often ask you to do something for me, Cass. That's usually your department – oh Hallie, just lend me a tenner! Oh Hallie, pick up my dry-cleaning for me, would you? Oh Hallie, take this inconvenient boy off my hands and shag him for me? Have you ever thought about giving not taking, Cass? I'm deadly serious this time – I needed Wonderwoman Herbert herself – and you've completely let me down. While you've been lounging around here with your mates,' she nodded tersely at Julian who just looked rather amused, 'I've been having eight nervous breakdowns rushing round trying to pick out Labour MPs like suspects in a lineup. Thanks for nothing.'

Cass looked at her appraisingly. 'Hey, take it easy! Who's been lounging? I'll have you know I have been using my time both wisely and well. I happened to pass a fringe meeting organised by T&W shop stewards, so I thought I'd pop in and spread the word about tonight. Sure enough, there were about thirty MPs there – well, I counted those I recognised anyway – and though I can't promise that they're totally impressed by tonight's fuck-up, at least they know about the shuttle buses between the two events. And I bought Alun off with the promise of free beers at the B&P stand for the rest of conference if he would go to the party tonight. So,' she beamed mischievously, 'did I do good or did I do good?'

Hallie felt terrible. The first time she could remember really blowing up at Cass since they were at school and she was in the wrong. How annoying was that?

'I'm sorry. I thought Alun hated Mandelson with a passion. Isn't he the last of the principled politicians? How on earth did you bribe him like that?'

'He reasons that he's not betraying any of his principles just by having a couple of beers – and I didn't say he was going to behave himself at the party.' Cass chuckled. 'He'll probably end up punching Peter Mandelson!'

'Don't worry about that,' Hallie assured her seriously. 'At least that would get us in the papers in a sympathetic light, rather than being the instruments of the unions' destruction.'

'Double-edged sword, that sort of media coverage,' Julian contributed. 'You don't want New Labour dogged by the sort of rifts that the Tories were crucified by.'

Hallie was about to snap, 'There's no such thing as bad publicity,' when she realised that she was speaking from her usual PR vantage point. Perhaps it was different in politics. 'Well, it may be a little late for that. Cass, I met your friend Wilbur Coolidge last night—'

'Wilbur was at that party?' Cass said sharply. 'Thank God I missed him. He's no friend of mine.'

'Really? He seemed to think so – he was asking all sorts of questions about you. You were right about one thing – he is absolutely drop-dead gorgeous. I'm not surprised you took up my challenge!'

'Hallie! Butt out, will you? You're so way off-beam it's almost funny. So he's playing it buddy-buddy, is he? Conniving bastard. Well, if he wants to play hardball, I can do friendly with the best of them.' Cass looked defiant.

By now Julian could sense so much juicy gossip going on, he was looking like the Cheshire Cat, eyebrows lifting wildly into his receding hairline.

'And,' Hallie went on, deciding that the only thing to do was to ignore Cass. 'He is going to do a little segment on this whole shenanigans, by sitting on the shuttle bus with his Hi-8 camera tonight, filming the to-ing and fro-ing.'

'People like Alun are going to love that,' snapped Cass. 'They'll think the whole thing was a Mandelson set-up. Don't walk into these traps, Hallie, it doesn't do our cause any good. You have to stop being so gullible, pumpkin. People like Wilbur Coolidge only care about a good story with plenty of juicy conflict. He'll just make it worse.'

'There's just no need for you to be so condescending, Lucasta Herbert.' Hallie shook her hair back like a ruffled Pekinese. 'Wilbur said that he would be able to convince the people on the shuttle bus that he's there as a sign of goodwill by B&P to prove that we're serious about trying to avert the effects of the clash. Wilbur said that you just have to flatter most politicians, especially if you do the goofily sincere American act, and you can get away with most things. And I just happen to believe him.'

'Wilbur says, Wilbur says,' Cass mocked. 'Well, I can see you're in good hands there, so I'll leave you to it. I have other things to do. Do you still want my humble help later on? No media star back-up from me, I'm afraid.'

'Of course I do, you—'

'Because I'm beginning to think that it's a good thing you've got God on your side nowadays. If I were you, I'd call him up and get him to send down a few miracles. You might need them later on.' Cass swung her legs off the desk and sauntered off into the milling crowd.

Julian whistled. 'Catfights,' he said gleefully. 'Love 'em.'

Hallie restrained a most unChristian urge to strangle the lot of them. Oh, to be back at HTB.

'Oh, the bliss of being back at home!' Nina presented her shoulders to Jerry for a massage. 'You have no idea how horrendous that was.'

'What did you expect? Them all to throw down their pens, throw open their arms, and tell you how much they've missed you?'

'Well, yes,' Nina admitted, 'I suppose I did.'

'Nin, every time I came and saw you at that place – which

luckily wasn't very often – you made me wish I hadn't. You were always too busy, too distracted, too much part of the little gang that sat at that bank of desks.'

'I know, but—'

'The *Evening Standard* is a newspaper, Nin-compoop! They've got deadlines to meet, pages to set out, people coming and going all the time.'

'All right, smart-arse, I get the message,' Nina grumbled, keeping a rein on her temper and settling back on his chest to look up at him. 'You know, I thought you'd be pleased that I had such a frustrating time, given that you didn't want me to go in the first place.'

'Nah,' he smiled, blue eyes crossing because their faces were so close together, 'don't want my little wife feeling downhearted, do I?'

Nina sat up straight and turned round. 'What did you call me? Your little wife? Well, you can fuck off and die.'

'Nina! Joke!'

'You can't let it rest for a second, can you? You have to put me down at every opportunity. Oh, fuck it. This little wife has to go and cook supper.'

Once in the kitchen, Nina leant against the cool door of the fridge. She knew she was a powder keg at the moment. She knew she had totally overreacted. But how could she explain to Jerry that almost every word he said annoyed her beyond belief? That even the way he ate, his knife and fork permanently hovering near his mouth, drove her absolutely fucking mad? That her reaction to his snoring was threatening to push her off the rails, it was so out of proportion to the crime?

This is marriage, she reminded herself for the fiftieth time that week. This is just one of those bad phases that every marriage goes through. It's an adjustment period, that's all. Two strong-willed, independent people suddenly being forced to share their lives twenty-four hours a day. There are bound to be teething problems. As ever, the repetition of these placebo proverbs calmed and comforted her. You're not unique, she told herself firmly, don't keep thinking you are.

The new problem was money. It was seven months now since Jerry had left the Army with his semi-precious handshake, and in that time, neither of them had earned more than a few quid. His Internet prescriptions business wasn't off the ground yet: all the targeted investors agreed that it was a great idea, but were still cavilling about the scale of their investment, the licensing rights to the site and other such obstacles. Nina was slowly getting together some features work but had just had to settle a whopping tax bill, for which she blamed Jerry.

'Don't bother with an expensive accountant,' he had dismissed, 'there's a website with all sorts of hints about what you can write off. You can do it yourself.'

So she had. The taxman, when he had stopped laughing, had promptly charged a grand more than she'd ever paid before, even though she hadn't earned as much, putting their joint account badly in the red and both of them in black moods.

Having no money was no new experience for Nina – years balancing the scraps and leftovers of a lowly journalist's income with her constant attempts at a media lifestyle had left her with a pecuniary nonchalance. In her book, as long as you could pay the rent and the basic living bills, anything left over should be treated as a bonus and spent with gusto. But Jerry, insulated from financial realities by seven years in the Army, was like a newborn babe in the world of the hard-up, wincing and wailing at each unexpected twist and turn. His parents had paid off the cottage's mortgage as a wedding present, so with their costs confined to the real basics of Babaji and the household bills, Nina was relaxed enough. Jerry, on the other hand, was getting altogether too serious about the situation. 'We have to start pulling our belts in,' he would announce with monotonous regularity, insisting that they had to put money away against all the rainy days they were going to come across.

'Why?' Nina had asked. 'Why put money away now – when we're not doing so well? Why not spend it now to cheer ourselves up during this bad time? We can save later – although I've never seen the big deal about saving for the sake of saving. What have we got to save for? If we want to go on holiday – we go for broke for a month or two, then jump in the car, cut a deal with one of the ferry companies and swing round Europe on a road-trip. It's just not a big deal.'

But it was useless. Babaji showed more signs of having

listened to her than Jerry. Suddenly she was getting lectures about leaving lights on, about buying groceries from Mrs Amin in the village instead of slogging to Waitrose in Marlborough, about having baths that were too deep, until Nina thought she would scream.

'And how much are we saving because of this?' she flung at him one day. 'A couple of quid? Get some fucking perspective on this, Jerry. In my humble experience, people who think that if you look after the pennies, the pounds will look after themselves – these people are only ever going to be thinking about those pennies because they're never going to make any pounds!'

Then that morning, while staring at her notes on her interview with Annabel Croft – including the part when her pen had slipped off the page, she had been that bored – she had heard police sirens wailing up towards the main road. They were such a familiar strand in the tapestry of London sound that it had taken her a moment or two to realise that this was the first time she had heard them since moving to the country. The realisation was enough to give her a strong pang of homesickness, enough to go through to the sitting room where Jerry was staring just as hopelessly at his computer screen, and announce that she needed to go to London, and he could scream all he like about the inconvenience and the expense.

Going up to London had also been a desperate attempt to get some work and to get away from the cottage before she really said something she regretted. The trouble was, that after her humiliating lack of reception at the *Evening Standard*, all she had wanted to do was cry on Cass's and Hallie's shoulders. When she remembered that they were both off at the Labour Conference, she had just felt even sorrier for herself. They were off having a great time and, as ever, she was out of the swing of things. But above all, she hated the fact that they were now her only frame of reference outside her marriage. She had been out of touch with all her old uni and media cronies for too long to be able just to ring them up on the spur of the moment – the urban scene they were in seemed to demand fixing diary details three weeks beforehand just to grab a quick drink.

So she had sat in Pret à Manger in Ken High Street tube

station, drinking espresso after espresso, unable to summon up the cash or the enthusiasm to go shopping, missing the faithfully loving presence of Babaji and conscious of feeling more alone than ever before in her life.

Worst of all, she couldn't even imagine a day when things would ever get better.

'If I hear "Things can only get Better" one more blinking time, I think I'm going to explode. That and "We're Comin' Home, We're Comin', Labour's Comin' Home," – every stinking shuttle journey!' Hallie slumped beside Wilbur as the minibus trawled along the seafront for what felt like the fiftieth time. Behind them, any fears about po-faced Old Labour die-hards were being dissipated by a fragrantly beery wave of bonhomie.

'Hey, you've done a good job,' said Wilbur. 'And so have I. Time to kick back and have a beer. Come on, I think you can give it a rest now.'

'Try and keep me away. But it's champagne for me, not beer, I am definitely New Labour in that respect.'

As they walked into the B&P party, Hallie turned to Wilbur. 'I've just got to sort out a couple of things. Do you need anything?'

'No, I'm off-duty now. I'll be fine,' he grinned lazily.

'Cass is here somewhere and was looking forward to seeing you.' Hallie repressed a smile. Cass would be furious. 'She's taller than most people here so you should have no trouble spotting her.'

'Cass is looking forward to seeing me?' He smiled again, ironically this time. 'In need of a punchbag, is she? Catch you later, Hallie.' And he sauntered off.

Hallie slumped, all perkiness wiped immediately off her face. It was so exhausting being constantly upbeat. Now she just needed to find a quiet space, change from her rather sensible Patrick Cox loafers back into her high-heeled Mary Janes, and stare into the middle distance for a minute or two before braving the scorn of Roland.

She could just hear him now – 'Did you have to get the Members quite so drunk to get them to come here, Hallie? We do want them to remember this evening, you know? If they wake up tomorrow with a thumping hangover, they're hardly going to thank B&P, are they?' Sigh. Jiggle change in pockets. Smooth beard. 'There's no need to be so friendly that you end up pouring drinks down their necks, Hallie. Perhaps it wasn't the job for a woman after all.'

Hallie gritted her teeth. It didn't help that she thought her new boss so repulsive he made her skin crawl. If she had to watch those little flakes of red raw skin underneath Roland's beard slough off and float down like tiny noisome snowflakes one more time, she would throw up. He obviously thought she was some empty-headed fashion mannequin – often speaking slowly, in words of few syllables, in his thin bank manager's voice. Never chock-full of confidence anyway, Hallie was beginning to doubt her own ability in this political quagmire. It was her own fault for thinking that, in the euphoria of a new era, her job as PR liaison with the public affairs teams of both B&P and Mandelson's crack squad from Millbank would be a caretaker role. Everyone loved Blair & Co, so it was just her job to keep it that way. But she hadn't bargained for all this underlying tension between the Old Guard and the New.

'It's Hallie, isn't it?' She looked up to see Julian Albarn peering down at her. 'What are you doing hiding behind the coat rack? Come and join the party – you've done a smashing job, sweetie. Everyone's having a ball!'

Hallie smiled at him. Repulsive Roland could wait.

Julian led her over to a raucous corner of the room.

'Hallie!' Cass had clearly forgotten all about their fight. 'Toptastic party, poppet. Here, have some champagne.'

As ever, Cass failed to introduce Hallie to anyone else. It was, Hallie decided, one of her more irritating flaws. But she looked spectacular – managing to carry off wearing high-heeled knee-high boots and a miniskirt together – if totally inappropriate. Next to everyone else's neat little two-pieces, Cass's long-sleeved, skinny-ribbed black and red striped top made her look like a bosomy Dennis the Menace. Hallie looked ruefully down at her own carefully chosen outfit, a powder-blue bouclé number, now rumpled from all the shuttle bus journeys and stained where one Welsh MP had stumbled while carrying a pint of beer, and sighed.

If she were to wear Cass's combination, she would look like a cross between a dwarfish Miss Whiplash and a rugby player.

'Well Cass is obviously not going to do the honours – where was she dragged up? – so I will have to,' said Julian. He swept her a bow. 'Hallie, may I introduce you to everyone? This is Ted Austin, who works for Medios.' Ah, so this was the faithful Ted-with-a-crush. He was sweet-looking. 'And this is Annalisa Smith.' This girl put even Cass in the shade. She hardly gave Hallie a glance. 'And her boss, Chris Phillips, Member for Shadwell.' An MP? He hardly looked old enough to get into a pub. He was also clearly in love with Annalisa, kept looking at her like a rabbit caught in her headlights. 'Wilbur Coolidge—'

'Yes, I know Wilbur,' Hallie smiled. Out of the dimness of the shuttle bus, he looked as incongruous as Cass, with his dusty black V-neck T-shirt moulding itself lovingly to his chunky torso. He was certainly no sartorial trailblazer, thought Hallie, thinking back to the finery of Reuben's three-piece tailored suits, but it all contributed to his rumpled sex appeal.

Julian's eyes lit up. 'Of course you do. Silly me. Oh, I can't be bothered with much more of this—' he gestured at the others. 'Lachlan McIvor, the lovely Warren Jameson,' and a list of other names that Hallie couldn't begin to take in.

'Anyway,' said Annalisa impatiently, ignoring Hallie's arrival. 'Cass darling, listen to this.' She put her long-taloned hand on Cass's arm. '*Harpers & Queen* might be doing a feature on "New Labour, New Lovelies" and they rang me up to see if I would like to take part—' she paused.

'Naturally,' supplied Julian.

Annalisa glared at an oblivious Wilbur. 'And the first person I thought of to do it with me was you, Cass! What do you think? It would be ever such a laugh! They would make us look even more dropdead gorgeous than we already are and we could have a scream doing it.'

'You have got to be kidding,' Cass said violently. 'Why on earth would I want to parade myself on some godawful photo shoot? I'm just a part-time researcher for Chrissakes! Why don't they feature some MPs?'

'Because they're all too ugly,' dismissed Annalisa. 'Oh! Except for you, sweetie.' She patted Chris Phillips on the arm, then giggled. 'Oh, I forgot, you're a man! Come on Cass! Say yes, gorgeous! Say yes, sexy! Say yes, beautiful!'

'Just say no,' quipped Ted. 'Not that you're not all of the above,' he assured an increasingly bemused-looking Cass.

Can no-one but me see that Annalisa is coked off her brain, thought Hallie disapprovingly? And it's almost as if she's flirting with Cass. What a silly cow.

'Hallie?'

She turned to see Roland looming over her. She gulped. 'Y-yes?'

'Peter wants to see you in two minutes. He's over by the bar. Don't keep him waiting.' He walked away again, his shiny suit reflecting back the overhead lights.

Hallie went white.

'What a charmer,' said Wilbur idly, then he looked closer at her. 'Are you OK?'

'This is it,' Hallie whispered. 'I'm going to get sacked. And by Peter Mandelson himself. Oh well, I've had a nice life.'

'Bollocks,' said Cass. 'You're not going to get fired. Don't be so quick to think the worst, Hal, that's just your bastard of a boss putting the fear of God into you.' She giggled. 'Oops, was that blaspheming? Gee, I'm sorry.'

Hallie ignored her.

'Don't be nervous,' Wilbur assured her. 'Just go find a mirror.'

'A mirror? Why? Do I look that bad?'

'Relax, Hallie, you look just great. No, go find a mirror. It's like a mantra thing. Tim Roth did this in *Reservoir Dogs*, just as he was about to go and mingle undercover with the bad guys. You point your finger at yourself, with thumb raised as if your hand is a gun.' Wilbur demonstrated, lounging as well as any gangster. 'Stare at yourself intently and say, "You are totally fucking cool . . . they don't suspect a thing." Then you'll ace 'em.'

'You are totally cool . . . they don't suspect a thing,' repeated Hallie.

'No, "You are totally *fucking* cool—"'

'Forget it, Wilbur,' Cass interrupted sharply. 'Swearing is against Hallie's principles. God doesn't like it, does he?' she asked Hallie.

'Hey, nice to see someone round here *has* principles,' drawled Wilbur, smiling at Cass.

Hallie ignored all this. She had just fallen in love again.

Cass was feeling uncharacteristically confused. Wilbur seemed to have forgotten all about their last encounter, and the harsh words they had exchanged, which was good, but which left her feeling uncertain about him. She wasn't used to feeling uncertain about men, and she didn't like it. Having been perfectly behaved and his usual laidback self, he now seemed more interested in talking to Hallie, who'd been glowing like a belisha beacon ever since her chat with Mandelson.

As Cass had told her, Hallie hadn't been fired. Quite the opposite. Mandelson had wanted to thank her personally for averting the crisis of the clash. It was just a goddamn party, Cass had thought unfairly, irritated that her friend was being, as usual, a drama queen. What a lousy job to have, nursemaiding fretful spindoctors and never, never being allowed to show anything but a bright and polished mask.

Cass laughed to herself humourlessly. It was not a job she could hold down for long: it had taken at least three days of speaking monosyllabically to a bewildered Alun before she had calmed down about him and Gwenny. She had given herself a real good talking-to, told herself that it was really none of her business, that she owed him some loyalty and that if he wanted to commit political suicide, she wasn't going to be the one handing him the bottle of pills.

In truth her change of attitude was more to do with the fact that she liked him so goddamn much. In the days before Conference, he had been more like a giddy kid than a politician, waving invites as they flooded into the office, choosing which ones to attend by making paper aeroplanes out of the covering letters. The ones that flew into the trash-can at the end of the room were the lucky winners. Until, that was, a disapproving Mags and Cass retrieved them and forced him to assess them according to his ministerial portfolio. He had then redeemed himself by ringing all the RSVP numbers personally and insisting that they added Cass's name to all the lists.

Mags had raised an impressed eyebrow at Cass. 'Doeshn't do that for everyone. Soft-hearted bashtard, though. Remember that.' It being four o'clock in the afternoon, she was almost down to the last of her tinned vodka and tonics.

Cass had smiled noncommittally and left it at that. It was hard to imagine being in a job where such petty dissembling came with the territory, like in public relations.

Now Hallie was being all peppy and bouncy, flirting with Wilbur and employing the usual weapons of coquettish dimples, sucked-in cheeks and a couple of extra shirt buttons undone to show her cleavage. They were tactics Cass had seen Hallie use a million times – giving her that copy of *The Rules* had backfired, just giving Hallie fuel for her fire. They worked, she couldn't deny her that but for how long? How long before the real Hallie would be allowed to show her face?

It was tactics like these, which revolved around what women believed men wanted, Cass thought savagely, that she was trying to deal with in her gender workshops. If she couldn't make headway with her best friend – how could she hope to make a living out of such advice?

'Cass, sweetie,' purred a voice in her ear, a warm, dry hand pressing insistently on her shoulder. She turned around to see Annalisa, dark eyes glittering wickedly. 'Let's blow this gaff and go and have some real fun.'

Annalisa, on the other hand, chuckled Cass inwardly, was the opposite of a *Rules* girl: she was a true *Code* girl – a straightforward party girl, chockful of *cojones*.

'Fun? Like what?' asked Ted, coming up to them.

'Dunno. Cass, what do you fancy?'

'Isn't there some big deal going on in the Grand? We could drink them dry. I'm so broke that I can't really afford to go anywhere we might have to pay for our own liquor.'

'And how *is* the view from that high moral platform of yours, Cass?' said Wilbur, overhearing.

'Is it hard to be so flawless, Wilbur?' she riposted airily. 'Can I come and worship at the altar of your perfection sometime? Or do I have to reserve space?' She looked pointedly at Hallie.

'I'll let you know if there's a cancellation,' he smiled, clearly enjoying this. 'But I—'

'Oh belt up, Wilbur, none of us are interested,' snapped Annalisa. 'Fuck me, you're so arrogant, it's incredible.'

Ted looked surprised, Cass noticed.

'Lachlan? Warren? Minnie? Oi, you lot, are you coming to the Grand with us?' Annalisa effortlessly ignored Hallie. 'Wilbur, I'm sure you've got bigger fish to fry, so I won't ask you.'

'Annalisa, honey, in my arrogance I have indeed arranged to meet some friends over at the Metro. It's a shame I can't come with you guys, but you know how it is.' He smiled infuriatingly.

'Hallie?' Cass broke in. 'Do you want to come with us?'

'I'm not sure. I may have to stay and help clear out the last few here – hang on a tick,' Hallie swung back to look up at Wilbur. 'Did you say the Metro? That's my hotel. If you could wait two minutes while I check with Roland that it's OK I go home, I'll walk back with you.'

She really wants Wilbur, Cass suddenly realised with a start. That would be right. He'll break her heart. That's why she wants him.

'OK, who's staying in seafront hotels?' Annalisa returned, triumphantly carrying three bottles of champagne. 'We've run out of coke, we're getting chucked out of here, and nothing else is open, so I propose, comrades, that we adjourn this meeting and repair to the nearest hotel room.'

'Seconded,' responded Ted, trying very hard to get his tongue round the words. 'My hotel, just down road. Can't remember name, sure'll come back to me.'

'Thirded,' added Cass unsteadily. 'Jeez Louise, I haven't been this bombed since graduate school. I never would have thought I'd be this wired at a goddamn political conference – I'm meant to have given coke up, for God's sake. I guess I'm going to need oxygen tanks to stand. It seems a hell of a long way up.'

She held out her hand to Ted but before he could focus on it enough to pull her up, Annalisa was there, giving him the champagne bottles and putting her arm round Cass's waist.

'Comrade Austin's room, it is then,' said Annalisa. 'I'll just put Chris,' she patted her comatose boss who was slumped, smiling blissfully, in the seat where she had been sitting on his lap, 'in a taxi.' She paused. 'I won't need to bribe the taxi, will I? No, no-one would believe he was an MP, so they won't think of telling the press about his state.'

Annalisa was beginning to sound bloody sober, thought Ted. They were a select bunch now, down to five – six, if you included the hapless Phillips – and Annalisa was without doubt their ringleader. Cass, himself, a tiny quiet girl from BT called Minnie and a strident woman called Roz, who had had them all in fits of laughter at – was it the fourth or fifth party after the one at the Grand? A raggle-taggle bunch, they were now the best and the drunkest of pals, Annalisa egging them on all the time.

Often, in mid-swig, Ted had looked up to find Annalisa's dark glittering gaze resting on Cass. If I didn't know better, he thought fuzzily, I could swear she was after Cass. Maybe she's trying to get to me through Cass. Hey, sweetheart, he wanted to say, you don't need to try that hard. Honest. I may be in love with Cass but I'm not exactly going to say no to a quick shag with the famous Annalisa Smith. After all, he didn't want to feel left out.

Walking into the hotel would have been a fine moment for any red-blooded male. I almost wish Wilbur were here to see this, thought Ted, four good-looking women on my arm. Him and his mantra, that was so much cooler than Ted's grandad's effort. Him and his effortless pulling ability. Yankee bastard. Well, he wasn't going home with Annalisa or Cass tonight. He, Edward Albert Austin, was. With both. So stick that in your pipe and smoke it, Coolidge.

Once through the door, Ted's hotel room seemed much smaller than before.

'Cass, darling? Champagne?' Annalisa popped one of the bottles with a flourish.

'You may have to give it me intravenously. I'm bombed.' Cass flopped down across the bed. Ted fell down on his stomach beside her. Roz and the BT girl followed, giggling.

Annalisa climbed up onto the bed and stood amongst them, laughing. 'Open wide, Roz,' she teased. 'Champers coming down. Minnie! Cass! Ted! Brace yourselves!'

Before Ted could turn himself round properly, he had what

was the most expensive cold shower of his life. He gasped, inhaled some champagne and choked, compounding the error by laughing until he thought his sides were split. Within seconds, they were a mess – the four of them holding up open mouths like hungry birds in the nest, Annalisa capering around like a rain god, as she poured the entire bottle down their throats – all of them giggling like maniacs.

When the last drop had spattered down, Annalisa joined them flat on the bed, wriggling her way in between Roz and Cass. 'Lie in a circle,' she ordered them, 'heads in the middle. Now we're going to play spin the bottle. Strictly sexual forfeits.' She span the empty champagne bottle on her hand. 'Minnie – it's you! OK, you have to kiss Ted.'

Bloody grand being the only bloke. Bloody heck am I going to get lucky if this is the forfeit every time, thought Ted fuzzily as he pressed his lips against a tremulously tittering Minnie's mouth. Who said twenty-eight was too old to play spin the bottle?

'No, come on,' commanded Annalisa sharply. 'Tongues too. Tell you what, let's try an experiment. Let's see if we can all kiss each other at the same time?'

The rest of them nodded solemnly as if this was the most natural idea in the world.

'What, just put our heads together and see what happens?' asked Roz. 'Why the fuck not?' She stared at Annalisa. 'I'm game.'

'I'm game,' repeated Minnie nervously.

'I'm game,' added Ted, dimly aware of some strange under-currents. 'Cass?' He nudged her.

'Huh? Yeah, OK. Count me in.'

Someone had turned the lights out. Perhaps they'd never been turned on. This was a silly game, Ted thought with the last shreds of his coherence, as they laughingly all tried to engage mouths at the same time. Our heads are too big. We need wedge-shaped foreheads, like segments on a pie-chart. Thoughts of the briefing he'd been working on for Frank popped into his head, with all its different pie-charts. Even as he was trying to get his lips to meet Roz's on the other side of the circle, a gusty chuckle bubbled out. If his Medios mates could only see him now – one bloke and four girls, all trying to kiss each other. They would kill him, they'd be so jealous.

He stopped suddenly. All trying to kiss each other? What was going on? This wasn't spin the bottle. As if in a dream, he saw Annalisa turn her head and kiss Roz squarely on the mouth. In the half-light, he could see Cass staring too. He nudged her but she didn't turn round. She just kept on staring.

Ted began to feel a little out of his depth.

'Thank you, thank you, thank you. You have no idea how close I came to just letting her get on with it. Is that very lazy of me?'

'No, you were just looking rather hypnotised there for a moment. What was she saying to you?' Hallie smiled sympathetically, trying to disguise the fact that she'd nearly decked the woman who'd been chatting Wilbur up for the last half an hour.

'Oh, I'll spare you the grisly details. Older women sure have wide-ranging imaginations, though. Even if they have slaved long and faithfully for the good of the Party, they've definitely had time for a little extra-curricular activity and learning on the side.' Wilbur grinned. 'Are all Party Conferences as debauched as this? I just think if this happened back home, the lawyers would be getting seriously rich on sexual harassment cases!' He looked more closely at her, his brow furrowing as he looked earnestly at her through hooded lashes.

Hallie could suddenly see what Cass meant by his Clooney look. It was devastating. She couldn't help her sudden indrawn breath. 'I don't know. It's my first Conference too, and probably my last.'

'I'm sorry, am I shocking you? I know this isn't really your scene. Cass says you've caught religion in a big way.'

Bitch, thought Hallie. Sorry God. Didn't mean it. 'Yes,' she said stiffly, 'although she didn't need to make it sound so much like a disease. I've just started going to church again after a few years of not going. That's all.'

'Sorry, that was my bad choice of words, not hers. You don't need to be ashamed of your beliefs, Hallie. Holy Trinity Brompton, isn't it?'

'Yes,' she said defiantly. 'It's the most fantastic church. And the people who go there are fabulous – they're just great, so normal, from all walks of life, company directors, secretaries, teachers – the whole spectrum. You know, I've been going to a few fringe meetings since I got here on Saturday on all sorts of subjects to do with the Church and church reform. I'm not sure why I did, actually. I think, in a way, it was to bring me back down to earth. Even a year ago I would've walked in, would've looked around, thought, what a load of beardy nutters spouting oversincere gobbledegook and walked straight out again. But I didn't. For once, I actually listened, instead of making that sort of instant judgement, and almost against my will, I found myself staying, even joining in a bit. They're really not so laughable, you know.'

Wilbur smiled lazily. 'I remember when I first started at the Oklahoma State Ballet. I was like the cocky East Coast kid – privileged background, three years being told I was brilliant at *Juilliard* – and there I was, dancing *corps de ballet* with these hicks in Oklahoma. I turned up there with the attitude that this was just a stepping stone for me, a necessary apprenticeship I could turn my back on as soon as I made the big time, and I really didn't need to make an effort to be liked by these people. So, before each performance, we used to have a prayer meeting, where everyone would hold hands and a different person each time would say a prayer out loud, all stuff to do with the show, people's families, injuries, that sort of thing. You can imagine it – there I was from this repressed, undemonstrative family background, a cynical New Yorker – I couldn't believe it. I used to be the one hanging back, arms folded. But, you know, my time there became very hard, and it only took a few weeks for me to realise that being surrounded by such strong, simple faith was better medicine than anything else. I may not be a practising Christian now, but I'll never forget those days.'

He was silent for a moment.

Hallie looked at him, marvelling. Cass was wrong. He wasn't too good to be true. He was just better than anyone either of them had ever come across before. In her heart of hearts,

Hallie suspected that Cass was not as adamant towards Wilbur's charm as she would have everyone believe. Therefore, to seduce him herself would be breaking the loyalty code the three of them had had since the turbulent days of teenage boyfriend-swapping.

But then again, Cass hadn't exactly been keeping to the letter of the loyalty law recently with her constant put-downs, teasing about HTB and inexplicable moods.

Hallie put the pang of conscience into cold storage.

'Are you going to join your friends, after all, or would you like to have some coffee with me?' She smiled invitingly at him, knowing full well that the hotel coffee bar was now closed.

Oh, the beauties of room service.

Every woman is curious about what it would be like to make out with another woman, Cass told herself, staring at the ceiling. What could be better than being made love to by someone who knows exactly what a woman wants because she too is a woman?

Whenever she, Nina and Hallie had had those 'What would you do if . . . ?' conversations, none of them had ever ruled out the idea of a little experimental lesbianism. They had then always rushed to qualify their daring openmindedness by adding that, of course, they wouldn't do anything with anyone they knew, so that they wouldn't have to see them afterwards. Then they'd spoilt the last vestige of liberality by making a bet that the first to 'dip their lipstick' as Nina had snickeringly put it, would scoop a thirty quid jackpot.

But until now nothing had ever tempted Cass to put her mouth where her money was – one party she had been to in New York had just made her laugh out loud, which hadn't made her any friends. She would never forget her previously well-adjusted wimmin's lecturer friend, Rhona, standing in the middle of the apartment wearing a floor-length, fur-trimmed, see-through black negligee, staring at Cass as if daring all comers (in her dreams, Cass had thought uncharitably) singing along to 'In the Navy' at the top of her hoarse, New Jersey voice, and flourishing the hem of her gown like a matador. Except that in this case, Rhona wasn't fighting off bulls, but bull dykes, who were there in their short-haired, tattooed, clichéd abundance. Cass had been amused but disappointed, kind of hoping that lesbians weren't so cleanly divided into the two extremes of aggressive whoa!men or the fragile flowers that Rhona was always trying to seduce.

If she was strictly honest with herself, Cass had to admit that she should have seen it coming. All night she had been aware of Annalisa's attention, her hand on her shoulder, arm, knee, the whispered comments in her ear, the unflinching holding of her gaze, the conspiratorial laughter for her ears only. If Annalisa had been a man, Cass wouldn't just have realised that she was being seduced immediately, she would have condemned the seduction as being hackneyed and unimaginative. But because it was coming from a woman, it had felt at first like being picked first for the netball team – here was a woman who had most of Parliament eating out of whatever body part she would let them near, but no! she wanted to spend time with l'il ole Cass. She wanted to be Cass's pal, and Cass felt both flattered and cool.

So when she had finally first suspected Annalisa's motives, her reaction had been not hostile but rather pleased. If she was going to be hit on by a woman, she might as well start at the top. Here was someone who was both gorgeous and self-avowedly voracious when it came to men. If she knew what she wanted – and let's face it, if she didn't by now, all those men were nothing more than a wasted opportunity – then surely she would know how to pass that on to another woman. Yes, thought Cass, as she intercepted another lingering look from Annalisa, I can roll with this, as it were. This is just one more of life's boxes to be ticked. Something for my biographers to grapple with and over-analyse.

Which had brought her, ever more titillated, to that strange moment when Annalisa had Pied Piperishly led them, skipping and giggling, to attempt that group kiss and had then pounced . . . but not on Cass after all, but on Roz. Up until then, Cass had imagined that any plans Annalisa had in mind involved just the two of them. Suddenly the agenda had changed. Roz and Minnie seemed to get the programme remarkably quickly which made Cass feel even more disorientated. As for poor Ted . . . at one point, Cass had sneaked a sidelong look, to see him wrestling between confused and lustful, with his tongue hanging out so far he looked like a dopey cartoon character, complete with thought bubble saying 'Wow! Guy's Greatest Fantasy! In Bed with Four Girls! Wow!'.

Then Annalisa had suddenly stopped kissing Roz and had turned to Cass, her perfect Cupid's bow mouth curving up into a knowing smile. 'Jealous?' she had whispered softly, stroking the side of her face with silky fingers and making Cass shiver with she-knew-not-what sensations. 'Don't be, sweetie.'

And then she kissed her.

Soft, soft lips, was Cass's first thought. Soft, soft lips which knew how to kiss. And kiss. And kiss. And hands that slid effortlessly under her top and round her back, snapping open her bra in one easy movement. And lips that wandered leisurely up her jawline to her ear, pausing there to murmur little sounds of desire, not manly moans but minute puffs of lust. And hair. So much hair. Fine, scented hair which crept in everywhere, softly whipping her face with silken lashes. And velvety soft, fragrant skin as familiar as her own. No lumps and bumps, just a curvy reflection of a body she felt she knew as well as she knew her own.

And then, more hands, more lips, more hair, more skin. Laughter had stilled to a silence punctuated only by those tiny sounds of arousal as everyone joined in. At first Cass had closed her eyes out of tipsy embarrassment, but then she opened them, even in her drunkenness wanting to record these strange events. They were all still half-dressed, but seeing Minnie kissing Roz as Roz caressed Annalisa's breasts as Annalisa kissed Cass as Cass stroked Ted's face, Cass could hardly believe her own eyes. As ever in moments of high drama, she began to think involuntarily of headlines: 'It's Party-time for Young New Labour', or 'Get Labour, Get Laid' or 'Five-in-a-Bed Sex Romp: Ex-parliamentary candidate admits having a hand in it'.

And that was what was wrong. The longer it all went on, the soberer Cass became. The soberer she became, the stranger she realised the situation was. But most disappointingly of all, as she came to, she realised there was little likelihood of her coming too. For all her talk, for all those shivery feelings as she'd realised what Annalisa was up to, for all that, in the end there was little genuine arousal. The more she was kissed, stroked and fondled, the more she realised what was missing: a man. It was as if the whole performance was just a warm-up act and that the main performer still needed to have a dick. So much for that. What a disappointment. She wasn't bisexual – she was only ever going to have half the fun Annalisa was able to have. She felt cheated, but there it was. She needed a man.

But of course there was a man there. Good, sweet Ted who tentatively placed his hand on Cass's arm, nervously inched forward to kiss her and then, when her eyes opened to see him only inches away, he flinched away as if she'd burnt him with her disinterested gaze. At that moment, Cass would have given anything to have been able to find him sexually attractive. But even in the middle of what was apparently turning into an orgy, she couldn't do that to a friend. She knew that if she'd slept with him, she wouldn't just have treated him like the bitch she was to her other unwanted sexual encounters, but she would also have tarred him with the memory of this strange situation, and been unable to be friends with him afterwards. Just like in that original pact she had made with Hallie and Nina.

Now, having run all these thoughts through her suddenly-racing brain, Cass lost interest in the whole scene as rapidly as things started to hot up between Roz, Annalisa and Minnie. For all her earlier fervour, Annalisa could obviously sense Cass's lack of passion. So she hardly demurred when Cass pulled gently away, and disengaged herself from the press of bodies. Ted too had been gradually sidelined, leaving him isolated on the other side of the bed. From either side, they watched; Cass half-fascinated, half-repelled, as clothes were peeled off and bodies manoeuvred between them. Suddenly, in the growing light of dawn, she caught Ted's eye. For a second, they stared warily at each other, then both of them looked down at the pornographic movie being enacted between them, then up again at each other. In the same moment, both were attacked by a crippling attack of the giggles, Cass having to shove her fist in her mouth to stop the gusts of mirth escaping from her. The next time she was able to look at Ted she saw him doing a thumbs-up over his shoulder at the door. She nodded, and quietly they both rolled out of bed, found what clothes they'd lost, slipped on their boots, grabbed coats and crept out of the hotel room.

They walked in silence to the lift and rode down without catching each other's eye. Walking through the hotel lobby, Cass felt as though they had signs above their heads: 'Recent Orgy-Goers – Video Available.' It was only when they emerged from the hotel's revolving door into the crisp, biting air of an October dawn that they dared look at each other.

'Lovely morning for it,' said Ted carefully. 'Glad to see the rain's cleared up. Shall we walk along the beach?'

'Yes,' replied Cass, feeling the need to grin biting into her jaw muscles. 'Hey, did you know they film *Baywatch* at this time of day? Imagine having to look all buff and suntanned at this time of the morning? Still, I guess California is a better prospect than Brighton in October.'

They crossed the road onto the beach.

'Yes. Funny old world. Strange what some people will get up to.' Ted scuffed the shingle with one foot, popping each bubble on a limb of seaweed.

There was a short silence.

'Ohmigod, ohmigod, ohmigod! Space-trip to the Planet Bizarro!' Cass exploded, her face splitting in half she was grinning so hard. 'What was that all about? What were we doing? Were we drugged? I mean, beyond the obvious. Did she drug us with some groin-altering hallucinogenic?' She started to lean on Ted like a drunken old ho, which was appropriate at least.

Ted too was laughing so hard, he could barely stand up himself, let alone support her. 'Jesus fucking Christ. When I caught your eye, I thought I was going to spontaneously combust.'

'Me too, me too,' gasped Cass. 'Oh Jeeee-sus, I am sooo embarrassed. It was like collective madness, wasn't it? I only recovered my sanity about half-way through and then all I could think of were the headlines!'

They were like school-kids who'd just completed a double dare, gabbling in spurts of nervous tension, a cacophony of catharsis.

'Yeah, it was crazy. All I could think was if only those Neanderthal bastards that used to beat me up at school, could see me now – they would be so fucking jealous.'

Cass pulled a face. 'I guess. But jealous of what? That was what I thought was so totally weird. It was so goddamn boring, wasn't it?'

'Depends on your boredom threshold,' Ted choked. 'It certainly beat the Ted Austin Average Night Out with the Lads – and will damn well stick longer in the memory banks!'

'I know, but all that hanging about, waiting for your turn in the line. Call me selfish, but I like to be the centre of attention. After a while I was, like, "Yeah, yeah, yeah, cut to the action. This is all very nice, but when are the guys getting here?" I guess I'm just not cut out to be a—' Cass caught Ted's hangdog expression and reddened. 'Oh Ted, you know what I mean. When I say, "guys", I don't mean that you're not, well—'

'Shut it, Cass,' said Ted heavily.

'Look, it was all wrong place, wrong time,' stammered Cass. 'That's not to say that one day ...' She hated herself for offering him false hope but she had to do something to get out of this hole.

'Yeah, well, perhaps not,' he grinned manfully. 'I mean, it would be strange – just the two of us, eh? Bit too much room! Bit bloody draughty!'

'Oh Ted!' Cass took a relieved swipe at him. 'But hang on a cotton-pickin' minute – aren't we meant to be morally outraged by all this? What we did is so far off the scale of acceptable behaviour, it's a joke! I mean, we were in an, in an—'

'Go on, you can say it!'

'Well, it was an – an –' Cass glared at a sniggering Ted. 'Goddammit, it was an orgy!'

Somehow just saying the word out loud made it seem even worse. Neither of them spoke for a moment, both gazing at their feet as they scuffed through the shingle.

'And they're still hard at it in my hotel room,' said a rueful Ted eventually, glancing back at his hotel. 'Let's hope they scarper before the cleaners arrive!'

Cass chuckled weakly. 'Did you book an alarm call?'

'No, thank Christ. I've just got to hope and pray that no-one from Medios decides to ring at sparrow's fart.'

Cass stopped and pointed ahead. 'Look, someone's doing tai ch'i on the beach – how cool!'

They walked a bit further and Ted squinted forwards. 'Hang on, that's Wilbur, isn't it?'

'Is it?' Cass's heart sank. If Wilbur saw her and Ted walking along the beach together at six o'clock in the morning, he was bound to jump to the classic misunderstanding. She wasn't sure she could cope with any more crossed wires between her and the guy. Perhaps they could just creep round the back of him.

Ted was looking at her intently. 'Perhaps we could just sneak past him without him seeing us – if it bothers you? Do you really hate him that much then?'

'Hate him? I don't hate him at all. He's a nice guy, when he's not being totally pleased with himself. I just don't want to be one of the scalps hanging off his tomahawk. Come on, let's be friendly,' Cass said lightly. 'Just not a word about you-know-what.'

'What, no boasting?' mugged Ted. 'So, what's our story? Been out on the piss all night – couldn't face going back to our hotel rooms – because yours is miles away, and you didn't trust me not to make a move if we went back to mine?'

Cass shot him a look.

'No, it's OK,' he protested. 'Hey, it rings true!'

'Ted, you have got to stop putting yourself down,' Cass started when she saw Wilbur suddenly collapse onto the sand. 'What the—? Wilbur?' She ran forward to find Wilbur lying on his back, his arms over his face, moaning quietly. She kneeled down beside him. 'Shit! Wilbur? Are you OK?'

Wilbur lowered his arms from his face. 'Cass? What the hell are you doing here?' he spluttered weakly.

Cass ignored this friendly greeting, looking anxiously into his face. He looked bad. Really bad. So pale underneath his suntan that she felt she could hold his head up to the light and see through it, the bags under his eyes deep enough to travel around the world with, the furrows in his forehead deepened as if in pain. 'Are you OK? Look, do you need an ambulance? Ted, call an ambulance!' Ted had just reached them.

Wilbur squinted past Cass at Ted. 'Ted? You too? Hey, let's party!'

Cass looked at him more closely. 'Hang on, you're just drunk.' She turned to Ted. 'Forget the ambulance.'

Wilbur stretched luxuriously, like a cat. 'Oh, the bliss of being allowed to do serious damage to your body!' He wagged a lazy finger at Cass. 'Not drunk, my sweet, but in an ambivalent state between loaded and hungover. I thought tai ch'i might tide me over the bad parts but all the blood seems to have left my body and gone straight to my head. Wanna join me on the sand?' He smiled guilelessly at her, almost cross-eyed in his efforts to focus on her.

'You need coffee, buster,' snapped Cass, hauling him to his feet. 'Ted, grab the other arm.'

'So what are you folks doing here at this time?' said Wilbur amiably, allowing them to lead him up the beach towards the centre of town.

'Same as you, mate,' said Ted, 'walking off a hangover. Cass's room is halfway to London and she refused to come back to mine just in case I pounced on her.'

Wilbur's eyebrows went up. 'Oh really? Same here. I had to avoid a predatory female. Hey, are we fussy or what, Cass? I mean, Ted here is a lovely guy. You two would make a lovely couple.'

'Enough with the matchmaking, thank you Wilbur,' snarled Cass. 'Haven't noticed you being exactly fussy, buddy.'

Wilbur smirked. 'Don't believe everything you hear, Cass honey.'

'Children, children,' reproved Ted, feeling like the kindergarten teacher in a playground scrap.

'I love hotels, you know,' Wilbur mused suddenly. 'For the first time since I came to this backwoods of a country I was able to drink through the night. Not excessively, just, you know, having a good time with my pals, shooting the breeze, playing some pool, not having to worry about – what do you call it – Final Orders? Last Rites? – whatever it's called. Hey, I love this Conference gig. I love the Labour Party. I love Brighton.'

He shook off their supporting hands, and skipped in front of them, facing them and walking backwards. 'In fact, you know, I feel great!' He turned to the seafront buildings. 'Brighton! I love you! England! I love you! Cass! I love you!'

Cass rolled her eyes.

'No, I do. You may be fucked-up beyond belief, but you're

bright and funny and you don't take any shit. And Ted! I love you too! I love you guys!'

Cass looked sidelong at Ted and sighed. 'Fruit-looped.'

'Am I hell!' Pulling off his leather coat and leaving it where it fell, without further ado, Wilbur ran ahead and hurled himself along the beach in a series of flip-flaps, somersaults and cart-wheels. Cass and Ted stopped in their tracks, dumbfounded.

'Ta-daa!' Wilbur struck an extravagant pose fifty yards away and launched into a wide circle of *grand jeté* leaps, legs almost horizontal as he floated around them. He finished with a complicated-looking, twisting flip-flap and landed steadily on both feet, eyeball-to-eyeball with an astounded Cass, breathing heavily but otherwise unscathed.

'And you didn't believe I was a ballet dancer, huh?' He smiled, thoroughly pleased with himself, sauntered over to his coat, shook the sand off it, put it on with a flourish, cleaned the brim of an imaginary fedora and tipped Cass a Bogart wink. 'Shall we call it a truce, little lady?'

Cass raised her arms in a helpless shrug. 'Wilbur, I can't compete with that. You win. Just don't go getting any other ideas. Let's sign the peace-treaty over breakfast. Ted can be the referee.'

Whoopee-fucking-doos, thought Ted irritably, now beginning to feel his hangover.

Well, that was Conference for you. Four days down, three to go. He wondered what could possibly be still to come.

9

e-mail to ss747@pipex.com
subject: The need to get out more often

I switched on the laptop today and read, as usual,
the suggested Tip of the Day. As you know, these are
usually handy little hints about word-processing,
the sort of things that make you say, 'Well, I never!
Fancy that!'. But not today: today's Tip of the Day
read, 'Plaid shirts and striped pants rarely make a
positive fashion statement.'

It struck me that my life has reached a pretty pass
when even the bloody computer not only knows that I am
turning into a walking advertisement for Oxfam, but
knows that I'm sad enough to read its bloody fashion
advice, take it to heart, and actually look down at
what I'm wearing, just to check. Then I laughed out
loud at my madness and sadness, and realised that
it was the first time I had laughed for days. I
occasionally hear Jerry laugh as he watches the
infernal television but I hadn't laughed myself,
not for days. I half expected him to run in and ask
me what the matter was, but he didn't.

It strikes me that I need to get out more often. The highlight of our week so far was a visit by a hoover salesman. When he rang up to offer us a *two hour* demonstration and free cleaning of all carpets, curtains, beds and sofas, I felt like a Fifties housewife, as if I should be removing my housecoat and patting my hair giddily into its headscarf. Then he confirmed the impresson by insisting that my husband had to be present throughout the demonstration. 'Why?' said I, dangerously, 'is he the only one who can understand the technical stuff?' The salesman just tittered politely. 'No, no, it's just that your husband won't understand how you can pay so much for a vacuum cleaner unless he sees for himself just how marvellous it is and just how many horrors are lurking undetected in your beds.' Well, I was sold then and there. In this cottage Jerry snores like the kraaken waking, you see, and I thought that if these undetected horrors could be removed, I might be able to get some sleep. Well, he came and we have been able to talk about little else for days. You could have flown to Mars with this thing, I promise you, it had that many attachments and twiddly bits. Watching him hoover our bed – not something we slovenly housekeepers do on a regular basis – brought us both out in horrified giggles. If we'd had a spare five hundred nicker lying around, let me tell you, we'd have signed up like a flash.

If you'd like a free house-cleaning – and two hours procrastination from your book – just let me know and I'll pass him on to you. Just make sure you can cope with the excitement. It was touch and go in the Kellman household for a while.

'Cass?'
  'Mmm?'

'Can I ask you a question?'

'Uh-oh.'

'Why "uh-oh"? It doesn't have to be a bad question.'

'It's three o'clock in the morning and we've been together since ten last night. If you preamble it with permission to ask it, then it is either a question I don't want to answer, that I dare not answer, or that I can't answer. Either way, you're not expecting to like the answer. Simple Psych 101, Hal.'

They were stretched out on a sofa each, in Hallie's flat, watching telly after a clubbing night at the Cross. For Hallie, it had been a controlled experiment, to prove to herself and to Cass that HTB hadn't robbed her of the ability to have fun. She never had drunk much, had done all her experimenting with drugs in her early twenties and had actually never gone clubbing to pick up men, so the Church hadn't changed anything in that respect. Now they were watching a Steve McQueen film, both straining to hear the great man at a volume deemed acceptable by a foul-tempered Beth, whom they had woken up by shouting at each other in their usual post-club deafness.

'OK, Cleverclogs. Bad question coming up. You truly don't like Wilbur, do you?'

'That's it? That's your question?' Cass yawned mightily. 'No, actually, I do like Wilbur. I like him a lot.'

Damn damn damn. 'Oh. Oh. Actually that wasn't *the* question.'

Cass woke up a bit, and looked at her sharply. 'Oh, now I get it. We're talking *like*, not like? OK, I don't want to jump into bed with him, if that's what you want to hear – and nor should you, if you want my advice. He is trouble, girl, plain and simple. Look at him, for Chrissakes, he's not only gorgeous, he's a nice guy, which is a very dangerous combination. He's also thirty-five years old – so I think he's probably worked out that he has fatal charm by now. Listen, the guy probably doesn't even mean to but he's broken so many hearts round Westminster that they're thinking of setting up a Coolidge Memorial next to the War Memorial in Whitehall. Now I don't want to be laying down wreaths for you, Hal, so quit lining up to be the next sacrificial lamb.'

'Wilbur says that his reputation is grossly overstated,' retorted Hallie, ignoring the fact that he hadn't said it to her – she had just overheard him defending himself to an MP one night during Conference.

Cass raised an eyebrow. 'He did?'

'Yeah, so thanks for the advice, sweetie, but I'm a big girl, you know. I just wanted to check for myself that you didn't harbour any ambitions in that direction because obviously I wouldn't start anything if I thought you wanted him.' Hallie conveniently forgot that she had already tried once.

Cass grimaced. 'Jeez, we sound like a teen-mag photo-story.' She flipped a careless hand. 'Take him, eat him up, and spit him out for all I care. Hey, if anyone can get through to the guy, I'd put my ten cents' worth on you, hon,' she added kindly, then spoilt it by going on, 'and if he does break your heart, you know I'm here for you.'

If she was honest with herself, Hallie knew that whatever she felt, Cass would have stood back and let Hallie get on with it. Cass never, ever fought for men: it wasn't part of her code. But Hallie's conscience was clear now, a little belatedly perhaps, but better late than never.

'Then again, you've always got your faith to carry you through,' teased Cass. 'With God on your side, yours will be a truly holy and blessed love!'

'Mmmm,' said Hallie absently, planning what she would wear for the date she had already fixed up with Wilbur for tomorrow night.

'Wilbur Coolidge.'

'Wilbur! Hi! Where are you?'

'Stuck in traffic somewhere in East London. Who is this?'

'Hallie! Hallie Templeton.'

'Oh, hi there. What's up?'

'There's been a slight change of plan about tonight, I'm afraid. Ted and Lachlan both have to work on this feasibility study for Blair's new Conference pledges. Medios are having brainstorming sessions all weekend apparently. And Cass did her usual double-booking and can't now get out of her other commitment. So I'm afraid it's down to the two of us.'

'Oh, that's too bad – shall we take a raincheck and reassemble another day?'

Hallie was just as determinedly nonchalant. 'We could. But my old boss here at B&P had tickets for the new play by Patrick Marber – did you ever see *Dealer's Choice*? – and she can't go, so she offered both of them to me.' She paused delicately. 'It's no big deal, but it seems a shame to waste them.'

And Coolidge gets slammed into the wall – he's going down, thought Wilbur resignedly. 'I agree, and I really should check out this famous British theatre scene, I guess.'

'Fantastic. Drinks beforehand at Soho House?'

'Nah, I'd better not risk it, just in case I'm still shooting. I'll meet you there at—?'

'It starts at seven-thirty at the Royal Court.'

'Shall we aim for seven-fifteen then? I'll be the one wearing no carnation at all,' he joked feebly.

'Fabulous. See you there. Sorry about the others not being able to make it – their loss, I suppose. Byee.' Hallie rang off.

Wilbur stared out of the cab window for a few thoughtful moments. Then he dug into his billfold for the scrap of paper that held all his useful phone numbers.

'Hello. Alun Blythe's office.'

'Is this the lovely Mags?'

'Who wants to know?'

'Mags, I'm sorry, it's Wilbur Coolidge, that presumptuous bastard from CNN.'

Instantly her tone softened. 'Mr Coolidge, are you trying to flirt with me?'

'Would I be so obvious? Of course I am.'

'Water off a duck's back, love – a bloody old and crispy duck. Now who do you really want – Alun, me or—' her tone cooled, 'Cass?'

'All three of you. My place. Half an hour. All tabloids will be there.' At last he'd made her laugh. 'No, is Cass there? I just have to check something out with her.'

Mags sniffed. 'Yes, she's loafing about here somewhere, getting under everyone's feet,' Wilbur could hear a muffled squawk of protest greet this remark. 'Here she is.'

'Hey, dude,' said Cass cheerfully. Then she paused, and said almost coldly, 'What do you want?'

'Easy, turbo! That is some Jekyll and Hyde impression you've got there,' said Wilbur dryly. 'And the ink hardly dry on our peace treaty. Shame on you.'

Cass laughed reluctantly. 'No, I'm just getting killer looks from Obergruppenführer O'Sullivan for hogging her phone all day.'

'Trying to untangle your busy social life, I guess?' Wilbur probed. 'Having double-booked tonight?'

She sounded puzzled. 'I have? No, I think I'm just going to that guy Warren Jameson's for dinner. Why, do you know something I don't?'

Gotcha! thought Wilbur. 'Well, just something Ha—'

'Hallie!' yelped Cass suddenly. 'Of course, I was meant to be going out with Hallie and – and—'

'Me,' supplied Wilbur helpfully. 'And Ted. And Lachie. And Lachie's girlfriend. Quite a gang, who have suddenly cancelled leaving just Hallie and me going to the theatre.'

'Well, what's wrong with that?' said a totally uninterested-sounding Cass. 'You like Hallie, don't you? Or is she not up to the Coolidge standard of date?'

'Whoa, mama!' said a stung Wilbur. 'Wrong track!' He pulled himself together. 'I'm delighted, as it happens. Hallie's a great girl.'

'Exactly.' Cass sighed. 'Now if I could just get you to describe us twenty-nine-year-olds as women not girls, I really could begin to talk to you again. I have to go, Wilbur. Catch you later.'

Wilbur looked at his mobile perplexedly and shook it as if not entirely convinced that it worked properly.

Cass frowned down at the phone. This was going to be tough. Remembering to be cool and aloof towards Wilbur when all she had wanted was to settle in for a really good talk, like that morning after the Night We Don't Remember (as she and Ted now referred to it) was hard enough. But when Hallie fucked things up by involving Cass in her devious little seductions without clearing the story with Cass first – now that was going too far. It was one thing stepping aside to avoid an ungraceful clash, but why did Cass have to embarrass herself by lying into the bargain?

'Cass, unless you're communing with the dead through that phone, some of us actually have work to do. Don't you have some Budget letters to write?'

Alun's secretary was capable of looking scarily like one of Macbeth's witches, Cass thought irrepressibly, as Mags loomed over her fiercely.

'Oh, Mags honey, let's go get a drink,' she suggested impulsively, 'it would cheer the both of us up.'

Mags drew back as if she'd been stung. 'What did you say?'

'I suppose it is kinda early,' amended Cass, glancing at the clock on the computer screen. 'Sun not being over yardarms or yardlegs or whatever it's meant to be.'

'How dare you?' spluttered Mags. 'Are you implying that I'm some sort of drunk?'

Cass looked nervously up at her. 'Look, I'm just going to get out of your hair here. You're right, Alun's left a ton of work for me upst—'

'You cocky little bitch. Honestly, you bloody Americans – you come over with your fancy talk and your oily charm and barge in here without so much as a by-your-leave. Then you have the fucking cheek to tell us what we should or shouldn't do.'

'Mags,' Cass looked round helplessly for some support, but everyone else was doing a good job of melding molecularly with their keyboards. 'For a start, I am as English as you are, I just lived in the States for most of my life. And second, I can assure you, the last thing I would want to do is offend you in any way.' She shrugged her shoulders and held up the palms of her hands in a 'why me?' gesture. 'What can I say? There are clearly some issues here that perhaps we should addr—'

'Oh, spare me the bloody psychobabble,' Mags snapped, 'don't think you can condescend to me, you snotty little whippersnapper. I may just be a secretary but you and I both know that your loyalty to Alun is not worth the paper your contract's written on, so when push comes to shove, I know where he'll be—'

'And where is that?'

Both Cass and Mags span round to see Alun leaning against the doorjamb.

'This is what I like to see,' he murmured wearily, 'my faithful team, standing shoulder to shoulder against the lubricious mauling by a hostile world. Who needs the Prince of Darkness's crack squad when I've got my own little rebellious guerillas here in the jungles of Dean's Yard?'

'Alun, I demand that you have some serious words with this little miss,' declared Mags imperiously, 'she—'

'Mags, belt up,' he cut in. 'I fully intend to have serious words. You,' he pointed at Cass, 'grab your coat. We're going for an early lunch. Mags, get us a table at the Atrium. Make sure we're outside, on one of those ground-level tables, not trapped in some gloomy corner.' Both of them gaped at him. 'Come on! Snap to it! Mags, tell Pimple-Chops over at the Ministry that I'm re-scheduling him for one-thirty sharp.'

Cass and Alun walked briskly through the back-gate of Dean's Yard to cut through to Millbank via Little College Street.

'Alun, I'm sorry if—'

'Save it for when we're sitting down,' he cut her off brusquely.

Fuck, thought Cass, there goes my Easy Street. Nice while it lasted.

'Now then,' he said when they were sitting down. 'What was all that about?'

'Well, I—'

'Actually, don't tell me. I can guess. Mags had a few too many last night and is feeling a bit fragile today. You breeze in – the embodiment of youth, beauty and energy – and, knowingly or unknowingly, you right royally piss her off. Bingo! Arma-bloody-geddon.' He looked at her questioningly.

Cass hesitated. Perhaps he hadn't heard the veiled reference to her knowing about him and Gwenny. 'Yes. I guess so. It suddenly blew up into this big fight. But I was using her phone and kind of kidding around so I can't really blame her for losing the plot a little.'

'So what was that comment about loyalty?'

Cass caught her breath. This was it. She was busted. 'L-loyalty?'

Alun gazed at her sadly, his face falling into slack lines. 'You're stammering, Cass. An experienced public speaker like you never stammers.'

He paused for a moment. 'Of course, I for one don't actually doubt your loyalty because I believe that you've known something about me and a certain nameless other person, for a few weeks now and you haven't told anyone about it. Have you?'

Wiping Wilbur from her mind for the second time that morning, Cass looked him firmly in the eye. 'No. I haven't told anyone. I didn't think it was any of my business.' She struggled with her curiosity. 'But how did you know that I knew?'

'That last day at Conference, when you were running round like a headless chicken at seven-thirty in the morning, trying to find me for that *TV-AM* interview, you left me a frantic message on my mobile. Did you know that one of your more endearing habits is that you talk out loud when you're sorting out a mess?'

Cass shook her head. 'That must be a new thing.'

'Well, just before you put the phone down after leaving that message, you mused out loud. "Where now?" you asked yourself. "Of course! Gwenny's room!" Trouble was, that also got recorded onto my message. Yet you didn't try me there? Why not?'

She quailed. 'I calculated that your being untroubled by knowing that I knew your little secret outweighed some chickenfeed interview that you were, in all probability, just late for and on your way to by then. Which you were, as it turned out.'

'Good judgement. You're right. I'd much rather you didn't know, but there we are. We must have been careless at one moment. Something to do with that Guildford seminar, I suspect, but there you go. Let's not talk about it again. You're right, it's my business and her business and as long as it's kept that way, no-one gets hurt. Do I make myself clear?'

'Crystal.' Cass rallied herself. 'Are you going to fire me now?'

He laughed. 'Sack the best researcher I've had in years? No, I'm going to buy you lunch, and you're going to run me through the details of your world domination plan again! How does that sound?'

Cass breathed a sigh of relief. This morning was turning out to have more swings and roundabouts than Disneyland.

'Zoran?' The head waiter turned his head enquiringly towards them. Alun did a well-practised bill-writing gesture, then turned back to Cass.

'Now, Frank says you're working much too hard, says you're putting him to shame in that office of ours, there from dawn til dusk, that sort of thing.'

Cass looked shamefaced. 'Oh God, I've been caught red-handed. Well, I have been working on all the stuff we agreed I should do – I must show you the drafts on all the Budget letters and I've roughed out a few thoughts for that Chamber of Commerce speech. But, to be honest, I've kind of had time on my hands so I've been putting in the extra hours on my dissertation. I guess I thought you wouldn't mind, as long as I was there to answer the phone and all.'

Alun leaned back in his chair and rubbed his paunch contentedly. 'Mind? Why should I mind? I usually have researchers who just sit around like lumps of clay, or who sit on the phone gossiping for hours, then go off and have four-hour lunches.'

'Well, I do that too!' Cass laughed.

'Yes, with Ted Austin, I hear.' He cocked an eyebrow at her. 'Nice lad, Ted, if a bit bloody progressive for me. No sense of his socialist roots, that boy, he's been listening to the likes of,' he looked round exaggeratedly, and whispered, 'the PM's PM, if you catch my drift, for so long he's lost his independent thought. Oh, when I think of the old days when Ted was working for Frank – the three of us used to have some right ding-dongs down the pub.'

Cass instantly felt dull and excluded. Why didn't she get invited to the pub for some political fisticuffs with the lads? Some things didn't change. Red-blooded men, even if they were in the red corner of politics, still ran an exclusive club – no goddamn women allowed within six yards of a pint of beer and 'a right dingdong'. Any remorse she had about not telling Alun about Wilbur quickly dissipated.

Then, as if her imagination had summoned him up, in walked

Wilbur with a dark-haired woman and two kids, just as the bill arrived on their table. Cass started guiltily.

Alun emptied his pockets onto the table. 'Where the bloody heck is my credit card?' Exasperated, he began to filter through the bundle of receipts, scribbled notes to himself, green Central Lobby request slips and other detritus.

'Alun, when are you going to get a wallet like everyone else?'

He smiled up at her and gestured at his wreck of a suit. 'And spoil the lines of my suit? No way, pet. Aha! Here it is. There you go, Zoran, usual tip. Be quick, will you? I have to be in Whitehall in five minutes.'

'Alun, we ordered coffee!' protested Cass, noticing that Wilbur's companion was both beautiful and strangely familiar.

'You stay, love.' Alun signed the credit card slip quickly but Zoran had been summoned away. 'Just bring back the receipt, will you? Now relax about Mags – she'll have forgotten all about your little spat by the time you get back. Just creep a touch softly around her for an hour or two and you'll be back to being blue-eyed girl. Look, I have to run.'

'Bye.' As Alun shambled across the marble floor of the atrium and up the stairs to the ground floor gallery level, Cass noticed that he'd left the contents of his pockets behind. 'Alun! Wait!' She scooped most of them up and ran after him, calling up the stairs.

He looked back badtemperedly. 'Oh, just leave that crap on my desk, Cass. I can't stop!'

Walking back to her table would take her right past Wilbur's. Mindful of her duties to Hallie, Cass hesitated, trying to work out where she'd seen his companion before. Suddenly it came to her and she frowned. What was the best way out of this situation? The best way for all concerned to come out with the right impressions?

'Hey, Wilbur, sorted out your social life yet, amigo?' she started as she stopped by their table, then she turned to his lunch guest. 'Now, unless Wilbur's going through an unusually narcissistic phase of his always eventful love-life, you must be his sister. Either that or he's started dating women who look like his sister, which, while I wouldn't put it past him, would be totally tragic. The family likeness is incredible.'

'Except that I'm beautiful and look years younger than I really am, and he's a played-out old wreck who looks fifty if he's a day,' grinned the dark-eyed, dark-haired woman, speaking with the most pukka American accent Cass had ever heard. 'Yes, I'm his sister: my name's Abigail Bingham. I'm visiting with Wilbur for a few days. How do you do?'

'Hi, I'm Cass.' She gave Wilbur a warning glance so that he wouldn't elaborate by adding her surname. 'Wilbur and I are both insignificant pawns together in the chessgame of Westminster.'

'Hey, I don't think we even make it onto the chessboard, do we?' He smiled. 'A better analogy would be that we're insignificant prawns in the ocean of British politics.'

Cass and Abigail groaned.

'Hey, don't knock it, babe.' Cass settled herself comfortably on the arm of his chair without asking. 'Being small is good. That way the sharks can't be bothered with us. But on the day of reckoning,' she grinned wickedly, 'the shellfish will arise in a great wave and engulf the killer whales.'

'Uncle Wow,' piped up one of the boys, 'I'm bored. Can I have a coke?'

Cass looked down at him and had to restrain herself from gasping. He was Wilbur in the miniature, down to the sweeping eyelashes and determined chin, but without the lines and marks of his uncle's thirty-five years. She looked up and caught Abigail looking at her curiously. Careful now, Cass, she warned herself.

'They're as like as peas in a pod.' She gestured between Wilbur and the little boy, grinning at the latter. 'Except that your Uncle Wilbur is a very old and wrinkly pea.' The little boy giggled. 'What's your name?'

Predictably enough, he went totally shy on her, doing his best to wriggle underneath the table.

'Yeah, very selfish genes us Coolidges have, I'm afraid,' said Abigail. 'My husband feels quite left out of the equation. This is Alec and this little one is Calvin, named after Wilbur, but without the burden of the Presidential connotations.'

Cass choked with laughter, waggling her hand at Wilbur. 'Your real name is Calvin Coolidge? No way!'

'Way,' he said.

'Well, your parents had a sense of humour, that's for sure! No wonder you went for the nickname option. So when are you going to be giving Clinton a run for his money? No, that can't be right. You surely must be a Democrat? So will it be Coolidge versus Dole for that Millennial Presidency?!'

'Yeah, yeah, go ahead, mock the afflicted,' he grinned back at her. 'Just 'cause you're going to rule the world, you think that gives you the right to sneer at us mere mortals. Why, you snob, Ms—'

'Don't you call me a snob, you WASPy dropout,' Cass interrupted quickly before Wilbur blurted out her name and Abigail put two and two together and came up with the John Connection. 'This is the guy,' she appealed to Abigail, 'who complained at Conference about the calibre of women who were hitting on him! Can you believe the arrogance of this guy?'

'Yes,' smiled Abigail.

'Here were faithful Party workers, slaving away thanklessly throughout the eighteen years of the Tory Dark Ages, who have ruined their eyesight proof-reading a million Labour campaign mailshots, spent their last few pennies on—'

'Cass, just get to the point.'

'And finally, they think they're allowed to have a little fun at Conference. Fun which includes a harmless flirtation with this,' she pointed scornfully at Wilbur, 'good-looking and unworthy lunk. This man whose camera hasn't been the only thing of his that has been rolling around the corridors of power—'

'Hey!' bridled Wilbur. 'I'm feeling litigious today, babe, and just remember that there are kids here.'

'But does he condescend to a little gentle sweet-talking of Betty and her friend Iris? Does he hell! I mean, heck! No, he gets himself rescued by his latest conquest, hides behind her skirts, retreats under fire, complaining all the while about these poor women's voraciousness, their bloodthirstiness. This brother of yours is just a spoilt kid, Abigail.'

'Tell her something she doesn't know,' sighed Wilbur. 'I used to threaten her with the worst sort of emotional torture if she – and all her most attractive friends – didn't come watch me dance. That way I hoped ballet would gather some kind of social cachet, even for us male dancers.'

'The most sickening thing, you know,' said Abigail to Cass, 'was that he succeeded. Never has junior ballet in DC reached the dizzy heights it did then.'

'Uncle Wow? You were a dancer?' asked little Calvin, wrinkling his nose. 'Sort of like Michael Jackson?'

'Sort of,' Wilbur assured him with a straight face. 'Just without the glove. Don't you remember me dancing for you when I lived with you in Washington?'

His nephew shook his head, lost interest and went back to his coke and his colouring book.

'Why Uncle Wow?' asked Cass, knowing that she should go back to her cooling coffee and let them get on with their meal, but somehow too intrigued by this incarnation of Wilbur Coolidge, Family Man, to wrest herself away.

For the first time since she'd known him, Wilbur looked almost embarrassed. 'I used to babysit all the time for Abigail and Bill during the day when I was working nights at the cable station in DC. Trouble was, I had no clue what to do or say to kids, so I would just fool around with them all day – dancing round the living room, *en pointe*, pirouettes, somersaults, all that stuff – and every time I caught their eyes, these huge, dark, impassive eyes, I would feel the need to offer some commentary, so I would strike a pose and say, "Wow!" Anytime they said anything or pointed to something, I would say "Wow!" because I couldn't understand or decipher what they'd said or pointed to. Basically, whatever happened, I just thought it safer to sail the "Wow!" course and inevitably it stuck – them naturally thinking that I was some strange Neanderthal creature that could only say its own name.'

'Yeah, well, that's great. I must get back to the office now.' Cass got up abruptly. 'I have battles to fight with some strange Neanderthal creatures back in Dean's Yard. It was great to meet you, Abigail. Wilbur, have fun with Hallie tonight,' she wagged a threatening finger at him, 'and look after her, otherwise you'll have me to reckon with. Bye, Alec and Calvin – you have a good lunch.'

Thoroughly repelled by her coagulating coffee, Cass swept all Alun's scraps of paper into her rucksack, and strode out, knowing that she was being rude but without meeting a surprised-looking Wilbur or Abigail in the eye.

Uncle Wow, indeed.

'So you can see, while I can flirt and even play the field to some extent, I have this damnable arrangement hanging over me that I haven't yet been able to get out of. It wouldn't be so difficult if Vanessa weren't the totally perfect Washington bride – my whole family just thinks she's so damn great – but how can you break an engagement off because you think they're too perfect?'

'Can't you just tell her that you don't love her?' Hallie was beginning to feel incredulous.

'Don't you think I've tried?' Wilbur threw his hands up in the air. 'She just says that's OK, that marriages founded on mutual respect survive much better than those conceived in heady passion and love.' He intercepted Hallie's Paddington Bear stare. 'And, yes, she does talk like that. It's tough to fight back on that plane, let me tell you.'

'But – but—' Hallie spluttered, 'there must be something—'

'Believe me, I've tried everything. That's really why I came to England in the first place, because I thought that removing myself from her – knowing that she couldn't bear to leave the East Coast – was the only answer. I still think that, but it's going to take a little time.' He looked down sorrowfully at his tensely clasped hands. 'And in the meantime, it just wouldn't be fair to get involved with anyone else. I may be a bastard but, God help me, I'm not that much of a bastard. So that's that.'

He looked back up at her disingenuously. 'Gee, I'm sorry, I've really been going on about my own problems, haven't I? Let's change the record, shall we?'

'Let's,' said Hallie with more vehemence than she had quite intended.

So that's that, she thought savagely, glancing at her watch. Not counting the three hours of the play – two hours and fifty-five minutes of which he had slept through quite unabashed – this had to be her most abortive date yet. For a start, he'd tried to wriggle out of dinner afterwards, but she was ready for that, saying she had to do research on one of Yen's competitors. Then they'd hardly got into the first sushi roll before he was asking her if he could cry on her shoulder. Oh yes indeedy, she had thought gleefully, you can cry on my shoulder anytime. Then she'd had to listen to him talk about this Vanessa creature for the next forty minutes. In her misery, Hallie had eaten all the sushi – Wilbur not having drawn breath since they sat down – and was now feeling well and truly sick. You can fool us for a while with this raw fish gig, her insides were telling her, but don't take the mick.

She could just picture Cass's face when she told her about this latest humiliation. Well, there was a simple answer to that dilemma. She wouldn't tell her.

'And then he made it all the worse by being utterly charming for the rest of dinner, paying for the whole thing, seeing me home in the taxi, and kissing me goodbye like any well-trained first date.'

'Tongue?' he asked, leaning over and swiping the last of her won ton.

'Tongue? No. As I said, well-trained.' Hallie looked at him reprovingly, and sat back in her chair, laden to the gills with Chinese food. This week's forays into the capital's oriental restaurants were playing havoc with her new *Marie Claire* diet.

He smiled wickedly. 'That's no first date tactic. Don't you remember our first date? I snogged the living daylights out of you. Half an hour of good lipwork I put in on that doorstep. No, it's the second date when you go for the tongueless lip-kiss. That completely confuses them.'

'But you didn't do that to me on our second date,' Hallie pointed out reasonably. 'You slept with me on our second date.'

He pointed a chopstick triumphantly at her. 'And therein lay the seeds of our destruction! If you'd been less delicious and I'd been able to hold out for the correct second date tactic, then who knows where we might have ended up?'

Hallie made a *moue* at him. 'I like to think I would have finally realised what a calculating creep you were. Anyway, are you sure you should be spilling these male secrets? Now that you've told me, aren't you going to have to kill me?'

'No, what doesn't kill you makes you stronger, as my good mate Nietzsche used to say on those interminable nights down the pub. And, my little Hallie, we need to make you very strong so that you can resist getting into tangles like this one.' He nodded wisely at her.

'The tangle that I'm in with you?' she challenged. 'Or the one I'm trying to get into with Wilbur?'

'Quite the little riposter today, aren't we? Seriously, for a minute – you don't perhaps think that it's maybe a bit incestuous, this whole thing with Dilbert.'

'Wilbur!'

'Whatever his name is. Whether you believe the Fiancée-Pining-in-America line or not, the fact remains that he's made it pretty clear that you're not going to get much of a look-in with him, so is it worth pressing the point and maybe alienating Cass?' He held up a hand as she opened her mouth to protest. 'No, little one, hear me out for a second. You think that secretly, she has the hots for this bloke?'

Hallie nodded.

'Yet you know that she would never stop you going out with whatshisname, because that's not her style?'

Hallie nodded.

'You don't think you're being a bit petty? Doing some pointscoring of your own? That Dilbert himself isn't just a tiny bit irrelevant to the whole equation? Why persist with him when you're on a hiding to nothing? You'll just get hurt yourself, when the original point seems to be to hurt Cass.'

'Not hurt Cass. I wouldn't do that. I'm just sick of Annie always getting her Gun. Ever since she came back from the States, she's been fairly unbearable – selfish, self-absorbed, man-hating, totally burying herself in her new political friends at the expense of her old, pre-States mates – yet old or new, they still throw themselves at her ungrateful feet. I even tried praying for her at a home prayer meeting the other day. The other members in the group suggested that whether she realises it or not, she might be a parasite on my good nature, and I sometimes think they may be right.'

He pulled a face. 'Doesn't sound very Christian.'

'Parasite is a strong word out of context – they were relating it to this Bible quote. Can't quite remember what it was. I'll look it up when I get home.'

'You're really into this religion scene, aren't you?'

'Yes, of course I am. You know that. I thought you understood all that the last time we met.'

'Is that why you won't come home with me this afternoon? I don't have to be at the hospital until ten tonight.' He stroked up the sensitive insides of her arms with his soft surgeon's hands.

Hallie shivered and nearly gave in. 'Sweetie, it's already three o'clock now and you know what I'm like about my Saturdays. It's my only shopping day. Now that's a religion that could give my Christianity a run for its money!'

He looked broodingly at her for a moment then shrugged. 'No matter, I did say I might meet Helen later on.'

Helen. This was a new name. 'Helen? Have I heard about Helen?'

'No, she's this new Health Trust Manager at the hospital. I'm not sure I like her much actually – she's very tall and rather strident – but she asked me out to dinner last week, and the least I could barter her down to was tea this afternoon. She was certainly persistent.'

'Poor you.' Poor Helen, more like. She clearly had no idea how to handle him. Hallie dismissed her from her mind. 'But don't think you can seduce me away from my shopping by playing on my sympathy.' She put index finger and thumb together on each hand and moved the right pair in a sawing motion over the left pair. 'This is the world's smallest violin.'

'Fine. Leave me to the tender mercies of some NHS Valkyrie. See if I care.' He grinned at her. 'I shall think of you while I'm giving her the first date treatment.'

Oh God, you'd better be grateful for this sacrifice, Hallie prayed firmly. She comforted herself with the thought of those new handbags in the Bill Amberg shop. If God and shopping combined weren't enough to distract her from her shameful and self-destructive lust for the man sitting opposite, then she was in deeper trouble than she'd thought.

'OK, OK, maybe, just maybe you're right. Maybe I am in deeper trouble than I'd thought. As you said, what good does that do me?'

Abigail paused in mid-lather of Alec's head, and looked at her brother thoughtfully. 'I'd like to gloat about the biter being bit, but without some sign of encouragement from her, you'll go off of her pretty quick. And the signals were more than clear there. There is no way on earth that she regards you in a romantic light. No woman who has the hots for you could be that buddy-buddy with you. You struck out there, bro.'

'It couldn't be some sort of sexual sparring?' he said hopefully. 'Being feisty to hide her true feelings?'

Abigail just had to give him that look she had been giving him for the last thirty-five years.

'No, you're right, I'm clutching at straws here. She didn't even fall for the Uncle Wow story, wasn't one tiny bit softened up by that one.' Wilbur tugged at the short front tufts of his steely-tinged black hair in frustration.

'Shame about that, since it's about the only true story in your repertoire. I can't believe you dragged the old Vanessa Defence out of the closet for that girl last night. I thought you'd retired that story long ago.'

'But I like Hallie so I had to find a way of letting her down gently. Vanessa's the best way of doing that. It's one of those ridiculous stories that are so unbelievable they almost have to be true.' Wilbur sprang up, suddenly electrified. 'That's it! Cass isn't going for me because Hallie's warned her off me. Cass would never fight for a guy, it just wouldn't be her. That's it!'

His sister looked sceptical. 'Believe in a sister's intuition, Wilbur. Cass is not interested in you.' She rolled her eyes. 'There had to be a day when that happened. Please don't now do the clichéd thing and fall for the only woman on this planet you don't seem to be able to get.'

Wilbur smiled lazily. 'Have I ever been one for the dramatic gesture? Give me some credit. No, I'm sure she's just playing a much deeper game than I thought. Well, I'm going to ring her, tell her that Hallie isn't even in the picture and see what sort of reaction that gets.'

'Your funeral.' Abigail scooped Alec out of the bath. 'Come on, short-stop. Bedtime for you.'

'Can Uncle Wow read me the Vanessa story before I go to sleep?' asked the little boy innocently. 'It sounds like a good one.'

Abigail giggled. 'All Uncle Wow's stories are good ones, Al, and I forbid you to believe a word of them.' She slid her brother a sidelong look. 'Now look what you've done!'

'Cass?'

'Wilbur, do you know what's going on? Something big's going down here. Frank's phone has literally been ringing non-stop all morning. It's bugging the hell out of me.'

'No, but did you hear how I screwed up my date with Hallie Friday night?'

Cass's voice was cautious. 'Well, I heard that it wasn't exactly lust in the dust – she said that you hardly spoke to her – something about what the President Calvin Coolidge said—'

'No, what was said *about* him – you must know the quote, "He didn't say much, but when he did, he didn't say much".'

'—but that you behaved like a perfect gentleman and took her home. When are you seeing her again?'

'I'm not. She's gone off me completely because of Vanessa.'

Cass sighed. 'And who's Vanessa?'

'Vanessa is my fiancée back in Washington.' There, that had to elicit a reaction.

There was a short silence.

'You mean, someone agreed to marry you?' Cass's voice was amused. 'That was brave of them. How did you talk your way into that one?'

Wilbur couldn't believe it. She thought it was funny? 'Well, it was a long time ago, before I even went to Juilliard, when I was still the blue-eyed Coolidge boy. We were kind of high school sweethearts except that she is the daughter of Pa's oldest friend so when I proposed in a fit of adolescent over-enthusiasm and she accepted, both of our families went stratospheric with excitement and have never let us forget it. I hardly saw her for the next few years, but she would never let me actually get out of the engagement and now it's a habit that has proved impossible to break.' He paused. 'I'm trapped.'

Cass snorted. 'Wilbur, when was the last time you used this bag of horseshit? Let me tell you, it's really showing its age. Are you telling me that Hallie seriously believed that you've been trapped in some kind of bogus engagement for nearly twenty years? Oh, pur-leese, give me a break! Let me take you on a little literary journey, pumpkin. Our fellow travellers? Edward Ferrers and Miss Lucy Steele. The time? Early nineteenth-century Plymouth. The book? *Sense and Sensibility*. You lifted this whole sorry excuse from Jane Austen, I'll wager you Lombard Street to a China Orange!'

For the first time he could remember in years, Wilbur was speechless. Then, almost against his will, a chuckle rose to his lips. 'Busted!' he choked out. 'In fifteen years, you're the only one who's totally called me on Vanessa! Totally busted!' He couldn't hold it back any longer, and burst out laughing.

Cass seemed unimpressed but he could swear he heard a smile in her voice. 'You've obviously never gone out with anyone who's read a book before, that's your trouble. I suggest a severe overhaul of all your stories if you're planning to lift your gaze out of the bimbo gene pool.'

'You know, Cass,' Wilbur said cheerfully, 'you are the most—'

'Hang on, Wilbur, Alun's just come in.'

Wilbur heard her cover the receiver and speak in muffled tones for a minute or two. What was going on? How could she put him on hold like this?

'Wilbur?' Cass's voice sounded strange, shocked. 'Listen, I have to go. There's been some terrible news.'

'What?'

'Frank Blackthorn just had another heart attack. Wilbur, he's dead. Frank Blackthorn's dead.'

PART TWO

10

For the first time in what seemed like months, it was a beautiful day. Alun closed his eyes at the cruelty of the weather, the sunshine mocking his longing for a deep, dark hole into which he could crawl. Why hadn't he pulled the curtains across? He had actually done better than usual he realised, looking at his watch. It was six o'clock. Finishing that bottle of whisky had at least given him a couple of extra hours' sleep, so for once he had beaten the birds to the punch. Lying on his back, his arms above his head in their usual waking surrender, he stared blankly at a ceiling that was both familiar and unfamiliar, his mouth dry and his eyes scratchy, but his mind already racing.

Today was Frank's funeral. If only he could drink another bottle to wash him through that ordeal. His best friend, and they were burying the sod. Alun still had to tell himself that it was true, because in his heart of hearts he couldn't believe it. In his mind's eye, there was a picture of Frank the day he had made his maiden speech in the Chamber, unbearded then, his green eyes flashing unholy fire as he had laid into Wilson's perceived softness on the utilities. Alun had spent most of the days since Frank's election coaching him, trying to make him see that, yes, they had a responsibility to kick the bums of their complacent Labour masters and remind them of their socialism but that there was a method to getting yourself heard here that would have been slapped down at the hustings.

'I've got three years' jump on you, pal,' Alun could hear himself telling Frank over a few bevvies that night before, in 1974. 'Trust me. Ranting and thumping might get you on the wireless but there's precious few in the Government'll give you more than the time of the day if you bring them down in public. Wit and then a wallop, that's my motto. And definitely no fireworks in your maiden speech. That's the convention. Lovely to be here, isn't it great to have the chance to correct something or t'other in the constituency, thankyou and goodbye. Save the big guns for when you've fooled the Big Men that you're a good bloke.'

Frank had nodded wisely, patted his friend on the back reassuringly, and had then stormed through his maiden speech like a miniature Castro, firing on none other than his own Prime Minister, turning an uncontentious Bill into a minefield of human rights abuses and safety whitewashes. Afterwards, at the Division, when both of them had dodged the Whips loitering in Members' Lobby in a strange moment of political British Bulldogs, and headed straight for the 'No' lobby, Frank had slapped him on the arm, grinning like a naughty schoolboy.

'Convention's for poofs, Al. I've never known a maiden I didn't want to set off a few fireworks with. Why be any different with my maiden speech? We're here to have fun, not join the fatcats – and what's wrong with tipping over a few bloody apple-carts? Can't have folks back home saying we've lost our bottle, can we?'

And Frank never had lost his bottle, Alun reflected. The quintessential backbencher, he had fought it out with Dennis Skinner, the 'Beast of Bolsover', for the joint title as the noisiest, most constituency-orientated of parliamentarians, never afraid to prick the balloon of Westminster pomposity, in whichever political colour it chose to manifest itself. And now he was gone, leaving a gaping void. In Frank, Alun was well aware, he had lost both his greatest friend and a political benchmark. Where he himself had lost fire and gained political kudos, Frank had never budged from the brio of his maiden speech and always stayed as far from Party patronage or any corrupting influences as he could.

Beside Alun, there was a stirring and a small sigh from the woman sleeping there. Alun's gaze flew to her face, re-focusing. Gwenny. For a moment he had forgotten she was there.

Gwenny. Frank's wife. His best friend's wife.

'Please,' she had begged him when he'd arrived at the house the night before. 'You have to stay here. Everyone's driving me mad – especially her.' She had pointed abruptly at Frank's first wife. 'Silly cow. I can see her eyeing up every bloody change I've made in this house, totting it up, then writing me off as a silly townie from Leeds who doesn't know the value of my shillings.'

'Don't be daft,' he had chided her, 'of course I'll stay.'

After nearly three years, it had become second nature to hide his feelings for her. Playing the grief-stricken friend had been no illusion and from there it was but one craven step to old family friend supporting distraught widow. It was expected of him, and several of Frank's old friends and constituents had taken him aside to pat him on the back, tell him that Frank was lucky to have had a friend like him. At that point he hadn't even felt guilty. He had almost forgotten that he and Gwenny were lovers – all that was buried in the fog blanketing everything but a central motor function to get on, do what was expected of him.

So he hadn't dreamt that she would come to him, when the old house was creaking uneasily into an early sleep, cold feet pressing into the backs of his calves as she nestled in behind him, the whisky bottle that had been between his fingers slipping noiselessly onto the carpet. He had watched the muzzy roll of the label before the bottle came to a silent halt, then turned to Gwenny.

'Ssh,' she had whispered, pressing her finger to his lips. 'I had to come. I'm sorry. I know I shouldn't. I just needed someone to hold onto, something to hold onto.'

But he hadn't been about to tell her to go away. Now that she was here, it seemed like the most natural thing in the world to have her there. He loved her – why should that have changed? Certainly in the forgiving blackness of the dark room – where he could run his hands over the comfort blanket of her familiar curves and breathe in her scent like life-giving oxygen, not see the new lines that grief and shock had etched into her face – he didn't even need to close his eyes to pretend that nothing had changed.

But Guilt had woken up at the same time as he and was squatting at the end of the bed, all bright-eyed and bushy-tailed, fixing him with a glittery stare. And lying beside him wasn't the Gwenny he had loved for three years, but his best friend's widow, a stranger with a sleeping face unpainted by the personality that had bewitched him. Alun felt a strange distaste for that blankness of expression – a defence mechanism perhaps, where Guilt was conspiring to help him find a way not to love her.

Then she stirred again and he watched her wake up. And as she opened her eyes and looked into his, for a moment, just for a split-second, he saw that she loved him, that nothing had changed, that there was a place within both of them that knew that, no matter what, they should be together. Then reality washed in, dousing that spark. Frank was dead. Everything was different.

With Gwenny, there was no stretching, no sleepy befuddlement. She opened her eyes, looked at her watch, sat up, got on. 'I have to go. Frank's sister will be in with her long face and early morning cuppa. Can you do me a favour?'

'Of course,' he said. 'Anything, love. You know that.'

She gave a little shake of her head, as if to repel his intimacy. 'I never thought to organise transport between the funeral and the house. But with so many coming down by train, there'll be a problem with taxis. Here's the number of a minibus firm. Can I leave it with you?'

He nodded.

'Oh, and Alun?' She still wasn't looking directly at him. 'Brian and a gang of others from Hebden Road came over yesterday. I need to talk to you about what they said, so can you stick around afterwards?'

'I asked Cass if she would drive me home,' – so I can drink myself back into numbness – lay unspoken between them, 'but I'm sure she wouldn't mind waiting a few minutes.'

'Oh yes, Cass. She's a great lass.' Gwenny walked to the door, then paused and turned around. 'Did you ever find out whether she knew about – about—?'

'No,' said Alun without hesitation. 'I mean, yes, I did probe a bit, but, no, she doesn't have a clue.' There was no point worrying her, spreading the circle of their guilt further. He trusted Cass.

'Good,' said Gwenny matter-of-factly. 'That's good.' And then she was gone.

The room suddenly seemed very cold, its brightness notwith-standing. Shivering into a foetal ball, Alun caught sight of the empty whisky bottle on the floor. Simultaneously he hated himself and longed for a stiff shot, both emotions slamming through him with vicious force.

God, he would be glad when this day was over. But when it was – what then?

Hallie looked round the faces in the conference room and wondered why she was there. Roland, the skin under his beard looking especially red and angry today, not meeting her eye. His boss, Kathryn, Head of Public Affairs at Bandwick & Parker, with her Kathleen Turner huskiness and challenging eye. And Mark, head of Mandelson's Millbank team, dapper and sleek-headed like his master, a bright-eyed little otter. A star-studded gathering. So why was she there?

'Hallie, sit down. We're not expecting you to get the coffee, you know!'

Trust Roland to come out with the sexist put-down.

'Hallie, before we start, we wanted to tell you that we were really pleased with your damage limitation at Conference. We've had several reports, from both trade unionists and MPs, that mention your skill in ferrying guests between the two events.'

'Thank you, Kathryn.' This was all two weeks ago, thought Hallie suspiciously, so why are they suddenly bringing it up now?

'Now, as you know, with Frank Blackthorn dying, we're into by-election time,' Mark said quickly, as if to say, enough of the soft-soaping, let's get on with this. 'Now, of course, Blackthorn's seat was a very safe one and we're going to have no difficulty at all holding onto it but there are various factors to consider. Now the press make much of the "honeymoon" factor, which is useful to us. So, while it's not vital, we should try and hang onto its coattails as long as we can since it makes our relationship with the media that much easier.' He looked at her to check she was following him.

Hallie nodded brightly. This was all fascinating but where was it going?

'Now part of that honeymoon is that, unlike the Conservatives and that pathetic Band-Aid of a leader they've landed themselves with, we take pride in how united the Labour Party is. Just like that night at Conference, we have to avoid the smallest suggestion of a rift between the old guard and New Labour. We've heard from our sources that Blackthorn's people may be putting up a very strong local candidate, and we have an equally strong suggestion from Walworth Road. Now it's obviously left to the NEC to decide on which candidate goes forward to fight the by-election. Whatever happens, it is vital that we run a flawless campaign. This time there can be no suggestion of any cash bungs or Whip involvement.'

He paused. 'There is no reason why this by-election should be anything but textbook stuff. The Conservatives have no policies yet and will be keen to attack us on the grounds that we are a user-hostile Government, given our recent tough promises, rather than on the detail of the pledges themselves. So it is clear that the campaign will be fought on public perception rather than politics. That is why we are willing to chance its management with a relative newcomer to the political scene but one who has proved her mettle in other fields where public perception is vital. Someone who has held her own under fire; someone that Peter himself has picked out for special praise—'

'What Mark is building up to, Hallie, like the true orator he is,' Kathryn laughed throatily, and looked piercingly at her, 'is how would you like to run the Bandwick & Parker end of the by-election campaign?'

Hallie felt the temptation to look round to check that they weren't talking to someone standing behind her. About to stammer 'Wh-who, m-me?' in a pathetically unprofessional manner, she took a deep breath and started again.

'Of course, I would be delighted,' she started humbly, 'but surely this is Roland's job?'

'Roland will of course be working with you at every stage,' Kathryn said smoothly, 'but he is so tied up with the national information campaign on the Conference pledges that we felt it was unfair to take him off that.'

Roland smiled at Hallie liplessly. 'We see the management of this campaign as largely a caretaker role,' he sneered. 'The only thing you have to worry your little head about is that you facilitate its conclusion without stretching our meagre resources.' He turned to Kathryn and Mark. 'But I would like to officially air a degree of misgiving that the girl is, indeed, capable enough.'

'Roland!' snapped Kathryn. 'Hallie does not need to hear your carping! We've been over this.'

Hallie made herself look perkier than she felt. 'It doesn't matter, Kathryn, I think Roland's reservations are valid. I would just disagree with one word.' She looked brightly at Roland, knowing that he was expecting her to take exception to him calling her a 'girl' – 'I challenge the word "capable" as giving the right impression – I may be inexperienced but I am quite capable enough.' She smiled at Mark. 'As you say, it's all a question of public perception.'

'Bravo, Hallie,' Kathryn said quietly.

Mark nodded approvingly.

I'll show you, you creep, she said silently to Roland, and you too, you smoothies, to Kathryn and Mark. She now knew why they wanted her to handle this campaign. Roland had let the cat out of the bag. They were so confident that the by-election would be a cinch that they wanted someone as low-paid as herself at the helm, so that, after an expensive election and a flashy Conference, she didn't put campaign funds any further in the red.

OK, she thought, you want a cheap, clean, uneventful by-election? You got it.

Would she have felt like this if she had gone to John's funeral? Cass wondered as she and Ted stood in a pew near to the back of the church. Out of the multitude of people who had tried to advise her at the time, all of them had agreed on one thing, that there would be a sense of closure, that that way she could say goodbye to John. But would she have felt the same sense of mixed guilt, regret and comfort in the simple rituals of prayer and song?

No.

What she was feeling now was, unsurprisingly, a pale echo of the gut-churning emotions she had felt over John's death. Here she felt remorseful that she hadn't liked Frank better, that she hadn't been able to see beyond the sexist joker; not the vision-blackening self-condemnation she had whipped herself with over John's death. The pity that she felt for both Gwenny and Alun was a poor relation of the burden of sympathy that she had carried for so many months and with such disastrous results for John's mother, the feckless Meredith. And she would never know about the comfort of the funeral itself since she hadn't been to John's; but here, on this sparkling October morning, with unself-conscious Northern voices booming hymns fit to rattle the rafters, she was conscious of a sort of peace stealing over her. If this was what Hallie was talking about when she talked about the Holy Spirit coming to her, then maybe this religious set she was getting herself so heavily into, wasn't so bad.

Ted, on the other hand, was quivering with tension, the veins and muscles in his thin face standing out like ropes, his knuckles white on the hymn book they were sharing, his dark, puppy-dog eyes staring into the middle distance. Cass had had no idea he had been quite so attached to Frank. In the week since Frank's death, he had been distracted even, hardly listening as she told him about the awful moments like when Paul and the other Dean's Yard attendant had come to empty Frank's desk in their shared office, Paul for once not cracking jokes at her expense but uncharacteristically sober and silent. Ted hadn't shown any signs of distress then, but now he was a mess. Perhaps he just didn't like funerals. She reached out impulsively and held his hand in a gesture of comfort.

His head swung round and inadvertently he looked her in the eye. Cass frowned. Rather than dejected, he looked almost . . . excited and pent-up, like a kid forced to keep a secret. He looked away again almost as quickly but clutched convulsively at her hand, refusing to let go of it. Well, some guys dealt with their emotions differently, she decided, going back to the long-forgotten tunes of her schooldays, losing herself in the openly emotional experience of two hundred people singing their hearts out in *The Day Thou Gavest*.

Having left family and close friends to be present at the actual burial, she and Ted climbed into Alun's car, Cass wrestling with the choke as badtemperedly as ever, accustomed as she was to low-effort American cars.

'So do you know the way back to the Blackthorns?'

Ted continued to stare out of the windshield, knee jiggling nervously.

'Hello?! Ted!'

'Sorry, what did you – er, do I know the way?' He looked around him as they pulled away from the church. 'Yes, I think I do. Um, left I think and onto the A64 for a start, then—' He drifted off again.

'Ted – what is *with* you? You're acting like an expectant dad in the delivery room! What gives?'

'Fucking hell, Cass, mind your own business!' Ted snapped.

Boy, he is upset, thought Cass, sensibly deciding to put a sock in it.

'Look, I'm sorry,' Ted pleaded after a moment or two.

'Hey, drop it,' she said easily.

'No, I think I need to talk to someone about this. It's doing my fucking head in.' Ted bit his lip nervously. 'The simple fact is, Walworth Road have invited me to stand at the by-election for Frank's seat.'

'Wow! Ted! That is fantastic!'

'Well, it is and it isn't. On the one hand I feel like a right toerag for even thinking about my own career when Frank's not even buried—'

'Oh come on, Frank would want this for you – you know he would!'

'Yeah, but it's not as simple as that. I still have to be accepted by the local Labour Executive, who apparently have come up with their own candidate.'

'Oh. That's bad, right?'

'Well, yes it is – but I reckon that if I can get Gwen's blessing on my candidacy, that might just swing it against their choice. She's no ordinary constituency wife – she was always considered Frank's equal by folks up here, even though she wasn't strictly a local herself when she married him. She's just as much a political animal as any local they could come up with, so her support would be invaluable. And it's not so unlikely that I'll get it – I mean I was working for Frank up here during the 1992 campaign, so people might remember me from then, and I'm from Skipton, which isn't a million miles away, so I'm not exactly a soft Southern bastard sent up by London blind.'

'So what's the problem?'

'I've got to get moving fast – damn fast – and I need to know that Gwen is behind me. Now that needs a face-to-face conversation, which basically means—'

'Oh, I get it.'

'Yeah – how can I ask her on the day she's burying her husband?'

'Well, I'll tell you what – Jeez, I'm a good friend – I'll put a good word for you in with Alun and,' Cass paused, 'I wouldn't be surprised if he doesn't then get a chance to square the whole thing with Gwenny.'

Ted shot her a sharp look. 'Why do you say it like that?'

Cass thought quickly. 'Well, he was Frank's best friend – she is going to listen to any advice he offers her, especially political guidance – it's obvious, dumbo.'

'OK, do it then. I suppose it would look a bit strange if I asked him myself, because I hardly know him any more. But play it very carefully, will you? You have no idea how touchy the whole subject of candidacy is. I don't want to put anyone's back up. It's too bloody important.'

'Hey, you got it! Just think if you win – Ted Austin, the Honourable Member for Heptonstall, Chairman of the Select Committee on Social Resources, Minister for Employment, Secretary of State for—'

'Cass, lay off, will you. You're jumping every bloody gun in the book.'

'Sorry,' Cass peeked a wicked grin at him, 'Prime Minister.'

'Cass.'

It took a good hour and a half before Cass was able to get Alun on his own.

'Alun, you know Ted Austin, don't you?'

'Yes, course I do. I told you. Him, Frank and I used to go down to the Marquis of an evening. Nice lad. Why?' He smiled wearily at her. 'Got something to tell me? Do I hear the pitter-patter of tiny researchers?'

'No! Nothing like that. I hardly see him these days.' Cass had already decided that she would downplay her closeness with Ted, judging that Alun might take her less seriously if he thought she was just running an errand for a friend. 'He's about the only person I know here, that's all. It's just that he's in a sticky position and I suddenly thought you might be able to help.'

Alun looked over her shoulder. 'OK, explain, but make it quick.'

As quickly and tactfully as she could, Cass explained Ted's dilemma.

'That's all very well and good, Cass,' said Alun irritably, 'but why should I put in a good word for Ted, when I disagree with about everything he stands for? He may be bright but he's no Socialist. And who is this local candidate? Maybe it's someone Gwenny knows already and would rather support?'

'You don't have to do a sales pitch on the guy, just check out with her if it's OK if Ted has a quick word with her about it. I just think he wants to avoid being insensitive. He seems like a pretty sensitive kind of guy all round.' Cass hoped she wasn't overplaying her hand.

'Oh, my heart bleeds,' Alun grumbled. 'OK, if I get a chance to talk to her alone before we leave, I'll trail it past her. Will that do? Can I go now?'

'Alun, you are a prince amongst men,' Cass smiled broadly, before remembering she was at a funeral. 'If I can help at all . . .' she offered more soberly.

Before Alun could suggest anything for her to do, there was the sound of a knife being tinkled against a glass.

'Excuse me, everyone! Excuse me!' It was Gwenny, holding her hands up in the air for attention. Having looked drawn and tense all day, she was now looking more feverish, flushed.

'Bugger!' exclaimed Alun. 'The eulogy! Already?' Grabbing myriad scraps of paper out of his pocket, he pushed his way through the crowd.

'Ted!' Cass hissed, as they all pushed into the living room. 'Ted!'

He turned and looked questioningly back at her. She gave

him a cautious thumbs-up. He smiled and mouthed, 'Thank you' over the heads of the crowd between them.

'Most of you here were able to call my husband "friend",' started Gwenny, 'and Alun Blythe was a faithful friend indeed—'

Depends on your idea of faithful, thought Cass.

'So he's going to say a few words. Mindful of politicians' idea of a few words, I have asked him to be short, so if someone could time him and let me know afterwards, I'll tell you if his and Frank's definitions of short were the same!'

She's cracking jokes? thought Cass. She and Ted raised eyebrows at each other over everyone else's heads. Perhaps she's had a few too many sherries.

As Alun, standing on a crate, began to speak, Cass was reminded of how seldom she got to see her boss in action. She had seen him make speeches to vast auditoria, had seen him work rooms at parties, and had witnessed him in action at lobbyists' lunches but the intimacy of this setting showcased his talents even more vividly. He soon had the room laughing as he described Frank's first weeks at Westminster, brought a lump to even Cass's throat as he told them what Frank had said to him after his first heart attack, and all in a few short minutes.

'Frank once said that convention was for tossers,' Alun concluded, 'which is why we decided to say these things back here at the house. Having a eulogy in the church may be the convention, but we thought there might be a bolt or two of lightning if we unleashed the true scallywag that was Francis Blackthorn in a holy setting like that. Frank was many things to many people – a lion on the political stage, a pussy-cat with his friends, a wildcat on behalf of you his constituents but let's remember him the way he was in this house, proud father with Iris,' he raised a glass to the boot-faced first Mrs Blackthorn, 'of two strapping sons, David and Tom, both of whom are, sadly, travelling somewhere in India at this moment, and devoted husband of Gwenny, who is known and loved by you all. To Frank – proud father and devoted husband!'

'Frank – proud father and devoted husband!' they all chorused, cheering.

Sailing a little close to the wind with this devoted husband bit, aren't you, Alun? Cass silently asked her boss. Sometimes she wished with all her heart that she had never found out about him and Gwenny, never had her illusions shattered so that she felt forced to second-guess so many of his comments.

Gwenny herself still looked flushed. 'Can I say one more thing?'

'We'd listen to you ower him anyday, love!' roared one appreciative voice.

'Thanks, Peter!' she called back, smiling, then held her hand up for silence. Just like before, the room went silent immediately.

That's quite a talent, thought Cass. She certainly has presence.

Gwenny suddenly looked grave. 'As you know, for the last nine years, Frank and I have been a rock-solid team, who believed in the same things down the line, fought for the same things together, and worked as a pair whenever possible. Now that team is down to one. My captain, coach and co-player has gone and I am at best a substitute player.' There was a poignant pause. 'But yesterday, Brian and the rest of the Hebden Road team came by to ask if I could bear to think about the forthcoming by-election. Of course I could, I said, what sort of wife would I have been to Frank if I hadn't thought jealously and hard about who could possibly replace him? Who did they have in mind as the local candidate, I asked them.'

Cass noticed Ted looking apprehensive.

Gwenny held up her hands in a humbly beseeching position. 'What they said right took the wind out of my sails, but the more I thought about it, the more sense it makes. Their suggested candidate would try her best to pick up the torch which Frank has been carrying for you all these years, she would shine it into the same dark corners he did, she would wave it in the faces of those that still need to listen. So I am humbly asking you – what would you say to me standing as the next Member of Parliament for Heptonstall?'

There was a shocked pause, then the room erupted into cheering. Through it all, Cass was conscious only of three faces. Gwenny's, triumphant and beaming from ear to ear at her reception. Ted's, shocked and despondent. And Alun's, also shocked . . . and horrified. And angry. Very very angry.

* * *

'So, were you ever going to discuss it with me? Or am I just totally incidental to the next Member for Heptonstall's plans?'

Gwenny ran her hands tiredly through her hair. 'Oh Alun, please, I'm very tired. It's been a long day. I tried, didn't I? I told you I wanted to talk to you before everything got underway. But then I couldn't find you.'

'I was gone for two minutes. Two bloody minutes in the next room. That's not what I call trying to find me, Gwenny.'

She shrugged, and carried on wrapping sausage rolls in clingfilm. 'Whatever you say. Does it really matter?'

Alun shook his head defeatedly. 'No. Why should what I say matter? The fact that I think you're insane for taking this on, that you haven't got the smallest clue what it all entails, that Frank would be spinning in his grave if he knew what—'

'How do you know that? How do you know?' she challenged hotly.

Alun stared at her. 'Because for the last couple of years, Frank hated politics. You must know that! If it wasn't for the constituents, he would have bowed out before the last election. In fact, I'm not sure why he didn't. He loathed the way the new party was going – you must remember his apoplexy when Blair rammed through the change to Clause 4 – for fuck's sake, he nearly dropped dead right there and then!'

'Alun!'

'And as for Mandelson and his crew – Frank would cross the corridor not to have to speak to them. Why, only the other day at Conference, I had to move in on a bust-up between Frank and Alastair Campbell. Frank was no more New Labour than I am but the difference was that he stuck to his guns, and I waved the white flag and got my thirty pieces of silver. It's as simple as that. And you're going to throw all that away?'

'No!' she cried. 'Didn't you listen to what I said out there? I'm carrying on the fight! Don't you think I know what Frank would want? Surely it's better that I go out there and stand for everything Frank fought for, than some young

Walworth Road idiot coming up and lisping about the third way?'

'You know him,' said Alun glumly. 'It's Frank's old researcher. I bloody nearly introduced him to you. You were supposed to be giving him your backing.'

'Ted? Ted Austin is the Walworth Road suggestion?'

Alun nodded.

'Ah,' said Gwen thoughtfully, 'well that's all right. He really is a whippersnapper. Should be no problem there.'

'Well, you seem to have it all worked out, but have you thought about what you do when you are selected and go on to win the seat? It's one thing being out of sorts with the front row when you're in Opposition but when they're in Government, it's a bloody different cup of tea!'

'I'll be a good constituency MP,' she said firmly. 'Frank and I always agreed that that was the most important thing of all. I don't care about the whole party politics thing – I don't want to be in Tony Blair's little gang – and I don't care about all of the hoopla.'

'And where do I come into it?' said Alun sadly. 'Do you care about me?'

She looked at him sadly. 'We've just buried my husband, Al. It's not fair to ask such things of me. Of course, I care about you. But you know how much I loved – for heaven's sake, how much we both loved – Frank. I know that he would have wanted me to do this.'

And I know how much he wouldn't have wanted it, thought Alun despairingly. I've had enough bloody conversations down the pub about it. 'And us? Are we going to be together? Ever?'

'Again, your timing's terrible, love.' Gwenny smiled thinly. 'Are we going to be together? Well, I would say that depends on whether we're going to be together over this by-election, wouldn't you?'

Alun wished he didn't feel quite so much the dog in the manger. What sort of choice did he have?

*   *   *

Nina and Jerry were in the kitchen, ranged against each other like the troops at Waterloo, Babaji looking from one to the other from the no-man's-land in between.

'Do you care about me? About what I think at all?' said Nina levelly.

Jerry glared at her. 'I left the Army for you, if you remember – that's how much I cared what you thought – and where has that got me? Anyway, I don't see why you're getting so over-excited. I haven't talked to anyone about any decisions. Nothing's changed – I'm just going to London to pick Uncle Martin's brains – so what is the big bloody deal? *You* went to London two weeks ago – against my wishes – but did you see me carrying on like a tragedy queen then? No!'

'But I wasn't giving up! I wasn't surrendering the best bloody idea I've ever had in my life just because a few fatcat investors refused to jump first! I was pushing for more work, not junking the work I'd spent the last eight months concentrating on!'

'How can you get more work? You haven't got *any* work!'

'You fucking bastard! I've brought more money into this household in the last few weeks than you have!'

'Unless you count my Army savings which you and your stupid fucking dog have been tapping into willy-nilly? Oh, this is useless!' He swiped the car keys off the kitchen table. 'I'm going to miss my train at this rate. I'll see you later. I hope for all our sakes you're in a better mood then.'

He ducked as she threw a Schwarz herb bottle at him. It missed him anyway and smashed a wall-tile.

'Ohhhhhh!' screamed Nina in frustration.

He looked at her seriously. 'Sometimes I think you really are mad, Nina.' And then he was gone.

Nina nearly smashed another tile to be symmetrical but restrained herself in time.

'Sorry, darling,' she crooned to a shaking Babaji, scooping him out from where he had been cowering under the kitchen table. 'Crap marksmanship. Next time I'll get him, not the kitchen wall, eh?' The little dog gave her nose a warning nip then, always quick to forgive, a swift lick. In response, she cuddled him as hard as she dared, stopping when he gave a smothered yelp. 'Let's go and see what we can find out on Daddy's computer, shall we?'

Going into the sitting room, she flicked on the computer and quickly logged on. Still cuddling Babaji with her left arm, she deftly clicked through to Jerry's homepage with the other. At least she thought she had.

Bing! pinged the computer. An icon flashed up on the centre of the screen. UNABLE TO FIND WEBSITE REQUESTED. PLEASE CHECK ADDRESS.

She frowned and tried again, typing the address out longhand this time.

Bing! UNABLE TO FIND WEBSITE REQUESTED. PLEASE CHECK ADDRESS.

Thinking hard, she tried to remember all the various URLs for the JK Enterprises Drugstore sites. All of them met with the same response. Finally, she connected up with one.

JK ENTERPRISES
OVER THE COUNTER DRUGSTORE
REGRETS TO ANNOUNCE THE HEIST OF ITS ENTIRE STOCK BY ALIENS. UNTIL THE USS ENTERPRISE MANAGES TO CATCH UP WITH THESE LIGHT-FINGERED, SIX-FINGERED BUG-EYED MONSTERS BUSINESS IS SUSPENDED.
LIVE LONG AND PROSPER?
I DON'T THINK SO.

Oh ho, ho, ho, she thought bitterly, very funny, Jezza. The bastard had lied. Again. So much for discussing some options with Uncle Martin. He *had* shut down the business without telling her, and after all that fucking bluster and indignation.

She sat staring at the screen for a few minutes before noticing at the bottom of the screen, her INCOMING MAIL icon flashing. Goody, some e-mails had arrived.

Reading through the six messages that had come in through the day, she immediately felt better. Two were the usual philosophical, amusing, in-depth rambles from an obviously procrastinating Steve. They were becoming almost manic in their e-mailing now. The day before, Nina had suddenly realised that she had spent two hours either reading or replying to the usual rich tapestry of observations, wry jokes and grumbles about the life of a freelancer. Even though they had only met that one time in Newbury, she and Steve had told each other everything about themselves – and this time, Nina didn't have to bother with the tissue of lies she had spun for BadBoy. Instead, there was a Platonic ideal to their relationship. Nina got her frustrations about her ever-more distant husband off her chest, while Steve gradually let fall details about his latest romantic disaster: an affair with his agent which, after three years of her using him and his country cottage as a retreat from ball-busting in London, had finally come to nothing when she had taken up with another of her clients. Steve had wryly observed to Nina that for an agent specialising in crime writing and gore-fests, she obviously didn't think it risky giving disgruntled ex-lovers and clients ample motive for knocking her off in a *crime passionel*. Nina had responded by downloading a Web page on Fifty Ways to Kill Your Lover (And Get Away With It), which she'd stumbled across when she'd idly typed in a HUSBAND KILL search, and had forwarded it to Steve.

The other four messages were from various people and organisations she had set up e-mail relationships with on her various trots round the Internet. It was as if the postman called four times a day, and never with the usual manila-clad bundle of bills. Never had she had such varied, funny, instantly intimate correspondence with people. Forget the puerile smuttiness of BadBoy – she shuddered that off as a bad dream – this was just larking about. But it was also fascinating. So far, she had exchanged essays with a fourteen-year-old teenager in San Diego called 'Crapola' on the 'sucks' rating of various nationalities in the world; swapped conspiracy theories with a UFO-spotter in Nevada; picked the brains of a Christian evangelist in Canada closely involved with the Toronto Blessing, so that she could see what Hallie was on about; and had had forwarded to her several of the Internet's equivalent of chainletters – except that these weren't to extort money but to amuse. Fifty ways to please a man, the ultimate tasteless collection of Princess Diana jokes, brain quizzes, optical illusions, even a companionable sheep which baa-ed, yawned and divebombed its way round her screen as she worked: all these and many, many more had found their way down the line to her.

One especially had made her laugh. It had started life as a

writing assignment, turned in by two students – Rebecca and Gary – at some American college's Creative Writing class. The professor had started by saying,

'Today we will experiment with a new form called the tandem story. The process is simple. Each person will pair off with the person sitting to his or her immediate right. One of you will then write the first paragraph of a short story. The partner will read the first paragraph and then add another paragraph to the story. The first person will then add a third paragraph, and so on back and forth. Remember to reread what has been written each time in order to keep the story coherent. The story is over when both agree a conclusion has been reached.'

Then the story began . . .

At first, Carly couldn't decide which kind of tea she wanted. The camomile, which used to be her favorite for lazy evenings at home, now reminded her too much of Larry, who once said, in happier times, that he liked camomile. But she felt she must now, at all costs, keep her mind off Larry. His possessiveness was suffocating, and if she thought about him too much her asthma started acting up again. So camomile was out of the question.

Meanwhile, Advance Sergeant Larry Harris, leader of the attack squadron now in orbit over Skylon 4, had more important things to think about than the neuroses of an air-headed asthmatic bimbo named Carly with whom he had spent one sweaty night over a year ago. 'A.S. Harris to eostation 17,' he said into his transgalactic communicator. 'Polar orbit established. No sign of resistance so far . . .' But before he could sign off, a bluish particle beam flashed out of nowhere and blasted a hole through his ship's cargo bay. The jolt from the direct hit sent him flying out of his seat and across the cockpit.

He bumped his head and died almost immediately, but not before he felt one last pang of regret for psychically brutalising the one woman who had ever had feelings for him. Soon afterward, Earth stopped its pointless hostilities toward the peaceful farmers of Skylon 4. 'Congress Passes Law Permanently Abolishing War and Space Travel,' Carly read in her newspaper one morning. The news simultaneously excited her and bored her. She stared out the window, dreaming of her youth – when the days had passed unhurriedly and carefree, with no newspapers to read, no television to distract her from her sense of innocent wonder at all the beautiful things around her. 'Why must one lose one's innocence to become a woman?' she pondered wistfully.

Little did she know, but she had less than 10 seconds to live. Thousands of miles above the city, the Anu'udrian mothership launched the first of its lithium fusion missiles. The dim-witted wimpy peaceniks who pushed the Unilateral Aerospace Disarmament Treaty through Congress had left Earth a defenseless target for the hostile alien empires who were determined to destroy the human race. Within two hours after the passage of the treaty the Anu'udrian ships were on course for Earth, carrying enough firepower to pulverise the entire planet. With no-one to stop them they swiftly initiated their diabolical plan. The lithium fusion missile entered the atmosphere unimpeded. The President, in his top-secret mobile submarine headquarters on the ocean floor off the coast of Guam, felt the inconceivably massive explosion which vaporised Carly and 85 million other Americans. The President slammed his fist on the conference table. 'We can't allow this! I'm going to veto that treaty! Let's blow 'em out of the sky!'

This is absurd. I refuse to continue this mockery
of literature. My writing partner is a violent,
chauvinistic, semi-literate adolescent.

Yeah? Well, you're a self-centered tedious neurotic
whose attempts at writing are the literary
equivalent of Valium.

You total $*&.

Stupid %&#$!.

With endless little snippets like this, Nina's fascination with
the mysteries, trumperies and fallacies of the Internet still
refused to wane, no matter how much turgid rubbish she
also waded through. She and Steve had explored the Web
together, confessing to each other their ignorance, working
out with each other how to use the tools available. Now, they
even had their own shared homepage, designed over hours of
frantic, panic-stricken e-mailing. 'This is quite a commitment,'
Nina had written teasingly in one of the final website-concerned
e-mails, 'moving in together and all that! Just keep your socks
off my radiator. That's all I ask.' It was easy, it was fun, it was
harmless, and every day she looked forward to her exchanges
with him more and more.

If only the same could be said of her marriage, she thought
bitterly.

Cass sunned herself on the Terrace, basking in the Indian summer
sunshine they were still getting. With the sparkling Thames on
her left, she closed her eyes against the lowering sun, wanting
to catch the last warm rays before it sank behind the Norman
Tower. This was the life. But why was Alun always so late?
She wasn't usually so impatient with him but this time she had
some great news. And it was all thanks to Wilbur.

Wilbur. Cass smiled to herself. Thank God, they seemed to
have come out of that brief moment when Cass could feel
herself falling for him. It had obviously just been her reaction

to Hallie's move on him. Now that that seemed to have hit the skids, relations between Cass and he were just about back to normal. It was intriguing, however, that Hallie had never told Cass about the whole Vanessa Defence rigmarole, and seemed happy to imply that she and Wilbur were still dating, when it was obvious that she knew the whole thing was dead in the water. Oh, the tangled web that wove itself when friends started getting incestuous with the same guy.

Now she and Wilbur were buddies again, which was good. She would miss him over the next few weeks. Whatever happened, whether Ted or Gwenny got the candidacy, Cass would surely be involved with the by-election campaign. But Wilbur's bosses at CNN had decided that a provincial British by-election wouldn't exactly wow their average Idaho potato farmer, so he would still be based back in London. She would just have to try and wrest him away from his harem for the occasional catch-up drink at weekends.

'Cass!'

She opened her eyes to see Wilbur himself striding towards her, with no less than three women in tow.

Cass grinned. 'Think of the devil!'

'You were thinking about me?' Wilbur looked delighted. 'Still nursing that monster crush on me, huh?'

Cass rolled her eyes. 'Back in your box, big boy. Hi there,' she smiled at the three women with him.

'Sorry, Cass, this is Joy, Pat and Tilly. They work with me. We're off to see Lord FitzPatrick,' Wilbur waved further up the Terrace, past the semi-permanent Marquee – 'he's our Sponsor for the Thanksgiving Party CNN are having in the House of Lords.'

'Right. Look, Wilbur, I need to have a word with you. I have great news and you're a genius!'

'Tell me something I don't know. I'll just go and get these guys settled in with Lord FitzPatrick, then I'll come back.'

A couple of minutes later he was back.

'Well, the old goat is happy now! Christ, I'm bushed,' he draped himself into a chair with enviable grace. Then he opened one eye and squinted lazily at Cass. 'Now what can this genius do for you?'

'Just let me know when they bottle that arrogance of yours. It would make great birthday gifts. No, I just wanted to thank you for reminding me to check up on Mrs Harrison.'

'Mrs Harrison?' Wilbur looked perplexed.

'The Lottery winner in Frank's constituency? Don't you remember, you suggested that since the Conservative candidate for Heptonstall is Boyd-Cooper's brother-in-law, it might be useful to know exactly what happened to that Lottery winner who was so ticked off with Boyd-Cooper and Avalon for invading her privacy?'

'Oh yeah, I remember now.' Wilbur frowned. 'So what's the deal?'

'Well, it's great news! I rang Mrs Harrison and you'll never guess what? She was kind of reluctant to talk at first, and wasn't exactly over the moon about the whole thing but it turns out that Boyd-Cooper wrote her like the tersest letter ever, passing her on to Frank Blackthorn. Frank then wrote a letter, apparently charm itself, promising to get Avalon off her back for good. But – and this is the best bit – Mrs H was so pissed with Boyd-Cooper's attitude and the Tories' generally cosy involvement with the old Anti-Christs over at Avalon that she ended up giving over half her winnings – nearly two million pounds – to the Labour Party Campaign Fund, to help them fight the general election. Two million pounds! Don't you think that is so great? That there are still people in this nasty, brutish world that are prepared to do things like that?'

Cass paused, but Wilbur seemed miles away, frowning as if in deep thought.

'I mean, Jeez, it was for people like Mrs Harrison that New Labour won this election – God, the excitement of being in an era where people give away millions just to help foster a political ideal. That's what it's all about! It was a shame, actually, because I never got to finish my conversation with her – Mags came in halfway through and hustled me off the phone – but even so far, this is fabulous stuff!'

Cass's eyes were shining. 'Don't you think? I mean, I know we can't use any of this because that would kind of defeat the point of Mrs H avoiding publicity in the first place, but it makes me feel so much better about this whole campaign. I've been so torn about the whole thing – you know, Alun and Gwenny – that whole scene, Ted acting like a spoilt kid with a tantrum, even my friend Hallie getting totally pious about the whole thing now that she is practically Mrs Mandelson.'

That briefly caught Wilbur's attention.

'No, I know,' she mugged at him, 'unlikely. But she is acting like she's bosom pals with New Labour High Command.'

'Talking of Hallie, did you ever tell her about the Vanessa Defence?' Wilbur asked absent-mindedly.

Cass frowned. 'No, I didn't. It's none of my business what you do to get women into or out of your bed.' Anyway, if Hallie wasn't even going to tell her that she and Wilbur were a non-starter, then who was Cass to muddy the waters by telling Hallie that he was such a practised heartbreaker that he had handy stories to get him out of every tight corner? Let her carry on thinking that Wilbur was some idiotic tragic lover.

'Fair enough,' said Wilbur equably. 'Thanks.'

Cass waved her hand impatiently. 'Hey, no problem. But stop trying to change the subject – anyway, this whole Harrison thing made me realise that no matter who gets the candidacy – Gwenny or Ted – it just proves that not only was Frank the greatest guy to his constituents, but that it's the big picture we should be looking at: that Labour is the sort of party that inspires people to do things like give away two million pounds! Don't you think? Wilbur?'

'Huh?'

'Are you listening to me? I know I'm being way too idealistic and naive again, but this is good soul-stirring stuff I'm coming out with here!'

'Yeah, sorry, it's just that – Mrs Harrison was the name of the Lottery winner?'

'Yes. Why?'

'You never told me that before. You just talked about "the Lottery winner". Now you say Harrison was her name, it rings like a huge bell.' He looked at her seriously. 'And not a good bell.' He glanced over her shoulder. 'Are you waiting for Alun?'

'Yes.'

'Well, here he comes. I have to go. Look, don't tell him about Mrs Harrison yet – leave it with me, and I'll check it out. I have a bad feeling about this. I'll call you.' He sped off before Alun reached them.

'Cass, love, sorry I'm so late. They've finally chosen the candidate for the Heptonstall by-election.' Alun sat down heavily in the chair just vacated by Wilbur and waved at the waiter to bring him a drink.

Cass sat up straighter. 'And?'

'Gwenny,' said Alun flatly. 'Of course.'

Oh, poor Ted, was Cass's first thought. What a shitty draw.

'Sorry about your friend Ted,' Alun went on, 'but he must have realised that he was never going to be chosen for a seat in our neck of the woods.'

Why, because he's a practising Labour councillor with eight years' political experience in one of the top think-tanks in the country compared to a House of Commons secretary with zero firsthand experience? thought Cass bitterly. Goddamn nepotism, that's all it was.

'Obviously, I am going to be giving Gwenny every assistance on this campaign.' Alun looked penetratingly at her mulish face. 'Now can I count on you for your support? I'll need you both up in the constituency and down here – but I do realise that this wasn't why you took the job. So I don't mind if you want to back out and get on with your PhD undisturbed. Just tell me now.'

Cass thought of her bare, echoing bank account, her debts to Trudie, the two months of work still left on her dissertation versus the loss of her salary from Alun. Then she thought of Mrs Harrison and her spirits rose – who was she to turn down the chance of working on a real-life political campaign when there was such idealism, such altruism to play for?

'No way are you leaving me out of this,' she assured him firmly. 'You never know, I might come in quite handy,' she added, thinking again of Mrs Harrison. 'I do have some campaigning experience, if you remember.'

'That's right,' Alun nodded. 'You helped out that Senator on his anti-guns lobbying, didn't you? What was his name again?'

Cass steeled herself not to blush. 'Carter Wylie.'

'Carter Wylie? Sounds like someone from a Western. Good bloke, was he?'

'Oh, you know, he was OK. A very persistent campaigner. Doesn't take no for an answer,' replied Cass, thinking of the stack of phone messages piling up back at Trudie's flat.

'Easy Street, Easy Street, we're back on Easy Street,' Jerry sang as he crashed through the back door.

Babaji scurried through to greet him rapturously.

Nina flicked off *This Life*, where Milly and Egg were thrashing through the last leftovers of their relationship and steeled herself. When Jerry hadn't come back after lunch with his Uncle Martin, she had gone through the gamut of anger, tantrums and, finally, the usual fear that he was lying in a gutter somewhere. She had raged round the cottage, composing each biting, acidic word of her 'I'm leaving you' speech until she stopped and realised that she was behaving like someone out of Jerry's Australian soap operas.

So now she was calm. She was married, she was grown-up, therefore she was calm.

There was a suspicious silence from the kitchen until the door opened and Babaji shuffled through, looking embarrassed and shifty. He hovered there, until a hand came through behind and shoved him forward into the room. 'Get on!' hissed a whisper from the kitchen.

Nina rolled her eyes. 'Babaji! Here! Come here! Good dog!' as the little dog bounded up onto her lap. Rolled into his collar was an envelope. Inside was a note. 'Press here for Good News' it read, with an arrow pointing at a circle in the form of a happy acid face drawn below.

Someone was going to have to tell Jerry to read some different women's magazines, if he thought this was the way to her heart, Nina thought, trying for the life of her to see the cute side of this. Sighing, she held the note up, so that anyone peeking through from the kitchen could see, and pressed the circle. Instantly, the door flew open and there stood Jerry, almost obscured by a huge bouquet of lilies.

'Ta-daaa!'

He fell into the room, fair hair flopping over his flushed face, bringing with him a warm, convivial smell of wine, cigars and a slight hint of garlic, as he collapsed on his knees at Nina's feet. Once there, he dropped the flowers into her lap.

'Hello, darling.' He grinned at her irresistibly, laying his head on her knee and looking up with that sidelong look that used to melt her every defence. 'Whatchudoin'?'

Nina resisted. 'Hello,' she smiled tightly. 'Just watching telly. How was your day? What's the Good News?'

'My day was fucking top banana! And I am pleased to announce, my darling wife, that all our problems are over! Today, the gods have smiled on us! They have descended from on high and pressed this into our sticky little paws!' He handed her a piece of paper.

'Jerry! What do you mean? Have the investors seen sense? Is the Drugstore up and running?'

'Just look at that.'

'But that's fantastic!' Nina opened the piece of paper excitedly. Then she frowned. 'A cheque? For nineteen hundred pounds. From Martin Kellman.' She struggled to retain her rapidly souring excitement. 'What's this?'

'That, my Nin-compoop, is just the start of our cushy future. I sold the laptop to Uncle Martin, a gesture of such extraordinary generosity that he offered me a job on the spot – with the firm, starting next week on the most enormous salary you could even guess at. We're in the money, We're in the money!' he sang.

Nina's smile was beginning to feel sewn on. 'You took a job with Martin? With the family firm? And sold the laptop? My laptop?'

'Now don't get angry, Nin, please,' he pleaded. 'I'm in too good a mood.'

She took a deep breath. Then another.

'It's OK, I'm not angry. Just explain what's going on. What about the Internet business? What happened to your, your *reservations* about joining the family business? About being a stockbroker? I mean, you've been avoiding it for nearly ten years – why suddenly change your mind? And I thought you weren't going to make any big decisions today? Or was that just another lie?'

Calm down, Parvati, she told herself. 'And where does selling my laptop come into it? If you're going to be paid such a megasalary, why do we suddenly need nineteen hundred pounds?'

'Okey-dokey,' he shook his head as if to clear it, 'just hold your horses. I'll work it backwards. Your laptop had to go, I'm afraid. While I was showing him some of my business ideas on it, Uncle Martin took rather a fancy to it and I needed the money to pay for being a gun on his shoot. One of his syndicate has dropped out mid-season, and he offered me his place. I had to come up with the spondulies then and there, and the laptop was the only thing I had. It's only fair really – after all, it was his wedding present you sold to buy it in the first place. As for the stockbroking, well, you know, Nin, there's a very good reason why the Kellmans have been stockbrokers for the last hundred and fifty years – because it makes money for us . . .'

Nina didn't hear any more. Her vision, hearing, thinking, feeling was obscured by a freezing fog, through which she could only detect Jerry's presence as a faint murmur far, far away. Then suddenly the fog lifted and in her mind's eye she saw her future crystal clear. She was the perfect country wife, with her meekly trained dog and her biddable commuter husband, moving into ever-bigger country houses with ever-more gracious gardens. There were children too, still with an unforgivably different tint to their skin but paler than her, on groomed ponies, and shiny bicycles. Manicured lawns and her working in the East shrubbery. Waving Jerry goodbye as he left at dawn and waving him hello as he returned just in time for dinner in front of *A Touch of Frost*.

It was a future where she could crawl into that Kellman pigeonhole, turn round a few times like Babaji in his basket, then settle down and call it her own.

It was everything she had always wanted.

Nobody should ever get what they had always wanted, she thought bitterly.

'Ted, don't be pathetic. What's the urgency, anyway? Before Frank's death, you were resigned to the fact that you were going to have to wait for a seat until the next election. Why is it so necessary to go for this seat? Now?'

'Cass, I'm serious. It is wrong, it is totally wrong that Gwen Blackthorn should even stand for Parliament. It's making a mockery of politics, going back to the bad old days of rotten boroughs, and you know it! And you! You're supposed to be Miss High Moral Fibre—'

'Oh, Ted, get over yourself! I'm working for the Labour Party here, not Gwen Blackthorn! If I dropped out of this campaign just because I wanted my pal to win, that would be just as morally wrong. Don't you get it?'

'But that's just where you're mistaken, Cass. You don't work for the Labour Party. You work for Alun Blythe and no-one else. Strictly speaking, it's actually illegal for you to work on the by-election, unless your wages are factored into the £3,370 expenses allowed for each candidate. Surely, your morals won't allow you to work illegally for someone who isn't even your employer?'

'Jesus, when will people stop bugging me?! I'm no more fucking moral than the next person! I believe that electing the sort of member who will further the Labour cause is what we should be fighting for – which is just as well you or Gwenny – and if that's naive idealism then that's too fucking bad. Just because I have ideals doesn't mean I am some kind of Vestal Virgin!'

'Well, yeah, from your performance at Conference, I'd say there was no danger of confusion on that score.' Ted's voice was bitter.

Silence.

'Cass, I'm sorry, I—'

'You bastard,' said Cass evenly. 'You'll regret that.'

'Cass, listen, that was a bloody stupid thing to—'

'Yeah, it was. I have to go now, I have a call on the other line.'

She hung up.

'Fuck! Fuck!' Ted swore at the receiver in his hand. Well, you stupid fucker, he told himself, you handled that well. Oh yes. Made for a career in politics, you are, with a temper like that. Well done, mate.

But how could he explain to Cass that – just for a few days between Frank's death and the funeral debacle – he had seen his prize within his grasp? And that the prize hadn't been Heptonstall but her, Cass Herbert. Somehow, his wish to be an MP had become entangled with his crippling lack of confidence when it came to seducing her – if he got one, then surely t'other would follow. That's why, when Frank's death brought this plum tumbling into his lap, he had allowed himself to believe that this dream had been pitched into the here and now.

That's why the urgency, Cass, he told her silently. For a moment there, I thought you were going to be within my grasp. How can I now wait four years to get another opportunity?

'A night in? For Cass Herbert? Shurely shome mishtake! I thought you were going out?'

'Trudie, you can talk, with your social life. Anyway, shut up, I'm trying to remind myself why the hell I used to watch *EastEnders*. It is so goddamn depressing. Doesn't anything happy ever happen to these guys?' Cass could see that her grandmother was itching for a heart-to-heart and was hoping to head her off at the pass.

It was no good.

'Come on, darling, switch that tripe off. We need a good old conflab.' Trudie took no notice of Cass's obstinate stare at the television, leaning over to turn it off herself. 'I'm not passing up this rare opportunity for us to talk, young lady, so don't even try to ignore me. For starters, not that I'm putting on any pressure, but is there any chance of you being able to pay me back any time soon?'

Cass winced. 'Sorry, Granda. No, not really. But there should be in the next few weeks. If I'm going to be working on this campaign, I'll be safely tucked away up in Heptonstall, not spending any money. How much do I owe you now?'

'Oh, not so very much. About six hundred quid.' Trudie wagged a finger at her. 'Always in the red, aren't you, my girl?'

'Course I am, I'm a Labour supporter, remember? Red is no longer dead!' chanted Cass cheerfully.

'What I can't work out is how you supported yourself for the last few months in New York. You know, after your Poppa – bless his stupidity – cut you off for turning down that Fellowship?'

Cass reddened and was silent.

'It must have been hard,' Trudie went on reflectively. 'Neither you nor Ricky ever had any sense of money. Now he doesn't need to up at Findhorn, lucky lad, but it must have been a shock for you out there in the Big Apple after years of generous allowances and those two years earning all that money as a management consultant, then suddenly being pitched into poverty.'

'Look, I managed, OK? I've already told you – I walked those stupid dogs and packed in as many workshops as I could find. Yeah, and some, er, friends spotted me the occasional month's rent.'

'Nice friends. Was one of them this bloke, Carter?' Trudie said shrewdly, waving the sheaf of messages. 'He sounds like a nice man over the telephone – if a little older than you. So why aren't you returning his calls? Do you owe him money? Is that it?'

'No!' Cass snapped. 'And I don't think it's any of your goddamn business. It's a free country. I don't have to speak to anyone if I don't want to. That includes Carter Bloody Wylie – and that goes for you too!'

'Keep your hair on, darling,' her grandmother said mildly. 'I just thought you could do with some good friends at the moment. Oh, I know that you're gadding about nearly every night but they're either your new hacky political friends like that smoothie Wilbur or old university acquaintances, not real friends. You've fallen out with that nice Ted, and you, Hallie and Nina seem to be at each other's throats more often than not these days. You never seem to talk to your New York friends much, even though they ring here so often – this Carter even said that he was just going to come over and confront you face to face – and even that charming-sounding Irish rogue – Devlin, is it? – even he seems to be giving up in the face of so much indifference.'

'Lecture over?' Cass said truculently. 'I'm touched that I'm nearly thirty and my grandmother is still feeling the need to choose my friends for me. And, anyway, I'm actually seeing the charming Irish rogue in a couple of – what did you say?' She broke off to stare at Trudie. 'Carter is coming over here? To England?'

'Don't you even read your messages? I don't know why I bother writing them down. One of the last ones said that he had some work trip coming up and he was taking advantage of it to drop in and catch up with you. Or something like that.'

'Christ, and I thought he was bluffing. Did he say when?' Cass began leafing frantically through the pile of notes.

'Oh, Lucasta, I can't be expected to remember every last blasted detail.' Trudie wiped her hands across her eyes tiredly.

'It's OK, here it is.' Cass scanned it rapidly. 'Oh, it doesn't say when he's coming. Goddammit.' She looked at her grandmother and frowned. 'Trudie, are you feeling OK?'

'Fine, darling. A little tired, that's all.'

Cass dropped all the messages on the table and gathered her grandmother into a huge hug. 'I'm sorry. I'm so fucking selfish—'

'Cass!'

'Sorry, so *very* selfish,' Cass grinned apologetically. 'Making you run round like a receptionist on speed. Are you sure you're OK – you've been tired a lot lately. Perhaps you should go to the doctor, get yourself checked out.'

'Oh pish-posh,' Trudie dismissed. 'It's nothing a few good nights' sleep won't sort out. I might just have to cut back on a few nights at the Crisis Centre, that's all.'

'Great idea. Then we can crash in front of the TV, rent a movie, pig out on popcorn and be total couch potatoes. How about one night next week, by-election permitting?'

Trudie smiled at her grand-daughter. 'Sounds exhausting. Maybe I will go to the Crisis Centre after all.'

'Don't you dare! Just think of all that time you'll have me captive to bug me about my finances, my career, my friends. You won't be able to resist it!'

And maybe, just maybe, she would finally be able to share all her problems with one person, instead of scattering them piecemeal amongst her so-called friends, Cass thought wearily, looking down at the messages from Carter. Alun and Gwenny's affair wasn't so very different to hers and Carter's – he was a married Senator, after all. How would she have felt to have had her foolishness splashed over every TV screen and front page? She would have wanted the full story, her reasons, to have been explained, but the media would never allow it, they never did. It would be the same for Alun and Gwenny. At the end of the day, Alun and Gwenny were good people – just as Frank had been – but caught in a situation that she knew only the external details about.

Bloody Ted could say what he liked but there were bigger things to play for here. Mrs Harrison had known that when she gave all that Lottery money to the Labour Party. Gwenny may not have the political experience of Ted, but she deserved to win the seat in Frank's name. She was no more a scarlet woman than Cass was, and Cass was going to do her best accordingly to help her.

11

The King's Crustacean pub, punningly near King's Cross station, had seldom seen a crowd like it. The low-ceilinged basement under the main bar was bulging like a convention of Jabba the Huts. It certainly felt like that to Ted, who had long ago lost any sense of his limbs still belonging to him, instead of just being a corporeal part of the crowd hemming him in. He wasn't entirely sure why he was there. Weeks ago, when he and Cass had still been on speaking terms, she had issued the invitation to come and watch a friend of hers play in a gig at this popular venue for emerging bands. In an effort to try and make it up with her, Ted had decided to come as per the original plan. It had worked only up to a point. Cass hadn't quite decked him with a good right hook when she'd seen him but nor had she decked him out in welcoming leis and sung 'Aloha'. Sometimes, he thought to himself savagely, he didn't know why he bothered to fly his pathetically fluttering flag for her. Never had she treated him with anything other than easy contempt and a sort of dick-shrivelling familiarity. Now was no different.

When he'd arrived, she'd been drinking with a huge group of people he didn't know, including the band who were yet to start their gig.

'Hey, Ted, what's up?' she'd greeted him casually, then turned back to the group without introducing him to a single soul.

Ted, his political poise abandoning him with that one move-ment of Cass's shoulder, had shuffled from one foot to the other, smiling noncommittally at the assembled strangers. Then the first set had started and here he was, still on the sidelines, grateful to be saved the necessity of introducing himself by the impossible volume of the five young lads thrashing it out at the end of the smoky, beery room. He might almost have enjoyed the nostalgically student feel of the whole sweaty exercise had he not been forced to watch Cass, in the smallest tank-top he had seen outside of primary school, giving it some welly to every last bump and grind of the impossibly loud band. Finally, one of the Blazing Sadlads, relaxed in the knowledge that their set was the last of the night, had taken pity on him and turned to him.

'Sure, and isn't it like Cass not to follow the usual conventions and be introducing us, then?' he smiled ruefully. 'Here,' he stuck out a nail-bitten hand, 'the name's Devlin. I'm with the band. I was about to get a round in – what can I be getting you?'

'Ted. Ted Austin. And, cheers, I'll have a point of,' Ted squinted at the pumps ranged along the bar, 'of McCaffreys.'

'Getting in the Irish mood for when we play, eh?' winked Devlin when he came back with the drinks. 'And how is it that you're here? Are you another of Cass's bleeding victims?'

Ted's shock must have shown on his face.

'Whisht, take no notice of me,' Devlin apologised quickly, 'I'm a daft eejit with a mouth that should stick to singing up there on stage. It's just that she has already ridden roughshod over my fragile little heart so I know how it feels.'

'No,' Ted pulled himself together, 'I just work with Cass. Well, we both work in Westminster. I'm a lobbyist.' He smiled twistedly. 'With an unusual interest in emerging talent on the music scene.'

'Right.' Devlin's tone was ironic.

'Hello, boys,' said a voice down to their left. It was Cass's friend, Hallie.

To Ted's surprise, a look of crucifying embarrassment flashed across Devlin's face. 'Well, and don't you even look like that gorgeous woman in those bra ads?' he said quickly, scooping Hallie up into his arms. 'How are you, my little darlin'?'

Hallie, Ted noticed, was also looking slightly abashed. 'Not bad, not bad.' She extricated herself from his embrace. 'I've actually been promoted since I, er, saw you last. I'm now director of PR liaison on the Heptonstall by-election campaign. Oh!' She caught sight of Ted's face. 'Gosh, I'm sorry. You're Cass's friend, Ted, aren't you? And I've put my foot in it, haven't I?'

Ted liked her honesty. 'We met at Conference if you remember,' he changed the subject before they had to explain the Heptonstall reference to a bemused-looking Devlin. 'I was at the B&P party when you got your Gold Medal for Good Behaviour from Peter Mandelson.'

'Now him I've heard of,' said Devlin, 'but if youse two are going to be yattering politics, I'll be off. There's a lovely lady over there that needs my attention.'

'Oh yes?' laughed Hallie. 'Booked the hotel suite yet?'

Devlin wagged a finger at her. 'She travels with me wherever I go, we make beautiful music together, and she never gives me any gyp – so don't you be mocking her.'

'Who, me? She sounds like the perfect girlfriend for you, Dev!'

'Girlfriend? Sure, and did I say anything about girlfriends? Who needs the ladies when you've got a beautiful guitar?'

Hallie and Ted laughed obediently as Devlin strolled away grinning.

'Quite the ladies' man, is he?' Ted asked Hallie.

'Up to a point. A very small point.' Hallie giggled. 'Sorry, ignore me. It's been a long day.' She glanced sidelong at him. 'You may not want to hear this but Gwen Blackthorn is proving to be a very intractable candidate in terms of anything Millbank want her to say. She's becoming quite a headache, to me at least.'

Ted began to like Hallie quite a lot. She was obviously a perspicacious woman. 'Sure – and whoiy would Oi not want to hear that?' he asked in a mangled Oirish imitation of Devlin. 'To be sure, it's music to moiy ears. Tell me more, tell me more.'

Hallie chuckled. 'I suggest that politics is a better career choice for you than impressions. It's actually nice to talk to someone who rates my opinions. Cass thinks I'm about one step up from Max Clifford on the political front.'

'Rubbish,' Ted said stoutly. 'She was boasting about you only the other day. Her very own high-powered Madame du

Mandelson, I think is how she described you. Of course that was before we fell out, when she was still talking to me, so don't quote me on that.'

'Yes, she mentioned the two of you had had "a blue", I think was how she put it.' Hallie looked over to where Cass was surrounded by a crowd of people, all of them whooping as the Sadlads finally began to tune their instruments up at the other end of the room.

She turned back to look up at him. 'Well, I don't want to get mixed up in all that – not tonight, anyway. Strange – I don't know any of the people she's with. She's such a constant enigma to me is Cass: supposedly my best friend, yet I often see her with a hitherto unknown new circle of mates. Without wanting to be rude, the chances of my talking to her tonight are slim at best so I certainly don't want to antagonise you!'

Ted grinned and shouted back at her over the starting music. 'I know what you mean. Not exactly conducive to making new friends this place, is it? Looks like we'll have to put up with each other.'

'What?' yelled Hallie.

'Looks like we'll have to put up with each other!' He bent down to shout in her ear.

'As the sheep said to the Virgin Mary!' she hollered back.

'What?'

She reached up and patted him on the shoulder. 'Never mind!'

Neither of them noticed Cass looking speculatively at them.

'You're kidding me!'

It was the day after Devlin's gig and Cass was nursing her hangover, when the phone had rung. After a few minutes of listening silently, she had been unable to resist this painful little interjection.

'I'm not,' replied Wilbur. 'You ring your Mrs Harrison, finish your interrupted conversation and hear it from the horse's mouth. I knew there was something fishy about that name, so I looked it up on the newsroom database. You'd better believe me, Cass. Blackthorn may have listened to her tale of woe and promised her he would get Avalon off her back, then when she gave the money to the Labour Party, he was the one who splashed her name all over the media and ended up getting Avalon way more publicity than they ever would if she'd agreed in the first place. It was a big story during the run-up to the general election – one of those pre-campaign feel-good spurts which occupy the public interest for, like, two and a half minutes.'

'But she gave that money to the Party because she hated Avalon so much. Frank must have known that!' Cass gasped.

'Of course he did, but this was an election campaign, Cass, how could he resist crowing about one of his constituents giving so much money to Labour coffers? And from a lottery win? Cass, the woman's a saint! Having a saint attached to your cause is good news for any party, even the Labour party!'

'But that makes Frank as bad as Boyd-Cooper!' said Cass slowly. 'Worse, in fact, because he not only dumped her in it, but he manipulated her to suit his own ends. That explains why Mrs H was so miserable on the phone – she probably thought I was going to bring the whole thing out all over again. Imagine winning such huge amounts of money twice in your lifetime – no wonder Avalon were so keen for her to take the publicity – even if the first windfall was through the pools.'

'And thirty years ago. It seems that she gave most of it away then as well. Only a year or so after she and her husband were plastered all over the papers in about fourteen different tabloid makeovers. That must be enough to put you off the media for life, so I'm not surprised she didn't want to go through the whole press circus all over again.'

'Nor am I. But hang on – the media this time never found out that she didn't want the publicity?'

'That's about the size of it, I guess. I suppose they looked at the old footage, at her and hubby grinning like idiots, and thought she would go for it second time round too. And you can bet that Gwen Blackthorn was in on it too. She was there on all those news-tapes as well, with her arm round that poor bewildered old lady, beaming away. Now that I watch it a second time, I should have realised that there was more to this than met the eye – for one thing, the Blackthorns spoke for Mrs Harrison: she hardly said a word – it's all kinda weird. Oh, and there's another thing—'

'There's more?' said Cass weakly.

'Well, it's easier if you do this from your end, because our computers are down at the moment. You guys must be hooked straight up to the HMSO Commons' Homepage and Hansard Online, aren't you?'

'I guess.'

'I'd be surprised if you weren't. Well, I'd check into Blackthorn's speaking and voting record on Avalon. He just looked way too buddy-buddy with the Avalon guys on that tape for my liking.'

'But it was Boyd-Cooper, not Frank, who was in Avalon's pockets – that guy in the pub told Mrs Harrison.'

'But remember that Mrs Harrison thought she was in Boyd-Cooper's constituency not Blackthorn's? What if the Avalon rep, who would have known who her MP was, had just said, "Your MP is in our pockets" and she assumed that he meant Boyd-Cooper but he was actually referring to Blackthorn.'

'Stop! This is getting out of hand! Suddenly Frank's the bad guy?'

'Just check it out, Cass, before casting your villains.' Wilbur sounded like he was smiling. 'You poor lamb – seeing the evil side of politics up close suddenly, aren't you? And made worse by you working on this campaign of Gwen Blackthorn's, huh?'

'You can say that again,' Cass said abruptly. 'Thanks, Wilbur, you're a honey.'

'I am?' His voice was thoughtful. 'Hey, call me when you get an update.'

'Will do. Bye for now.'

Cass put the phone down and stared out of the window. Out of the corner of her eye she could see Frank's desk, unnaturally tidy now, a silent eavesdropper on these shenanigans. Poor Mrs Harrison. Little did she know that in addition to being Avalon's reluctant winner and Frank Blackthorn's mascot saint, she had also been a totem of idealism for a misguided Labour researcher who needed to wise up.

Ignoring the pile of letters that she and Alun needed to get out of the way before they went up to Heptonstall next week, she stood up determinedly and strode downstairs.

'Mags,' she demanded abruptly, as she went into the secretaries' room, 'are we logged onto the Internet?'

'Fuck knows,' said Mags unconcernedly. 'Doubt it. See for yourself.' She stood up and gestured at Cass to sit in her chair.

'Are you sure you don't mind?'

'Oh, you've made an old woman happy, you have, by supporting Alun on the Heptonstall by-election. You can do whatever you like today, love, it's a great day for the Party as we used to know it. Raise the Red flag, hey?' She headed out of the office, singing merrily.

'Thanks!' Cass called after her and sat down, pushing her legs out to get them under the desk. There was instantly an anguished howl. 'Fuck!' Cass bent down to see the malevolent face of one of Mags's Staffordshires peering out at her. 'Sorry, Gillie, or Sunny, or whichever the hell you are, you ugly little shits.'

'But if you kick my dogs,' Mags popped her head back round the door, 'I kick you. Your choice, chuck. Do you want a cuppa?'

Needless to say, the Blythe Empire didn't have a modem to its name, let alone was it hooked up to the Internet, and nor was Marnie, or any of the others in the room. Cass marvelled at this as she wandered out of the room in search of someone who was. She still couldn't get used to the idea that this was the hub of the nation yet most of it – from the architecture to the people inside – seemed lost in the 1950s.

'Paul, my prince, my hero, my luscious love-bucket.'

Paul the Attendant, as he always introduced himself, looked up, owlish eyes blinking suspiciously through aviator reactolites. 'This is good. You must really want somefink. How can I help you, my little Yankee-doodle-dandy?'

'Do you know anyone round here who's logged onto the Net?'

It was a strange peculiarity of the House of Commons attendants that they knew everything about everyone, from Ministers right down to what the secretaries' children were up to. Paul pondered for a minute, then nodded.

'Siobhan – do you know Siobhan? Blondish hair, red-framed big glasses?'

'Works in that office by the photocopying room?'

He nodded. 'I remember there being a whole load of excitement when she got all her Internet stuff – the world and his bleedin' wife were popping down there to,' he bent his knees and held up his hands like a born boardie, 'surf the Net. 'Course, everyone soon got bored with it, but I fink she still has it for e-mailing and that sort of stuff.'

'Thanks, Paul, you're an angel,' she patted him softly on the shoulder.

He blushed slightly. 'Pleasure, treasure.'

In the world within a world that was the Palace of Westminster, Siobhan was surprised to be asked by a complete stranger if Cass could use her computer, but, bemusedly, she said yes. After a fair amount of fiddling about with Siobhan's Compuserve set-up, Cass managed to change the log-on details and, using her old Columbia University account number, was able to access the Net. Typing HANSARD at the search engine prompt, she quickly found the HMSO website and was into the Commons Archives.

Only five minutes later and she had more than enough food for thought. That's what made the Internet so insidious, she thought, leaning back in her chair and taking a deep breath. In the bad old days of *Hansard* transcripts, it would have taken someone, with a plastic ruler and red Bic biro, weeks to piece together what she had achieved with a couple of clicks on the SEARCH button. To the casual eye, Frank Blackthorn was no more interested in Avalon and the National Lottery than the next man, yet he had spoken up in their defence on almost every possible occasion – in the Horse Race Totalisator Board Bill in February that year, in the Sport for All Debate in June, the list went on and on – as well as tabling no fewer than fifteen Lottery-related Parliamentary Questions and Early Day Motions in the last session. Furthermore when, on a hunch, she matched up his name with Boyd-Cooper and Avalon, it turned out that Boyd-Cooper had done the same. Perhaps Boyd-Cooper was Blackthorn's pair. But if he was, then on the three-line whip votes on Lottery-related subjects they should have neutralised each other either by both not voting, or both voting according to the Whip. Yet on three occasions that Cass could see, Blackthorn had gone against the Labour Whip to vote alongside Boyd-Cooper in favour of Avalon.

In a way, she was amazed that the *Sunday Times*, in their

self-appointed role as sleaze-hounds, hadn't put this material together themselves. Frank hadn't declared more than one free lunch in Le Touquet in the Members' Register of Special Interests and yet it was becoming obvious that there was some sort of relationship between him and Avalon. Then again, Frank hadn't been in Government – not like Jonathan Aitken and his habit of giving out the Saudis arms contracts like Mars Bars: 'A jump jet a day brings the baksheesh my way'. And what was one bent backbench oldtimer when there was the likes of Mohammad Sarwar bunging his way into the House?

But it didn't make her position any easier to digest. She decided to go back to Alun's office to get her head round this whole situation. Once there, she spent a few minutes tidying his desk, mindlessly following a tidy-mind-tidy-desk dictum.

One thing was clear as day: she was mired in a conflict of interests. On one hand, she already found this by-election doctrinally unpalatable, resting as it did on an Old Labour foundation, not the new ideas she personally followed. But those were just personal quibbles which were unprofessional and irrelevant.

Yet everything she had found out discredited Frank Blackthorn's memory as a Grand Old Man of the Party and of the constituency. This in turn weakened Gwenny's candidacy for Cass, since she was running on a 'More of the Same' ticket. Alun and Gwenny's affair was bad enough in itself, but on the grounds that she had behaved no better with Carter, she had persuaded herself to come to terms with that. Put together with this gradually unravelling business surrounding Mrs Harrison, however, and the whole campaign was as potentially scandalous as any Hamilton-Aitken-Mellor combination. Either it would come out, dragging Blair's government through the mud and bringing the honeymoon period to a premature end, or it wouldn't – and she would have colluded on a Tory-style cover-up.

On the other hand, what were her options? Trash her personal loyalty to a man she still admired, lose her job and kibosh any contacts she might have been able to extract from working here, by blowing the whole thing wide-open? And even if she did decide to spill the beans how, exactly, was she supposed to do that? Was there any way she could keep herself and Alun out of it? Was it hypocritical of her to want to keep him out of it? Was that not a cover-up in itself?

She shook her head. This was hopeless. She had to stop being such a drama queen and get this into perspective. It was just a goddamn by-election in a safe seat. No-one would care. Then something Carter once said came back to her.

'Never underestimate the media, Cass,' he had joked, 'they've got woodlice with notepads hiding under every stone you've ever visited. Always assume the worst, assume that they know everything and you're halfway there. But the million-dollar-question is, are they going to use their information? And that's also the answer, honey. Never give them an excuse to use that information and never, ever give them a victim. Without a victim, there is usually no story. Who cares if some Congressman is diddling his campaign manager? Oh, his wife doesn't know and isn't going to stand by him – instead, she's going to go berserk if she finds out . . . alright! Now we've got a story!'

The trouble was, there were victims here. A political victim – Mrs Harrison. A personal victim – Alun, because Cass would lay bets he didn't know about Frank's extra-curricular activities. And Cass herself – a victim of her own idealism.

On impulse, she dialled Hallie's number. If her friend was now so high up the political beanstalk, she would surely be able to toss a few magic beans of advice down Cass's way.

'Hallie Templeton's line. This is her executive assistant—'

'Karenza,' she said impatiently, cutting through the trilling spiel. 'Is Hallie there? It's urgent.'

'And who shall I say is calling?'

'Karenza, it's Cass!'

'Cass?' Had the woman had a lobotomy? 'Oh, *Cass*! Silly me! Hang on, she's just here.'

Hallie was laughing when she came onto the line. 'Karenza, eh? You've got to love her! So, what can I do for you this fine morning? Have you talked to Nina lately?'

'I talked to her and Jerry last week and I've left a couple of messages this week. Is that good enough for you, little Miss

ACAS? More to the point, just exactly how long did you talk to Ted last night?'

'Oh, stop trying to change the subject!'

'OK, OK, anyway I didn't call to chat. There's some serious shit going down here. Can I trust you not to go anywhere else with this?'

'Cass. Please. Do you have to ask?'

Cass ran quickly through the whole story, as well as her thoughts on what she could and couldn't do but without telling her about Alun and Gwenny's affair. After Alun's chat to her in the Atrium restaurant that day, she couldn't bear to mouth off to anyone else about that. Then she waited for Hallie to respond.

Finally Hallie spoke. 'Well, I think, first off, that there is good news as well as bad here—'

'Hal, cut it out with the fucking PR-speak!' snapped Cass. 'Just get to the point.'

'OK, we blow the gaffe – it's a good opportunity for Blair to oversee the final sinking of Old Labour. Alun isn't deeply involved at all, so it's only Gwen Blackthorn who is left out in the cold.'

'Yeah, but how do we do that?' said Cass querulously, 'will you be able to keep control of the whole thing? And keep me out of it?'

'To be honest I don't know,' Hallie admitted. 'I doubt it. Mark and Mandelson will take it over.'

'Fuck. OK. Look, promise you'll sit on it while I think about it?'

'Yes, OK, but Cass – why are you so bothered about it? Just because your boss is giving this Blackthorn woman a helping hand doesn't have much to do with you, does it? Why are you in such a tizzy?'

Thoughts of Alun and Gwenny embracing, her last fight with Ted, that stack of messages from Carter piling up at home, the weary dignity of Mrs Harrison's voice on the phone, Mags's change from dragon to pussycat, a memory of Frank's jocular leering, the spectre of her unfinished dissertation – a jangling tapestry ran through Cass's mind.

'Long story, Hal, really long story,' she said dryly.

* * *

As she filled a bowl of water for a panting Babaji from the downstairs loo, Nina looked at herself critically in the mirror. All these head-clearing walks she was taking with Babaji were at least making her look better. Now that summer had finally chosen to skulk in – this being the muggiest October in years – she had a becoming flush to her sallow cheeks, and her body looked less marshmallowy. It wasn't quite a good enough trade-off for everything else.

She braced herself for the upcoming confrontation with Jerry. So far she hadn't dared go into the kitchen, having heard the familiar strains of his beloved Australian soap operas coming from the television in there. Instead, she hosed down her hot cross dog, who'd paid the price for her walking deliberations by having to keep up as she marched unseeingly through field after field, his little legs getting tangled in the long grass. It had been as if he knew she was in need of cheering-up as he did his 'up-periscope' impression time after time, bouncing up above the top of the grass to see where he was going, then turning expectantly to make sure she'd noticed and was smiling at him.

'There you go, darling,' she finished off the hosing with a kiss and backed off before he shook all the cooling water off again, 'you can dry off out here, while I go in and face the music.'

Babaji shook himself vigorously, looked sympathetically back at her, and rolled onto his back beseechingly. Nina's heart lurched with love for him. Why couldn't she love Jerry so unconditionally? Perhaps it was because Babaji didn't lie to her, didn't go behind her back, wasn't condemning her to a cryogenically frozen life as his little-wife-in-the-country.

She took a deep breath and opened the door into the kitchen. The dying strains of *Neighbours* was her cue. It was time to follow the script she had been planning so carefully on her two-hour walk.

'Hi, darling,' Jerry said, switching off the television. 'That was a long walk. Are you tuckered out?'

He was acting the same as he had for the last few days. As if nothing had happened. As if nothing was wrong. For a moment, Nina's resolve quailed. Wasn't it just easier not to cry over spilt milk, let that water flow under the bridge, take the rough with the smooth and all the other clichés of the ebb and flow of married life? How could she argue with someone who didn't realise they'd done something wrong?

Then she saw the Corby trouser press in the corner, dusted off and brought out of its regimental retirement in time to get his civvie suit shipshape for Monday, and her determination hardened. He bloody well should have realised the effect his sudden change of plans would have.

'Jerry,' she said firmly, 'we have to talk.'

'We do? OK, what about? Do you want a cup of tea?'

'No I don't. This is serious.' Fuck, she had to stop sounding like a drama queen.

Jerry barely refrained from rolling his eyes. 'Oh God, do we have to go over all this again? Look, Nin, we'll be fine, you'll see. Once the money starts rolling in, and we're more settled, we'll be able to go back to how we were. We've been spending twenty-four hours a day together – it's no wonder we're getting on each other's nerves a bit. Hey, you should be glad I'll be out from under your feet!' He smiled pleadingly at her, his clear blue eyes shining from under a lock of blond hair.

'No,' Nina said again. 'No, it's all more than that. We've got to stop kidding ourselves, Jerry. I don't know what went wrong but this – us – marriage – it's not – well, it's as if we've started out on the wrong foot, somehow – and something's not working, quite.' Even as she heard herself, Nina knew that she was diluting her intended message.

Jerry looked pained. 'Nina, darling, what are you on about? Started out on the wrong foot? We've been going out for ten years – I don't really see how we can suddenly start on any foot at all!'

'You read about it all the time,' Nina retorted. 'Couples go out for years, then get married and suddenly it's all over—'

Jerry laughed mirthlessly. 'So now we're all over? Well, forgive me if I disagree. I still love you.'

'Do you? Do you really?'

'Oh, for God's sake—'

'So why go behind my back with this whole Internet business? Why suddenly start treating me like some fucking three-year-old moron? That's not love, that's—'

'Nina, if you're just going to start hurling abuse at me then there's no point in attempting to have this conversation. You're talking complete bollocks. There is nothing wrong with our marriage that a little space and clear-thinking won't fix.'

'Says who?'

'Says me, for Christ's sake! I'm hardly going to bring in a bloody committee!'

Nina pounced on this. 'And what if I disagree? What if I say that there is a hell of a lot wrong with our marriage – are you just going to tell me that I'm wrong?'

'Well, someone has to,' Jerry muttered.

'What? What the fuck did you say?'

'It was a joke, Nina! Do you remember those? Back in the days when you used to have a sense of humour?'

By this time, Nina didn't know where to attack first. 'You're joking? Our marriage is collapsing and you're joking? Well, forgive me for thinking that this was an amusing conversation for you!'

'Oh, stop being such a bloody woman about this!' Jerry exploded. 'You know that's not what I meant – you're just being a drama queen. Christ, you have no idea what a good thing we have going here – you're so determined to pick a fight that you're being totally illogical, jumping on anything that gets your goat. What, is it that time of the month?'

Nina, appositely enough, saw red. 'Well, that's not something you're likely to know about, given the last time we had sex!'

'Now don't you dare bring our sexlife into this!'

'What bloody sexlife?'

'That's enough!' Jerry slammed his hand on the table. 'What? Am I not *bad* enough for you, is that it?' He glared piercingly at her.

She went very still. 'Wh-what do you mean by that?'

'Oh, I know all about you and your Badboy,' he scorned. 'And you dared to get hot under the collar about my stumbling little recces with Honolulu Hotlips or whatever her name was?' He held a hand up to his ear, mimicking a phone receiver. 'Hello, pot, this is kettle – hey, you're black.' He wagged a finger at her. 'Pretty saucy stuff, Nin, though I say so myself. You must have been disappointed when Badboy turned out to be more of a BadGirl.'

Nina could hardly breathe. 'You knew all about that? And you never said a word?'

'I was waiting for you to say something to me. Anyway, I thought it was all rather amusing, the way it turned out. It was harmless smutty fun. Now Steve, on the other hand, is all a bit more threatening.'

'Steve? You've been reading my e-mails as well?'

He cocked an eyebrow at her. 'Nina, we are married – what's yours is mine and all that, remember? Of course I did. Well, after the BadBoy fiasco, I had to keep a weather-eye on you, didn't I? Couldn't have you copping off with any old virtual Tom, Dick or Steve, could I? But then you did seem to be getting rather cosy with old Stevie so I just did something about it before a situation developed.'

'Did something about it?' Nina stopped. It was all becoming clear now. 'My laptop. You sold my laptop. So that I have to use your computer for all my e-mailing. So that whole story about shooting with Uncle Martin was another lie?'

Jerry looked pained again. 'Nina, I haven't lied to you. The whole Uncle Martin thing is true. It was all a rather lucky coincidence. And there's no harm done, is there? I mean, it's all out in the open now – and you're free to e-mail from our machine here. Bingo! No situation!'

'Fuck you!' Nina blazed. 'How fucking dare you snoop around behind my back? And then tell me there's no harm done? We're married, Jerry! We're supposed to communicate with each other!'

He sighed. 'Oh, don't for pity's sake go turning this into a whole analogy about marriage. I think we should end this conversation now, Nin, and have that cup of tea. We're just going round and round in circles.'

'Stop fucking deciding things for me!' she screamed. Nina Parvati was back with a vengeance, sweeping aside Nina Kellman with hardly a second glance. '*I* think we've hardly started this conversation! If there's anything we should end, it's this marriage!'

Jerry stood up then and pointed an accusing finger at her. 'Nina! Get a grip! We are not, I repeat, not, having this conversation! I'm going to the pub and when I get back I hope you've calmed down and then we can talk sensibly.'

'Jerry, if you run out like you usually do, it's our marriage you'll be running out of,' she warned him, her voice shaking.

He snatched up the car keys. 'Just watch me. You're talking emotional bullshit, Nina, and we both know it.'

'I mean it!'

'Oh, grow up,' he said cruelly, pausing by the kitchen door. 'Listen to yourself. You sound like a spoilt child. And you say I treat you like a three-year-old – is it any wonder?'

Nina screamed in frustration as he slammed out of the house. She heard the revving of the engine and the fast crunch of gravel. He was doing it. He was calling her bluff. She slumped down at the table and put her head into her hands. Then, just as suddenly, there was an anguished howl and the noise of the car stopped as abruptly as it had started.

Her heart froze. What had that noise been?

The door burst open. Jerry stood there, his face as white as a sheet, his lips bloodless.

'Nina—' he started. 'Oh Nina, I'm sorry . . .'

'What is it?' Nina jumped up. Then the realisation struck her like a train.

Babaji.

'All quiet on the Northwestern front, Hallie? The good folk of Heptonstall not giving you any problems?' Mark's silky smooth voice brooked no disagreement.

'No, no,' Hallie assured him obediently. 'I thought we might be in danger of the usual LibDems by-election offensive but what with their guns being spiked by the pact and the fact that they've put up a very weak candidate there are no discernible barriers there. William Hague is going back up there next week to rally local Tories—'

'Well, that's brilliant then – that closet-case prat will be doing our job for us. At least we won't have to send Tony in on this one – not like Uxbridge. Ooh, now that was a PR nightmare!'

'We're having a few problems getting through to Gwen Blackthorn to square up the bullet points in our brief, but they're just logistical. Nothing I can't handle. We'll win this one for Blair all right.' And when Cass stops dithering and lets me get on with it, you'll see how much of a triumph this by-election is going to be. A total undermining of Old Guard quibblings.

'Oh, I wouldn't be too much of a stickler for Millbank policy out there in the sticks, Hallie.' Mark sounded almost bored. 'I think the voters of Heptonstall fall into the category of our less sophisticated Labour supporters. Just steer clear of obvious pitfalls in backwaters like this – law and order, strong local unions, that sort of thing. Oh, Peter's paging me – I have to go. Keep me posted, Hallie.'

As Hallie put the receiver down, she was thoughtful. 'Karenza?'

Her assistant looked over from her desk. 'Yeah?'

'Tell me honestly. What's the word out on the street about this by-election campaign?'

Karenza looked knowing. 'Well, I don't know about any flipping by-election but I do know that Kathryn & Co are fed up with Roland being so queeny and precious about his Labour Party links. It was bad enough when Blairy-poos was just on the other side, but now that he's, you know, in charge of things and all, Roland has apparently been ever so hoity-toity about how important he is to the B&P account. Which is really funny when you think how much he got his knickers in a twist at your Conference knees-up. So me and the girls reckon that because this election thingie is such a doddle, they're just testing you out on something safe to see if you can knock old Roly-Poly off his perch.'

Hallie felt cold with apprehension. The stakes on this assignment were starting to look larger than she'd feared. Rather than just being an opportunity to say 'nur-nur-ni-nur-nur' to Roland, it looked like she might be playing for a bigtime promotion. It also seemed that everyone was far more interested in keeping this election safely on the straight and narrow than anything else. With their leader's 93 per cent popularity rating safely in the bag, the Blair team seemed uncaring about whether this was won on New or Old beliefs so long as it didn't rock the boat.

That morning, Gwen Blackthorn's election agent had said to her, 'Listen, love, I was Frank Blackthorn's agent for twenty years, through Harold Wilson, Jim Callaghan, Michael Foot, Neil Kinnock and John Smith, before His Toothsomeness ever pitched up. Up here they don't care which faddy little ideas are top of the pile – as long as it's red on the door, they're coming in. Don't complicate the issue, lass, believe me.'

Doctrinal sophistications were clearly too rich for their blood. It seemed that the Heptonstall electors themselves didn't give a tinker's about New Labour, Old Labour, whatever. If she was to try and expose the Blackthorns, with their Old Labour beliefs and corruptions, might she not just bring down New Labour as well? It was all getting too risky.

She dialled Alun Blythe's number. It rang a couple of times, then obviously switched onto another line.

'What?' said an aggressive voice, thickly.

'Er, is that Alun Blythe's office?'

'Secretary. Speaking.'

Hallie gulped. So this was the infamous Mags. It sounded like she was well through her booze supplies. 'I'm sorry to bother you but is Cass Herbert there, please?'

'Just call me a bloody switchboard,' the slurring voice grumbled, 'she's gone home. And I'm trying to go home so don't make me take a message, I beg you.'

'No, no, don't worry—'

'Hang on a sec, I lied. I can see her sloping past the door now. Cass!'

Hallie winced away from the receiver as Mags bellowed unreservedly.

'It's yet another call for you,' she heard Mags say. 'But that's OK – because I live to be your receptionist.'

Cass sounded uncharacteristically meek. 'I am so sorry, Mags. But think how boring life would be if I weren't here to bug you. Hello? This is Cass speaking.'

'Yikes a-lordy, Cass, that woman sounds like an absolute ogre. Now listen, I've been thinking about this whole Blackthorn deal and, while I sympathise with your, you know, ruined ideals and Ted's disappointment and all that, it's my professional opinion that we have to hold fire on this. The only thing they care about at this end is a quiet election campaign. The Heptonstall voters don't care about New Labour or Old Labour – they just want the next best thing to Frank Blackthorn, and what do we have, really? Nothing substantial – just one disappointed Lottery winner and a few suppositions.'

'I guess,' Cass said doubtfully.

'And if we're left to our own devices, what do we know about breaking scandals? One thing's for sure – if the media do get hold of this, they will do exactly what they want with it – either ignore it because it doesn't suit them to slag off a Grand Old Man of the Labour Party, or they'll go berserk with it – savaging New Labour willy-nilly and ending the honeymoon period on Blair's government just like that, irrespective of the fact that neither Blackthorn was ever New Labour or ever will be.'

'Wow, Hallie, you're good at this, aren't you? Now I know how you are when you do a presentation,' said an impressed-sounding Cass. 'Hey, I'm convinced. To be honest – hang on, let me just check everyone's gone – yes, I think so – and I know this doesn't exactly sit well with my rep as knight avenger of the moral state of the nation – I wasn't looking forward to stepping into the firing line. Which discreet City company would employ a gender consultant who'd just had her face splashed all over the papers for attacking a female political candidate?'

'Aren't we grown-up?' agreed Hallie. 'Taking decisions based on something other than our emotions.'

'Or other than our ideals,' Cass added glumly. 'Poor Mrs Harrison.'

'Well, not that poor – she's still got a couple of million.'

'Hallie, that's not the point. She's still the loser here. And we're just sitting back and letting it go.'

'Nina, he's gone.'

It was Jerry, his arm going gently round her shoulders.

'Come on, darling, you can't do anything more for him.'

Nina was sitting in the driveway. The October sun was still warm on the back of her neck, but inside she was as cold as a tomb, the warmth leaving her as quickly as it was leaving the stiffening body in her arms. She couldn't take her eyes off Babaji. He was surely sleeping. There wasn't a mark on him except for one small streak of blood coming from his nose. He couldn't be dead.

'Come on, Baba,' she whispered, nuzzling him behind one woolly ear. 'Let me tickle your tummy. OK, no more puppy training. I promise. You can stop playing dead now. Come on, sweetie.' Come on, open your eyes and wink at me. Lick my cheek when you think I'm not looking. Give me that condescending glare of yours. Please don't leave me. Please don't be dead.

'He must have been sleeping in the shade underneath the car,' Jerry repeated numbly. 'I just didn't see him. Christ, what a mess. Poor little dog. Oh God, Nina, I'm sorry. I'm so sorry.'

Nina stood up abruptly, shrugging off the heaviness of his arm, still clutching Babaji's body.

'Well, I must bury him.'

'No, no.' Jerry looked horrified. 'Nina, no. I'll do that. It's the least I—'

'In the long grasses behind the stream. I've never buried anything before. I wonder how deep you have to dig.' Nina started to walk purposefully to the ramshackle little garden hut.

Jerry looked after her helplessly. 'Wait, I'm coming with you.'

'No! I want—' Nina stopped and shrugged. 'OK.'

A few minutes later, they found a suitable site. Without saying a word, Jerry took the spade from Nina and began to dig. Nina continued to hug Babaji closer to her, her arms crossed round the little body like a shield, her nose dipping occasionally to nudge at the dog's head, her gaze blank.

'There,' said Jerry quietly, after a few minutes, 'it's ready.'

Nina sank her head into Babaji's fur and breathed in one last ration of his sweet, summery, still puppyish scent. She looked at the open grave. She couldn't put him in there – it looked clammy and dank. She wanted to remember him above the ground, not underneath it; his ears flying, not drooped; his teeth bared in that wickedly ecstatic grin, not slack-jawed; his little eyes darkly bright and knowing, not sunken and closed.

'His blanket,' she said suddenly. 'I'll get it from his basket.' And before Jerry could say or do anything, she was half-running, half-stumbling back to the cottage. As she came through the trees she stopped. The cottage was bathed in the limpid light of an autumn evening – every window a gilded slash, the very last of the roses glowing palely in the last golden rays of sunshine. She had never seen it looking so beautiful, so peaceful, such a haven. Only one note rang false. In the drive stood the car, parked wildly askew, its driver's door still open. She stared at it dully.

Someone must shut that door, she said silently to the dog in her arms. Otherwise the battery will go flat.

'So this is what you learned in your five years in America?'

Cass surveyed the coffee table. 'OK, we have beers, we have chips, we have dip, we have popcorn, we have all remotes to hand, we have a movie in the VCR—' She glanced up at her grandmother. 'What do you mean?'

Trudie laughed. 'Well, this is more like a religious ritual than a simple night in front of the telly. I mean, I never even knew you could buy popcorn that just went in the microwave like that!'

Cass rolled her eyes. 'Hey, get with the beat, Baggy. Now, snuggle here with me on the couch, and get ready for the Herbert Movie Extravaganza.'

Trudie folded her large frame onto the sofa and put her feet onto Cass's lap with a blissful sigh. 'You're right, this was a brilliant idea. I feel guilty about leaving Naomi in the lurch at the Crisis Centre, but a little selfishness never did anyone any harm. Now what have we got?'

'What do you feel like first? Sex and silliness or classy period drama?'

'Sex, please,' winked Trudie. 'I'll try and cast my mind back.'

The doorbell rang. Cass and Trudie looked at each other non-plussed.

'For Chrissakes, Jehovah's Witnesses, at this time of night? Surely not. Hey, let me up, I'll get it.'

Cass stood up and went downstairs to the front door. OK, so maybe her first thought had been that it might be Wilbur, come to hear what she was doing about the by-election but really because he couldn't keep away from her. That was fine, she was allowed to be foolish. After all, she hadn't returned his last message for a couple of days now, so it was probably her guilty conscience talking, reminding her that only a coward would be shirking telling him about her decision not to rain on Gwenny's parade. She would, she decided as she unlocked the deadbolt on the front door, grasp the nettle tomorrow and call him. That's what friends did, wasn't—

Then she stopped, dumbstruck, staring at the man on the doorstep.

'Carter!'

He stepped forward and pulled her into a hug, her head fitting automatically into its habitual nook in the hollow of his neck behind his ear. 'Oh Cass, it's so good to see you again. Over four months! It's been too long, babe, too long.'

For a brief second, Cass breathed in his subtle aromas of Givenchy soap and expensive shampoo, felt the solid luxury of his cashmere-clad bulk, then she pulled back abruptly. 'Carter! What the fuck?'

Carter shrugged and let go of her arms. 'Well, at least you remembered my name,' he quipped weakly. 'I was beginning to wonder. I guess you've forgotten how to use the phone, huh? And when was the last time you checked your e-mail? If you did, you wouldn't be looking so surprised that I'm here.'

'Surprised? You bet I'm surprised! What in hell are you doing here?'

'Because I have something to tell you – hey, can I come in, or are you going to keep me out here like a lovesick Romeo all night?' He reached forward to tuck a lock of hair behind her ear.

'Cass – who is it? Oh, hello!' Trudie appeared behind Cass, eyebrows raised at the sight of the expensively-dressed, imposing stranger with his patrician forehead and silver temples, just lowering an immaculately manicured hand from her grand-daughter's face.

Carter bowed slightly. 'Good evening, ma'am. If I'm not mistaken you must be the delightful lady who has been so kindly putting up with my many calls.'

'Oh, spare us the Yankee-boy charm,' snapped Cass. 'Carter, this is my grandmother. Trudie, this is Carter Wylie – sorry, *Senator* Carter Wylie – come all the way from good, old Washington DC to honour us with his presence.' And put that in your pipe and smoke it, she told her silently.

'Please ignore this querulous child,' Trudie smiled at Carter. 'She's a changeling. It's the only explanation. You must be tired after your flight – please, come in, let me take your coat.'

Trudie had a wickedly mischievous look familiar to Cass since boyfriends immemorial. It had always been the same – she would softsoap them totally, then, if she liked them, by that time they were already more than half in love with Trudie, let alone Cass. It was the same treatment if she didn't like them but in amongst the honeyed charm would be a few choice words about how aggressive, competitive and tough Cass was – and were they sure they knew what they were taking on? Before Cass had a chance to rebut, the poor callow youths would be running for their lives.

As Trudie ushered Carter up the stairs, twittering beguilingly about the mess and their aborted vid-session, Cass sighed. What had she done to deserve a grandmother as cunning as Trudie? No flies on her? She was a one-woman swat team when it came to her grandchildren and their lovelives.

At least she was distracting Carter from whatever it was he had ominously come to tell her.

But not for long. After a few minutes of giving him the strongest whisky-and-water Cass had ever seen – 'We don't do rocks in this country, I'm afraid, so you'll have to have it the way nature intended, with just a splash of water,' she had told him – Trudie said something uncharacteristically grandmotherish like there was some sewing she just had to take care of, and left them to it, Cass staring moodily out of the window onto the leafy Clapham street below, Carter strangely nervous, shooting his cuffs edgily.

'I like your new hairstyle,' he said, after a pause. 'It's very hip. And it shows off the way your temples move when you talk. Not that you've done much of that yet. Cass—'

Cass took a deep breath and turned round.

'You shouldn't have come, you know,' she said shortly. 'I don't care what kind of senatorial junket you're using as an excuse, you shouldn't have come here. For Chrissakes, I've told you a million times that this,' she spread her hands apart sharply, 'whatever we had, this affair, is over. It should never have begun—'

'But it did,' interrupted Carter implacably. 'And we fell in love. No! Wait!' he held up his hand to stem her interjection. 'It may have started out as a reaction to the whole Meredith

– John horrors but are you really gonna sit there and tell me that's all it ever was? Those times in the George Inn? Skiing in Vermont? Not to mention just those precious ordinary moments sitting up on Capitol Hill arguing the toss on everything from Szechuan food to Nato commitments in Europe?'

Cass shook her head. 'Isolated moments when we forgot about everything else going down, Carter, and you know it. Anyway, let's not go there. It's pointless toiling down old paths – it happened, and I have to live with that – but that's all I have to do. What did you think? That even though I left the States for the sole purpose of ending it, that after a few months, I would have pined so badly that I'd suddenly change my mind?'

Carter came up close to her. 'Just look me in the eye and tell me you don't miss those mornings when Meredith was away and we would lie in bed, facing each other eye to eye, just like we are now,' he whispered softly, one hand going up to stroke the tender skin above her elbow.

Cass shivered but held his gaze with her own glare. 'You said it, Carter – "when Meredith was away". You said it, but you just don't get it! You're a married man. You're a Senator of the United States of America. You have responsibilities. Not to me, to your wife! I had a temporary aberration – but it's over! Getting involved with a married man is not part of my gameplan – how many times do I have to tell you that?'

'How about an unmarried man?'

Cass stared at him. 'What?'

'Honey, you heard me. That's what I came here to tell you. I've left Meredith.'

'You've left Meredith?' As she choked the words out, Cass felt an almost paralysing sensation creep over her. 'Why?'

Carter laughed wryly. 'You have to ask that? My darling, isn't it clear to you yet? I love you, Cass. That's what this is all about. To be with you, I've left Meredith.'

The doorbell rang.

Cass was off like a horse from starting gates. 'I'll get it!' she bellowed, before Trudie made it out of the kitchen, and sprinted down the stairs, praying this time that it was those Jehovah's Witnesses. Maybe they could attribute some sort of divine order to the madness waiting for her upstairs.

But no such luck. It was Nina.

'Nina!'

'Hi, Cass. Can I come in?'

Cass clutched her forehead. It was obviously going to be one of those nights.

'Oh Christ, Nina, I'm sorry, it's not such a good time right now. If you came back a bit later, maybe, but it's all just too – anyway, what in hell are you doing here?'

Nina looked at her expressionlessly. 'I've left Jerry.'

Cass would curse herself for it later but the tide of anger that flooded through her was unstoppable, directed as much at Carter upstairs as her hapless friend.

'You've left Jerry? Well, that's just fine and dandy. Shit, what is *with* everyone all of a sudden? Does marriage mean nothing at all these days? What happened to "until death do us part"? One fucking fight and it's marriage, where is thy ring? One lousy flirtation and the party's over? Well, fuck that – do I look like I care?'

She was shaking with rage now. 'If you're doing this for attention, Nina, you've come to the wrong person. I may be studying psychology but I don't do marriage counselling. Not my subject, babe. I know I'm your friend and I'm here for you on anything else, but I introduced Jerry to you, remember? *He's* my friend as well, so don't you dare involve me in your little spats, OK? Fuck, one lousy moment and you're off!'

Cass struggled to sound coherent. 'Marriage isn't a toy, Nina – you can't just throw it away when the batteries go flat! You're obviously having one of your blues – just swallow that Parvati pride, climb back into the car and drive home before it's too late. Don't throw this marriage away, Nina, you know that's not what you want!'

'Yeah, yeah, okay,' Nina was backing away. 'Maybe you're right.'

Cass relented suddenly. 'Look, do you want to come in, have a cup of tea and give Jerry a call? Let him know you're OK?'

'No!' Nina said violently. 'Don't want to disturb you.' She turned and stumbled back to her car.

'Fuck!' cursed Cass under her breath. 'Nin! Come back! I'm sorry – I shot my mouth off! Let me explain! Please?'

No answer as the car pulled away jerkily.

'Fuck!' Cass said again, and slammed the front door with unnecessary force.

'Is anything wrong?' Carter was standing at the top of the stairs. 'Who was that?'

'I'll tell you what's wrong,' snapped Cass, striding up the stairs two at a time. 'You are! You are so wrong, buster, that it's frightening. And, oh boy, are you out of line! I've just alienated my best friend because of you and if I were her, I don't think I would forgive me in a hurry. How fucking dare you stride in here, waving your dick around and telling me that I should be grateful because you've left your wife? She buried her only son less than a year ago and you've left her? Well, Mr Fucking Compassion, you can stop thinking with an aching right wrist now and start using your ears to listen to this.'

She pulled him into the sitting room again and kicked the door shut behind her. 'What makes you think I would want a man who walks out on his grieving, frankly unstable, wife for an unknown prospect five thousand miles away and twenty years younger? Is this a good prospect for me? No, but you're too goddamn arrogant to see that, aren't you? I don't want you. I don't want you married. I don't want you single. I have moved on, Carter, and my life does not involve you. Can you not understand that?'

But Carter was just looking at her admiringly. 'Oh, it's this fire, this passion, that I've missed, babe. You have no idea how miserable it's been in that house since you left – and you don't understand how determined I am that you *will* come back to me. I don't care what it takes, or how long I have to wait. These past few months made me see that. You're right. I'm nearly fifty. I'm a Senator. So goddamn what? All that means is that I've done what I wanted to do, I've got enough money so that I don't worry where the next buck is coming from, and now I've found the person I want to spend the rest of my life with. So you're mad at me – that'll pass. The important thing is – you love me and I'm going to stick around until you realise that.'

Cass could hardly breathe, let alone scream in frustration. Then the phone rang. She stared down at it in disbelief. 'Oh, this is a fucking farce!' she screamed, snatching up the receiver. 'What?'

There was a pause. 'OK, so I'm guessing this isn't a good time to call,' said a calm voice, goodnaturedly.

Wilbur. All at once, Cass felt like she'd come to rest on a sandbank in the middle of a storm. Perversely she also felt like crying. 'Not great,' she said gruffly, missing Carter's sudden frown, 'but keep talking.'

'Just thought you might like to know that I've been doing my own little bit of digging – I found some tape of Blackthorn and Mrs Harrison being interviewed together on local news – it's a doozie, Cass, you're not going to believe it – he was practically harassing her on camera: hearty slaps on the back and squeezes of the knee, while she barely says a word, just flinches every time the interviewer turns to her. Not that Blackthorn lets her get a word in edgeways. You are going to eat this up. I'll bike it round to you tomorrow—'

'Oh, that's wonderful, you're wonderful,' said Cass shakily. How could she tell him that she wasn't going through with the revelations after all? Especially now that Carter had turned up to complicate her life even more.

Wilbur's voice sharpened. 'Cass, what's up? You sound—'

'Hey! Car—' Cass reeled in shock as Carter gently took the phone from her.

'I'm sorry,' he said urbanely, 'could she call you back later? She's kinda busy at the moment. Thank you so much.' And he placed the receiver back on its rest.

'I'm sorry – I could sense you were getting distracted and it's important we give this our full—'

But he got no further because Cass punched him hard in the face.

'Ow!'

'Fuck!' Cass said simultaneously, rubbing her knuckles agonisedly and feeling as shocked as he looked.

'What in hell did you do that for?' he bit out, rushing over to the mirror above the fireplace and looking at his face. 'Are you insane? I have to go to top-level NATO meetings at SHAPE tomorrow.'

'Oh, relax,' snapped Cass. 'I've never hit anyone before – I probably hurt myself more than I hurt you. And I'm not insane, I'm suddenly feeling totally sane.' She paused, looking thoughtful. 'You know, there's this guy called Paul who's an attendant at the House – the House of Commons – who says that I'm far too tough and confident for my own good. That I probably frighten men to pieces. And I said that he was absolutely right. But it occurs to me that I only actually frighten off the ones *I* like, in a kinda masochistic way. I'm sure we could blame it on something to do with my Poppa and his string of wives. I mean, you're not frightened off by me, are you? I just hit you in the face – and yet you still love me, don't you? Or think you do.'

Carter caught her eye in the mirror and laughed ruefully. 'Oh yes, I still love you. But then maybe I'm the masochistic one.' He tapped his cheekbone gingerly and said nonchalantly, 'So who was that on the phone that provoked such a strong reaction?'

'Oh no-one in particular,' Cass said, reluctant to bring Wilbur's existence to Carter's attention. Then she had an impulsive idea and spoke without thinking it through. 'Just the man I love.'

Carter whirled round. 'You're lying!'

Cass steeled herself to look him clearly in the eye. 'I wish I were. Because I really am the masochistic one in this respect. I'm in love with him, but I've frightened him off so much that he now thinks I'm his kid sister. So, haven't we got a pretty situation here? I should introduce him to you for the circle to be complete.'

There, that would fix him, she thought, looking with weary satisfaction at Carter's shell-shocked face. What an inspired cover. The arrogant swine hadn't even imagined that she might have found a rival in this poxy little country. The trouble was, as she spoke the words, she had a horrible realisation that she might never have spoken a truer word. Falling for Wilbur?

If that meant what she thought it meant then she was, indeed, in big trouble.

Nina got to Marble Arch before she realised where she was going. Instead of heading down the Cromwell Road to get back onto the M4, she had been driving blindly towards her and Hallie's old flat in Maida Vale. So she set off once more round the laborious roundabout, with its endless ring of traffic lights. Round and round the mulberry bush, she sang tunelessly to herself. Round and round the old Jerry-bush. Since she'd been ten years old, Cass had been the one Nina went to with the important dilemmas. Whether to lose her virginity to that wimpish but persistent Simon Kager. Whether to go to university or head straight into journalism. Whether to marry Jerry.

Where Hallie had been the one to bitch to about life, Cass had been the decisive force. But this time, Cass had pushed her too far, hurling abuse at her on the doorstep, ordering her to go back to Jerry without even listening to what Nina was saying. Her usual blind submission had propelled Nina back into the car and heading westwards but here she was now at Marble Arch – being guided by another force: a last flicker of rebellion.

I won't do it, she thought defiantly, and went round again for good measure. I won't go back there. She still didn't quite know why she'd left at all. As they'd come silently back from burying Babaji, she'd walked over to the car, intending to close the driver's door, then found herself slipping behind the driver's wheel, turning the keys in the ignition, putting it into gear and driving slowly out of the drive. In the rear-view mirror, she'd seen the horrified face of Jerry fade away to the sky as she hit the downward patch of gravel just before the road. Then she was gone, turning automatically to drive to London, robotically following signs to South London, Clapham then – recognising the landmarks of the Common, Sainsbury's and the disused car lot – to Trudie's house.

So she didn't know why she'd left. But what was the point of going back when there would be no black, furry face to welcome her ecstatically, just Jerry's guilt and her own irrational hatred. As he'd bent to put the last sods onto the grave and had then looked up at her with that hangdog expression that already seemed carved into his face, she had had the strangest urge to grip his head and push it hard into the soil, thinking, guilt won't get him back, you fucker. She knew that because she was the one who was actually guilty. She had killed Babaji as surely as if she'd been the one driving the car, and now there was nothing there for her.

Hallie. She would go to Hallie's flat in Islington.

Fifteen minutes later she was there. As she parked down the street, she heard a door slam and saw Hallie rushing down the street towards her, looking almost furtive in the gloom of the autumnal evening.

'Hallie?' she said, getting out of the car.

'Nina?' replied an astonished Hallie. 'What are you doing here? Where's Jerry?' She stared at Nina. 'Sweetie, what's wrong?'

Nina took a deep breath, all too mindful of Cass's reaction the last time she said these words. 'I've left Jerry.'

Hallie's eyes nearly popped out of her head then. 'Oh no!'

'Please don't lecture me! Cass bollocked me, and I just want – I just want—' Nina swayed slightly.

Hallie grabbed her arm. 'You poor lamb. You're coming in right now. Come on.'

'B-but weren't you just going out?'

An expression of pain crossed Hallie's face. 'Just to church, and then dinner with, with – a friend.' She clutched Nina's arm harder, and bit her lip. Then she led them back into the house, face hardening as she saw her flatmate's face, dismayed at her early return.

'Hallie, what's going on? You know Slammer's getting here any minute. You promised you'd let us have the place to ourselves tonight. I mean, I own this place – is it too much to ask that I can be alone in it at weekends?'

'Beth, don't start!' Hallie said pugnaciously. 'Just give us the kitchen to ourselves, OK? Here, take your scented candles into the bedroom. You wouldn't want to eat dinner anyway, would you? You might put some weight on. You might even get as fat as me.' Hallie almost laughed as Beth gave her a horrified look then quickly checked her reflection in one of the many mirrors. 'Bitch from hell,' she muttered under her breath.

'Right,' she said once they were settled in the kitchen, a cup of tea for her, a steep vodka for Nina, fags lit for them both, 'what happened? And don't worry about Cass – she's got her own problems at the moment – and you can rest assured that however much of a mess you're in, I've been there.'

It was the sudden sympathy that did for Nina. 'I fucked up, Hallie,' she sobbed, bursting into tears. 'This time I have really fucked up.'

Hallie's face crumpled and she too dissolved into tears. 'I'm sorry, sweetie, I know I'm meant to be strong for you – but so have I!'

12

The bottle of vodka was empty. Now they were cracking into Beth's precious bottle of Limoncello.

'We have been the most terrible friends, haven't we? No,' Hallie shook her head, 'don't bother to deny it. That weekend we came down a few weeks ago, you might as well have been the butler, we paid so little attention to what was going on inside your head.'

She got up to light her umpteenth cigarette from the toaster. 'The really awful thing is that Cass and I were busy discussing amongst ourselves how much we thought Jerry had changed – but we never even stopped to consider how much that impacted on you.'

'Impacted? You make Jerry sound like a meteorite,' Nina smiled twistedly.

'Sorry, PR-speak, but you know what I mean. It's bad enough when your friends are in dodgy relationships – but it's like there's a taboo over discussing issues inside a marriage. Take sex just as one example – the number of times Cass and I have dissected sexual disasters, penis sizes, fantasies, range of vocab when talking dirty – everything basically – but because you're married we would never ever ask you about your sexlife.'

'Lucky that,' muttered Nina. 'Nothing,' she said quickly to Hallie's inquiring look. 'I know what you mean. I felt the same way. It was as if I had passed through some one-way door, like

317

coming out of the side exit of the cinema. You can either hang back and hold it open, while people walk past you as if you weren't there, or you can let it slam behind you and be left in this dark deserted alley that seems rather a let-down after the bright glittery lights of the cinema you've just left.'

'But if you walk on a bit further, you come out into the lights and bustle of the street,' Hallie said softly. 'Question is, did you send Jerry on to fetch the car, or are you taking the bus home alone?'

Nina half-laughed, half-choked. 'Oh Hallie, I love you. Never one to leave an analogy unflogged.' She looked around the kitchen, at the remnants of the cobbled-together feast they'd just had and all the colourful detritus of two single women living together and compared it to the tidy functionalism of the kitchen at home. Here there were brightly coloured invitations, silly postcards, make-up, cotton buds, silk scarves. Back at the cottage, there was nothing but some lawn-mower manuals and Babaji's puppy-training schedule. Babaji. Her heart clenched.

'Uh-oh, empty glass. And pass us another fag, will you? Christ, I've missed all this so much. You know, perhaps Cass was right that time.'

'Oh, Cass is always right,' said Hallie crossly. 'When in particular?'

'When she said that going to weddings was the same as going to a funeral – you never saw your friends again after either.'

Hallie grimaced. 'Yes, I remember that now. So much for the holy sacrament of marriage.'

Nina looked intently at the burning tip of her cigarette.

'But seriously, what are you going to do next? I mean, this isn't,' Hallie hesitated, 'well, it isn't the end for you and Jerry, is it?'

'Oh God, no,' Nina said automatically. 'It's just that, with everything that's been going on, Jerry's new job, the whole Internet thing, my career, I feel like I've been in a stormy, fucking claustrophobic teacup of change and confusion. I think when I married Jerry, that I thought the whole marriage deal would just be more of the same, and it wasn't, and that has done my head in. Now I just want to sink myself into some sand for a while. Is that very cowardly of me?'

Hallie shook her head sympathetically.

'Also, I just can't quite bear to go back at the moment.' Nina felt her lip start to quiver dangerously. 'I know I shouldn't have got so attached to him. He was just a dog, after all, but going back there and not being mauled to death by the enthusiasm of this little black thing hurling himself at me – well, I just couldn't . . .' Her voice tailed off, and she began to cry again.

'Oh, Nina.' Hallie just stroked her friend's shoulder.

'I'm sorry. I never cry. I'm probably about to get the curse,' Nina sobbed. 'God, if a bloke ever said that to me, I'd clock him one.' Then she remembered that last fight with Jerry and its aftermath and she cried harder. 'Oh fuck, I'm turning into one of those hysterical women I hate so much. Maybe I've got some hideous, mentally-wasting disease.' She looked hopefully up at her friend. 'Maybe I'm dying?'

Hallie smiled encouragingly. 'If that's what you want, sweetie, then a wasting disease it is.'

Nina hugged her, and shook her head. 'Thanks, Hallie, you're an angel. What I would do without you and Cass – oh God, I wish she was here—'

'So do I,' Hallie said grimly. 'I'd give her a piece of what-for! Turning you away like that – what sort of friend does that? Someone has to tell her—'

'No, Hallie, please don't,' Nina wailed. 'What's happened to us? We've been friends for nearly twenty years – why are we suddenly falling apart? Why has everything changed?'

'The only thing that's changed is Cass since she got back from the States.' Hallie shook herself. 'No, I didn't say that. Oh, it's so hard to know what's what sometimes. It seems like none of us have had much fun with each other since we were all back together again. I mean, before Cass went away, we never, ever fought. We hardly even disagreed. I know that we're approaching our thirties and everything, that we're all set in our ways, know our minds, have gone our separate ways but it's all very different from the good old Bikeshed Blasters days, isn't it? I just pray that He shows us the way out of all this sooner or later.'

'He?' said Nina. 'Who?'

'God,' said Hallie simply, then she paused, with a look in her eye that Karenza would have recognised as her Broody Chicken look, which preceded the hatching of one of her better ideas. 'God,' she repeated. 'Now He might just have the answer. Why don't the three of us go to church this weekend? Praying and worshipping together will surely bring us closer.'

There was an agonised pause, as Nina wondered how to deal with this unexpected turn in the conversation.

Then Hallie broke down, flopping onto the table with her head in her hands.

'Oh, who am I kidding?' she sobbed. 'God hasn't provided me with any answers, so why should He for anyone else?'

It was Nina's turn to put her arm round Hallie's heaving shoulders. 'Come on, I'm meant to be the crybaby round here and this is the second time you've burst into tears since I got here – what's wrong?'

'I'm sorry. It's just that I'm such a hyprocrite, and a liar, and a – a – a bad person,' choked Hallie.

For the first time in what seemed like weeks, Nina had to restrain a smile. 'I don't believe that for a second, Hal. How could you, of all people, be a bad person?'

'But that's just it – *of all people*. Even my own best friends don't believe that I could be anything but a goody-goody.' Hallie's voice was bitter.

'Hey, hey,' Nina calmed her. 'What are you on about?'

'Even while I've been going to church and preaching to you both about how clean and holy we should all be – all that time, I've been lying to you and Cass. Solidly, for the past ten months.'

'OK,' Nina said slowly, 'what about?'

'Reuben!'

'Hmm,' Nina murmured noncommittally.

'You remember when I turned up on New Year's Eve like a lost waif – when Cass had come over and I was spending the weekend with Reuben and I was meant to be standing you both up? Well, you know I told you how I dumped him because he was such a nightmare that New Year's weekend that I realised there really was no future in it? And that was when I came over to the cottage?'

Nina nodded.

'Well, that was just the first lie. He tried to dump me beforehand, but I forced him into that one last weekend. To go back to the good, old days, I said. One last fling, going out with a bang not a whimper, as it were. So I only had myself to blame when it all went horribly wrong. But I couldn't admit it to you and Cass, because you were in the first flush of married love, and Cass – well, she hardly knew Reuben and although it was awful what happened to John, she's never been chucked, has she? How would she know what it was like?'

'So you felt like neither of us would understand if you admitted that Reuben had been the one doing the dumping? Oh Hallie, for fuck's sake. You may think that Cass and I are the last of the great heartbreakers but I've spent nearly all of my adult life with one man – and look where that's got me – and look at Cass! Do you really think it's the mark of an emotionally well-adjusted person to go off to the States with her hand luggage bulging with condoms, then come back swearing off men altogether? Anyway, lying to us about who dumped who, is no great crime—'

'But I've been lying to you ever since!' cried Hallie. 'Once I'd bent the truth that time, how could I tell you that I was still seeing Reuben – in fact, still, still—'

'Sleeping with him?' said Nina calmly. 'Yeah, we thought so.' Again, she almost laughed at the look on Hallie's face.

'You knew?! You and Cass knew?! And didn't say anything!?'

'Hallie, for the last few months, we have been listening to you giving us a blow by blow – quite literally – account of every man you've fallen into bed with. And yet every so often, there would be a night when you'd go AWOL and if Cass or I tried to get hold of you then or ask you where you'd been afterwards, you'd bite our heads off for being nosy. It hardly took Sherlock and Watson to work out what was going on. Reuben was – is – the great love of your life – so it follows that he would be the only man you cared about keeping stumm on.'

Hallie shook her head. 'But I shouldn't have been doing it with Reuben at all, let alone lying to my best friends about it. The Church is so clear on this – sex under these circumstances always leads to conflict and dishonesty. And they're right. But I also knew how moralistic Cass would be and with you being married, I was convinced you would take a dim view of my intelligence. Besides, Reuben isn't the love of my life – I just can't seem to stop sleeping with him. I know it's empty, it's automatic, I just can't break the habit. In fact, I'm seeing him more than ever. It's like, when I started going to Holy Trinity I gave up the whole singles' scene—'

'Which is a good thing.'

'But that just made me want to see more of Reuben. It was like that entire exercise, the Hallie Goes Mad in Singleland exercise, simply served its purpose as a distraction from Reuben. Now that I've stopped, I'm getting obsessed all over again. And you know him, he's so easygoing. As long as I don't try to move our "thing" up a gear, it's fine by him how many times I want to swing by and go to bed with him.'

She began to sound hysterical again. 'I feel totally schizo-phrenic, Nina. Look at tonight – if you hadn't turned up I was on my way to church, then after that I was going to sneak off and bonk Reuben. It's all such a mess! I pray for hours each day but it doesn't seem to make any difference. I'm too ashamed to talk about it on Alpha nights – everyone else there is so genuinely good, kind and well-meaning.'

'Hallie, Hallie, so are you!' Nina interrupted. 'Now just calm down, will you? Calm down, calm down,' she added in a bad Harry Enfield Scouser impression. 'You're the kindest, loyallest person I know. Now don't bite my head off, but it seems to me that the only effect HTB has had on you, is to wind you up beyond belief and just make you even more fucked-up than you already were. Is that really what you want from your God?'

'You don't understand. HTB is the best thing that's ever happened to me – it's made me see where I've been going wrong, what I should be looking for in life, where my priorities lie. It's turned my life round.'

'Yeah, in one big fucking circle!' said Nina brutally. 'Listen to yourself, Hallie! You're sounding almost brainwashed, you're unhappy, you're still sleeping with Reuben, but you're now feeling worse about it instead of at least getting some unashamed enjoyment out of it – and now tell me how your life has turned around?'

'But – you don't – you haven't been to HTB – you don't know how – how amazing—'

'I'm sure it is – it's friendly, filled with people who are secure in their own certainty – that's always attractive. But, Hal, *you're* not certain, are you? You're as fucked up as I am, as Cass is, and it's frustrating not being able to sort it all out with your Churchy friends, eh? For fuck's sake, Hallie.'

'Nina, please, it's like watching *Goodfellas*, listening to you,' protested Hallie.

Nina flicked her hand impatiently. 'OK, OK, but listen, Hal, I'm Catholic – don't you think I would love to go to some priest, fall on my knees and say, "Forgive me, Father, for I have sinned, I have left my husband" and for him to reply, "Say these twelve Hail Marys and your marriage will be saved"? But it doesn't work like that – of course I would like to save my marriage, but whatever is going on between Jerry and me relates to us as people, not as two halves in some religious equation. It's the same with you – you have to look at yourself as an individual before applying some formula to your life, whether it's religious or social or whatever. Look within yourself and ask why you're still sleeping with Reuben, why you're still seeing him – is it nostalgia or do you believe it's leading to something? Is it you deciding to have sex with him, or him deciding to have sex with you? Can you really—'

'Stop! Please! I get the picture!' Hallie laughed weakly. 'How did we get to psychoanalysing me to within an inch of my life, instead of cheering you up?'

Nina smiled crookedly. 'This may sound awful but do you know how much of a relief it is to consider someone else's problems instead of my own? I am so sick of me, of my life, my little tragedies. If it's all right with you, I would just like to take a holiday from me for a while.'

'Go right ahead, ride on the merry-go-round that is Hallie Templeton, sunbathe in the glow of my glaring errors, dissect my every move if it makes you happy,' Hallie said mock-wearily.

'Hey, Doctor Cass would be proud of us,' quipped Nina feebly.

'As long as I don't have to be proud of Doctor Cass,' retorted Hallie.

*   *   *

Cass looked again at the map of Heptonstall, then around nervously, to check that no-one else from the Hebden Road team was following her. She didn't even want to think about all the canvassing she was meant to be doing. She still had the whole tranche of Sunsets to take care of – Sunset Avenue, Sunset Street, Sunset Crescent and so on – but she had to satisfy her own curiosity, put a face to the name of Mrs Harrison. She still hadn't told Wilbur that she and Hallie had decided to drop the issue. She couldn't face talking to him with the knowledge of her inconvenient crush on him banging a Homer Simpson-like litany of 'Doh!' round her brain, let alone brave his scorn at her decision. Perhaps meeting Mrs Harrison face to face would reassure her that this was all a fuss about nothing.

The trouble was that Cass was beginning to have a bad feeling about this by-election. Having braved pitbull dogs, rabid children and a chilling wall of indifference, the only real conclusion she had gleaned from the past two days canvassing, had been that Heptonstall voters didn't give a damn about New or Old Labour policies, they just wanted someone they knew. Frank Blackthorn had clearly been revered round here by the older folk, but largely in his role as a jobs-for-the-boys union man in the best tradition of the bad old days. He had also been their MP for twenty-three years, meaning that the younger generation had never known anything else. Nor did they seem to want to. Now that Frank was dead, anyone with the name Blackthorn would do.

Having worked only on the slick, stage-managed, media-obsessed lobby campaigns of Carter's office – with their infomercials, press conferences and staged rallies – Cass had also been unprepared for the pub-centred foot-soldiering of a British by-election. No wonder Alun had been so keen to help Gwenny out, she had thought uncharitably as she tramped through the streets to yet another Fox and Hounds rendezvous – it meant he could spend his whole day in a pub. From there to working men's clubs to WI coffee mornings, it was clear that the accent was on back-slapping more than laying out any political agenda. The previous afternoon, Cass had been sent off to loiter outside a local primary school, to catch the emerging children with happy-face stickers saying 'Go with Gwen!' then their parents with electioneering leaflets. The whole exercise had made her feel sick.

Manipulating kids with dumb stickers just so you could get the attention of their parents was not Cass's idea of high politics.

Nor was Alun and Gwenny's increasingly obvious relationship. While in front of the party workers, they were propriety itself but when they were alone with Cass, it was a different matter. How stupid did Gwen think she was? Cass thought bitterly. Alun had told her that Gwen didn't know that Cass knew about them – but how was Cass supposed to profess ignorance when they were behaving like lovesick teenagers? For Cass, watching Gwenny being downright coquettish and Alun doing his devoted puppy act, it was like witnessing the start of just another of her Poppa's disastrous marriages.

The final straw had come the night before. Cass – who was staying at Gwen's house, as cover for Alun, she suspected, who was also staying there – had come in from a late night at the pub with her fellow campaigners, where she had managed to put the circumstances of the by-election out of her head, and fall into the beery conviviality of the election trail. Creeping into the house much later, she had wandered blearily into the front room to watch some latenight TV. Putting her keys on the coffee table, she had suddenly seen them. Ripped condom packets, empty little husks of lust, two of them, right there on the table. It was like having the fact that your parents still had sex shoved down your throat. There was something rather gruesome about the thought of Alun, with his crumpled suits and beer belly, having sex there in the sitting room, not once but twice. It certainly hadn't made her feel any better about this election campaign.

Yet still she went along with it. What had happened to all her high ideals? For the first time since she'd left the John situation behind in America, Cass was beginning to feel ashamed of herself. It was an uncomfortable and sinkingly familiar sensation. Shaking her head, she rang the bell.

'Hello. Mrs Harrison?'

'That's right.' The woman who answered the door looked friendly, if cautious.

Cass showed her her canvassing ID card. 'I'm canvassing for Gwen Blackthorn and the Labour Party in the forthcoming by-election and I was wondering if—'

'You look fair tuckered-out, my girl. Tell you what, come in and have a cup of tea, put your feet up. Mrs Blackthorn won't mind and anyway, we won't tell her, will we?'

Cass felt drawn into the woman's simple kindness, like a tug into a whirlpool.

'I was really just going to ask you if you wouldn't mind sticking this small poster in your front window, but thanks, Mrs Harrison, I'd love to come in for a minute.' And find out just what lies behind all this Avalon business, she thought silently.

She followed the middle-aged woman, resplendent in her housecoat and tan-coloured pantyhose, into the small kitchen at the back of the house, which smelt of warm, damp cookie mix and kitty litter. The windows were fugged up, the heat almost overpowering. Cass wondered how long she would be able to stay awake.

'Now you sit yourself down there, in front of the fire, and make yourself at home,' said Mrs Harrison.

'Thank you, but I really can't stay too long.'

Cass was handed a cup of tea as brown as a ploughed field. 'I shouldn't worry about your canvassing, lass, round here there's few as would vote anything else but Labour.'

So why have they sent me round here? thought Cass resentfully. Don't Alun and Gwenny trust me with the tricky areas? She rubbed her hands, feeling the rawness from posting too many flyers through too many scrubbing-brush protected mailboxes. Did these people want clean letters or was it some sort of anti-hooligan device?

'Now that's a funny accent you've got, dearie,' said Mrs Harrison, settling herself into the armchair opposite Cass's and holding her gnarled fingers out to the fire. 'Is that a London accent? It doesn't sound much like those EastEnders people on the telly but happen you're not so common as they?'

'It's partly London,' admitted Cass, 'but I spent the last few years and some of my childhood in the States so the accent there rubbed off on me. My father's American, although I don't see too much of him.'

'Oh aye, America,' Mrs Harrison said doubtfully. It was clear that Cass might as well have said Mars. 'That's nice. So how did you find yourself up here in Heptonstall?'

'I'm researcher to Alun Blythe, who's MP for one of the Leeds constituencies, and he's helping Gwenny – er, Mrs Blackthorn – with the by-election campaign.'

'That's nice of him. Researcher, you say? Wait up, didn't I speak to you a few weeks ago?' Mrs Harrison withdrew suddenly, a wary look settling over her finely-drawn skin with its dusty smattering of scented powder. 'You haven't come to speak to me about all that Lottery business, have you? Because I'm fed-up to the back teeth—'

'Mrs Harrison, hang on! No! I promise, I'm just here as Mr Blythe's researcher, helping him to canvass for Mrs Blackthorn. Nothing more.'

Mrs Harrison sighed with relief and pressed on, obviously wanting to abandon the subject. 'I remember I met one of Mr Blackthorn's researchers at the election five years ago. Now, what was his name?'

'Ted Austin?'

'That was it. He was a nice lad.'

'He still is. He's really successful now, and just missed getting elected himself at the last election.' Cass hesitated, then decided to test the waters just one time. 'In fact, you know, he was next on the list to stand for Heptonstall if Gwen hadn't decided to run for office. Of course, he's much more New Labour than either of the Blackthorns . . .'

Mrs Harrison nodded absently. 'Isn't that nice? We'd have liked a lad we know. But Mrs Blackthorn will do just as well, I suppose. Not that I would know anything. I don't really go in much for politics, whatever you might think from me giving over that money to them. But my Alf always thought Mr Blackthorn was a grand man. Alf was Shop Steward over at the plant when Mr Blackthorn was first appointed the local Union head – and Mr Blackthorn always saw him right. Straight as a die, he was, that man, but it never stopped him putting a few contracts the plant's way. That's why I was glad I was passed onto him after that horrible man, Mr Boyd-Cooper, was so rude to me. I thought that my husband would have been glad to put the whole business into Mr Blackthorn's hands. Not that Alf was around by then. But I was so lost. Didn't know what on earth to do. I thought he might help, seeing as how he was now a proper politician and all.' She stared unseeingly into the fire.

And, instead, he screwed you over, thought Cass bitterly. She searched hurriedly for something to say.

'I'm so sorry, is your husband passed away now?'

Mrs Harrison closed her eyes for a second. 'No. Maybe. Who's to know?'

There was silence, Cass kicking herself for opening up this can of worms.

'Mrs Harrison,' she said softly after a moment, 'please forgive me, I had no business prying. I think perhaps I'd better go now.'

She stood up, and went to get her coat from where Mrs Harrison had hung it on the back of the door. As she did so, a framed photo on the wall caught her eye, and she paused. It was a black and white print of a much younger Mrs Harrison and a man in his late thirties, standing in front of an instantly recognisable monument. Mrs Harrison was anxiously incongruous in tightly knotted headscarf and light belted mac. The man, by contrast, was dressed only in a sleeveless tie-dyed T-shirt, baggy pants and a big careless grin. If Cass hadn't known better, she would have thought he looked stoned.

'Is that the Taj Mahal?' Cass heard herself asking. 'It looks gorgeous.'

Mrs Harrison came out of her reverie to look at the photo. 'Aye. It is. Why? Have you been there yourself?'

'No, but I've always wanted to. My Poppa always told me I should try to see it at night, then at dawn, to get the contrast.'

'And the blessed lack of tourists at that hour, compared to the crush later on,' Mrs Harrison said, 'even in them days. The place was packed by the time we got there, because I was late getting up. Alf never could abide with my tardiness of a morning.' She came and stood behind Cass, her finger reaching out to stroke the photo almost absent-mindedly. 'He was a lovely-looking man, wasn't he? That's the last photo I have of him. Doesn't he look daft in those silly clothes?'

'Er, well, I guess tie-dye was really hot in the . . . Sixties?' Cass hazarded.

'Oh, the Swinging Sixties were nearly over by then, not that I ever noticed them in the first place, not up here in Heptonstall,' the older woman said ironically. 'That picture was taken in 1969. A year after we won the pools. Three days before Alf left.'

'Left for where?' Stop asking goddamn questions, Cass cursed herself. What is with you?

Mrs Harrison looked at her sharply. 'You really don't know, do you? You just found that letter I wrote to Mr Boyd-Cooper, and that's all you've got to go on. You never spoke to Mr Blackthorn about it, did you?'

Cass decided to come clean. 'To be honest, I forgot all about the letter until Frank died. And then when I first spoke to you, I guess I was so excited by the noble altruism of you giving all your money to Labour, that I didn't exactly listen to what you *didn't* say. Then something a friend said made me follow it up.' She shrugged helplessly. 'You won't believe me, but I thought then that it would be better to let the whole thing drop.'

'Quite right.' Mrs Harrison patted her on the shoulder. 'You're a good lass. You weren't to know.'

Cass looked at her searchingly. 'But what wasn't I to know, Mrs Harrison? That Frank and Gwenny Blackthorn betrayed your trust? Because I personally think that their behaviour throughout this whole affair . . . well, I think it stinks.'

'Heavens! You do feel strongly about it, don't you? No, I can't blame Mr Blackthorn. It was all my fault. I should have known better, after that first time.' She looked at Cass with a kind look in her tired eyes. 'Now I can see you're all confused, you poor lamb, so take your coat off and sit down. I think it's about time you were set straight on a few things.'

Cass was jolted out of an uneasy head-dipping sleep by the unwelcome sound of her mobile ringing. She prayed that it wasn't Alun or Gwenny. There was no way she could face talking to them, let alone explain why she had taken off back to London without even telling them face-to-face, just leaving a note at Gwenny's house. She squinted at the screen, but it registered no number, just a flashing 'Call'. Given that Cass had programmed all her customary numbers into the phone only a few days ago, who else could be ringing her? Her heart sank. Carter. Carter – who still wouldn't believe that it was all over, including the shouting. Bloody, bloody men. She punched the receive button savagely.

'Now that's better – you finally got a cellular phone?'

'Einstein lives,' snapped Cass. 'Look, I told you before. If you don't leave me alone, I'm going to get tough!'

'But Cass, you always get tough with me – I wouldn't have it any other way!'

'Oh, Wilbur! It's you!' Cass squeaked uncharacteristically, praying that no-one on the train could see how red she was blushing.

'Whoa! Come back from the bats! Who did you think it was?' Wilbur's tone was teasing.

But Cass was recovering quickly. 'Just another asshole who won't stop pestering me,' she said coldly. 'I must have a sign above my head saying "Jerk-offs apply here".'

'Hey, don't think I hadn't noticed you weren't returning my messages. I just wanted to know where we were on the Blackthorn thing—'

'Yeah well, can't talk right now,' Cass said repressively. She had to get the whole garbled story straight in her mind before sharing it with anyone else.

'Oh, Alun's with you?'

'Yup,' lied Cass.

'OK, we'll meet in Oblivion at ten. You'll be able to make it there by then?'

'Yes, but—'

'No buts, Cass. You can't avoid me for ever. I'm way too determined.' Wilbur clicked off the line.

But not so determined to jump my bones, thought Cass savagely, cursing herself once again for wishing that he would. Such a cliché, she berated herself, falling for a man who doesn't give a damn.

Then again, the most clichéd thing now would be to carry on acting like she hated him. Then he would know for sure that something was up. It was time for Friendly Cass to come back from holiday.

She still couldn't believe the story Mrs Harrison had told her, the bare facts of what Cass had already known unravelling like the mere outer layers of an onion. Nearly thirty years ago, Alf and

Aud Harrison had won the pools, collecting over twenty thousand pounds in prize money. Alf had revelled in it from the beginning, welcoming in the reporters, delighting in the makeovers, the chat show appearances, the conspicuous consumption.

'I never felt comfortable with it, myself,' Mrs Harrison had told her, 'but I went along with it for our Alf's sake. He was like a kid in a sweet shop and who was I to tell him to slow down a bit? We'd never had much money before – though we'd never gone hungry – and it was fun not having to care any more, but it were the papers that got to me after a while. It was like they got bored with the good-time story and wanted something more? Had it changed us? Had we abandoned our friends? Did the town hate us now? Why hadn't we moved out of Sunset Hill Road? All that sort of thing.'

She sighed. 'Alf took it so personal, as if he thought that the reporters themselves thought we were the sort of muck who would be changed by a bit of brass and he started to get really down in't mouth. So it was me who came up with the idea of travelling round the world. My fault, you see? I thought it would be champion to get away from all the hoopla, the razzmatazz, and get back to being ourselves.

'But I was so wrong. The press found out and thought this was your typical pools-winners-go-mad story. In those days, they had stringers everywhere, so wherever we went – Paris, Venice, Rome, Beirut, Cairo – we'd have some blighter following us with a flash in his camera and a lick in his pencil. And poor Alf became more and more withdrawn. So then we went further off the beaten track, to Morocco and Tunisia to start with, and soon we lost them. Alf was making all these strange new friends – hippies, you called them then – and we started to follow the hippie trail, out to Nepal first, then down into India. I was hating every minute of it by this time. I was twenty-eight years old, remember – far too old to suddenly become some flower child. I didn't want to smoke their silly pot and I didn't want to sit cross-legged in the dirt and talk about the overthrow of the establishment. It all sounded like a lot of time-wasting rubbish to me. But Alf loved it. Here were people, he said, who didn't care about money. They didn't want to know if he'd been poisoned by the pools win, they didn't want to stick a camera in his face every time he went outside, they just wanted to be his friends. Yes, and have their bills paid by you, I told him. Cupboard-love friendship, that's all it was, for all their fine talk. Well, that was the first of many rows we had in India. He told me how I was a misery-guts who didn't know how to enjoy herself, that I hadn't enjoyed getting the money in the first place and that I wasn't joining in the fun and games now that we were travelling around, that all the reporters were right: that I'd changed since the pools win, become more selfish. And I thought it was those stupid drugs talking so I took no notice, thought it would blow over.'

She looked reflective for a moment. 'But it didn't. Because he left me. I woke up one morning in some godforsaken guesthouse near Jaipur and there was a note saying that he'd gone on with the others, that he wouldn't tell me where he was going because he didn't want the press to be able to follow him. Such melodramatic rubbish. And that was that.'

'You mean that was the last time you ever saw him?' Cass had said, astonished.

Mrs Harrison looked almost fond. 'My Alf was always a man of his word. For a while I would get wires asking for money to be sent to some bank or other but once I'd given away the pools money, I had none to send, so they soon dried up. He's probably dead now, shouldn't wonder. But it was a shame he never knew about Peter.'

'Peter?'

'I came back to Heptonstall straight from India. Alf had taken every penny we were travelling with, so all I had was my plane ticket back to England. I was so glad to be home that it took me a few weeks to realise that I was expecting. I was overjoyed, to tell you the truth, even if I had given away all the pools money, because I knew that this way I would always have a bit of Alf to remember him by. And when Peter was born, I didn't care about anything else except him. And I've had a good life since, so I can't complain. Until Sandra – my daughter-in-law – made me buy that dratted lottery ticket. You see, it was my fault again. I had told Peter everything about his dad and I knew that he blamed the pools win for his not being around. I knew that he banned Sandra from buying a lottery ticket, so why I let her persuade me to buy one instead I will never know. Then when

I won, I didn't even want to claim it except that I knew Sandra and Peter were struggling. So I did, but on the strict condition that there would be no publicity, and it was Sandra's and my little secret. She didn't want much, just enough to get by, and we would pretend that some long-lost uncle had died and left her some money. Peter was satisfied by this and everything was just tickety-boo. Until that horrid man from Avalon came and dragged me out to the pub. And he went on and on about how he'd found out about the pools win and how it would be such a great story – "The Double Winner" and all that – well, you know the rest.' She looked exhausted.

'But did you tell Mr Blackthorn all this?' Cass had asked, aghast. 'Surely when he heard about your husband, he realised that he couldn't break your confidence.'

'Oh, but I'm sure he didn't,' stressed Mrs Harrison. 'You see, it was my fault again. At first I didn't tell him about Alf – he was being so nice and kind anyway, and I don't like to wash my dirty linen in public, you know – and no-one else had picked up on the aftermath of the pools win business. Both Mr Blackthorn and the Avalon people just assumed that I was a widow and I let them believe that. And Sandra and I had agreed that there was just too much money to keep, so we'd already given half of it to the Labour Party Election Fund. I just think Mr Blackthorn was so excited about that part of it, that he forgot about how serious I had been about not wanting publicity. Who would take any notice of a silly, hysterical old lady who doesn't want to share her good fortune with the world? So finally, I did tell Mrs Blackthorn about Alf, and she was very understanding and promised she would tell Mr Blackthorn to hold fire.

'Trouble was, I think it was too late by then. The press already had the story, and suddenly I was being splashed all over the papers and the television. And, you know, the Blackthorns were so nice that I almost wouldn't have minded, except for, of course, Peter found out that we'd been lying to him all this time.' She looked crestfallen and, suddenly, very old. 'And now he's not speaking to me. Sandra smuggles my grandchildren in to see me occasionally, but it's not the same. Now I just feel like, because of some poxy money, I've lost both my husband and my only son. And it's all my own fault.'

But it isn't, Cass had wanted to cry. Frank Blackthorn should never have betrayed you. And Gwenny Blackthorn is just a fucking hypocrite. But to have blurted this out would have ripped the last shreds of dignity from Mrs Harrison, shown her that she'd been used, and made a fool of. It would have been the final cruelty.

Hallie toyed nervously with the silver cross round her neck, then resolutely dropped her hand. Nina was right, she wasn't going to think about Holy Trinity tonight. She wasn't going to let guilt interfere. Nor was she going to let thoughts of work intrude. She was just going to concentrate on enjoying her evening.

'Hello, peeps.' Hallie felt a kiss being dropped on her head. 'Am I late?'

'No, no, I was early,' Hallie assured him.

Reuben wagged a finger at her. 'You should never admit to that, you know. Did your mother never tell you how to play hard to get?'

Hallie looked levelly at him. 'You know perfectly well how hard I am to get.'

'True enough, my love, true enough.' He smiled and picked up his menu. 'Now, isn't this all very posh? What are we celebrating, by the way?'

'We're celebrating the fact that four months ago, I won the Bandwick and Parker Annual Sales Conference Eddie Prize, which was a meal for two at Aubergine.'

'Do I want to know what the Eddie Prize is? It sounds suspiciously AbFab to me,' he mused. 'No, I don't think I do. Hang on a tick – four months ago? Why the delay?'

'No delay,' she assured him. 'I rang the next day to make the booking. This was the first date they could do!'

They both looked round their surroundings – at the beige and mirrored, dimly-lit decoration, the tinkling of expensive cutlery over well-bred, hushed conversation, the sparkle from an average four glasses per person.

'You're joking. That's obscene. I would have told them what they could do with their precious restaurant,' he said seriously.

'Yeah, well, feel free to leave if you feel that strongly about it.'

Reuben stared at her. 'Hallie? Are you all right?' He reached out for her hand, sliding his thumb and forefinger over her skin with the familiarity of habit. 'I'm sorry – was I being a jerk? Not much of a fall-back, am I?'

'What do you mean?'

He winked at her. 'Don't play the innocent with me, Templeton. You only invited me yesterday, remember? Who am I replacing? Who stood you up?'

Hallie battled between anger that he should assume she'd been stood up and anxiety that he not discover the truth. That she never had invited anyone else but had been so unwilling to admit to herself that she only wanted to take Reuben that she had left it to the very last minute to capitulate. So she lied.

'You know me so well,' she sang ironically. 'OK, so you've discovered my little secret. You are actually a figment of my imagination. I wouldn't be dining at an expensively chic eaterie like Aubergine with a short, curly-haired doctor who thinks nothing of teasing me within an inch of my life. I'm actually here with a tall, dark George Clooney-lookalike television reporter who hangs on every word I say, compliments me on my new haircut,' she tossed her newly trimmed, newly blonded locks, 'and thinks that I am the wittiest, sexiest, most desirable woman since Madame Pompadour.' So there, she added silently, and I don't care if it's not exactly true.

Reuben gazed at her admiringly. 'And *I'm* the figment of your imagination?! What's the name of this gorgeous apparition?'

'Wilbur. Wilbur Coolidge. He works for CNN.'

'Wilbur?' Reuben snorted. 'What kind of name is that?'

'It's a nickname. He's actually called Calvin Coolidge.'

'Oh, the President that Time Forgot. Any relation? Wait a minute, isn't he your friend Cass's main squeeze?'

'No,' she said shortly. 'They never got it together and now they're into the Friend Zone.'

'Still – it's all a tad incestuous, isn't it? Careful, Hallie,' he wagged that finger at her again, 'you don't want to start picking up friends' leftovers – that's not a healthy way to go.'

'And this is?' Hallie suddenly didn't want to talk about her fictitious date with the patently unavailable Wilbur any more. 'Anyway, while we're on the subject of being stood up, how come you're available on a Thursday night at a moment's notice? Or have you left patients dying of neglect while you're here stuffing your face?'

Reuben laughed. 'So far, I'm the one dying – of hunger. Do you think if we speak in the same comedy-French accents as the waiters, they'll be fooled into thinking we're posh enough to serve?' He waved ostentatiously at a passing maître d'. 'No, you're right – I too was stood up. Not that I care, really. It was just that bird from the hospital – I think I told you about her. Helen.'

Hallie nodded vaguely. 'She sounded like a bit of a pain in the neck.'

'Well, yes, she is, I suppose. But she's certainly persistent. Doesn't take no for an answer, and certainly doesn't take any shit. Last week, I tried to back off, saying that I wasn't free for a few days, so she cancelled tonight's date and this new Shakespeare production we were meant to be going to tomorrow night in a sort of tit for tat, saying that until I got my head together and put in some commitment, then I could go and take a running jump.'

She sounds like a nightmare, thought Hallie comfortably, she hasn't got a clue how to handle the commitment-phobic Reuben. Since they'd broken up, she and Reuben had had the same string of Pop-Tart relationships – for two minutes they were piping hot and tasty, the next they turned unpalatable, stale and full of artificial additives. Even though two dates in a row sounded uncharacteristically romantic for Reuben, this Helen seemed destined to go the same way. Blink and you'll miss her, she said to herself.

'So this week I asked her to go out with me. Am I mad or what? This girl has a weird effect on me. I mean, I'm not sure I even like her. Not like I like you, anyway.' Again, his hand crept forward to slide over hers.

Even while revelling in his touch, Hallie felt the smallest twinge of presentiment.

'Zo, Mamzelle, you are rrrready to orrrder maintenant, non?' Finally, a waiter was bending over her.

'Yes, foie gras and the lamb for me,' Hallie said dutifully, 'and blow the diet. Reuben?'

'Now, tell me about the sea-bass,' he said challengingly, a wicked look glinting in his eyes.

'Oh, ze sea-bass, 'e is verrry, verry nice, prepared on a mousseline of—'

Reuben smiled brightly at him. 'Yes, I can read the menu. But what is a mousseline when it's at home?'

The waiter explained in excruciating but incomprehensible detail, then proceeded to give the rest of the menu the same treatment, describing everything without exception as 'verry, verry nice'. In their attempts not to laugh, Hallie and Reuben avoided catching each other's eye, but underneath the table, a shaking foot was slowly creeping up her leg. Hallie started to turn crimson.

'Mamzelle needs a drrrink of water, p'raps?' The waiter stopped prattling to stare anxiously at her florid face.

'What Mamzelle rrreally needs is a rrright good s—' Reuben broke off with a yelp, then rubbed his foot and glared aggrievedly at Hallie. 'Sip of wine. Sip of wine. Now, let me see.' He looked archly at the wine menu. 'I think . . . yes, the Chateau Haut Briand – why the hell not?'

Even to Hallie's untutored ears, this sounded expensive. He showed her the menu – £976 leapt out at her like a cricket bat. The waiter started trembling, his eyes widened, and his hands clutched his order pad convulsively.

'On second thoughts,' mused Reuben, 'naah,' he waved his hand dismissively, 'I'm not in the mood for red. Let's just go for a Chablis, shall we, dollface?'

Hallie thought the waiter was going to faint from disappointment. As for her, she was back to battling both the giggles and that straying foot again. The trouble was, she decided with the last shreds of rational thought, that Reuben was too damned irresistible for his – or her – own good. Even if he did seem to have forgotten that she didn't drink.

'What an unreal story! So the scene we have so far is Frank Blackthorn – Hamlet's father, if you like, except he's no blameless victim, but an Evil Genius casting his shadow over the rest of the protagonists. Gwen Blackthorn as Gertrude – outwardly Miss Perfect, but underneath a manipulative bitch. Alun as a hapless sort of Claudius – bewitched by his sexual lust for Gertrude. And, last but not least, Mrs Harrison – a tragic Polonius perhaps, being stabbed behind the arras, or Ophelia, driven mad by the evil Lottery bosses and the media.' Wilbur's dark eyes were sparkling. 'God – this is great! Cass, we could win prizes with this stuff!'

'You're enjoying this way too much, you sick puppy,' Cass waved her beer at him mock-sternly. 'Trouble is, you've hit the mark with your analogy. I'm Hamlet here, and I'm dithering. In fact, I'm being more decisive than the man in tights – I'm saying, "Enough already. We can't go through with this, so why start?" '

Wilbur looked around the crowded Oblivion bar, with his hand cupped to his ear. 'I'm sorry? Did I hear you say we can't go through with this? Cass, are you insane?'

Cass smiled apologetically. 'You're going to hate me, I know, but I just don't think I can go through with it. You weren't up there, Wilbur, it was weird, like another century. It was like they couldn't give a damn about ideas, policies, anything like that, just so long as they get Gwen, someone they know.'

Wilbur stared at her. 'And you don't think they deserve to know that Frank was a lying cheat filling his own pockets, that Gwen not only knew about that but was too busy screwing another MP on the side to care, that there are Blackthorn victims here? Or have you forgotten Mrs Harrison?'

'But that's just it, don't you see? You're being a typical journalist – running away with yourself. For the last goddamn time, we can't bring Mrs Harrison into this! That is the last, the very last thing she would want! And we can't bring Alun into it! Even I can't afford to bring myself into it!'

'You just don't get it, do you? Don't you realise that everyone – but everyone – in the media already knows about Alun and Gwen? That they're the worst kept secret since Joan Ruddock and that guy Frank Doran? I didn't want to tell you because I knew you would want to keep Alun out of it, but you can't, Cass, he's already in it up to his neck, and there's a flock of vultures just waiting to put a run-of-the-mill infidelity hiccup together with a genuine fledgling scandal, to make a godawlmighty stink. Don't you want us to be the ones handling it? But oh no, you just give me all this stuff, you just cry on my shoulder, "Oh Wilbur, what am I gonna do? I'm so confused!"' Wilbur's voice was mockingly falsetto. 'Well, let me clear some of that confusion for you, lady. I make my living from reporting on politics, Cass, but you won't let me do anything with this goldmine of a story. So, what *do* you want me to do?'

Cass stared at him, trying to take in the enormity of what he was saying about Alun and Gwenny. 'What else can we do? You said yourself that more often than not CNN yank your pieces in favour of stories about two-headed chickens in New Mexico. What makes you think they'd even be interested in some poxy British scandal? This is not Watergate, Wilbur – we're not Bernstein and Woodward and we have no Ben Bradlee to tell us how to handle this. Neither of us is senior or influential enough to keep control of this for more than two seconds once it's out. Besides, you know perfectly well that without my input, there is no story – because without me there *is* no Mrs Harrison and Avalon.'

'So you're just going to sit on the whole thing? Get Gwen elected and who cares that Ted would have made ten times a better Member of Parliament? Have you seen him lately, by the way? He's a wreck.'

Cass pointed an accusing finger at him. 'Don't you fucking dare try to make me feel guilty about that!'

'Hey, Princess Touchy, who's even trying? Seems to me you're doing a pretty good job of that all on your own!' Wilbur stared her down. 'So much for those pretty principles of yours, huh? Into the ropes at the first dirty punch. I have to say I never had you pegged as the cowardly type, Cass. Just goes to show how wrong us guys can be when it comes to figuring out the *weaker* sex.'

'Fuck you! That is just not fair!' But Cass was having trouble meeting his gaze. 'You have no idea what you're talking about! Don't you think I wish I could do something about it—'

'So why don't you? Come to that, why can't you afford to bring yourself into it? What have you got to lose?'

Cass clutched her forehead. 'Jesus, this is nothing to do with you – why am I telling you all my personal business?'

'Cass! This isn't your personal business, this is—' Wilbur started, then as suddenly he stopped, and a look of dawning realisation came over his face. 'Oh, I get it. Carter. Carter Goddamn Wylie. You don't want to embarrass him.'

'No! That is absolutely not it—'

'Oh, bull!' Wilbur was losing it now. 'Of course! How could you be the one to reveal Alun to be an adulterer when you are one yourself – we couldn't have the perfect, flawless Cass Herbert shown to be the hypocrite she is, could we? Just one question, Cass, why did you come here in the first place? You'd be much better off setting up your precious consultancy in the States, so why not do your contacts-gathering in political circles over there. Hey, as the mistress of a Senator, you sure got the in!'

'Christ, you're such a typical man!'

Wilbur laughed shortly. 'Not much I can do about that, honey.'

'Just use your goddamn brain! Why do you think I left the States? Doh!' Cass said tightly, in her most vicious Homer Simpson impression, right down to the dangerously squinted eyes. 'It was to get *away* from Carter, you moron!'

'But—' stumbled Wilbur, obviously wrong-footed, 'that was him on the phone the other night, in your apartment. I recognised the voice. And you thought it was him ringing you on the cellular this afternoon.'

'That's because he's a moron like you who needs things explaining in words of half a fucking syllable. He wouldn't accept that it was all over and – oh, what's the use in explaining?' She gave up and put her head in her hands. 'If you want to think I'm a politically self-serving tart, then what do I care? Go right ahead! My two best friends think I'm a lowlife who deserves to be shot, so why should you be any different?' She started to battle the tidal wave of tears that was threatening to sweep over her. She no longer cared what Wilbur thought.

After a minute, she felt rather than saw Wilbur get up and come round to sit next to her on the sofa. Then an arm crept around her shoulders. She pulled her gaze up to see Wilbur looking at her thoughtfully.

'C'mon now, Cass, don't cry,' he murmured, smoothing her hair away from her face. 'What is this all about?'

'I'm not crying,' she managed weakly, 'I don't do crying. It's just that my allergies are terrible and I'm tired and—'

'C'mon, let go of it.' He smiled gravely down at her. 'Tell your Uncle Wow. What is the story between you and Carter?'

Cass took a deep, shuddering breath and sat up straight. 'I never loved John, you know,' she started, looking defiantly at him. 'We just went out for a while: just fun, no strings. That's what I thought, anyway, even though he apparently thought that I was the love of his life. Then I finished it, when this became clear to me, because I knew I would never feel the same way he did. No big deal. Or it wouldn't have been if he hadn't died.'

She sighed. 'Christ, I'll never forget that nightmarish weekend at Meredith's cabin in the Rockies. Every time I had tried to end it up until then, John would change the fucking subject, duck out, go off to class, whatever. So I thought maybe being alone with him at the cabin would give us the space to get everything said. But when I finally got him to listen to me, I was so pissed at him that it came out all wrong, much more aggressive, I guess, than I had intended. And then he stormed out and said he was going climbing with Matt and the other guys from Jackson, to clear his head. Little did I know that when he got to the Centre, they'd blown him out, so he just hooked up with that guy, whatever his name was.'

'Rod, I think,' supplied Wilbur softly.

'Yeah, Rod. Poor guy. Anyway, when I saw the way the weather was going, I called Meredith and told her what had happened, and asked her if she knew Matt's parents' number so I could find out where they'd gone climbing. Then Matt answered the phone and that was just the start of the next nightmarish twelve hours until they found Rod, sitting half-frozen by John's body. Then, having to wait at the morgue until Meredith and Carter turned up and having to look her in the eye and seeing the blame there. "If you hadn't of dumped him, this would never have happened!" That's what she was saying inside, and she was right, but she couldn't bring herself to say it out loud. But it didn't make any difference then because that's what I was saying to myself, every minute, every second—' She broke off and clenched her fists.

'Hey, take it easy. You don't have to go on with this if it upsets you—'

'But that's just the point!' Cass turned on him. 'It didn't upset me! Not in the way you mean! It never did! Why should it? Up until the moment I heard Matt's voice on the phone, John had been nothing but an annoying presence outstaying his welcome in my life!'

Wilbur winced.

'Go ahead, wince! It doesn't make it any less true! Yet, because John died, he has had some sort of automatic status conferred on him – everyone assumes that he was some kind of hero beyond criticism and that I must be grieving for him, carrying a torch for him. But he wasn't – he was an insecure, attention-grabbing boy who took life way too seriously – in your heart of hearts you know I'm right – and I have never grieved for him, not for one second! I have never felt one iota of noble emotion for him – only guilt, anger at an only son being taken away at the age of twenty-seven, self-pity, sorrow for his mother – all these,' she paused.

'But anger most of all. Anger that I would have to carry this catastrophe around for the rest of my life when he should have been one of those boyfriends whose name you can hardly remember a few years later. Anger that it should have been me that pushed him into his death when I'd done nothing but try to spare his feelings in the weeks before that. Anger that I couldn't grieve for him. I never have. I couldn't – that really would be hypocritical – and that's why I couldn't go to the funeral. I would have felt such a fraud, sitting amongst his mourning family, and I did have the feeble but genuine excuse of my first ever gender workshop. So I wrote Meredith, explaining why I couldn't come and trying to set out my complicated feelings for John and my observations of him. Then, when I heard that they'd read the letter out at the service – only the flattering parts, if you remember – I realised that this could never be avoided – this gallstone of guilt blocking everything else in my life – unless I faced the lion in its lair.

'So I went to see Meredith in New York and tried to explain

all these churning, awful feelings. Tried to tell her about my guilt. Tried to get her to blame me. Then at least I would have had something to fight against – like when you condemned me out of hand when we first met. But she wouldn't. She was so obsessed with talking to her grief counsellor that she couldn't have a similar sort of conversation with me, yet she wouldn't let me go, made me stay at the townhouse with her, kept breaking down and wailing that I couldn't go, I was her last link to John, all that emotional bullshit. She was a mess. And Carter – Carter was the one who listened, who was also being alternately shut out and clung to by Meredith, who missed John but couldn't talk about it to Meredith because she became instantly hysterical. We were like shipwreck survivors clinging onto each other to survive and it seemed like he was the only one who understood about me and John, and like I was the only one who understood about him, John and Meredith. And so, in the middle of this claustrophobic environment, we became close and,' she looked directly into Wilbur's eyes, 'yes, we made the massive error of taking that closeness one step further. It seemed logical at the time, as if the three of us were the only ones left in the world – and the only way we could get any joy out of what was left was with each other – Meredith by leaning on Carter and me, and Carter and I by having an affair. In a funny way, it felt like otherwise I was always going to be in the red with the Coolidge Clan, that I was in debt to John's memory and that by making one member of his family happy, I was somehow making up the balance.'

She smiled ruefully. 'The trouble was that as the weeks went on, I realised that these were all the wrong reasons for sleeping with someone married, old enough to be my father and in the public eye. To cut a long and boring story a little shorter, he on the other hand had concocted a whole tranche of all the right reasons he thought we *should* be together. The only way I could end it was by cutting loose from him and Meredith, and coming here. End of story. Except that he went for the Epilogue approach and turned up at Trudie's the other day, swearing undying love and telling me he'd left Meredith—'

'He has?'

'Not any more. I threatened him with all sorts of punishments and exposures if he didn't pull his head out of his ass, and get back to her before she noticed that he was gone. At the heart of it all, he loves her – that's why he was so upset when she shut him out after John's death, he just needed a ten-gallon wallop in the right direction. That's why I can't go on with this Blackthorn thing – we made a sort of deal, that I wouldn't go public about anything to do with us, if he went back to Meredith like a good boy. If I expose Alun and Gwen, then the press do some digging on me, they'll blow Carter and me straight into the *National Inquirer*, then the delicate state of play between him and Meredith will collapse. After John's death, I couldn't ruin her chances of happiness all over again. You do understand, don't you?' She held his gaze pleadingly.

'Cass Herbert, you fraud. Underneath it all, you're just a big softie.' Wilbur relented. '*Il faut que le coeur se bronze ou se brise,*' he added softly.

Cass looked up with raised eyebrows, almost smiling. 'Say what?'

'Balzac – the heart must bronze over in order not to break,' he explained. 'Or something like that.'

'Nice repertoire,' she said lightly. 'Bet you say that to all the girls.'

'Cass,' he reproved gently. 'Don't.' Then he grinned. 'All except the French ones – they'd be able to tell how bad my accent was.'

Cass shook her head mock-despairingly.

'No, all I'm saying is, of course, I understand. I won't pester you any more about it. Blackthorns – be gone!' Wilbur went through an elaborate charade of bundling up papers in his hands and throwing them away, then turned back to stare intently at Cass, his dark eyes boring into hers. 'But what about you now?'

'What do you mean?'

'Now that you've sent Carter packing, back to the marital home – what happens to you? Who's there for you?'

'Oh me? Who cares? To be honest, the whole idea of caring for anyone ever again fills me with horror. That way you don't get hurt when they die or leave you. I felt totally twisted with hate and bile and anger when John died – imagine what real grief and pain must feel like.' Cass patted his hand almost cheerfully. 'Old Dame Cass, they'll call me, when I go to collect my OBE from the Palace for my pioneering work in gender studies.'

'OK, but it doesn't have to be that way, you know,' Wilbur said softly, giving her his Clooney look. 'Now that we've got all that emotional baggage unpacked, how about we start to see, you know, how the future looks . . .'

'We?' she teased. 'Since when was there a "we"?'

He said nothing, just looked at her calmly. Cass could feel him waiting for her to make a move. She held her breath, her stomach suddenly in freefall, longing to be able to be the one to reach out and touch him.

She couldn't, wouldn't, wanted to.

Impasse.

'Forget Aubergine, that place was Ratatouille by the time we left!' Reuben grabbed hold of Hallie's hand as they trotted up the street towards the Fulham Road as fast as Hallie's new gossamer-soled stilettos would allow. 'It was the Chaos Theory all over again – put two cocky young Jeff Goldblums like you and me in with a load of dinosaurs like that and bam! Steven Spielberg couldn't have done better!'

'The maître d's face when you threatened to sue over the loss of your non-existent coat!' gasped Hallie. 'Then when you quoted French poetry at him and he didn't understand it.'

'To be fair, it was medieval poetry,' admitted a grinning Reuben, 'so he didn't stand much of a chance, but I still reckon that when he went into the kitchen it was,' he pulled a face and went into his best 'Ackney accent, ' "farkin'elw, we've got a right pair of tossers aht there. You'd hardly Adam and Eve it." '

'Lucky neither of us had soup,' Hallie giggled, as they climbed into a taxi. 'Gob City behind the scenes.'

'Yeah, forget spitting – if he hadn't had to open the wine at the table, I bet he would pissed in it after that Chateau Haut Briand stunt.' Reuben collapsed into the taxi and pulled Hallie into his arms so that she lay lengthways across the seat.

She adapted to the position with the ease of long practice and they lay there in companionable silence, Reuben stroking her hair absentmindedly, both of them watching the passage of floodlit landmarks past them, the V&A, the Royal Albert Hall, the bright lights of Harvey Nichols, the uplit glories of the Britannia at Hyde Park, Marble Arch. After a while, Hallie noticed that they had turned off the Marylebone Road to head towards Primrose Hill. Now that she came to think of it, Reuben had not even asked the taxi to go on to Islington. Well, that was one decision that had been taken out of her hands.

When they got back, Josh was still up, flicking through the satellite channels still in his muddy tracksuit, football kitbag spilling its guts beside him.

'Wotcher bro,' he greeted them without looking up. 'And how was the little woman?'

'Josh,' warned Reuben.

Hallie felt sick.

Josh looked up and didn't bat an eyelid. 'Hey, Halster. All right? No, Reuben, did you work your medicine man magic on that little old woman that was brought in yesterday?'

'Oh. Yes. Sort of. Hey, how did the Spurs match go?'

Hallie still felt sick.

'Oh, we wiped them out. Three-nil. Did it with our eyes shut. Hallie, have you heard about my glorious football career?'

Hallie shook her head. 'Don't tell me you've been picked from obscurity by Tottenham Hotspur?'

Josh laughed. 'Close, but no bananas. Nah, this is the Harry Hotspurs – a bunch of mostly unemployed Shakespearian actors like me. We play under the Westway, most weeks. It's a laugh.'

'Hey, you should play the Westminster Wobblers in a charity match,' Hallie said, ignoring Reuben's hands against head 'let's go to bed' gestures and sitting beside Josh on the sofa. 'Is there anyone famous in your team? Toby Stephens? Mark Rylance? Anyone like—'

'Pur-leeze,' groaned Reuben. 'Enough networking. C'mon, Hallie, let's go to bed.'

'I want to watch telly with Josh.'

'There's actually nothing on,' said Josh, not wanting to get caught up in this, 'I'm going to bed myself.' He stood up. 'Oh by the way, some girl called for you, bro.'

Reuben frowned repressively. 'Uh-huh.'

'I think she said her name was Helen. What a stroppy cow! She nearly bit my head off when I said you were still out.'

Hallie smiled.

'And she said that you hadn't called her today, when you said you would, and that she wanted a damn good explanation. I tell you, I was shaking in my trainers by the time she was finished. What a demanding bitch!'

'You may be right,' said Reuben good-naturedly, steering Hallie determinedly towards his bedroom. 'I'll have strong words with her on your behalf. Goodnight.'

'Cheers, bro. 'Night, Halster.'

'Night, Josh.'

Once inside the bedroom, Reuben dipped his head to hers and kissed her, long and thirstily. Then he turned away and started shrugging out of his jacket and shirt.

'Wait,' Hallie said suddenly. 'I don't think I want to do this.'

Reuben paused, belt drooping, half-undone. 'Why?' He looked at her, puzzled. 'This isn't anything to do with that Helen bird, is it?'

'No, no,' she assured him.

'Because you would really be barking up the wrong tree if you thought I wanted anything to do with her. The woman's a nutter! Typical product of the NHS trust system, if you ask me.'

'It's nothing to do with her. It's to do with me. I don't think I can go on like this. We broke up ten months ago, Reuben, and I can't go on kidding myself any more. The truth is, I think I've—'

Reuben gathered her up, wrapping his arms across her back. 'I know.' He kissed the top of her head. 'I've been seeing this coming all evening. Look, if you want us to start going out with each other again, then I'm prepared to give it another go.'

'What?!' Hallie pulled back and stared at him.

'I mean it. I was a fool to end it last time and I acted like a shit over New Year. The truth is you've kept me sane over the last few months, when I hardly deserved a polite word from you. Work has been a nightmare and you've been a constant lifesaver. I'd be an even bigger fool if I let you get away a second time.'

Hallie struggled to say something tough and coherent. 'H-hardly very romantic.'

'You want romantic?' he purred, bending down to nuzzle at her neck. 'What would you say if I told you how jealous I've been about all these Devlins, Sauls, Wilburs? I sometimes thought you were making them up just to torment me.'

'Torment you?!' she gasped, her hands going up of their own volition to cup the back of his curly head. 'But that's—'

'Ridiculous. I know. I had no right.' His long, surgeon's fingers were now edging slowly but surely inside her shirt. 'Hallie, you have no idea what you do to me. Those baby-blue eyes of yours are deadlier than you think. And these,' his hand was now firmly ensconced round her breast, 'they're enough to reduce a man to tears. You truly don't know how sexy you can be, do you?' He looked up at her, his dark eyes bright indeed. 'So, what do you think, Hallie? Will you take me back?'

If her knees got any weaker, thought Hallie suddenly, her thighs would slop down to her ankles like Josh's baggy old games socks. 'I-I-I—'

'Tell you what,' he wheedled, turning her gently round and pulling her towards the bed. 'Think about it in bed. Let's see if I can't persuade you.'

That was all it took for Hallie to make her decision.

Everything was perfect, thought Nina, as she sat on the steps of Theberton Street, red-faced and puffing, relishing the bite of the autumn air on her tingling skin. To her left was the rush and bustle of Upper Street, Young Fogeys mixing with New Literati, Meedja types and every other label currently on pundits' lips. Garishly coloured Conran-wannabe restaurants with nonsense names like The Road or Faster, Pussycat! sat side by side with grimly-persevering, grimy-fronted hardware shops. The smells were of diesel and leaf-rotting gutters, with a faint whiff of curry from the Tandoori Star on the corner. She had a grazed palm, aching insteps, a bruised knee and a heart that was still beating like the clappers from her rollerblading sortie, but Nina was almost beginning to feel happy. To be in London felt – okay.

At least she was keeping busy. In the last few days, Nina

had coaxed most of her old contacts out for a drink or coffee at the least. She had spent hours in the library – cursing the laboriousness of old-fashioned research after the speed of the Internet – and had blagged her way into the cuttings library at Northcliffe House. Still not quite able to think of returning to travel writing, she had taken the first step by coming up with pages of UK-based ideas. Now all she could do was wait to see if she would be commissioned. She had just been paid for her Primrose Path columns – although she rated the chances of them ever seeing the light of newsprint at zero – so she wasn't facing immediate money worries. And if at times she felt like the opposite of a swan – all furious activity on the surface, frozen stillness underneath – then she would think about that tomorrow. And tomorrow was a country she didn't have a visa for at the moment.

At least Hallie had left her well alone. Nina had been half-afraid that Hallie would dive into a Save Our Nina campaign with her usual enthusiasm and vigour but, luckily for Nina, though perhaps not so luckily for Hallie, she was so distracted by her various career and lovelife entanglements that she had little emotional energy left over. So the matchmaking, predatory clubbing and P.O. Boxing that Hallie had placed such faith in herself were put on hold for the moment, leaving Nina to her own, much welcomed, devices. Even better, usual peacemaker Hallie had not tried to solve the situation between Nina and Jerry since that first tearful night, and now had no qualms about shielding Nina from Jerry – making sure that Nina never answered the telephone, telling her firmly to check through the spyhole whenever anyone rang the doorbell – without asking any questions.

Less puffed now, she leant down to undo the straps of the dreadful Beth's rollerblades, realising that she would have to get them fully aired out before Beth came home from work and realised that she had been using them. The situation between Hallie and Beth was beyond ridiculous – they had segregated food in the fridge, Beth's marked with skull and crossbone labels (given by Hallie tongue-in-cheek for Beth's birthday, but received straight-faced and immediately put to good use) saying 'Hands Off My Crow Pie!', and had roster times for morning showers, washing up and bill-paying. If both of them were in, Hallie would have to sit in her room – Nina suddenly understood why Hallie had been so keen to hit the singles circuit – anything was surely better than being banished to a silent bedroom. And Hallie had to make all her telephone calls on her BT Chargecard.

When Nina had arrived, she had soon sussed this out and had pointed out to Hallie that her staying was just going to make matters worse.

'Don't go,' Hallie had begged her. 'The trouble is that I haven't got the time or the energy to fight back at the moment, but if you can bear it, you can be my official mascot of protest. One of these days, I will get round to moving out but until then I don't see why the selfish cow can't put up with a wounded lamb for a few days.' She had looked sidelong at Nina. 'I know it offends your notion of "not wearing your heart on your sleeve", or whatever the expression is, but if you *can* give the odd wounded lamb impression, that would be fab.'

So, when Nina had been alone with Beth, she had embarrassed both of them by attempting to cry on Beth's shoulder.

'I'm so sorry to burden you with my problems, even just by staying here,' Nina had sobbed carefully, 'but I just don't have anywhere else to go. Even my mum won't see me.'

Of course, that last part was almost true – Nina's mother had been so ecstatic when her half-breed and therefore disadvantaged daughter had married someone from the Right background, and so appalled when Nina told her she had left Jerry, that the stiff little house in Brook Green would have been anything but the unquestioning oasis that Nina had found with Hallie. 'I won't outstay my welcome – you have to tell me the moment I become a pain in the neck.'

'No, no, that won't do,' Beth had assured her heartily. 'You'll soon pull yourself together and get back on your feet. Time is a great healer – and sport, of course . . . have you thought about coming along to netball practice with me next Tuesday? Of course, some rent would be nice – I know you're sharing Hallie's room, but three people use three times as much hot water and so on.'

And Slammer doesn't? Nina had wanted to ask, before

remembering how Hallie had told her that Beth's boyfriend was only on nodding terms with soap and water, believing it to be unmanly to smell fresh and clean.

Easing her feet out of the skates with a sigh, Nina failed to notice the unfamiliar car drawing up in front of her, or the person stepping out of it, until it was too late.

'Hello, Nina.'

It was Jerry. He was standing at the bottom of the steps. 'This is a stroke of luck, actually seeing you in the flesh. And with no protectors.'

Afterwards, Nina realised that she must subconsciously have been expecting him, because she was so unshocked by his sudden appearance. Mind you, at first glance, she might not have recognised him. In his three-piece pinstripe suit and new short haircut, gone was the easygoing, hair-flicking Jerry with whom she had fallen in love. Then she saw the bags under his bloodshot eyes, and the strain in his jaw, the wanness under the remnants of his summer tan and the grim set of his mouth, and Nina's heart ached for him, for her, for Babaji. Still she didn't say anything.

'A silent Nina. Now there's a thing. Those steps look comfortable. Can I join you?'

Nina nodded, and shuffled over.

'So, strange times, eh?' he said equably. 'Funny old world. One minute, you're happily married, the next minute your wife was has left you without a backward glance. Ker-blam! Out of the blue! Bit of a shock, really.' He turned suddenly and grabbed her by the upper arms. 'Nina! For Christ's sake, say something!'

Nina shook herself free and moved further along the step. 'You haven't said anything worth replying to yet.' Her voice was cold, almost unrecognisable even to herself. 'Whose car?'

'It's a company car – I'd have been a bit stuck without it, wouldn't I?' he said savagely. 'I waited on the doorstep for nearly thirty-six hours, you know, waiting for you to come back. I thought you were dead in the gutter, smashed under some central reservation. I couldn't believe you would leave me – just like that. How many times can I apologise for Babaji?' Jerry cried. 'It was an accident! You can't punish me this hard for something that was an accident. It just wouldn't be like you!'

'I'm not punishing you,' Nina said steadily, staring straight ahead into the middle distance. 'And how do you know what is like me? I'm not sure even I do. Who is Nina Kellman? Nina Parvati was easy: she was wild and crazy, but at the heart of it all she knew that the thing she craved above everything else was belonging. Doing the right thing. Fitting in. And she fell in love with you, and you were perfect. By your side, she *could* belong, be one of them. But Nina Kellman? She's someone altogether different. I don't like her, actually. She's selfish and self-obsessed and she has no focus except that feeling of arrival, of being where she aimed for. But where was she to go from there? She couldn't stay static.'

Nina turned to Jerry and looked him in the eye for the first time since he'd arrived. 'I didn't leave you out of the blue, Jerry. And it's nothing to do with Internet chatlines, e-mail flirtations, or even you lying to me about your job. It's just me. I'm sorry. I married you for all the wrong reasons and since then it's just been a struggle to match expectations with reality. I just can't go on pretending. I don't know who I am now but I'm not the same person you married and it's not fair to either of us to pretend that I am.'

'But that's natural,' he snapped. 'Marriage changes people – don't you read your own bloody magazines? And as for being unfair, don't you think I get a say in this? That afternoon, when you blew up at me, you didn't let me get a word in edgeways. Don't those vows we said to each other mean anything to you? Look, I will do anything to keep you. If I have to, I'll change. If it's that important to you, I'll chuck in this bloody job. I'm prepared to do all these things. But Christ, it's as if you don't even want to try!'

She took a deep breath. 'I don't.'

'What?' Jerry suddenly looked on the brink of tears.

'For once in my life I'm not going to do what I should. I'm not going to just fall in line and do what is expected of me. I'm not going to try and mend a marriage which I no longer feel I am in. Look, this is coming out all wrong but I'll give you the simple version. Nina Parvati loves you. Nina Kellman loves you. I'm just not sure I love you, because I'm not sure who I am. That's the only way I can explain it.' Nina plucked at the escaping threads of her jumper sleeve agitatedly.

Jerry looked like someone had let the air out of him. 'Do you know something?' he asked her tiredly. 'That is the first conversation we've had in about four months where you haven't said "fuck" at least five times. I've just realised how much you usually swear. That's Nina Kellman, is it?' He shook his head. 'I can't pretend I understand a word you're saying, so I'm just going to ask one question – are we over?'

Nina clutched her head in her hands. 'I don't know!' she wailed. 'That's what I've been trying to tell you!'

'Well, that's good enough for me. I'll wait for you. Not for ever, but I will wait,' he said heavily, scraping his hands through what was left of his hair. 'What about your stuff?'

'I'll leave it with you for the time being. I just need my clippings file and my passport, just in case I get some work.'

Jerry sprang up, shocking her. 'You're back to travel-writing already? I don't believe it! How can you think about gadding off when our marriage is collapsing around our ears?!'

'Just like you can get all dressed up, jump into your company car and go to your new job!' she bit back.

'That's not the same,' he raged. 'That's just a job.'

'And travel-writing isn't? Oh, piss off, Jerry!'

'Fine! I will.' He strode over to the car and pulled something out. 'There! I got this for you, you self-centred bitch.' He shoved it into her hands.

She looked down. It was her laptop. 'You bought it back.'

'Yeah. Fat lot you care, but you'll need it for your glorious travel-writing career. And here,' he thrust a wrapped parcel at her, 'I also bought this for you. I hope you like it.'

And he stalked away, got into his car and drove off with a melodramatic screech of tyres.

She unwrapped the package.

'Oh, you complete fucking bastard,' she said slowly.

Hallie came round the corner from Upper Street, with a spring in her stride. Ever since she had woken up that morning, she felt like she'd had a smile on her face. Even the concerted efforts by Gwen Blackthorn and Alun Blythe to ignore every piece of campaign material sent up to them by Walworth Road and plough their own idiosyncratic path couldn't blacken her mood. She should get propositioned more often.

As she got closer, she saw Nina in a huddle on the front step.

'Nina?'

Nina looked up and it struck Hallie anew how dreadful her friend looked. Where once she had been compact and fit, now she was both wasted and slack-fleshed, her olive skin blotchy and discoloured between tan and stress rashes, her dark hair dull and tangled.

'Look.' Nina handed Hallie what she had been hunched over.

It was a framed photograph of Babaji, blown up into almost unbearable detail, showing off his white grin up at the camera, the sparkle of black eyes behind an irrepressible fringe of woolly hair, his tail a blur behind him. With it was a card – some anonymous Impressionist scene of blues and mauves – and inside, in Jerry's spider-on-acid handwriting, an inscription. 'I loved him too. I miss him and I miss you. Come back to us. All my love, Jerry.'

'Oh,' said Hallie uncertainly. 'Jerry's been here, then?'

Nina nodded.

'Well, it's a nice thought. Isn't it?' asked Hallie.

'It's the most blatant fucking emotional blackmail I have ever come across. I can't fucking believe he thought I would fall for it.'

'Well, maybe it's true,' Hallie suggested, then when she caught Nina's glare, 'but, you know, then again, maybe not. Bastard. That's what I say.'

'Better,' said Nina with a half-smile.

'Do you know what?' Hallie said with sudden vigour. 'Do you know what I think we need? And it won't even cost us because we can wangle it through the New Business account.'

'No offence, but I'm not in the mood for one of your posh dinners,' Nina grimaced.

'No! A weekend at a health farm! There's one down in

Hampshire called Forest Mere which we've just taken on as a short-term client until they have their grand new opening after some massive refurbishment programme. Come on! I know it's all cosmetic but you know what they say, healthy body, healthy mind. Let's face it, we both need it! Say yes! Say yes! Look, it's only Friday afternoon – I'll ring them up and see if they can squeeze us in tomorrow. Come on, you know it makes sense.'

This was what Nina had been dreading: Hallie in Crusader mood. But now that it came to it, she found that she wanted nothing more than to be swamped by someone else's decisiveness and sink into some pampering. Maybe it was putting off the evil moment of dealing with her marriage, but, hey, what was wrong with that?

'OK,' she said finally. 'As long as you don't expect me to be in a good mood.'

'No, no,' Hallie dismissed the idea with a wave. 'I'm in a good enough mood for both of us.' She winked at Nina. 'And I'm not going to tell you why until we get there, so you'll have to be in suspense until then!'

'Fuck me, is everyone into emotional blackmail, or what?' grumbled Nina. 'What if I tell you that I'm far too miserable and self-obsessed to care about your petty little happinesses?'

Hallie stuck her tongue out at her. 'Pig. Believe me, you'll be impressed by this petty little happiness.'

'Try me,' said Nina blackly.

13

'Now this was a good idea.' Nina stretched out luxuriously on the sofa cushions, making sure not to smudge her toes' nail varnish and smoking exaggeratedly to avoid denting her fingernails.

Hallie and Nina were sitting in the Smoking Room at Forest Mere Health Spa in Sussex, with its appropriately tobacco-coloured hessian walls and the deliberately un-room-freshenered aroma of stale smoke, guiltily puffing on a sneaky fag between treatments. They had had facials, manicures, pedicures, steam baths and it was only half-past one. So far they hadn't done more than waggle their toes to dry them but Nina couldn't remember the last time she'd felt so deliciously exhausted.

'Hey, just doin' my job,' drawled Hallie. 'I'm the Good Ideas Girl, remember? Gig-a-gig all the way. Just save your strength for the algae wrap.'

Nina giggled. 'Sounds like a different sort of gig. Ladies and Gentlemen!' She threw her arms open, 'Put 'em together for Al Ghee and his Rappers.'

'If I'm going to be spending the whole weekend with you, sweetie, your jokes had better improve,' threatened Hallie. Then she smiled, looking past Nina. 'Oh look, there go the three mush-keteers.'

Nina turned round to see the three middle-aged ladies they had shared their table with at lunch, during which they had hardly drawn breath yabbering to each other, while spooning up some specially prepared liquidised pap with every appearance of enthusiasm. They were walking across the lawn outside, down to the lake, still in their white Forest Mere dressing-gowns, still chattering away.

'They've been here for three weeks,' Nina said incredulously, pulling her own white robe tighter across her chest. 'How do you suppose they've got anything left to say to each other?'

'I know,' marvelled Hallie, 'I work in PR – and I've never heard such seamless smalltalk.'

'I don't know about smalltalk – that conversation about hospitals, it was like some macabre form of one-upmanship about how many hospitals they had each been to!'

'Yes,' Hallie chuckled. 'What was that about "Oh, the King Edward – I've been there. Was it my hysterectomy or my varicose veins that I had done there? Yes, that was very nice"? Unbelievable!'

'Bloody funny though. When that very bejewelled one was going on about walking in here with thirty-two pats of butter strapped to her hips and how "a pat off a day has kept the mirror at bay!" I thought I was going to do the nosetrick with my beansprouts.'

Hallie giggled. 'Yeah, you know when we were in those steam cabinets? While you were asleep—'

'Fuck knows how I managed to do that. Now I know how tomatoes feel when you're told to skin them in posh recipe books.'

'Well, I was trying to keep from fainting by talking to the woman on my right – the one in full makeup – and she was coming out with some classic stuff. She was talking about going into the hairdressers this morning and coming smartly back out again. "Just too Mrs Tiggywinkle, darling," she said. "Mind you, I am the woman who goes on holiday with her hairdresser – eat your heart out, Cherie Blair! – after all, anything's better than going with your husband, isn't it, dear?" and I felt too weak with heat and laughter to do anything but nod.'

'But, hang on, wasn't that the woman with the husband and son here? So she does sometimes come on holiday with him.'

'Husband and *step*son,' stressed Hallie knowingly. 'And you saw her and the stepson together at lunch – I reckon there's something funny going on there.'

'That's nothing – what about that fucking ancient-looking Lebanese woman and that gorgeous young bloke she's with. I assumed they were grandmother and grandson or something but I distinctly heard him call her *habibti*, which is, like, darling sex goddess in Arabic so he must be her toyboy. Fucking gross.'

'Nina – we are in a temple of health and calm, a refuge of tranquillity and serenity. I will not let you curse your way through the whole weekend. And how on earth would you know what darling is in Arabic?' Hallie said accusingly.

With Nina's dark skin, it was often hard to tell when she was blushing. Not so this time. 'Oh, the things you pick up on press trips,' she said airily.

'Things or men?' Hallie arched an eyebrow at her.

Just then the door swung open on its fire-door hinge and a dazzling vision came into the room. All that glisters *is* gold, thought Nina dazedly.

'Hello, girls,' boomed the roughest, huskiest, biggest voice either of them had ever heard. 'Mind if I join you?' Without waiting for an answer, a large, swarthy-skinned woman crossed the room and deposited herself heavily on one of the remaining lowslung olive sofas, leopardskin legginged-legs swinging akimbo to reveal three perfect rolls of leopardskin T-shirt-clad flab. 'What a perfectly horrible room. They're punishing us smokers, aren't they?'

Hallie and Nina tried not to gape. Never had they seen so much gold outside a Ratner's window. There had to be six chains on each well-curved arm, rings on every pudgy, red-taloned finger, and a Mr T profusion of necklaces sitting on a pair of bosoms big enough to breastfeed the Less Developed World. They watched as she opened her gold Prada handbag, took out – what else – a gold cigarette holder and threaded into it a dark cheroot.

'Would you like a light?' Hallie asked finally.

'Angel, thank you. Would you like some of this?' She plucked a bottle of Evian out of the depths of the handbag and held it out to them.

Nina shuddered. 'No more water, thank you. I'm swilling with the stuff after that steam bath.'

'Oh bugger that, darlings, this is Absolut.' She unscrewed the top and took a slug without even wincing.

'Oh! Oh, right,' stammered Nina, feeling like a giggly schoolgirl. 'No thanks, all the same. I think I'd pass out if I had vodka.'

'Suit yourself. I think I'd pass out if I didn't,' shrugged the woman genially. 'If my husband's going to send me here, I've got to have my laughing gas!'

Hallie and Nina didn't dare catch each other's eyes.

'So is your husband here with you?' said Hallie politely after a short pause.

This provoked a hearty guffaw, followed by an explosion of coughing and a fearsome jangling of chains and bangles. 'Lordy, no! This is my holiday from him! And he really would have a heart attack.' The kohl-rimmed eyes turned speculative. 'Now there's a thought. I'd make ever such a merry widow!'

Hallie turned wide-eyed to a frantically jaw-clenching Nina.

'Just having you on, angel!' There was another guffaw, and more billows of smoke from the cheroot. 'No, I love it here really! Come about once every couple of months for a week – Mona's little treat, I call it. It gives me a chance to dress down for a few days. I mean, no-one cares what you wear here, do they? So, I leave most of my jewellery at home and just slop around here in this old T-shirt and leggings. I just have to dilute the first day or two with a few slugs of this stuff. Now, what's the time – quarter to! Oh my goodness, I must fly. Bye, angels!'

And as suddenly as she had arrived, she was gone.

'What the—?' started Hallie, then she caught Nina's eye, and couldn't carry on. For the next few minutes they rolled around on their respective sofas, not caring about their sticky nail varnish, as they laughed themselves out.

'Dress down?' gasped Nina after a few minutes.

'Left her jewellery at home?' riposted Hallie breathlessly.

'I thought that people who came to health farms were your towelling-headband-wearing, lycra-clad, whippety-thin ladies who lunch?' said Nina when they had both recovered. 'I never thought there'd be so many mad characters like her here, let alone weird combinations of toyboys and wicked stepmothers. This is brilliant, Hallie, you're bloody clever to have brought us here! I haven't laughed like this for a million bloody years!'

'And do you know what?' mused Hallie. 'For the first time since you arrived in London we have had an entire morning without mentioning either Jerry, Reuben or the by-election – in fact, we've had a boy-free, work-free zone, which must be a mi—' she broke off as she saw the shadows racing back into Nina's face and could have kicked herself. 'That wasn't quite so bloody clever, huh?' she said ruefully. 'Me and my big mouth.'

'No, don't worry,' Nina assured her. 'I genuinely haven't thought of Jerry all day and you're doing a fab job of cheering me up – considering you've got enough on your own plate. By the way, what did happen to you the other night when you had dinner with Reuben? I haven't spoken to you properly since then.'

Hallie shrugged but couldn't keep the smile off her face. 'Oh, nothing earth-shattering. We went to Aubergine, had an overpriced but delicious dinner taking the mick out of every waiter in the place, then I was whisked back to his place.'

'So far, so predictable,' said Nina dryly.

'Yeah, but then things started getting interesting, because just as we were starting to get into kit-off time, I started to have second thoughts. So I said, thanks, but no thanks.'

'Strong-minded. But where's this impressive happiness you were taunting me with yesterday?'

'Well! Then he practically fell on his knees and told me he wanted to go out with me, wanted to give it another chance, that he thought I was the sexiest thing ever.' Hallie paused. 'Now I come to think of it, I wish I'd taped it – then I could just play it back to myself whenever I'm depressed or bored.'

'And? And?' questioned Nina, trying to repress a quiver of envy.

'And I still said no!' Hallie cried triumphantly. 'And the amazing thing is I meant it! For the first time, I meant it! I just told him that I felt it was no longer appropriate for us to sleep with each other. At best, he was kidding himself that he wanted to go out with me, and at worst, he was doing what Karenza is always telling me men do to her: basically lying to her, telling her what she wants to hear so that they can get into her knickers. I mean, I don't think Reuben was doing that, but, you know me, naive to the last.'

'Wow,' said Nina thoughtfully. 'Wow. Those Holy Trinity people really have got to you, haven't they?'

'No! You don't understand,' Hallie went on excitedly, 'it genuinely had nothing to do with my faith. Well, nothing to do with what HTB has taught me specifically. I just think I really have outgrown him – that from now on we can just be friends. I don't even regret what we've been doing for the last few months – which must prove to you that it's nothing to do with HTB – in fact, I think I needed to do it, to outgrow him. Sleeping with him, especially so surreptitiously and infrequently, was some sort of catharsis, to flush him out of my system. You know,' she went on, carried away with her own enthusiasm, 'perhaps you should try it yourself!'

'What, sleep with Jerry until our marriage is out of my system?' Nina asked dryly. 'I don't think so, somehow.'

'Sorry,' said Hallie more soberly. 'Baroness Brainless, that's me.'

'Might have been fun trying, though,' added Nina in an attempt to lighten the sudden heaviness of atmosphere. 'Pity I can't stand the guy!'

'Nina!' Hallie was shocked. 'Really? You hate him?'

'Not hate. Just can't be with him at the moment. It might be me – as I said to him, I don't know who I am at the moment, so how can I know if I still like him. But what I do know, is the me that is calling the shots at the moment, can't stand to have him anywhere near me.' Nina shuddered. 'Just the thought of him laying his hands on me makes me sick – because those were the same hands that drove the car over our dog, that buried Babaji, that signed the contract for this moronic job of his. I know, I know,' she caught Hallie's warning look, 'I'm getting irrational again, aren't I? But I can't help it. When I think of him smarming up yesterday with all his promises of change – if he had to – and the emotional blackmail and that final *coup de grâce*, giving me Babaji's picture like that – in that melodramatic way, driving off with all his tyres screeching – oh! I just want to – to – throttle him!'

'OK, anger is good,' said Hallie soothingly. 'Throttling is fine. That's anger. We can work with anger.'

Nina barked with reluctant laughter. 'Oh, Tosis, I love you.

What would your churchy friends say if they heard you saying that throttling someone was fine!'

'What the ear doesn't hear, the heart doesn't grieve over,' Hallie was brisk. 'Anyway, you know what I mean. And don't call me Tosis, otherwise I'll use my influence to get you turned into a Gazarene swine: then talk to me about bad breath!'

Nina looked at Hallie, amazed. She'd never heard her joke about HTB before. Perhaps their influence was waning.

'Come on,' she said, glancing at her watch, 'enough psycho-analysis for one day. It's two o'clock. What have we got now?'

'Cripes,' said Hallie, jumping up. 'We can't be late for—' she looked at her appointment card – 'our Tummy Toning class. Uh-oh, that sounds like work, not pampering. That can't be right.'

'No, and nor is this,' Nina leaned over and poked Hallie in the stomach. 'Think of all those babies you're going to have. For them you're going to need the best sort of linoleum on that pelvic floor.'

'For babies, you need a man before a pelvic floor,' muttered Hallie gloomily.

'Ah, but think of the men you can pull with flat stomach muscles and a vaginal grip like a Dustbuster,' quipped Nina.

'Nina! How do you –!' Hallie sounded scandalised, then she smiled. 'Heyyy, welcome back, girlie. Sex-talk rules!' She looked closely at her friend. 'You're doing them right now, aren't you? I know a pelvic exercise face when I see one: Karenza and I spend whole afternoons in the office with that pursed up, constipated look.'

Nina blushed. 'And you're not?'

Hallie laughed. 'I'm laying parquet flooring as we speak. None of this tatty linoleum for Hallie Templeton. You forget, I'm fussy now! I'm now a girl who *can* say no!'

Cass bowled along the motorway on the scooter, praying that Trudie would never find out that she'd taken it so far outside London. A few times, she received strange looks from the drivers she was overtaking, possibly because people in Jaguars and Mercedes didn't expect to be overtaken by a well muffled tall person in open-face helmet and goggles riding a pistachio green Vespa scooter. Well, it was their problem for driving so goddamn slowly. She had her bike test – Nina and she had snuck out when they were seventeen without telling anyone and had got it – so she had just as much right to be on the motorway as they did. Fuck 'em.

Sitting there, staring grimly ahead, just the sound of rushing air in her ears, Cass was finally beginning to achieve some semblance of calm. She felt that she had sunk so low into confusion and fury that, beneath the muddy waters, she had at least hit the solidity and security of rock bottom. The various rocks lobbed into her pool over the past few weeks had settled there with her, forcing her to consider them all.

Yesterday's events – Cass eased the padded goggles away from her left eye with her gloved hand – had at first just been another of those rocks. It was only when she had remembered that Trudie was spending the night in hospital for some tests, had swallowed her pride to ring Hallie and Nina to apologise, and been told by the harpy Beth that they were both away for the weekend – it was only then that Cass had started to panic.

It seemed that she had been so obsessed by her own problems that she had pushed away everyone on whom she usually depended: Carter, Hallie, Nina, even Ted, Wilbur, Trudie. It was a shock for someone who considered themselves independent from everyone, for Cass to realise that she was just like everyone else: she needed someone to lean on. From there, in the uncharacteristic silence and darkness of St Luke's Avenue, Cass had got herself really worked up. I push everyone away, she had berated herself. If anyone gets too close, I just push them away. I haven't got the courage to deal with anyone face to face – that's why I wimped out on Wilbur. I knew it was a critical moment, but I didn't run with it. All I had to do was move my hand a few inches and he would have been mine. But I didn't.

Then there was Hallie and Nina. After nearly twenty years of friendship, surely she couldn't have succeeded in pushing them away as well? It was this question that had tormented her through the witching hours of the night, making her scratchy and bad-tempered the next morning when she had gone to see Trudie in hospital.

'I think I might just stay here for the weekend,' her grand-mother had announced, looking carefully at Cass. 'All these years I've been paying my BUPA contributions – I might as well cash some of it in. Isn't it a great place? King Edward would have been proud, that's what I say. Even the food is good. Can you imagine? No way am I going home for baked beans on toast after this, let me tell you. Cass?'

'Hmmm,' said Cass absently. 'So long as you're happy. Whatever.'

'Fine,' said Trudie briskly. 'I'll stay here until Monday, then they can run as many tests as they damn well like. Now you run off and do whatever you're busting a gut to do.'

'Hey, I'm not leaving you, Granda,' said Cass suddenly. 'It's the weekend. I don't have to go anywhere. They can live without me in Heptonstall, that's for sure. I'm not going to waste my weekends for Gwenny Goddamn Blackthorn.'

'Look, darling,' Trudie said firmly, taking her grand-daughter's hand. 'No offence, but scat, will you? You look like you have the burdens of the world on your shoulders. Go and unload them, my darling, get your life back in order. That's all I'm doing here, after all. We'll meet and compare notes on Monday. How about that? Do we have a deal?'

'OK, deal.'

Once she had bullied Hallie's and Nina's whereabouts out of a reluctant Beth, Cass had hardly thought before leaping on the scooter and heading out onto the A3. Now, as she passed Guildford, she shook her head at her folly, causing the bike to wobble alarmingly. Was she crazy? She didn't even know where she was going, just the name of the nearest town, Liphook.

She was in luck. Liphook was tiny and everyone in the pub knew where she was talking about, falling over themselves to give her directions. A mere hour and a half after leaving London, she was skimming over the speed bumps into Forest Mere, rounding the gentle curve of the lake, pale gold now in the fading light, up to the red-brick Surrey-style main house. Pushing open the heavy arched front door, it had taken only a minute to find out that they were in a line-dancing class in one of the outbuildings. Wiping the dead bugs off her face with a grimace of distaste – now she knew how a windshield felt – Cass walked stiffly through the car park as directed.

As she neared the building, Cass could hear country music bowing and scraping, accompanied by a couple of half-hearted whoops, a ragged line of claps and an irregular thumping of feet. She crept up the stairs and hung back in the porch, watching the fifteen or so linedancers from the concealing darkness there. Hallie and Nina were in the back row, laughing their heads off. Hallie had scraped her blonde hair up into a minuscule ponytail while Nina's was, as usual, escaping from a messy knot on top of her head. Both their faces were red and shiny – only Nina's still showed the strain of the last few weeks and months – and their eyes were slitty with concentration and mirth, as they slapped their heels, slid clumsily along the floor in their socks, and clapped above their heads.

'Yee-haar!' cried the teacher in a strong Northern accent, as the music came to an end, and clapped.

'Yee-haar!' chorused the class, and clapped.

'Yeeeeeeee-hyarrrrrrrrr!' screamed the gold-covered, leopard-skin apparition next to Hallie and Nina, and snapped her fingers. 'Yeah! Right on!'

Hallie and Nina nearly collapsed with laughter. Watching them, Cass felt like a stranger, like she'd never been part of their enchanted duo, that if she were to open the door now, they would merely be made uncomfortable by her presence.

'Mona!' gasped Nina. 'You're not Miss Piggy and this isn't the Muppets' version of *Saturday Night Fever*, you know! This is line-dancing – this is country – dosido and face your pardners, that sort of thing!'

'Oh lawks, do I care?' trilled the vision in an oddly deep voice. 'I'm dancing! I'm actually dancing! It's a miracle! You know, I do believe in miracles,' she growled, 'look at me! I have to!'

She struck a balletic pose, her short, stubby arms arched above her head, her thighs in her leopardskin leggings quivering as she did poor man's pirouettes into the middle of the room. 'I'm sure you can tell, actually,' she explained to a captivated Nina and Hallie, 'but in a past life, I used to be a Siamese cat. My swami told me that.'

Everyone else was now filing past Cass, out into the cold

evening air outside. Quite unself-consciously, Hallie put her arm round Mona – as far as she could – and hugged her. Again, Cass felt a twinge. If only she had Hallie's knack of getting on with people immediately. The only way Cass got on with people from the word go was if they fancied her.

'Mona, you are a star!' grinned Nina. 'A star!'

'So who wants to be a dead planet?' grumbled Mona. 'High time for a drink and a fag, don't you think, girls? Hello? Who's this?' She was the first to notice Cass stepping awkwardly into the room.

'Cass!' shouted Hallie giddily, then she frowned. 'Cass? What are you doing here?'

'Hi, Cass,' said Nina aggressively. 'To what do we owe this honour?'

To her horror, all Cass suddenly wanted to do was hightail it out of there. These were her friends, for Chrissakes. If she couldn't face them, who could she face?

'I just – I just—'

'Wait a minute,' Hallie said, drawing closer, 'what's this? You have a black eye!'

'What?' Nina came over. 'So you have!'

'A doozy,' agreed Mona, putting on some reading glasses and squinting at it.

'Full marks for observation,' said Cass abruptly. 'Hi, I'm Cass,' she stuck her hand out to Mona, 'and you're – Mona?'

'Mona by name, Mona by nature,' she agreed, looking at her curiously. 'Are you joining these girls on their therapy weekend?'

Cass glanced at Hallie and Nina. 'I guess.'

Hallie frowned bemusedly. 'How did you – I mean – who told – well, why are—'

'Is that the time?' Mona interrupted. 'Well, I have to try and squeeze my bulk into the kiddy-sized showers they have here. Which sitting are you on for dinner?' she asked Nina and Hallie.

'The second one, I think,' Nina told her, then looked sideways at Cass, 'that is, if we can get her in as well.'

'Well, I'll see you in there in full warpaint.' Mona bustled out of the dance-room, turning just as she reached the door. 'If you need concealer for that black eye, Cass, pop along to my room – forty-four – just down the corridor from your friends.'

There was silence in the vacuum left behind her, as the three friends tried to avoid catching each other's eye in the myriad mirrors around them. Eventually Cass cleared her throat.

'Do you guys mind me joining you? I probably should have called before I left but it was kind of an impulse decision. I just jumped on the scooter and tore down here.'

'You came here on the scooter? On the motorway?' Hallie looked incredulous. 'Surely that's not legal?'

'It is actually,' Nina assured her. 'As long as you're not on the L-plates and over 50 cc.'

Both of them looked at Cass.

'Of course we don't mind,' Hallie said eventually. 'I'm just looking forward to the explanation that goes with it, aren't you, Nina?'

'An apology wouldn't go amiss either,' Nina added shortly.

'OK, OK, I get the point,' Cass said bitterly. She knelt on the floor and flung her arms out in the air. 'I am sorry for yelling at you the other day, Nina. I am sorry for being a terrible friend to you both. I am sorry for—' her mind went blank on what she could apologise to Hallie for, 'I am sorry for introducing you to two bastards like Devlin and Wilbur, Hallie. Sorry, sorry, sorry.'

Nina looked over at Hallie, then down at Cass.

'Kiss my feet. Come on, I have clean socks on. Kiss my feet. Then I'll know you're sorry.'

'Kiss my ass!' snapped Cass, standing up. She should have known that this would be a failure.

'There!' said Nina triumphantly turning to Hallie. 'I knew it was too good to be true! For a minute there I thought Cass was actually being penitent! Hah! She's so selfish, she wouldn't know how to be apologetic.'

'Nina,' reproved Hallie, 'now you're just being petty. Come on, let's go up to our room, get changed for dinner,' she looked inquiringly at Cass who shook her head, 'well, us two will get changed for dinner, then all three of us will thrash it out over the lamb cutlets.'

'Lamb cutlets – I thought this place was a health farm!

Shouldn't you guys be on lentils and chickpeas?' asked a surprised Cass.

'Not in the special dining room – and we thought it was hardly worth starving to death in the Light Diet Dining Room just for a weekend. Mushroom terrine, lamb cutlets and rhubarb crumble. Very small helpings thereof,' added Hallie. 'I mean, honestly, cutlets. Even the word is small. Why can't we have lamb cuts? Although we might be able to get a couple extra if we pretend it's for that black eye. How did that happen, by the way?'

'I'll explain everything over dinner, and don't worry about the eye – just talking about raw meat has made me feel better already,' Cass smiled tentatively at Nina who stared neutrally back at her. Well, it was better than outright hostility.

'So, come on, when are you going to tell us about the black eye?'

Hallie picked bad-temperedly at the remains of her rhubarb crumble. 'Fascinating as your stories about life on the campaign trail are, I personally came down here to get away from all that. And why did *you* come down here, Cass? Because I don't remember you being part of the plan, actually – you know, I don't remember you being part of any of our plans since the night you decided friendship was less important than some programme on the telly—'

'Hallie! Take it easy! What are you talking about? What night? What programme?'

'Yes, slow down, Hallie,' said Nina. 'If anyone's going to get bolshy about that night, I think it should be me. I was the one being turned away from my best friend's doorstep at the lowest moment of my life.'

Cass stared at the two of them. So much for no outright hostility. 'Oh,' she said heavily. 'That night. Well, it was nothing to do with the TV – there was nothing on worth watching that night!' she quipped weakly. 'That's why Trudie and I had planned a vid session.'

'God!' Hallie swore. Nina stared at her in surprise. 'You really take the biscuit, Lucasta Herbert. You swan down here, gatecrash what is meant to be our pampering, healing weekend, looking

like a battered wife and acting all mysterious and important –
with your political anecdotes and your little jokes – and just
like always, we're supposed to dance like trout at the end of
your line. Well, bugger that. Both Nina and I are fed up of
you being a selfish Miss Perfect with your own cryptic little
agenda. Best friends tell each other things, Cass, that's the deal.
So either you tell us what's going on or you get out and go back
to London!'

There was a tiny silence, everyone else in the dining room
holding their breaths and their cutlery, as Hallie and Cass stared
at each other.

'You think I have a "secret agenda" do you, Hal?' Cass said
softly. 'Unlike yours with Reuben which is just out there – up
in lights – for all to see.'

Nina and Hallie exchanged looks. Cass saw and narrowed
her eyes.

'Oh, I see. Only Cass isn't allowed to know what's going. Well,
it was a cheap shot, so I deserve that, I suppose. Good to see that
hypocrisy isn't just my domain though, Hallie. Because you're
right, I haven't told you stuff. Stupid really, I didn't want to
admit my failures. Little did I know that if I had, you would
have liked me better for it. So you want to know everything?
OK, let's go for a walk and I'll tell you everything.'

So she did. As they walked around the lake then sat on the
steps of the gym, their breath emerging in clouds in the cold,
bright-mooned night, she told them everything. John, Carter,
Alun, Gwenny, Frank, even Mrs Harrison – the whole mess of
personal and political complications that had brought her to
this point were included. She even told them about the Night
We Don't Remember the Orgy at Conference, but in the same
calm measured voice with which she had just told them about
Frank Blackthorn's links with Avalon. The only thing she left
out were her feelings for Wilbur, because even she couldn't put
those into words.

Finally, when her voice was about to give out, Cass stopped
and held out her hands. 'That's it. That's why I wasn't there for
you that night, Nina. That's why I didn't tell you everything
about Alun and Gwenny, Hallie, because I knew that you would
have to tell your bosses and eventually he would be punished,

yet I had effectively behaved in the same way so how could I be the one to spill the beans? And that's why I'm down here, guys. I'm no Miss Perfect – I actually never was, but I obviously tried to make it look that way – and I've screwed up. I know I'm not exactly flush on the calling-in favours front but that's why I'm here: I realised that I can't sort myself out – can't sort this whole mess out – on my own. I need your help, guys.'

In the hard blue light of the moon, Cass could see the stunned faces of her friends. Inside her, an irrepressible voice hissed, 'Well, that showed 'em!'

Nina was the first to clear her throat and speak.

'So how did you get the black eye?'

For a moment, Cass stared at her. Then, almost against her will, a smile crept across her face, reflected by answering grins spreading across the faces of her friends. Within seconds, the three of them were hissing with laughter, clutching their sides and each other as their hysteria mounted, sniggering and snortling like the ten-year-old Bikeshed Blasters they used to be.

'That's all we wanted to know,' gasped Nina, tears pouring down her face. 'We didn't want to know any of that crap about your boss. We didn't want to know your deep, dark secrets about your affair with a married man – although bonking your dead boyfriend's grieving mother's husband, is a new one on me! – all we wanted to know was how you got your black eye – and you didn't even tell us. Aaaaha! Aaaaha! Ow! My stomach muscles!'

'Mine too!' Hallie gulped. 'It must have been that Tummy Toning class! Oh heavens above! What a night!'

'You bitches from hell,' choked Cass. 'Here I am, spilling my guts, laying bare the foundations of my soul, and all you can do is laugh at me and my afflictions. Great friends, you are!'

'Please,' begged Hallie. 'Just put us out of our misery.'

'Well, I was in the House yesterday, sitting in Mags's office but at one of the other secretaries' desk because they were away—'

'And, please,' Nina implored, 'make it short. I'm freezing my arse off out here.'

'OK, OK. I was on the phone to that guy Lachie – you know, Hallie, the one at Conference who worked with Julian Albarn

– and he's so right wing, it's funny. So we're having this joky conversation about the by-election and he is, like, totally taking the piss out of Tony Blair, calling him a shark-toothed wig mannequin and suchlike. So I'm responding in a similar vein, saying things like "Oh, but how can you say that? Tony's got such a nice smile, he's such a handsome boy. That's why I'd vote for him," in this silly cheerleader's voice. And all the time, one of Mags's dogs – she has these three smelly little Staffordshire pooches – is poking around my feet and, like, licking my ankle. Well, without thinking, I pick my leg up and shake the pesky little fart off, catch Mag's eye, see her face like thunder, so I put my hand over the receiver and apologise saying, "Sorry, Mags, but Smithie was licking my goddamn ankle." Then I go back to my conversation and think nothing more of it.

'Trouble is, it's five o'clock in the afternoon by this time and Mags is loaded to the gills. Oh, and she's truly Old Guard – fucking hates Blair. So anyway, two minutes later, Lachie and I have upped the ante on our fooling around and I am practically saying that Blair should be anointed a saint – all still in this stupid voice – when suddenly, out of the corner of my eye, I see something flying towards me. So I turn to see what it is, duck, and instead of taking it harmlessly on the arm or shoulder, I turn right into it and – *voilà*!' She pointed to her face. 'One shiner!'

'But what was "it"?' asked Hallie, agog.

'A dog bowl. A heavy ceramic dog bowl. Sunny Jim's ceramic dog bowl, to be precise.'

'So this Mags—' Nina was beginning to relapse into laughter again.

'Yup. Mags threw a dog bowl at me. Oh, and I forgot to mention that it was full at the time. So there I am, bruised, bleeding, with Chunky Pal all over my face, and all I can hear is Lachie at the other end of the phone, doing this Derek and Clive race commentary – "and it's Blair in the lead, taking the country to the dogs, and Mandelson is coming up behind – well he would, wouldn't he – hotly pursued by Chris Smith – hey, that'll put the cat amongst the pigeons," and so on, and I'm just sitting there, speechless, literally looking like a dog's dinner!'

'Stop!' pleaded Hallie. 'I can't take much more.'

'Hey, go ahead! Laugh. This is, after all, the seat of British politics. This is where the country is governed, so it's obvious that having a dog bowl hurled at you is going to be your everyday hazard. And so it would seem,' Cass smilingly ignored the fact that the other two were now in hysterics again, 'because I stood up, told her she was a maniac, and went straight to see the Serjeant at Arms.'

'As opposed to the Major at Legs?' giggled Nina. 'I'm sorry, go on. This is priceless.'

'The Serjeant at Arms is kind of like the principal of the House of Commons – in charge of discipline, admin, all that. So I barge into his office – it's Friday, so he's not that busy – and make an official complaint about Mags. Anyway, he looks totally unsurprised, gets up, strolls over to some filing cupboard, says "Mags O'Sullivan? Alun Blythe's secretary? Ah, here we go!" and he pulls out this file so thick and heavy he can hardly carry it back to his desk. Then he grins at me, almost embarrassed, and says, "She's been working here thirty years so we have quite a file on complaints made about her." Quite a file! This thing is thicker than my dissertation, I kid you not. Of course, I should have known that making a complaint was totally pointless – Mags is employed by Alun and unless she does something dangerous or unlawful, he's the only one with the powers to sack her.'

'So chucking a heavy stone object at someone for no reason at all – that's not dangerous or unlawful enough?'

'Apparently not. In the States, I would probably be set for life – I could have sued everyone within a five mile radius. I'd never have to work again. Sometimes there are good things to be said for US litigation! Anyway, it was obvious to me that Alun would never fire Mags – those two are such a double act and he depends on her.'

'But she's a drunken maniac!' said Hallie, with all the indignation of someone who rarely drank.

'Exactly. And yet Alun would still never fire her. Which got me thinking. Who's the weak link in this whole political mess, both because he's too innocent and kind for anyone to enjoy bringing him down and because, at the end of the day, he's too goddamn gutless to stop his lover making a fool out of him?'

Cass held out her hands helplessly. 'Alun is. All this time,

I've been dithering and blithering, because I like the guy and didn't want to see him destroyed by this—'

'And because you're Cass Herbert,' Hallie pointed out. 'One day Ruler of the Planet and Crusader for the Moral Majority. Don't underestimate your idealism, Cass, it's nothing to be ashamed of. When you found out Mrs Harrison gave all that money to Labour, you told me that this by-election wasn't about Old Labour versus New Labour, or Gwen versus Ted, but a fight to protect the faith that people like Mrs Harrison had in Blair's cause. Now Mrs Harrison may have been let down by Frank Blackthorn but that doesn't change the fact that before that she had wanted to give her money away to Labour – not some charity, but to Labour – don't lose sight of that!'

'Exactly. Which is why I can't go on just ignoring the fact that this whole by-election is plain rotten. That's not idealistic of me, it's just naive. I don't want to destroy Alun politically but it's naive to want him to get off scot-free – although I can't help feeling that someone is going to use this apparent media knowledge of Alun and Gwenny's affair at some point. But why should *I* go to all these lengths and cover-ups to protect him? He wouldn't protect me by firing Mags, would he? He would do anything for a quiet life, believe me. He'll probably just take me out of the firing line for a while – make sure I stay in his office upstairs until she's calmed down. And that's what we've got to do with him. He's the weak link. If we can take him out, he takes out Gwen, and in comes Ted. Bingo! Problem solved.

'The thing is,' Cass continued, '– and I'm sorry if this is boring for you, Nina—'

'Boring!? You're fucking joking! I'm not even cold any more!'

'– you and I have been considering this whole thing on far too big a scale, Hallie. This isn't *House of Cards* and we're not ministers and mandarins, able to topple our enemies with a couple of well-placed phone calls. We're the little people of politics and, as I said to Wilbur or Ted weeks ago, we don't have the smallest clue how to leak a scandal.'

'And, as I said to you at the beginning of all this, there's no way we'd be able to retain control of it once it got out,' Hallie pointed out.

'Exactly. So somehow, we have to persuade Alun – oh, and preferably without me losing my job – that the rest of the world is piecing together this scandal, without the rest of the world doing any such thing. We have to keep it quiet – but convince him that every last part of the scandal is being sung out from the treetops. Apart from anything else, the whole problem of Carter staying back with Meredith kind of hinges on me not being pulled into any sort of limelight or under any sort of media investigation. So we also have to think about that – *and* make sure that you come out of this smelling like roses, Hallie, so you can replace that jerk of a boss – *and* make sure that Ted gets elected in the end.'

'And how are you going to do all that?' asked Nina.

Cass rolled her eyes. 'Fuck knows. That's what I've been wracking my brains about ever since I sat and worked it all out in the Serjeant at Arms's office yesterday.'

'So we have to think up a Foolproof Plan,' Hallie joked.

'How about a thirty degree proof plan?' giggled a voice out of the darkness.

All three of them jumped like nervous deer.

'Sorry, we didn't mean to startle you!' Two women stepped out of the shadows, carrying a large icebox. 'It's just that we spotted you at dinner-time and we reckoned that you were the ones to ask to our little soirée.'

'Soirée?' asked Nina faintly.

'Yeah, we have got so much booze in this cooler that we don't know what to do with it. We'd sort of hoped that there might be some tasty men to have some fun with some forbidden alcohol, but every bloke here seems to be either geriatric or a toyboy!'

'Oh, so you spotted that too, did you?' laughed Hallie.

'Yes, gruesome, innit? Anyway, what do you say?'

Cass looked at the other two, who shrugged noncommittally.

'Have you got any champagne in there?' asked Hallie.

'Will Möet do?'

'You betcha!' Hallie grinned at her friends. 'I'm in!'

'What the hell! Me too,' said Nina.

'And me!' said Cass, feeling her black eye tenderly. 'You know what they say about hair of the dog . . .'

Their new friends couldn't understand why the three of them fell about laughing at this.

'Great clean-up weekend, Halster,' said Nina dreamily from the depths of her vodka-filled toothmug. 'Hey, I sound like Darth Vader. "Luke,"' she intoned echoingly, ' "I know what you're getting for Christmas." "How, Mr Vader?" "Because I felt your presence." Oh, good joke, good joke. Crrrrskkkk,' she started clapping, 'and the crowd is going wild.'

'Nina, sweetie, you're rambling. Come on, Cass, what about Wilbur?' Hallie persisted, draining the last few drops from the champagne, and trying to look nonchalant. 'I've told you I got absolutely nowhere with him, so you can tell me what's going on with you two.'

Cass sighed and pulled her head up from the pillow with difficulty. 'Truth?'

Hallie grimaced. 'I think I can take it.'

'I'm nuts about him. Crazy about him. Can't stop thinking about him. For the first time since I was eighteen years old, I'm in love.'

'Who were you in love with when you were eighteen?' Nina slurred curiously.

'Julian Pears. Do you remember him? He was that banker friend of Ricky's. Gorgeous but a total shit.'

'Julian Pears!' screeched Nina. 'He was awful. He wasn't a shit, he was just dull! In fact, he still is. I met him a couple of years ago at one of Jerry's regimental balls. He's married – can you believe it – to someone called Flavia. Do you get it? Flavoured Pears? Oh never mind. Cass, how could you fall in love with him?'

'How could I fall in love with Wilbur?' countered Cass gloomily. 'That's just as doomed—'

'Hang on a sec,' interrupted one of their new friends, breaking off her own tipsy ramblings with Mona, whom Hallie had recruited to the 'soiree'. 'Did you just say Julian and Flavia?'

'Julian and Flavia Pears. That's right,' said Nina. 'Why, do you know them? Poor you!'

'In that case, it has to be the same couple,' laughed the woman, whose name, if Hallie remembered rightly, was Cockie or Cookie or something bizarre like that. 'She had a face like a wet Sunday? And he's pleased with himself?'

'Sounds right.'

'Christ, what with Hallie working at my old company Bandwick & Parker and now this – what a small world! I went to their wedding a couple of years ago. You remember, Ro, that time I pretended to be Drew's wife? Long and boring story,' she warned the others, who were beginning to look interested.

'But you're married now, right?' asked Hallie, damping down the usual jolt of jealousy when confronted with people who were married.

'Yeah, we both are, but Rowena won this weekend in a sweepstake at work and her husband refused to come, so we decided to make it a girls' weekend out. We just couldn't stand the idea of an alcohol-free weekend, hence the cooler.'

'One bottle of Möet, a winebox, vodka and 12 bottles of tonic,' said Cass admiringly. 'I must gatecrash these alcohol-free weekends more often. And as for being caught by that therapist when we snuck in the back way and saying, "Insulin. It's my insulin." – that was a master stroke.'

'Once a scammer, always a scammer,' smiled Cockie.

'Well, hey, you deserve every drop!'

'Make the most of it while you can, huh, Cockie?' laughed the other girl, flicking her cloud of bright red hair back over her shoulder.

Cockie blushed.

'Oh, are you pregnant?' blurted out Hallie, blaming her sudden wish to cry on the champagne she had drunk.

Cockie glared at Rowena. 'Why can't you keep your big mouth shut, Spader? No, I'm not,' she told Hallie, 'but Ben – my husband – and I, we, well, we've decided to go for it. What the heck, it's fun practising.'

'Sorry,' mumbled Hallie. 'It's really none of my business.' Determinedly, she turned back to Cass, before she betrayed herself by becoming enviously weepy and maudlin. 'But seriously, Cass, what are you going to do about Wilbur?'

'Do? Do? Nothing! I had my chance the other night and I

blew it.' She had already told them about her big showdown with Wilbur.

Nina snorted. 'Don't be so melodramatic! You had your chance and you blew it! What, do you seriously imagine that someone who's as obviously in love with you as this Wilbur sounds, is going to be put off by one tiny setback? Don't be ridiculous! This is real life, you know, not some cliffhanger in *Home and Away*. He's not going to suddenly fall out of love with you just because you didn't grab him and shag him when you should have done.'

'Yeah, but I don't know if he's in love with me in the first place, do I?' Cass pointed out. Then she smiled. 'Although I'm pretty sure he is . . . It's just that I'm in unknown territory here – we're too similar, in a way – we've both had it way too easy in the past, and neither of us is used to making the running. And please don't look at me like that, Hallie,' she begged her friend, 'I know how terrible that sounds, but how many times do I have to tell you – it's no easier to be me, than it is to be you.'

About to retort, Hallie suddenly realised that perhaps Cass was right. The playing field may be different, the rules might be out of whack, but the end result was the same: Cass was trying to get her man, the same as Hallie. She looked at Cass with a new perspective. All that jealousy over all those years – and yet they were both in the same place. In fact, Hallie was better off, with her new certainty about Reuben, than Cass, floundering in her new emotions for Wilbur. There was definitely a poetic justice in Cass falling for her male equivalent: both of them were clever, arrogant, charming and far too good-looking for their own good, yet both were surprisingly inept at making their own moves.

'I reckon it's easiest to be me,' said Mona suddenly, from her prone position on Cockie's bed.

The others turned to her in surprise, as she heaved herself up into a sitting position. On her face were corrugated wrinkles where her chains had been pressing into her dimpled flesh while she'd been lying down. Her heavily highlighted hair was matted and tangled, her eyes bloodshot but still sparkling and her fabled warpaint had smudged down her cheek.

'You're still treating men as if they are the ones in control, as if they have their fingers on the button, when the only button their fingers should be anywhere near is the one between your legs,' laughed the older woman coarsely. 'Look at me – I'm a wreck, aren't I?'

The others demurred.

'No, I'm fat, and I'm common and I have dyed hair and I wear too much makeup, and I have terrible taste in clothes; I wear too much jewellery, and I make fun of my husband,' Mona said baldly. 'But the truth is, I have been blissfully married for nearly thirty years to a man who adores every inch of me, has never denied me anything and makes me feel like a princess every day I'm with him.'

Hallie felt the hairs stand up on the back of her neck and a lump form in her throat.

'The trick is to let them think that they're in control but you actually do all the running. Like me coming to this place: I let him think he's sending me because I'm a fat, old woman who needs to be bullied and nannied into taking exercise and dieting. But in fact, coming here every few weeks gives me this fabulous holiday away from this enormous family we have, away from doing the accounts of the family business and away from the disapproving looks of whichever daughter-in-law is thinking I'm eating, drinking or smoking too much – and best of all, David pays! Likewise I may only show him certain pages of certain credit card bills but it doesn't matter, because it's a small deception, I'm in control of the whole thing and it's worth it for the end result.'

For the fifth time since she'd arrived, Mona tried to light her cheroot before remembering that this was Cockie's and Rowena's bedroom. Instead she took a healthy swig from her trusty Evian bottle and raised it to the assembled company. 'Here's to small deceptions!'

'Small deceptions!' A ramshackle collection of toothmugs, bottles and dainty teacups were lifted.

Suddenly, Nina sat bolt upright. 'Small deceptions! That's it!'

'That's what?' asked Cockie.

'What's it?' asked Hallie simultaneously. They looked at each other and sniggered tipsily.

'What do you mean, Nina?' Cass asked.

'Small deceptions! That's the answer with the whole Alun thing!'

'Another man? You lot!' said Rowena admiringly. 'Cockie, doesn't it make you want to be single again?!'

The two of them laughed uproariously. Hallie suddenly hated them.

'Let's talk about this later, hey, Nin?' Cass warned, with the last unpickled vestige of sobriety.

'Yeah, okay, boss.' Having expended such effort on that sudden burst of clear-headed inspiration Nina's eyes were now crossing and uncrossing. 'Just remind me tomorrow of what I said, will you?' she mumbled. 'Small cedep – deped – deceptions. And the Internet. Jerry's not the only one with cyber-cred.'

Cass and Hallie looked at each other over Nina's gently subsiding head. The Internet? Cyber-cred? They couldn't wait to hear how this involved Alun.

The three of them floated head to head in the pool, arms linked companionably, buoyed up by the foam attachments round their biceps, gazing up at the ceiling. By some miracle, they had the indoor pool all to themselves.

'Ow,' said Nina after a while. 'So much for a health farm. I'm in pain here.'

'That water is slapping awful loud against the side,' agreed Cass.

'Have either of you ever been to the Saatchi Collection in St John's Wood?' Hallie asked absently. 'There's a permanent exhibit there, which is a whole room half-filled with sump oil, except for this little spur of a high-sided iron gangway into the room. It's amazing because you walk to the end of the gangway thinking that you are walking out on a plank suspended in mid-air. You're not, of course, it's just that the reflections of the skylights above in the oil below is literally so perfect and complete that it looks like there are skylights above and below you. It takes a surprisingly long time to work it out – it's only when you blow on the surface of the oil and see the reflected skylights ripple that the optical illusion is destroyed.'

She paused, her voice disembodied in the sepulchral gloom of the brown-bricked pool room. 'I feel like that exhibit. If someone were to blow on my surface, the illusion that I am a functioning human being would be exploded.'

Silence.

'Good. I was wondering where all that was going,' commented Nina, then stopped as if the effort of speaking were too much for her.

'How long ago did we ring them?' asked Cass nervously.

'About an hour and a half ago. They won't be here for a while. Don't worry, Cass, you'll be fine. Just be nice.'

'That'll confuse him,' Cass said dryly.

'Is there a Miss Herbert here?' said one of the aqua-clad fitness staff, coming in from the stairs.

Cass jerked her head round, straight into Hallie's face, who yanked her head back to clonk it against Nina's. Through the chorus of pain, the spluttering and the flailing, Nina saw two tall figures come in behind the staff member.

'I hardly even dare ask what you guys are up to,' said the stockier of the two in a soft American accent. 'Hey, Hallie, how are you? Hey, Cass. And you must be Nina. I am very pleased to meet you.' He came to bend down by the side of the pool. 'I'm Wilbur.'

Without really thinking, Nina put up her hand for him to shake. He took it with a raised eyebrow, looking down at her through thickly carpeted lashes. Nina gulped. He was unbelievable looking despite being, as Cass had described, thoroughly rumpled and greying. She could suddenly appreciate how it was that Cass had fallen so completely for him – and what was holding her back from telling him. Perhaps it was the charm that flooded out of him in waves as palpable as those now lapping against the side of the pool.

'You're very early – you must have driven down at the speed of light,' she heard herself saying breathlessly. Small wonder he had such success with women, there had to be some sort of magnetic field around him which scrambled female brain circuits.

'I have a motorbike – and having wasted a few minutes persuading Ted to ride pillion on it – we made it down in good time, through the rest of the Sunday morning traffic. Actually it was a lot of fun.'

'Although I now know rather more about Wilbur's body than I ever wanted to, having been clinging onto him for dear life for the last sixty miles,' said the other man dryly, turning from saying hello to Cass and Hallie. 'Definitely got a bit of a spare tyre round the middle there, mate.'

'Thanks, Ted. Always a pleasure.'

'I didn't know you had a motorbike, Wilbur,' said Cass shortly. 'Is there no end to your collection of pulling toys?'

Nina rolled her eyes at Cass, who glared back. Back to the drawing board of the Cass Herbert Charm School then, thought Nina ruefully.

'It's not going to work.' Cass peeled a tangerine listlessly, her bruised eye now an interesting prism of blues, reds and greens.

They were sitting in the chintzy splendour of the drawing room of Forest Mere, having just come out of lunch, during which Cass had been all too aware of her shiner, from the whispered comments of the other diners to the naked curiosity of Ted. She could feel him wanting to ask but beyond their short conversation on the phone that morning and the flurry of hellos down at the pool he hadn't seemed able to talk to her and a question about the black eye was hardly going to be a great opener. As for Wilbur, Cass couldn't tell whether he'd noticed or not, since his face was expressionlessly friendly towards her as they chatted through lunch.

'You'd have thought that Cass was the separated wife round here, with that black eye, wouldn't you?' Nina had said finally and loudly. Oh, thank God for the telepathy of friendship, exulted Cass inwardly. 'But in this case the truth is definitely stranger than bloody fiction, eh, Cass?'

'Really?' asked Ted, to no-one in particular.

But recounting the Mags story again had broken the ice in more ways than one. Not only had it made everyone laugh – even Nina and Hallie, which was no mean feat, considering the average level of hangover – but as she came to the end, Cass had felt Wilbur's hand brush over hers, so imperceptibly that she almost thought she had imagined it.

'It can be hard dealing with a nutter,' he had murmured smilingly, looking sidelong at her. 'I advocate extreme caution. It should be worth it in the end.'

His hand had lit the match. His words had fanned the blaze. Cass felt instantly lit up from within, simultaneously cursing herself for behaving like such a goddamn girlie and buzzing with sensation and delicious tension. Then, like a piece of newspaper that flares up and suddenly crumbles when tossed onto a fire, she had started to doubt his words.

When he talked about extreme caution, was that a warning to her about his emotional shortcomings? When he said it should be worth it in the end, was that 'should' as in 'will' as she had at first inferred, or 'should' as a warning for her not to bother with the caution unless she really thought it was worth it. When did she suddenly turn into the sort of woman that over-analysed every word that was said to her, she berated herself furiously. She didn't do this. She had never needed to before, so why start now?

Then, as Nina started to explain her ideas, all the internal wrangling had teamed up with Cass's hangover and she had started to feel mighty peculiar. Now her black eye was joining the party and throbbing dully, reminding her that in her present state she was unlikely to attract even Mike Tyson – even if she offered him a free nibble on her ear. Soon, she had sunk into her present zombie-fied state, able to appreciate the brilliance of Nina's Grand Plan, without actually believing that it would come to fruition.

'It won't work,' she repeated. 'Alun is a technological dinosaur. He'll never go for it.'

'That's exactly why it bloody will work,' Nina replied robustly. 'Anyone who wasn't a computer caveman would see the holes. Trust me, it'll work.'

Hallie looked up from her notebook into which she had been busily scribbling notes. 'I agree. Just. If I can keep the Millbank minnows out of the flow, then I think I can carry it off from my end. After all, Alun's only met me once through Cass. His more dominant impression will be of me at the B&P Conference Party when he watched me being patted on the back by Mandelson.' She looked across the room. 'But what do you think, Ted? After all, if you're not happy with it, then we might as well pack up and go home, because if you're not around to pick up the pieces, who knows who the By-Election Panel would select to replace Gwenny.'

Ted stopped pacing around the grand piano and spread his hands out wide, muscles of all descriptions ticking away in his jaw. 'Didn't Hitler, Stalin and all that crew – didn't they always meet up for their treaties and what-have-you in, like, health spas? Wasn't Yalta some seaside health resort? Is that why we're here?'

'For Chrissakes, Ted, cool your fruits and spare us the histrionics,' said Cass witheringly. 'We're here because I gatecrashed their weekend here. We just thought it would be nice for you to get out of London for a day, and, if this satisfies your cloak-and-dagger urges, because it's discreet. No-one knows who we are here – and my name isn't even on the booking, so there's absolutely no link to Alun. It would be pretty pointless, if, after all this, we did end up having a scandal on our hands.'

She lay back on the sofa and clutched her still-aching head. 'Anyway, what's the big deal? The end result is you win – you get to be Member for Heptonstall. What do we get out of it? Nina and Wilbur – zip, diddly, bubpkes. Hallie – promotion at best, the sack at worst. Me – I keep my job or I lose my job and possibly get bad-mouthed throughout the City, which scuppers me for my consultancy. But you? If it doesn't work, you're totally unaffected. If it does work, you get to govern the country, achieve your dearest dream. So quit being a primadonna.'

Ted held up his hands in a surrender pose. 'All right, all right. Point taken.' He shook his head. 'To be honest, I'm gobsmacked. Where you've come up with this daft harebrained scheme is beyond me.'

He started to tick points off on his fingers. Cass could suddenly see how he must be in meetings. It was kind of frightening, watching Good Old Ted metamorphose into someone taller, stronger and far more compelling. Any minute now he was going to go green and start ripping through his shirt.

'This so-called plan of yours relies on a network of people who don't know what they're being pulled into – and assumes that they're not going to wonder why they're being asked to do these things then put two and two together themselves. Its crucial element is a medium which none of us, with the amateurish exception of Nina and Wilbur, have much experience of. It's vital that it all happens within a forty-eight hour timeframe otherwise the whole thing falls flat on its face. And even more importantly, that within that time, Alun doesn't lose his head and confess all to the world's media. I don't need to tell you that if that happens, we're fucked, he's fucked, and the only happy people are media people.'

He stared round the room – at Wilbur leaning easily against the mantelpiece, Hallie sitting, ankles crossed neatly in an armchair, Nina perched on the edge of a chair, hanging onto his every word – and Cass, slumped on the sofa, eyes closed, to all intents and purposes, asleep.

'Look at us,' he said abruptly. 'We're a pretty sorry bunch, aren't we?'

'Speak for yourself,' muttered Cass. So she was awake.

'I'm the only one with any political experience to speak of and I'm the only one who can't be seen to have anything to do with this whole bloody scam.'

'So?'

Ted sighed. 'So, it is amateurish, hastily conceived and worst of all, the whole blasted plan rests on one foundation: the gullibility and vanity of an MP.' He paused. 'Which is exactly why I think it'll work.'

'What??' they choroused.

Now he had their attention.

'Fuck it,' he crowed, 'it's flawed but it's brilliant! Nina, even if it doesn't work, I'm giving you a job at Medios as soon as blink! And if it does, you can take over my job there! Cass, Hallie, Wilbur – you lot are the salt of the fucking earth. I have no idea why you're all willing to do all this for me but what can I say? What can we lose? Let's have a fucking crack at it!'

'Yes!' Hallie punched the air. 'Sorry!' she giggled. 'Getting a bit carried away there.'

'Hallie, you can get as carried away as you like,' promised Ted, 'when we're in that town hall, watching them empty those ballot boxes out onto the trestle tables. Until then . . .'

'I know,' she dimpled. 'Loose lips sink ships. Don't worry.'

They smiled complicitly at each other.

'Ted, I have to say, I'm impressed,' said Cass. 'I began to see what we were fighting for there for a minute. I almost feel we should toast the occasion. Mineral water anyone?' she grinned.

'Good vintage is it?' said Wilbur.

'Then can we go to our yoga class?' pleaded Nina. 'We've still got a fucking raft of treatments to get through before we leave.'

'And we insist that you boys join us,' said Hallie. 'It's not so threatening, you know. Mrs Conway, the lady who teaches it, is amazing. She must be eighty if she's a day. So I think you could probably manage it.' She glanced at Ted challengingly.

'Hey, I love yoga,' Wilbur defended himself, going seamlessly into an impeccable Stork Looking at the Moon. 'See?'

'He used to be a ballet dancer,' Cass explained to an amazed-looking Nina. 'Show-off,' she grinned at Wilbur.

He bowed so low his head touched his knees. 'Of course. It has to be useful for something! Now come on, are we going to toast the Good Ship Ted and all who sail in her?'

They raised their glasses.

'To – to Project Yalta!' said Cass, laughing.

'Project Yalta!' they cried.

14

TUESDAY

'Hello, 602088.'

Cass snatched up the phone receiver to take it off speakerphone, and looked round Alun's office one more time to check that no-one could listen in to her conversation. This was just the first of many calls she had to make that morning. Project Yalta was underway.

'Mrs Harrison – hi, it's Cass Herbert again. I am so sorry to bother you so early on a Monday morning—'

'That's quite all right, love, I know why you're ringing and you're not to worry. I posted them last night, right after I spoke to you, so you should get them tomorrow.'

'Oh Mrs Harrison, you are an angel.'

'Well, I don't know about that – I will just be glad to see the back of this whole sorry business.'

'I know, and I can't tell you how grateful we are for your help. I know how hard this must be for you.'

'It's not hard, lass. I just hope I can trust you to do the right thing with them. Aud Harrison believes in trusting people – but you know how I've been let down before.'

'Mrs Harrison, you don't need to go on. You can rest assured that at no point will your name be brought into anything we do.

I just wish there was something we could do to change what happened.'

'Bit late for that, love. It would be nice to think that Peter might talk to me again, but I won't be holding my breath. I'm just grateful to you for opening my eyes to the Blackthorns. As I told you, after you left last week, I sat in my kitchen until the fire went right out, thinking about what you said. And you were dead right – they did betray my trust. I don't believe that that Frank Blackthorn had any intention of getting dratted Avalon off my back – all he cared about was his blessed feel-good story. Well, the Frank Blackthorn my Alf used to work with would not have been like that. I think it was that fancy piece he married after Iris that changed him. Conning me with her nice words and cosy hugs! She's the one that needs to get her comeuppance. Mr Blackthorn will have been judged by a higher Power than me, but I just don't think it's right if Gwen Blackthorn takes over where he left. It's time for a fresh broom, and you made me see that. No more of this muck, that's what I say.'

'You are so right, Mrs H, and I hope it won't embarrass you if I say that it's people like you who make me want to fight battles like—'

'Hush, you'll make an old woman blush. Now, get on and do all your cloak and dagger stuff. I'll speak to you when it's all over. Goodbye, young Cass.'

'*Andrew Kerr and Tamsin Macpherson are out being highly paid, busy and successful actors at the moment, so leave a message after the beep and when we've taken our curtain calls we will ring you back. If you are ringing to offer us work we will also declare our undying love to you. Bye now.*'

'Andy, Tamsin, it's Cass here. I've thought of a way you can make up for that Born Again Virgin gag. Did I ever tell you that that wasn't even my car, but my boss's? Well, now I need your acting skills to play a little scam on the same boss. He's been complaining that even though he's a bachelor, none of the papers are interested in his sex life because he's not good-looking or young enough. So me and his secretary have decided to send in some pretend paparazzi to quiz him about his reputation for being a Ladies' Man, sowing wild oats on the campaign trail, that sort of thing. It's all just a practical joke – harmless stuff – but guess who I thought of for the paparazzi? Call me asap. Sooner, even.'

'Hello – the Minister for the City of London's Private Office. Can I help you?'

'Hi, can I please speak to Spotty – er, to Neil? It's Cass Herbert, Alun's researcher.'

'Hello, this is Neil Fry. Can I help you?'

'Neil, it's Cass Herbert. How are you doing?'

'Well, we are very busy so—'

'Which is exactly why I'm calling. Neil, I'm worried about the Minister.'

'Yes?'

'Yes. Worried that he's letting the rope go slack on his ministerial duties while he helps out on this by-election. I know it's a quiet time in the City at the moment, but I think that is ideal for him to start a contact programme with key City figures. Show that he's not just there to hassle them when things hot up.'

'I certainly don't think the Minister "hassles" anyone.'

'Er, no, 'course not. But you know what I mean. What do you say, you and me cook up a way of getting him down from that campaign?'

'I must say, I'm intrigued as to why you would want to do that.'

'Neil, honey, where are you from?'

'Er, Kent, originally. Tunbridge Wells.'

'You're kidding! I love Tunbridge Wells! All those cute teashops, and there's such great climbing round there . . .'

'You like climbing? Really? It's one of my favourite hobbies, actually.'

'No way! Well, we should meet up at that climbing wall in Shepherd's Bush one of these days. It's awesome. Anyway, my point is that Heptonstall is not Tunbridge Wells, Neil, and to tell you the honest truth, I am motivated a little selfishly by the fact that I am bored out of my brains up there. Do you think that very shocking?'

'Er, n-no. And I think you may be right about the need for a contact programme—'

'You do? Fantastic. What are you doing for lunch today?'

'Well . . . I suppose, nothing that can't be put off.'

'Neil, you are a Prince amongst Men. If you get me out of that pitiful backwater, I will love you for ever!'

'Er, right. Yes. Right.'

'Fantastic! See you at one o'clock at that wine bar opposite the Whitehall theatre.'

Hallie glanced surreptitiously at the back of the taxi driver's head. He probably couldn't hear her conversation, but it was best to make sure. Quickly, she leant forward and closed the panel of glass, before dialling swiftly on her mobile.

'Hallie Templeton's line. This is her executive assistant Karenza speaking. Can I help you?'

'Karenza, it's Hallie. Look, can you speak?'

'Hallie, 'course I can! Oh, I see – you mean, can I *speak* speak?'

'Yes, you idiot.'

Karenza's voice went hushed. 'Well, Roland is in a meeting, and no-one else is within hearing distance. Why? What's going on? And where are you?'

'On my way to Millbank. Just another briefing. But it reminded me of something you need to do. Can you book the small conference room for the whole of Thursday afternoon? Just say it's for a Cosmopole presentation, or something. For God's sake, don't mention it to Roland. And can you ring Alun Blythe? Don't go through his secretary – unless you really have to – but ring him direct on his mobile – which is 0973 798217—'

'Hold your horses, say that again!'

'Karenza, you are writing this down, aren't you?'

'I am now. Keep your hair on. Did I tell you I've had my hair done? Eight different colours of skunk stripes – just wait til you see it, you'll be so jealous yours will go green. Right, what do I say to this Andy Black bloke? Who is he anyway?'

'Karenza, his name is Alun, A-L-U-N, Blythe, B-L-Y-T-H-E. He's an MP. You're ringing to confirm an appointment for him to come to B&P at 4 o'clock on Thursday afternoon. If he gives you any gyp about not knowing anything about it, say that it's been in his House of Commons diary for ages, and that you've already confirmed it with his secretary. Her name is Mags O'Sullivan.'

'But you told me not to ring her!'

'I know.' Hallie sighed. How was Project Yalta ever supposed to get off the ground with line-troops like Karenza? She pressed on doggedly. 'But she's so permanently pissed that she'll never know you didn't ring her, so just pretend to him that you did. Believe me, it's not worth trying to make sense with her at the moment. Simply make sure Blythe knows how important it is that he turns up. You can make up some cock-and-bull story if you like. Just get him there.'

'OK, anything else?'

'No, not at the moment. Just, whatever you do, make sure you don't tell Roland or the rest of the desk about any of this.'

'Ooooh, very cloak-and-dagger, I must say. What's this all about?'

'If I tell you, I'm afraid I'll have to kill you.'

Silence.

'Karenza, I'm joking! It's orders from on high, from Kathryn and the Millbank boys, if you must know, and it's all to do with the plot to turf Roland out, so not a word, OK?'

'I knew I was right about Roland being handed his cards. Oh, I do love it when a good rumour comes together!'

'OK, well, just get on the case, will you? I should be back in the office by twelve.'

'See ya, Hallie! And bring us a Snickers back, would you?'

'Karenza, that's cruel. You know I'm on a diet.'

'Look, it's going to take blackmail to get me to rat on Roland. Rat on Roland – d'you geddit?'

'Blackmail it is then. One Snickers bar coming up.'

'Cheers, Hal, you're a doll.'

Cass peeked into the office. As she had hoped, everyone was out, attending a Dean's Yard meeting for one of the other secretaries' leaving party next week. She walked casually over to Mags's desk and flipped open the diary. Having scrabbled around for one of Mags's characteristic 3B pencils, she sharpened it and sat down to reap the profits of her hours of practising Mags's handwriting upstairs. She had found that if she crossed her eyes slightly and tried to recreate how she had felt on Sunday morning down at Forest Mere, it worked wonders. After a few minutes, she was satisfied and had nearly finished. Mags would never know that she hadn't written in the diary entry with her own hungover hand.

'Hello there, young Cass! Taking your life in your hands, aren't you?'

Cass's hand jerked across the page of the diary. Looking up in horror, she relaxed slightly, as she saw that Marnie had already sat down at her desk on the other side of the room.

'Hey, Marnie. Not out with the others?' As soon as she spoke, Cass could have bitten off her tongue. She was obviously not cut out for all this sneaking around. Normally she would have had the presence of mind to avoid referring to the Olympic Flame's habit of never going out.

Marnie looked sharply at Cass. 'Are you being lippy with me? You're lucky I don't have dogs otherwise I might be chucking something at you myself one of these days. Really, Cass, you're a sweet girl, but you do need to watch your tongue – you know that Mags has been summoned to see the Serjeant, don't you?'

Cass nodded.

'Well, you watch your back, that's all I'll say, because she has really got it in for you now. You should have left well alone, in my opinion.'

'What, let her get away with this?' Cass pointed angrily at her black eye, no longer swollen but a picturesque blend of colours. 'Marnie, she could have blinded me!'

The older woman shrugged. 'Yes, but she didn't, did she? And what has this precipitous flight to the Serjeant at Arms done? Nothing, that's what! Nothing will change, you know, it never does round here, except that you've made an enemy of Mags. Big mistake, my girl, big mistake.'

Cass stood up, closing the diary and putting it back carefully in its usual place. 'I just can't let these things go, Marnie, it's not in my nature to stand back, shrug and say shit happens. But I appreciate the words of advice.'

'Oh, the impetuosity of youth! Get on with you! Oh and Cass?'

Cass turned round from the doorway.

'I'm sure that when John Major saw you on Friday, he thought you looked good enough to eat. After all, he always was the underdog!'

Cass laughed reluctantly. 'Been working on that all weekend, have you, Marnie? Good job!'

'Cheeky bugger! Be off with you!'

Shaking slightly from her close shave with Marnie, Cass crept back into Alun's office. On the other side of the office, Frank's desk was still not filled. Nor would it be until the result of the Heptonstall by-election was known. That was just over two weeks away. Fifteen days for them to change the Labour candidacy, then make sure that Ted actually got in, without the rapacious media smelling even a hairy hint of rat. She took a deep breath and looked down at her list of calls. Next up was Julian.

'Julian Albarn.'

'Julian, hi, it's Cass.'

'Queen Cass – salutations! Broken any more hearts lately?'

'What can I say? Papworth is overflowing. Look, Julian, I need you to do me a favour.'

'Favours are just treasures that I can lay at your milky-skinned feet, my darling.'

'Someone's in a good mood today!'

'It's called sex, darling, and lots of it. Do you remember Timmy Stourton? Michael Portillo's Special Adviser, back when he needed one?'

'Yes, vaguely. A bitter little queen, as you described him, if I recall.'

'Bitter no longer – he's ripened into the sweetest plum anyone could wish for. Oh, I'm feeling positively moony.' Sigh. 'Anyway, what's this favour?'

'Kind of macabre, actually. Can you find out which books Frank Blackthorn took out from the Commons' Library recently – on gambling specifically.'

'Certainly, my darling. But why me?'

'Because if I ring up, they'll start beating me up about all Alun's non-returns. To be honest, I could do without the hassle, what with all this by-election shit, and all.'

'Okey-dokey. But why do you want to know?'

'Oh, Gwenny Blackthorn asked me to check it out. Something about her having some up in Heptonstall and she couldn't remember which ones were due back.'

'Well, who's La Blackthorn's lackey now then?'

'Tell me about it. Any minute now, I'll be doffing my cap to her.'

'Isn't that your boss's department? Oh, I'm sorry, I thought you said "boffing".'

'Julian!'

'Sorry! I forgot – that Secret! The Secret that Nobody Knows.'

'You are an evil man, Julian Albarn. Talking of which, how did you know all that stuff about Spotty Neil Fry? Him being into climbing and all that?'

'Need you ask?'

'Neil's gay?! Oh dear, I just spent five minutes flirting with him.'

'Wasted effort, darling. I really should ask someone to take a look at that gaydar of yours.'

'You may be right. Let me know about those books, will you?'

'I shall get my moles on the job right now, Queen Cass.'

'Love you, pumpkin.'

'And you, my liege.'

'Newsdesk.'

'Wilbur?'

'Hey, Cass. What's up?'

'Ready to rock and roll?'

'Diary fixed?'

Cass smiled, forgetting that he couldn't see her.

'You bet. Piece of cake. There is one extra detail that will totally clinch the deal, however. I was surprised by one of the other secretaries so my hand slipped just as I was writing your stuff in so—'

'No sweat – I'll think of something. Oh, and before you ask – I biked round that video clip to Hallie's apartment. Are you sure that Nina can do the necessary with it? She can't possibly have that powerful a PC, can she?'

'You don't know Nina Parvati, I mean, Kellman. She's a resourceful chick.'

'And a very good friend to you and Hallie. Gotta go, my producer's going ape.'

'OK, catch you later. Oh, Wilbur!'

'Yep?'

'I know I shouldn't be saying this, given everything that's at stake, but in a Nancy Drew-ish kind of way, this is fun, huh?'

'Cass my darling – life with you is never dull, that's for sure!'

e-mail to ss747@pipex.com
from: nk@jkenterprises.demon.co.uk
subject: Urgent! Urgent! Urgent!

Steve – sorry I've been out of touch lately. Lot of things happening at this end and I've only just got hold of my laptop again. How's our homepage? I must make some time to check it out. And dare I ask how the book is? Deadlines coming and going like confetti?

Steve, I'm sure you're busy, but I need your help in a Big Way. Do you have Pagemaker or any of the other desktop packages used by the nationals? If you do, could you e-mail it to me – or give me the URL where I can download it from the Net? Also, can you remind me how to encode a site? Nothing too complex, just some-thing to keep out the casual browser. Finally, do you know where in London I can hire a scanner? I remember you telling me about a great software-hardware hire shop somewhere off Tottenham Court Road, but Jerry has wiped my mailroom clean so I wasn't able to check back on that. Do you think they'll have anything to help me get a clip of video onto a website?

Thanks for all this – knowing you, you'll jump at the chance to procrastinate for a few hours – but thanks anyway.

Like an eager little puppy, I will be checking my e-mail every few minutes, so hup-to!

big hugs
xx N

P.S. Guess what? I left Jerry.

'My, my, we are a busy bee today, aren't we?'

Cass flinched guiltily from the photocopier. 'Oh, Paul, it's you! Shit, you gave me a fright! Just come in, will you, and shut the door behind you.'

The attendant did as she ordered and squinted quizzically at her. 'Hiding from someone?'

'You betcha. You know that Mags was called in by the Serjeant at Arms this morning, don't you? Even though she knows and I know that he won't be able to do anything except rap her knuckles, I still don't rate my chances of survival if she sees me.'

'You poor fing. I still can't believe what she did.' Paul hauled himself up to sit beside Cass on the workbench. 'Mind you, it wasn't half funny – the two of you storming out into the hall, just as John Major walked in, you covered in dogfood, and nose bleeding all over the place, her screaming blue bloody murder. Poor bloke must have really regretted being thrown out of Downing Street at that moment!' He chuckled, his round face crumpling into plump folds.

'Don't remind me,' said Cass gloomily. 'Marnie and Geraldine keep running up to Alun's office to tell me what else Mags has been saying about me. They think it's all so goddamn amusing that they keep cutting out coupons from newspapers for, like, 10p off a can of Winalot, or something and saving them up to give to me.'

She shuffled the papers out of the photocopier without Paul

noticing what they were. 'Mind you, because of that madwoman, I'm soon gonna need all the help I can get, so I'll be taking any coupons I can get my hands on.' She draped herself across the photocopier with the limpness of despair.

As she had hoped, Paul took the bait. 'Steady on, darlin', what's she done now?'

'Just landed me in all piles of crap. Oh boy, am I going to be in trouble when Alun finds out about this. What it comes down to is sabotage, pure and simple. She,' Cass held up her hands in parenthesis, '*forgot* to pass on a message from Spotty Neil – you know, from Alun's Private Office – that I was then supposed to get to him. It's all totally complicated – suffice to say, after the business with Mags and the dogbowl, Alun might just think it easier to let me go.'

'But that's unfair,' said Paul indignantly. 'You can't help it if Mags goes off the deep end and starts lobbing heavy objects at you. Come on, this is your Uncle Pauly here, what's it all about? Can I do anyfing to help?'

'Oh Paul, my Prince amongst Men, I don't know. It's all kind of a mess. If only you worked Central Lobby instead of Dean's Yard, you could maybe save my bacon but, otherwise, I'll have to depend on my native charm.'

She smiled bravely but hopelessly at him. Then she crossed her arms in front of her and hunched her shoulders, looking down at the floor with a slight wobbling of her chin. She had practised this routine, with Hallie's experienced tuition, all last night when they had been rehearsing this particularly shaky part of the project.

Cass was beginning to respect her friend's psychological understanding of certain situations better than many of the papers she herself had written over the last five years.

'It's like being a blonde and driving a car,' Hallie had insisted. 'It's social conditioning – men and brunette women alike expect you to behave like a moron – so why not profit from that? I can guarantee you that in a car-race from one side of London to the other, I would beat you every time. How? Every time there's an empty right-hand-turn-only lane, I shoot up it, go into my shrugging, "silly me, aren't I blonde?" routine every time, get let in by some eye-rolling male and am quickly on my way. Same with bus lanes, roundabouts, any filtering measure. Works like a treat.'

Hallie wagged a finger at her. 'This will be the same, mark my words. Especially from you – you're usually such a tough cookie that this will really throw Paul off his guard. Don't get trapped into specifics, just talk doom-ladenly, with lots of those looks we practised, all downcast eyes and wobbling chins, and he'll slip on his shining armour before you can squeeze out that first tear.'

'Hallie, please! Enough already!' Cass had laughed. 'Every feminist bone in my body is rebelling.'

'Why? This doesn't go against what you're preaching in your gender psychology – this isn't just acting how men expect us to, because it's not gender-specific: you could try this on certain types or ages of women with the same result – it's reacting to a situation in a way that will be most advantageous to you: in this case, forcing a response from the deeply instinctive need to protect something that is vulnerable. Tell me that's wrong!'

Cass had shaken her head. 'There must be a thousand arguments against that – not least, a certain loss of dignity – but do you know, it makes a certain twisted sense in this situation, so I'm willing to give it a try. Let's go through it again.'

Now she peeked up at Paul through her eyelashes. Was it working?

'Hey, my little Yankee-doodle-dandy, this isn't like you. It's not so hard to swap a shift with someone. Look, I'm sure I can call in a few favours with my mates over in Central Lobby and squeeze into me old penguin suit. If it's so important that I'm over there, I can do that. What do you want me to do?'

Cass shook her head slightly, marvelling. Hallie had hit the nail on the head.

Ted paced up and down his small office like Steve McQueen in solitary. It was now Tuesday afternoon: exactly two days since they'd toasted Project Yalta and he felt like he was going insane with the inactivity of just waiting for everyone else to finish their preparations. He hardly had a clue what was going on – occasionally one or other of the team would ring him and put him in their part of the picture, but this was like stray pieces of jigsaw puzzle when you've lost sight of what the original picture looked like. One thing he was sure of. Cass, Nina, Hallie, even Wilbur – all of them had assigned tasks, but he had nothing to focus his mind on, except the growing certainty that they were way out of their depth here. This, this, Heath-Robinson approach to the very real issues of nepotism, corruption and sex raised by this by-election was surely not the way to tackle the situation. As far as he could see, they were trying to please too many masters, resolve too many issues and fight on too many fronts, and with an arsenal made up of blissfully unknowing dinnerladies, attendants and drunken secretaries. It was madness.

'Ted!'

Ted whirled round to see his boss at the door.

'Can I have a word?'

'Yes. Yes. Sure.'

'Ted, this childcare brief.' He held up a spiral-bound booklet. 'All I can say is that I hope that whatever has been occupying your time over the last couple of days was as interesting as this piece of work suggests . . .'

Ted looked at him blankly.

'Work it out, Ted. Look, we've been patient with you, Ted, but you have to let it go, put your own personal political ambitions on the backburner until the next election. We need you to concentrate on the tasks at hand – like this childcare paper. Remember, we present it in Brussels on Monday. That's less than a week, Ted, less than a week. Now, pick up your game, boy.'

And he was gone, door shut carefully behind him, leaving Ted still staring at where he had been standing.

Wilbur cracked his knuckles and prepared to go to work. If he'd been wearing a black suit, narrow black tie and shades, he would have been a deadringer for Michael Madsen in *Reservoir Dogs*. He just hoped that chopping off someone's ear wasn't going to be required in Project Yalta.

He took a deep breath and punched in some numbers into his desk phone quickly.

'Alun Blythe's office.'

'Mags?'

'No, it's the fucking Pope! If you know me well enough to call me Mags, you know me well enough to know my voice.'

'Aah, but I would feel cheated if you didn't swear at me. A little brightness would go out of my day if you were all bland and polite. Mags, it's Wilbur Coolidge from CNN.'

'All right, all right, no need to give me your vital statistics as well, I know who you are. What do you want?'

'Just confirming everything's OK for my interview with Alun on Thursday?'

'What interview?'

'The one for my Oldtimers' collage segment. Remember? We talked about it towards the end of last week? Mags, you wrote it into the diary, I know you did, because I remember you cursing because you snapped the lead in the pencil and your hand slipped right across the page.' Wilbur thanked Cass silently for remembering to give him this vital little detail.

There was the rustle of pages.

'Er, yes, you're absolutely right. Eleven forty-five on Thursday morning. I'd completely forgotten. Am I a senile old bag or what?'

'Nah, we wouldn't have you any other way. Just as long as Alun's there: it's very important, otherwise my ass is grass. Can I leave it with you to make sure he turns up on time?'

'Er, yes. Righto. Leave it with me. Don't you worry.'

'I trust you implicitly, fair Mags. Irish fire is tempered by Irish honesty into Waterford crystal, is it not?'

'Prettily said, you Yankee flirt. Nearly enough blarney for an Irishman there.'

'Hey, you say the sweetest things.'

e-mail to ss747@pipex.com
from: nk@jkenterprises.demon.co.uk
subject: Thank you! Thank you! Thank you!

Steve – you are an angel! May your wings always be white and fluffy and your image be always on the best sort of Christmas cards. Thank you sooooooooooooooo much for talking through exactly what I want with the Tottenham Court Road people – I would have hardly had a clue. And thanks so much for telling me about Crayon: who would ever have thought there was a website that allows you to create your own newspaper? Brilliant! Everything is now scanned in and the links between the sites are working better. Looks like the video clip will be up and running by tomorrow morning, then I can encode the site. Now we just need a few tweaks on the material and all will be hunkydory.

Thank you even more for not asking any more questions about what we're up to. As I said to you on the phone, it's nothing illegal – more of a practical joke on a friend. Just a very involved practical joke . . .

I feel like I've been staring at a computer screen for so long that I've forgotten what a non-digitised world looks like. When you said something in your last e-mail about autumn being over and it just being a darkening decline into Christmas, I realised I hadn't looked out of the window since Sunday. I swear there were still leaves on the tree outside my window then. There aren't now.

I've been reading over the backlog of e-mails you've been sending over the last three weeks (three weeks? Has it been three weeks since I left Jerry? Unbelievable) and I hardly know what to say . . . they're magnificent, and touching, and funny (how do you manage to have comic timing – in an e-mail??!!) and they have added colour to my presently monochrome world. Without getting too profound – I haven't got time to be deep, as my friend Hallie has been known to say in moments of crisis! – I feel rather like that tree outside my window. One minute I was apparently green-leaved and blooming, but frost nipped me in the bud and suddenly I was stripped bare, leaving me exposed and, if not dead, then in hibernation.

Does this make any sense?

xx N

P.S. Out of the blue as it was, I have been giving some serious thought to your question in 'A Proposition' . . .

Cass's dialling finger was beginning to ache. She looked at her list of calls still to make. Not that many to go now, then she could head off to their Briefing Meeting at Wilbur's apartment.

'Hello, hello, hello! Chris Phillips' office.'

'Annalisa, hi, it's Cass Herbert. I need a favour—'

'Cass Herbert! Where have you been for the last few days? Have you been avoiding me? Scared I might try and seduce you again?'

'Shit, Annalisa, broadcast it to the whole entire world, why don't you?'

'Relax, gorgeous, I'm the only one here this afternoon.' She giggled. 'I was actually doing a quick line when you rang. There's an old photo of the Queen in this office that's perfect for snorting off – now is that a buzz or what? Now what can I do you for?'

'Jeez Louise, Annalisa, you really like to push it to the edge, don't you? One of these days, that search for the ultimate shocker is going to wear you out. Well, I was going to ask you to do me a little scam as a favour, but I'm beginning to think better of it now. It's way too boring for a thrills junkie like you.'

'Oh, go on, tell me. I love a good scam.'

There was a short pause.

'OK, but first you have to swear total and utter secrecy. And, Annalisa, I mean it. No kidding around.'

'Ooooh, sounds important. OK, I promise. I promise, on my most treasured possessions – my pack of condoms – that I will not breathe a word to anyone ever. Will that do?'

There was reluctant laughter from Cass. 'You are unbe-fucking-lievable. Yeah, that'll do. OK, here's the scam: I need you to seduce someone.'

'And that's a scam? Talk about a bleedin' busman's holiday.'

'Annalisa . . .'

When Cass had finished explaining, Annalisa butted in.

'What if he doesn't turn me down? I do have a pretty good track record, you know.'

'Annalisa, you are the Daley Thompson of political sex, I have no doubt, but this man is in love – do you even know what that means?'

Pause.

'No, don't reckon I do. What a sob-story, eh? So what's in it for me?'

'Er, helping to steer the course of history? Advancing the cause of New Labour?'

'In other words, nothing. Oh well, I'll do it for you, Cass. It's weird, you know, I've never been friends with a girl before. I've only ever been able to sleep with them or bitch about them before. What makes you so different, do you think?'

'Given that one day I am hoping to be a gender consultant, I would like to think it was my carefully acquired understanding of what makes women tick.'

'Nah, I reckon it's more because you didn't write me off as a silly tart when you met me – yet you don't take any of my shit. That makes you a pretty rare combination. Oh, and, of course, you're gorgeous. That helps.'

'Thanks. I think.'

'De nada. Speak to you later.'

'You did what? Are you insane? Annalisa?! Right, that's it. Call the whole thing off!' Ted raked his hands through his hair frenziedly. 'There is no bloody way I'm going through with any plan that includes that smacked-out little tart.'

They were having a council of war at Wilbur's flat, a dark-panelled, warped-floored bolthole in Covent Garden. A rented flat, it was obvious to Cass that the dominant decorative theme was book-based. There were books everywhere, leather-bound

Towers of Pisa leaning over Empire State buildings of colourful paperbacks. She looked at one pile at random – *A White Merc with Fins, Snowcrash, Deadmeat, High Fidelity, Disco Biscuits* – noticing absently that it matched almost book for book the well-thumbed heap in the corner of her own bedroom – Wilbur was clearly as muddled a sci-fi-cult-pulp-drugs-and-violence-fiction nut as she was. With difficulty, she tore herself back to the discussion underway.

'—she's like Cass's actor friends, Andy and Tamsin, Ted sweetie – Annalisa just thinks it's a practical joke,' Hallie was saying soothingly. 'And like Wilbur's librarian friend Sarah – she thinks she's taken Cass's advice to bend Alun's ear while she can, nothing more. And Paul the Attendant. None of these people know anything about the real Plan – just enough to feel that they are being entrusted with a tiny piece of a harmless scam.'

'Yeah, but Annalisa's not interested in being a bit player in someone else's game, she likes to run her own game,' said Ted frantically. 'She's such a devious little floozie herself, she's bound to know something's up.'

Cass looked at Ted with barely concealed irritation. They were all doing this for him, at the end of the day, yet he was consistently the doubting Thomas of their little posse.

'Ted, you're talking bollocks. Calm down. Annalisa doesn't have a political bone in her body. There is no way she'll put her part of it together with Gwenny's campaign. Especially since nothing is going to happen. And she's not a smackhead, by the way,' she dismissed, 'so stop exaggerating, Mr Worry-Wart.'

'But she does take cocaine,' Hallie interjected, 'I'm sure of it.'

Cass, Ted and Nina turned and stared at her.

'Hallie, honey,' said Cass gently, 'everyone does coke.'

'Well, we don't,' Hallie pointed out. 'Do we?' She looked harder at the others, who were shaking their heads indulgently. 'Do we??'

'Guys, no offence, but can we take a raincheck on the *True Confessions* here?' said Wilbur amiably. 'After all, we were plotting the overthrow of the World As We Know It, last time I looked. And Cass is right – using Annalisa is risky but could be an inspired touch. It will totally unsettle him, throw him off-beam just in time for the big showdown on Thursday. And best of all it might stop him calling Gwen to unburden all his problems.'

'Shit, I never thought of that,' said Cass. 'With the benefit of perspective, Gwen might be able to point out that this whole thing is smoke without fire. Christ on a bike. Do you think he will call her? Shall I try and fix it so that she's out tomorrow?'

'No, Gwen's way too canny for that,' mused Wilbur.

'And what happens if he doesn't turn her down? Have you thought of that? You say, he's in love but this is a girl who can take men's trousers off with her teeth before she's been introduced to them, for Christ's sake. I mean, Wilbur, you've seen Annalisa in action!'

'You were there too, Wilbur?! Was I the only one NFI?!' gasped Hallie.

'Where?' he said, nonplussed.

'Hallie, just zip it, will you?'

Nina and Cass began slowly but surely to get the giggles.

Ted's eyes bulged. 'What?!' He turned on Cass. 'You told them about Conference? You told them! You daft bitch! I don't believe it!'

Cass shrugged guiltily. 'Girl talk, Ted, you know how it is.' She struggled to keep a straight face. 'But, hey, don't have a cow – you came out of it very well – so to speak.'

'Christ! With friends like you . . .!' Ted got up and grabbed his overcoat. 'Well, fuck the lot of you. This is a fucking farce. If this whole thing was an elaborate way to set me up, consider it a job well done. Now, if you'll excuse me, I have to go and drown my political ambitions in fifteen pints of beer.' He glared at them with loathing and stalked out.

Hallie jumped up. 'I'd better go after him.'

'Leave him,' advised Wilbur. 'Pre-wedding jitters, that's all. We're all nervous – that's just his way of showing it. Poor guy is the only one not doing much to contribute, it's probably driving him nuts.'

'No, it was me who put both feet in my mouth and waggled them around. I'll just calm him down then I'll come back. I'll leave the door on the latch, so don't worry about letting me in.' Hallie bustled out.

Nina and Cass looked at each other, eyebrows raised, both thinking the same thing.

'So,' said Wilbur, with a crooked grin. 'I'm not even going to ask what all that was about. As we were saying . . .?'

'I think, crossed fingers, we're pretty much all set, actually,' said Nina. 'Cass, what's left?'

'OK, I have to talk with Marge, Arthur and whichever police officer is on duty at St Stephen's.' Cass thought hard. 'Check with Paul that he's still on for Thursday. I've already ordered the books from the Commons Library, so once I've called her tomorrow morning, all you have to do, Wilbur, is drop some hints with Sarah.' Her hand flew to her mouth. 'Shit! I totally forgot to call Avalon. Fuck!'

'Hey, it's not the end of the world,' Wilbur assured her, 'just do it first thing tomorrow morning. The chances are they'll return the message promptly anyway, so you'll still be OK.'

'But if I've forgotten to do that, what else have I missed?' fretted Cass. 'Ted's right, this is totally farcical. Who do we think we are, anyway? Christ, the arrogance of playing around with people's lives like this as if it was some dumb adventure.'

'The Famous Five Go Mad In Westminster?' joked Nina.

'Nina, I'm not kidding – there are so many things that could go wrong—'

'And they probably will,' said Wilbur sharply. 'Stop being a drama queen, Cass, it doesn't suit you. Small deceptions, remember? The whole deal is that it doesn't matter if one or two things go pear-shaped – it's the cumulative effect we're aiming for here. As long as we each just get on with our thing, keep cool and don't lose our heads, nothing can go wrong. It may not work – we've always known that – but one or two hiccups do not a disaster make.'

He grabbed her by the shoulders and stared sternly at her. 'And as for playing around with people's lives, my love, that was already out of your hands when Frank Blackthorn screwed Mrs Harrison over, when Gwenny and Alun started having their affair and when Gwenny started getting Thatcheresque delusions of grandeur.'

'You know, Gwenny does kind of remind me of an early Margaret Thatcher,' mused Nina. 'You are clever, Wilbur, are you sure you've only been working in politics for a few months?'

'And this from the woman who designed this whole plan having never been anywhere near politics?' he smiled at her, then turned back to Cass.

'I know you're uncomfortable railroading Alun into all this – but haven't you stopped to think why we're all doing this? It's because there's something fundamentally wrong with the status quo as it is – and I bet you a hundred bucks that Alun knows that. You told me he looked as shocked as anyone when Gwen announced her candidacy. The circumstances may not be *that* scandalous, *that* shocking – there's no Irangate here, or private parts that need to be identified – but the difference is that this time we can do something about it! Us! The little people of politics! OK, so we're not moving and shaking, but at least we're nudging and wobbling.'

Nina chuckled, but Cass seemed hypnotised by Wilbur's rhetoric.

'Think about it, my darling; if this all works, Alun keeps his job, gets the girl and stays out of trouble. You may not believe it now but he may even thank you for it, one day. So don't ever think you're arrogant because that's the last thing you are. You may be an obnoxious, opinionated heartbreaker but you're also brave and kind and one of those rare people who actually gives a shit about integrity . . .' He paused. 'Why are you staring at me like that? I'm rambling here, aren't I?'

'A little,' said Nina briskly, standing up and putting her coat on. 'I'm off. Cass, I'll bike the laptop over to the House of Commons as soon as I'm satisfied that the Tottenham Court Road bods have done their funky stuff up there in cyberspace, and that all the pages link up OK. Then all you have to do is practise your sleight of hand with the mouse, and you'll be laughing.'

Cass tore her gaze away from Wilbur, and grimaced at Nina. 'Look at my hands,' she grumbled. 'They're shaking so much I won't be able to pick my nose, for fuck's sake, let alone do this mouse-flicking business.'

Wilbur wrapped them in his own strong hands. 'Simmer down, babe. You'll be fine. What? Superwoman Cass Herbert – nervous? Don't be. You've been a powerhouse of industry so far, putting the rest of us to shame. You'll do great. You can't fail. You're too good.' His dark eyes bored into hers, as she held her breath.

'Oh, why don't you two just get on and fuck each other!' came a sour voice from the doorway. It was Ted – with Hallie – both white-faced with cold, soaked through and out of breath, shaking their coats and stamping their feet.

Cass tried to spring away but Wilbur's hands held hers firmly. 'If only I could, Ted,' his gaze never left hers, 'trouble is, she won't have me.' He finally let go of her and turned to Ted, his tone teasing. 'Apparently, someone told her I make Casanova look shabby when it comes to playing fast and loose with women's affections. So, you see, she doesn't have the monopoly on gossip, does she?'

Ted shook his head. 'Point taken. Hey, I came back, didn't I? Hallie has done a great job of stroking my ego and generally making it impossible for me to get away unscathed.' He grinned at Hallie, who dimpled back.

Nina laughed and threw her hands in the air. 'If any of us get through the next two days unscathed, it'll be a miracle. And I'm not just talking politics,' she added naughtily. 'Ahoy, boys and girls, tangled webs dead ahead! Hallie, I think it's time you had a word with the Big Guy – I think we need a few prayers to tide us over the coming storms.'

'Don't take the mick, Nin,' Hallie said automatically, but her tone was abstracted, her hand still feeling the imprint where Ted had held it as they'd run breathlessly through the cold rain.

15

'Well, if it isn't the Born Again Virgin? Getting any action yet?'

Cass couldn't believe her luck. It was Mick, the policeman who'd seen her car that day she'd come from Andy and Tamsin's. Ever since then, in his gratitude to her for giving him the best Westminster story of the summer, Mick had been one of Cass's greatest fans. He was the perfect man for the job she was about to give him.

She grinned widely at him. 'Put it this way, if I was a cat, I'd be running out of times I could be Born Again. And that's just the way I like it.'

'I think it's deliberate cruelty, meself. You're depriving us of your fatal charm and beauty. What we in the Force like to call, withholding evidence. I may have to take you in.'

Cass gave him a pained look. 'Mick, it's seven-thirty in the morning. The sun has not even yet risen in the land of the sexual innuendo.'

He looked shamefaced. For about two seconds. 'What, the land where the one-eyed man is king, you mean?'

She couldn't help but laugh. 'Tacky. Tacky but quick. I have to admit it.'

'So what are you doing here this early?'

'Just getting the mail. Alun's back from up north for one lousy day, so I thought I'd try and clear the decks before he arrived. We're doing our best to cheer him up today. He's convinced that he's not doing enough to help up at the by-election, that he's a spare part and that Gwenny is just putting up with his presence because of his friendship with old Frank Blackthorn.'

'Sounds like someone does need to cheer him up,' agreed Mick.

'Yeah, so if you do see him, can you make a special point of congratulating him on the campaign so far, and emphasising how highly Gwen Blackthorn must rate him, and how glad she must be that she has him by her side, with Frank dead only these past couple of weeks. Something like that, anyway.'

'Something like that,' the policeman repeated dryly. 'Let's just hope there isn't a queue for tourists trying to go past if I have to say all that to Mr Blythe alone. I'll do my best, my love,' he hastened to assure her.

'Thanks, Mick, you're a doll.'

Slipping unchallenged round the X-Ray machines, Cass trotted into the Policemen's Café – Plod's – to brief Marge on her cholestorol speech. Then, nipping out into New Palace Yard, through the Speaker's Car Park and turning right into the Star Chamber courtyard, she strode through, her boots ringing on the revolving metal disc used by the Post Office van-drivers to turn their vans round in the narrow space. She passed through the tiny door there, briefly considered junking the whole thing, going downstairs to the Thomas Cook office there and not stopping til she'd reached Rio, then walked past the cash machines into Arthur's tiny lift. It was one of the mysteries of Westminster, as to why this lift rather than any of the others, should be manned, but manned it was, by Arthur, whose amiable, wrinkled face seemed as much part of the fabric of the House as Pugin's most splendid wall decorations.

'Hey, Arthur, what's up?'

'Fine, t'ank you. And you?'

Cass pulled a face. 'Could be better. To be honest.' Her face suddenly perked up and she looked down into his kindly black face. 'Hey, you might be able to help, actually. It's my boss, Alun Blythe – you know him.'

He nodded gravely.

'Well, he's coming down today and he is, like, so depressed at the moment that I feel like paying people to cheer him up. If he happens to come in here, could you make a special point of saying something nice to him?'

Arthur looked alarmed. 'Sure t'ing. But like what?'

'Oh, I'm not sure,' Cass said carelessly, getting out of the lift. Then she turned back and held the doors open with her hand. 'But you know he's helping out at the Heptonstall by-election? Well, you could say something like how you saw a snippet about it on the news and how you thought Mrs Blackthorn was a smashing-looking woman and how you'd vote for her in a flash, and how she must very grateful to have Alun's support. How about that?'

Arthur looked at her doubtfully. 'Okay, I'll give it a try,' he promised hesitantly. 'If I see him, mind.'

'Arthur, you're an angel,' Cass reached down and kissed him on his cheek, feeling the heat of his blush as she did so. 'Alun will be so touched.'

Well, she thought, as Wilbur said, it's not the end of the world if he doesn't do it, at least I've tried. Just another cog in the finely-oiled machine that is Project Yalta. One other thing struck her and she turned back again just before the lift doors closed.

'Sorry, Arthur, but you know the roof terrace up here?' She pointed above her head. 'Is it still open in winter? I wanted to get some pictures in this incredible Fall light we're having at the moment.'

'I believe it is, yes,' murmured the patient lift operator.

'Thanks a ton, hon.' Stop laying it on so thick, she berated herself as the lift doors slid together, the poor guy looked ready to faint with embarrassment.

So much for Wilbur's high talk about preserving the integrity of politics, she thought ironically. It wasn't even nine o'clock in the morning and she'd already prostituted herself so many times she was beginning to get jaw-ache from grinning so winningly at anyone who crossed her path.

*   *   *

Cass glared forbiddingly down at the phone, willing her hand to get on and dial this next, most difficult call. Not only was she going to have to pretend to be someone else, she was going to have to lose all traces of her transatlantic accent. 'Bottle,' she said with her best glottal stops. 'Don't lose your bottle. I'm going to make a call. Not a cahl, but a corl. To Avalonn, not Avalawn.' Right, she thought, here goes.

'Good morning, Avalon.'

'Hello, can I please speak to Geoff Burnell. My name is Gwen Blackthorn.'

'I'll put you through to his secretary.'

'That would be grand.' Stop talking like an extra from *Emmerdale*, she rebuked herself. Don't overdo it.

'Good morning, Mr Burnell's office. Can I help you?'

'Yes, my name is Gwen Blackthorn. Mrs Gwen Blackthorn. Can I speak directly to Mr Burnell please? He will take my call.' And if he's in the office yet, at 9.02am, then I will eat my dissertation, vowed Cass.

'I'm afraid Mr Burnell isn't in the office at the moment, Mrs Blackthorn, but could I take a message?'

'Yes, would you tell him that I am looking forward to building another special relationship between Avalon and the NorthWest when I am elected Member of Parliament for Heptonstall. Just like my husband Frank did, of course. In fact I would like to think that, as in so many areas, I can merely step into my beloved husband's shoes and maintain the close contact between him and Mr Burnell. I would very much like to speak to him on a Lottery-based issue this morning if possible. So if he could ring me on 0802 756895, that would be most kind.'

'Right, I have that, Mrs Blackthorn. *"I am looking forward—"'* and the secretary repeated the whole thing back to Cass.

'That's right. Thank you so much. You've been most helpful.'

'OK, guys. Listen up.'

Wilbur was having his usual morning briefing with his crew: cameraman, soundman and line editor.

'I'm going over this today because we're scheduled for an early start tomorrow morning. I am just warning you that tomorrow, with Alun Blythe, we are running a dummy interview – maybe without even tape in the camera. There is a point to this – that Clinton piece he did for us was good, but he doesn't give much away. What I want to do is warm him up. I'm doing some research on a big City scandal so we'll need him on hot form when I break that story – that's why I'm going to try and crack him tomorrow, get him to lose his temper, get something human out of him. I'm prepared to say anything, true or not, to try and get a reaction from him.'

Wilbur smiled at his loyal crew. 'I guess what I'm trying to say is – take no notice of what I say.'

The cameraman turned to the soundman. 'So, no change there, then!'

It was one of those crisp autumn days, spritzed clean by the rain of the night before, that Alun loved best of all. When he could feel the fizz of cold air up his nostrils, the delicious shiver of a Siberian blast, converted from perishing to bracing by the golden prism of pale sunlight, and the ethereal emptiness of the air, compared to the downy heat of summer humidity.

So why was he sitting on a train? Unable even to see the beauty of the day through the dirty-fingernail opacity of the train window? Forced to come down to London by his acne-strewn Private Secretary, with some half-baked idea about a contact programme? Where was the justice in that?

That morning he had lain in bed, feeling the warm ivy cling of Gwenny in his arms, and he had had a moment of never wanting to leave. 'Goodbye, Ministry. Goodbye, Leeds,' he had murmured no louder than a breath, into her glossy dark hair, 'Goodbye Westminster. Goodbye poky flat in Kennington. Goodbye Kirkridge Hill. Hello Heptonstall. Hello Gwenny.'

'If you dribble much more nonsense into my hair, it'll go curly in a silent protest,' grumbled a sleepy voice, 'and I won't be able to do anything with it all day.'

'You won't be able to do anything with *me* all day,' said Alun mournfully. 'I have to go to London, remember. No, don't get out just yet. Stay here, love, just a moment longer.'

She took no notice of him. Back went the covers. Out she got. In came the cold air. Gone was that cosy refuge. He sighed. Another day, another day.

Alun came to with a start, realising he'd fallen asleep, probably with the requisitely humiliating number of head-nods and drool. His mobile phone was ringing. Eventually he gathered enough presence of mind to answer it.

'Er, h-hello?' His voice came out unnaturally high and squeaky.

'Gwen? Hello, this is Geoff Burnell. And how is the lovely Mrs Blackthorn?'

Alun stared at the phone. Don't say he'd come out with her phone and she had his. He looked more closely at it. No, it was his. So why was Gwen being rung on his phone? Curiouser and curiouser. And how did he know the name Geoff Burnell?

'No, I'm sorry, this is not Mrs Blackthorn. This is Alun Blythe. I think you must have my number muddled with hers.'

'Oh, Mr Blythe!' The man sounded almost comically taken aback. 'Oh, I am sorry. My secretary must have passed on the wrong number when she took the message from Mrs Blackthorn.'

'No problem. I am working with Mrs Blackthorn at the moment, on the by-election, so if you would like to give me a message for her, I can easily pass it on. Perhaps she actually gave you this number by mistake. Hang on, let me get a pen.' Alun dug into his crammed pockets for a pen and spare-looking scrap of a paper.

'That would be kind. Could you just tell her that I received her message this morning and that, yes, I too hope that our special relationship will continue. It is always important to Avalon to maintain our links with our MPs. And, you know, Mr Blythe – that also goes for you, you know. Avalon's doors are always open.'

Geoff Burnell. MD of Avalon. Of course. That's why the name was familiar.

'Thank you very much, Mr Burnell.'

'Oh, call me Geoff.'

'Geoff – and I will pass on the message when I next speak to Gwen.'

'Thank you again, and sorry for disturbing you.'

Alun hit the END button and looked bemusedly at the phone. What had that been all about? What special relationship was he talking about? And how come he was on such cosy first name terms with Gwenny?

'Alpha One, this is Alpha Bravo Three Zero.'

Cass sighed deeply down the phone line. 'Nina – get real, will you?'

'Sorry, just feeling rather giddy this morning! I'm with Wilbur now on the corner of Parliament Square – looking as dowdy a librarian as I can manage. The depressing thing is, it wasn't that hard. I biked the laptop to you before I left Theberton Street so it should be with you any minute.'

'Cool banana. I can take it straight off the courier because I'm going down in a minute to intercept Alun when he comes in off the train, to persuade him to go to Plod's. It shouldn't be too hard. He almost always has breakfast there.'

'Sod's fucking law if he doesn't today. Hang on a tick,' there was a mumbling in the background. 'Oh, Wilbur says that he will ring Sarah in the Library as soon as Alun goes to his meeting with Spotty Whatshisname and tell her that he'll be going to the message board at, what, eleven?'

'That's right, and impress on her that that's the only time she can catch up with him for the next few weeks.'

'Fuck me, this is all so cloak and dagger, isn't it? It's fucking wicked. I also talked to Trudie, by the way. She said Andy and Tamsin had just left your place which she was very glad about because she couldn't remember for the life of her how much you'd told them. They got the Ladies' Man practical joke story, didn't they? Anyway, Trudie and her friend Graham have been practising every silly voice they can manage for the Mags Scam. You should hear Graham's impression of a *Sun* hack – it's hysterical. They've done about five calls so far. I did a couple myself before I left. Fuck, Mags is scary to talk to, isn't she? I was expecting the verbal equivalent of a dogbowl to come flying my way any minute. In fact this whole thing is deliciously terrifying, isn't it? Christ, I'd forgotten how imposing and scary-looking this place is – like some wedding cake on acid. Yikes, what the fuck are we doing??'

'Hey, slow down there, Floyd!' cried Cass, laughing. 'You'll be fine, pumpkin.'

'As you will be. Good luck with Alun.'

'Thanks, hon. Let's wreak havoc! See you in Yalta!' Cass cried with nervous exultation, replacing the receiver.

'Yalta, eh?'

Cass whirled round in guilty shock. 'Alun!'

'That sounds like fun. If you're into dachas and grain vodka. Well, the latter gets my vote – can I wreak havoc with you? Much more fun than going to see the Spotty Youth.'

Alun was leaning against the doorjamb, grinning broadly.

'Oh, that was just a friend,' yapped Cass wildly, thinking fast. 'And Yalta is a bar we're going to tonight. Just a bunch of us crazy kids, acting like Russian Revolutionaries. Apparently, that guy Orlando Figes might do a reading from his new book.' Careful, Cass, don't get too elaborate with the lying. Keep it simple, stupid.

She couldn't help but stare at his face. After the past few days of plotting and feuding, she hadn't expected him to look so normal and familiar, his pockets still trailing detritus like Jason dropping crumbs to find his way out from the Minotaur's Maze, his face as crumpled, world-weary and kind as ever. Instead, in an effort to quash her conscience for mucking about with his life, she had demonised him into someone more like a cross between Quasimodo, Beauty's Beast and Inspector Morse.

'By the colour of your face, I would say he was slightly more than just a friend. Hey, don't blush, Cass! And there I was, thinking you were a tough career woman for whom romance was low on the agenda. I'm so glad to find out I was wrong. Love is a wonderful thing, hey, Cass?'

He wandered over to Frank's old desk and sat down there, leaning back in the solid chair and lacing his hands behind his head. 'You are a dark horse, Cass. I have absolutely no idea about your life outside this place. And now it turns out you have a boyfriend. Honestly, you know everything about me –

well, nearly everything – and I know next to nothing about you except how many degrees you have – much less informative than meeting some of your friends. I don't think I've met any of your friends, have I?'

Well, that's lucky, she thought irrepressibly, given that nearly all my friends are involved in some way, in this complicated little plot against you.

'Although I noticed you were having quite a razzmatazz at Conference. You were in a tight little bunch there. That Ted Austin was one of them, if I remember. I suppose you don't see much of him these days. Wasn't that what you were saying at Frank's funeral?'

'Yes, that's right. And I haven't laid eyes on him since then. I guess he's still a bit sore about the by-election candidacy,' she said dismissively, desperate to get off the subject of her Conference cronies, before he put her together with – in the worst scenario – Hallie. 'And I wish it were as exciting as being a dark horse,' she said instead. 'The sad truth is that I have no life to speak of outside this job, beyond my dissertation, my consultancy plans and my grandmother. And definitely no boyfriend. Much simpler that way, believe me.'

'You may well be right.' He smiled indulgently. 'Gwenny can be a right handful at times, let me tell you.'

Please don't! she said inwardly. How can you speak about your mistress when you're actually sitting at her dead husband's desk? Her heart hardened and she looked at her watch. Time to get him moving, before Wilbur and Nina died of cold on that draughty corner of Westminster Bridge.

'Alun – I wouldn't be doing my job if I didn't remind you that your meeting with Spotty Neil is in only half an hour.' She smiled half-apologetically at him.

'Yeah, yeah, keep your hair on. Plenty of time. He'll expect me to be late. Would hate to disappoint him, poor joyless lad that he is.'

'Knock, knock.' It was Paul, carrying a parcel. 'A courier just delivered this for you, Cass.'

Cass held her breath in horror. The laptop! Shit!

'Anything exciting?' asked Alun as she unwrapped it.

'Oh, just my laptop, back from the menders,' she improvised.

'I thought I would use it to surf the Net this afternoon – gather some material for that speech you're giving next week, log onto *Hansard* online and pick out some stuff you've already said.'

'You can do that?' Alun said uninterestedly. 'Well, isn't technology amazing? Well, I suppose I'd better slope over to the Ministry; give Spotty Neil the thrill of explaining this pesky contact programme he's got such a bee in his bonnet about. He's already planned the first one – did I tell you? – for Thursday lunchtime. The boy's keen, I'll give him that.'

Bless Neil, she thought, you really came through with the goods. I almost forgive you your snottiness.

Then she started. 'Are you not going over to Plod's for breakfast?'

'Oh yes, good idea. Yes, I have a few minutes. Why, do you want to join me? Be my guest. It would be nice to catch up. I could pump you some more about this potential new boyfriend of yours.'

'No, I've had breakfast. I just wondered if you could get me a Diet Pepsi?'

'Next thing, you'll be wanting me to deliver it on rollerskates with a tray and a Martini smile,' he grumbled. 'If I remember, I will, how about that?'

'Good enough for me,' she nodded. Then, as he reached the door she remembered the rest of her brief. 'Alun! Before you go, there's something you should know. There's probably nothing to it, but an awful lot of people have been ringing you on this line this morning.'

'Oh? Did they say who they were?'

'Well, quite a few said they were journalists and the rest sounded like it as well, but they wouldn't leave messages, just wanted to know when you were coming back from Heptonstall, how long you'd been up there, that sort of stuff.'

He frowned. 'Funny. Mags said the same thing. Wonder what that's about. Oh well, I'm sure we'll find out, eh?'

'If any more ring, what shall I tell them?'

'Oh, the usual stuff – I am around but you don't know quite where. And try and get out of them what they want.'

'Will do. Hey, are we still having lunch?'

'Oh yes. It'll have to be a late one. See you in the Marquis at two?'

'I'll be there.'

'Wilbur, it's Cass. He's on his way. Hurry!'

'Christ, that was quick. He didn't take much persuading, did he? OK, I'll take Nina in through the Great Hall, leave her in Plod's and then nip back out through New Palace Yard to catch up with him at St Stephen's. We'll let you know how it goes later. How is it your end?'

'Nerve-wracking. It's no longer make-believe. There I was, just lying away to my boss – and I suddenly realised that this isn't exactly going to be your average day at the office, is it? Now I'm all bunched up.'

'I'll give you a massage later on. How about that?'

'Wilbur, stop flirting with me and get on with it, otherwise you'll miss him.'

'Yassir! Am on my way! Over and out!'

As Alun crossed the lights across Millbank to the St Stephen's Entrance, he saw Wilbur Coolidge hurrying along from the river side. Alun nodded politely as they walked towards the Entrance together, Wilbur fishing out his pass, Alun not bothering.

'Busy times, Wilbur?' he asked courteously.

'Pretty busy, pretty busy,' nodded Wilbur. 'Not quite by-election pitch, though, I guess.'

'Morning, Mr Blythe,' nodded one of the policemen on the door. 'I hear that Mrs Blackthorn is doing well up in Heptonstall –' spect you're pleased about that aren't you? She must be glad to have you with her – I mean, Mr Blackthorn's only been dead a few weeks, hasn't he?'

Alun stared at the policeman. Why was he saying all this? What did he mean by it? 'Er, yes. Thank you. It all seems to be going very well.'

Going through the arch and up the stairs, he caught Wilbur's eye. Was it his imagination or was there a gleam of interest in what

Wilbur had just overheard? Alun summoned up a nonplussed grin, and shook his head bewilderedly.

Instead of walking past the X-Ray machines, Alun swung off left and into the Great Hall, his metal-tipped shoes echoing hollowly through the massive medieval stone hall. He frowned slightly when he saw that Wilbur was following him – what was a CNN TV reporter doing going to Plod's?

But when they walked into the sunken cloisters of the shabby little caff, Alun was relieved to see Wilbur greeting a tired-looking, dark-skinned woman already there.

'Hi, Menina,' he heard Wilbur saying, 'sorry I'm late. How are you doing? Hey, Alun, let me introduce you to Menina Parvati, she's just started working in the Library. Menina, this is Alun Blythe, MP for Leeds South.'

'Hello,' Alun smiled politely, thinking that she wasn't nearly pretty enough to be the infamous Wilbur Coolidge's usual type. 'Commons or Lords?'

'Commons,' she replied. 'I'm sorry – did you say your name was Alun Blythe?'

'That's right.'

'Isn't that funny, I was just writing you a letter about those books on gambling and the National Lottery that you ordered. It was asking when you will be able to bring them back.'

The poor girl actually started to look flustered. It sounded like she took her job too bloody seriously, Alun thought, glancing surreptitiously at his watch.

'It's just that, what with that poor Mr Blackthorn's death, they've been out of the library for months now and, well, there might just be others with an interest in the issues beside Mr Blackthorn, God rest his soul, and now you. It's funny actually, you've ordered exactly the same books as he did – are you thinking of taking over his mantle?'

Alun looked sharply at her. 'What on earth do you mean?' he snapped, more coldly than he had intended, noticing with dismay how Wilbur's interest suddenly sharpened.

'As a sort of unofficial spokesman for Avalon,' she had said, surprised, 'well, not FOR Avalon exactly since he would have had to register his interest then, but I did notice that he had an admirable interest in the issues surrounding the National

Lottery. It looks like they'll miss him over there, especially now Mr Boyd-Cooper's gone as well.'

'I'm sorry, there must be some mistake. I never ordered any books from the library. And, if you'll excuse me, I must be getting on – I've got a long day and I must get some food to set me up for it. Nice to meet you, Menina, and welcome to the House of Commons. Wilbur,' he nodded at the man, and moved into the queue.

'Marge,' he said, when he reached the hot counter. 'One of your best and biggest bacon butties, please, love.'

'Now, Mr Blythe – that's not the sort of food you should be having at your stage in life!'

'Pardon?' Alun looked startled.

The dinner lady wagged her finger at him affectionately. 'More than twenty years you've been eating my bacon butties and I think that gives me the right to have a few words. I mean, it's no way to get fit for that campaign trail, is it? I'm told that there are people up there in Heptonstall who are worried about your level of cholestorol. Things change, Mr Blythe, when you get older and you'll be no good to Mrs Blackthorn if you drop dead of a heart attack, will you?' Alun flinched as she winked at him. 'On the campaign, that is. So I've made you up a nice salad bap. That'll keep you going. And good luck to you and Mrs Blackthorn!'

'What?!'

'Well, in the by-election, of course. Although you don't need luck up there, do you? I hear it's all sewn up for Mrs Blackthorn. That's nice.'

Alun was speechless, helplessly aware of that CNN guy's eyes boring into his back. How many other journalists were listening to this innocently condemning prattle? He paid quickly and left, stuffing the offending salad bap into a bin as he went up the stairs to the door.

As he walked, he felt the hairs stir on the back of his neck. His antennae for trouble had never let him down in his twenty-six years in politics, and they were beginning to twitch now.

*   *   *

Cass was staring at the laptop's screen with her best cud-chewing expression, when her phone rang. She snatched it up.

'Progress report?' said Nina's voice. 'I'm freezing my fucking arse off underneath the taxi lamp on the corner of Parliament Square, as arranged, with no sign of your loverboy Wilbur. Marge did her cholesterol lecture brilliantly and Alun's just stormed off with a bug up his arse. I'd say the seeds were beginning to push out some roots.'

'Well, at this end I had a deeply scary moment,' said Cass and told her about Alun eavesdropping on the end of their conversation. 'I tell you, it's one thing planning this whole thing out – it's quite another actually telling barefaced lies to your boss. I'm not sure how much more direct confrontation I can take – and we haven't even got started on this whole Internet thing. Shit, Nina, you're right, this is goddamn scary stuff!'

'I know. I could hear myself prattling inanely on,' Nina sympathised, 'desperately crunching in all the things I had to say and hearing them come out sounding so contrived and awful. As Menina Parvati, I don't think I should be giving up my day-job.'

'But don't worry, Cass,' she went on, 'the Internet stuff will be a doddle. Being able to concentrate on the techie stuff will take your mind off the,' Nina put on a melodramatically deep voice, 'elaborate tissue of lies and deception, woven as if by ants from insubstantial threads of gossip and innuendo. Tune in next week for the next nail-biting episode of *Politics: The Little People*.'

Cass laughed admiringly. 'Wow, you rock! Don't suppose you could swing by my office over here and hold my hand while I screw up the courage to start the ball rolling at the Marquis?'

'Of course I will, but I don't think that's wise, you know? If Alun sees us together, he may start doing his mental arithmetic.' There was a pause. 'Fuck me, I never thought I'd see the day when I would be the one giving you advice.'

Cass laughed again, slightly bitterly. 'And that I would listen to it as well, huh?'

'Amazing. Spooky. Changing the habit of half a lifetime.'

There was another little pause then Cass rushed into a little speech. 'Hey, Nin, I know this isn't the right time to say this but you know how sorry I am about that night when you turned up at St Luke's Avenue, don't you? I would do just anything to take those few moments back and relive them.'

'I would do anything to take a few of the preceding months back and relive them, believe me,' Nina said dryly. 'But, yes, I do know – and I'm sorry too, that I put you through all that shit in Forest Mere.'

'Oh Christ, don't apologise for that. I deserved worse. What I definitely don't deserve is you giving me this unbelievable amount of help at the same time as dealing with a collapsing marriage.'

'Collapsed, Cass. Collapsed, I'm afraid. I'm beginning to realise that.'

'Oh. Oh. Oh, well, you know, that sucks but these things happen. Onwards and upwards and all that.' Cass hesitated. 'Hey, can I come up with any more clichés at this emotional juncture of our friendship?! How about – there are plenty more fish in the sea? I defy you to beat that.'

Nina burst out laughing. 'Doctor Cass, is this what your clients have to look forward to?!' Then she quietened. 'But you're right about one thing – this is quite an emotional juncture of our friendship, isn't it? For you, me and Hallie. We've been friends since we're ten and yet this is the first time that friendship has had to change, has had to weather some piss-awful stormy weather.'

'I don't know,' said Cass lightly. 'Hallie was at great pains to remind me the other day of the time I apparently nicked some boyfriend from you and we feuded pretty badly then.'

'Bobby Wallis!' cried Nina. 'I can't fucking believe you don't even remember snogging him. Hang on a sec, why *am* I friends with you, you nicker of pimply-boyfriends?'

'Because none of us will ever find better friends,' Cass said quietly. 'Ain't that the truth?'

'Got it in one, pal,' agreed Nina solemnly. 'I don't lie, cheat, dress up in bad clothes to pretend to be a librarian and spend three days staring at a computer screen for just anyone, you know. I must be mad.'

'We all are,' confirmed Cass more cheerfully, 'and I tell you what, when this is all over, we are going to go totally wild and nutty. Extreme clubbing action. Drugs. Insanity. Seeing in the dawn. When was the last time we did that? Got totally caned and held each other's heads over the toilet bowl?'

'Oh, you really know how to sell me on an idea. Anyway,' Nina's tone was teasing, 'I have the strangest feeling you're going to be too busy being wild and nutty with someone else.'

'Yeah, don't think I didn't notice the "loverboy" reference,' Cass chuckled. 'You noticed last night then?'

'Notice! I still have the scorch marks from being too close to the action!'

'Yeah, when he started holding my hands and giving me the motivation spiel, I did think I was going to spontaneously combust . . . but the trouble is, we just get on too well now. I have this awful feeling that maybe we've gone too far – that we've stepped into the Friend Zone . . .'

'Doo-doo-doo-doo, welcome to the Friend Zone. Naah, no chance. Ross-and-Rachel style *Friends* maybe – but I have never seen such sexual chemistry between two people.'

'Oh that!' dismissed Cass. 'I know that! But what if that's all it is? Chemistry and habit?'

'Now who's sounding like a fucking smackhead?! Anyway, so what?! For a start, you just said so yourself, the two of you just get on so well and, as my father says, it's vital you have the lust and excitement part to start with – you've got the rest of your lives to work the rest of it out.'

'Nina, your parents have been divorced even longer than mine have.'

'Yeah, but you know what my father's like when he's pissed, and the number of times he's boasted about the unbelievably good sex they always used to have – you must remember how embarrassing he used to be. No, the problems there came from my mother being a totally repressed debutantey snob – who was swept off her feet by fantastic sex but could never cope with the fact that she'd married an Indian—'

'—and has made you pay for it ever since,' interjected Cass.

'Yeah, I suppose she has,' said Nina slowly. 'Anyway, talking of sex, are you thinking what I'm thinking about Hallie?'

'Her and Ted – you bet! What a perfect combination – why

didn't I think of that months ago, instead of setting her up with Devlin. What a disaster that was!'

'Do you know,' mused Nina, 'Hallie and I were convinced when you came back from the States that Devlin was going to be some hugely significant feature in your life – all that meeting on a plane, him tracking you down, begging you to come to Dublin and sending you the tickets – it was all so romantic, but he just turned out to be a big red herring, didn't he?'

'More of a little red herring,' said Cass wickedly, 'according to Hallie.'

Still smiling over her conversation with Nina, Cass glanced at her watch and moved on to her next call.

'Neil? Cass here. Is Alun still with you?' Say yes, she prayed. Say yes.

'Yes. He's just about to leave. Would you like to speak to him?'

No, I'd like to suck his dick, you moron, she thought irritably. 'Yes. If it's not too much trouble.'

'No trouble. Minister, it's your researcher.'

'Alun, sorry to bother you there but they just called here from Central Lobby to tell me that there are two journalists hanging about there, sending messages like green confetti to try and track you down and could you at least drop by the message board to pick up their details.'

'Bugger it,' swore Alun. 'Names?'

'Um, Andy Macpherson and Tammy Kerr.' They'd really put a lot of effort into some aliases there, she thought crossly, like swapping surnames was going to pull the wool over anyone's eyes, 'From something like the *Mail on Sunday*, doing a story on parliament lotharios, apparently. Alun, what's going on?'

'Cass, I have no idea. I'll swing by the message board now on my way to my 11.00 meeting in Little College Street. Then I'll be out of touch until I see you at two.'

'Two in the Marquis.'

Cass dialled again immediately.

'Wilbur? Cass. He's just leaving Neil so he should be in the Members' Lobby just in time to bump into Sarah. Let's just pray that the Attendant there really has been putting Andy and Tamsin's messages on the message board. Are you on the roof terrace?'

'Yup. It's amazing. Nina and I are enjoying the view. And don't worry about the message board – that's the way the system works isn't it? So why should this time be any different? Look, I'll go down to Central Lobby, tell Andy and Tammy to send their final message and get the hell out of there, just in case Alun takes it into his head to confront them, then wait until he's well clear of the House, and smuggle Nina out.'

'Perfect.'

'I am, aren't I?'

'Pull your neck in, big guy. Just don't use Arthur's lift to go back down from the roof terrace. I'm kinda hoping that Alun will use it to get into the Members' Lobby by going in through Star Chamber courtyard. Hopefully he'll go that way to avoid going anywhere near Central Lobby. Then, you never know, Arthur might also come up with the goods.'

'But remember – it isn't the end of the world if he doesn't. I reckon we've laid enough little landmines as it is. Alun will soon be getting the message that something's up, believe me.'

'Landmines, Wilbur? That's a very politically uncorrect analogy to use these days.'

'Focus, my darling, on the matter in hand, and I promise to make a donation to the Princess's Memorial Fund when this is all over.'

'Jeez, you're cheezy. See ya.'

Something was definitely up, thought Alun as he hurried through the House of Lords. Walking swiftly across Parliament Square and into New Palace Yard, he had avoided the main way to the Members' Lobby, going up there instead via the little used lift from the corner of Star Chamber courtyard. Even Arthur – sitting placidly in the lift, with his wooden arm and gold-toothed smile, even Arthur, for heavens' sake, had gone into some weird speech about how lovely Gwen was and how 'you, Mr Blythe, you're bein' a good fellow to her, standing by her side in that election' and had wished him all the best. Arthur who had previously never said more than mornin', afternoon and evenin' and seasonal greetings in all of Alun's years at the House.

By now he was so jumpy about Gwen that he could have sworn that there were some bloody knowing looks flying around the Whips' Office, as he nipped in to say hello. Then, outside the Whips' Office in the Members' Lobby, he was standing at the message board, trying to make head or tail of all the messages from journalists he had never even heard of, from papers that were never usually interested in City goings-on, when he was tapped on the shoulder by a girl he knew worked in the Library. 'Mr Blythe, just a word on the gambling texts you've ordered. If you could return them to the Library within the due date, I would be very grateful. Mr Blackthorn had them for so long that we—'

'Yes, I've heard all this,' he started testily, when he was tapped on the shoulder by one of the white-tied Central Lobby attendants.

'Mr Blythe – I don't know if your researcher tracked you down, but there are two very persistent journalists from the *Mail on Sunday* waiting for you in Central Lobby. Andy Macpherson and Tammy Kerr. Would you like me to—'

'Just say you can't find me, there's a good chap, I'm already late for my meeting.' Ignoring the librarian completely, he took off quickly up the corridor towards the Library. He would have to go down and round by the Dining Corridor to avoid Central Lobby and dodge out through the Lords. What the bloody hell was going on? Why was he being doorstepped right here in the House of Commons? Surely they hadn't found out about him and Gwenny? And what was all this about gambling books, and him taking over Frank's mantle as Avalon champion? What was all that about? Did any of this tie in with that phone-call to Gwen from Avalon that he had intercepted on the train that morning? It seemed such a long time since the morning. Christ, he needed a drink.

'Christ, I need a drink.' Alun sank onto the leather banquette next to Cass.

'I'll get you one. Pint of Theakston's?'

'Yes. And another one to keep it company. Here, here's a tenner. Fill up whatever you're having.' He picked up her glass and smelt it. 'Whisky? You, Cass? At lunchtime?'

She looked uncharacteristically nervous, raking her hands backwards and forwards through her still-short black hair. 'Dutch courage. Back in a sec.'

Waiting for her to get the drinks, Alun looked up wearily to see the most amazing-looking girl staring at him. She looked, he mused, almost like a young Gwen, with that shining straight dark hair and a figure that men would go to battle for. He felt the temptation to look over his shoulder to see if there was someone behind him she could really be staring at. Now that he came to think of it he vaguely recognised her.

'There you go.' Cass put the drinks on the small table. 'Mike asked if we wanted to move upstairs like you usually do, but I thought we were fine down here. Is that OK?'

'Great. I'm avoiding my usual haunts. Now, tell me why you need Dutch courage. I'm the one being hounded by media hacks and strange librarians. What's your problem? Mags being throwing things at you again?'

Cass took a deep breath. 'No. Because I think I might know why those reporters are hounding you. And you're not going to like it.'

'Cass? Cass Herbert?'

Both of them glanced up in surprise, to see the young Gwen-lookalike gazing warmly down at Cass.

'Annalisa. Hello.' Cass's voice was cold.

'Fancy meeting you here,' the gorgeous girl said, her eyes flashing provocatively. 'Mind if I join you? My friend's late. Is this your lovely boss?'

'Gee, it's a shame, Annalisa, but we were just on our way upstairs—'

'Rubbish. You've only just sat down.' Without further ado, she sat and held out her hand prettily. 'Hello there, I'm Annalisa Smith, Chris Phillips's secretary.'

'Oh right, how is Chris? He's a nice lad. Alun Blythe, by the way. So how's Chris settled in? I haven't seen much of him in the Chamber, but then I haven't been there much myself lately.'

Five minutes later, Alun looked up to see Cass making frantic throat-slitting motions behind Annalisa's back and pointing upstairs. He sighed. The only fun he'd had in an otherwise terrible day and his researcher seemed determined to spoil it. He stood up resignedly.

'Well, Annalisa, it's been lovely to meet you but Cass and I have serious affairs of state to discuss upstairs. All to do with dogbowls, isn't it, Cass?'

Annalisa smiled maliciously. 'Yes, Cass, I hear you and Mags O'Sullivan are great Chums these days. Or is she your Pal?'

Cass stood up abruptly. 'Funny to the max, Annalisa, watch my sides split.'

When they got upstairs, Cass turned to him. 'Christ, I'm sorry about that, Alun. I couldn't get rid of her any quicker.'

'Why get rid of her?' he grumbled. 'Bloody pretty girl.'

'And practically a call-girl.'

'What?'

'Alun – you must have heard of her! She's slept with most of the Tory MPs – and by the looks of it, she was about to add a Labour scalp to her bedstead.'

Inexplicably, Alun felt a tiny thrill of pride. Of all the Labour MPs that were younger and better-looking than him, she had chosen him. He must remember to tell Gwen. 'Oh stop your exaggerating, lass,' he said gruffly. 'Who made you my mother?'

'Yeah, well, who made me the bearer of bad news is more to the point,' she snapped. Then she stopped, horrified. 'Alun, I am so sorry. That was totally out of line. It's just that I – well, you know I said I was going surfing on the Internet this morning?'

'Whatever that actually means,' he smiled. 'Yes, you did mention it. Something about references for next week's speech.'

'Yeah, well, I couldn't remember the website address for the *Hansard* Online homepage, so I logged onto Alta Vista and typed in your name to get there that way. But then Java threw up all these other matches that were nothing to do with *Hansard*.' She broke off, looking at him quizzically. 'This means nothing to you, right?'

'Nothing at all,' he admitted cheerfully, trying not to dribble toasted cheese down his shirt. 'But I'm sure it's all very interesting.'

'Well, I'll show you when we get back to the office but basically there, large as life, Alun, for about forty million people to see worldwide, are, like, pages and pages of this website, devoted to you, the Heptonstall by-election, your affair with Gwenny, Frank's links to an Avalon scandal and Gwenny's collaboration over its cover-up.'

Now she had his attention.

'OK, here we go. Look, the way I got there was to use the Alta Vista search engine and type in your name, because Alta Vista is more streamlined and quicker – but the grandpappy of all search engines is Yahoo. The way information is displayed on the World Wide Web is a bit like Ceefax – some of the main pages have, like, banner headlines advertising hot other sights – so if we go to the main Yahoo page—'

Flick, flick with the mouse. Cass held her breath and prayed he hadn't noticed that she'd actually just opened a FAVOURITE site direct from the toolbar. She glanced up at him and saw that his face still showed the same blank incomprehension and shock it had displayed since she'd dropped the bombshell at the Marquis. She couldn't believe that it was actually working.

On the screen in front of them, was a page that, to all but the most expert eye, looked like the index page of the Yahoo search engine. Along the bottom, flashing red, then yellow, then blue, was a banner which read: BY-ELECTION SCANDAL! CLICK HERE!

'Now the good news is that this particular Yahoo page is dedicated to UK users only,' said Cass, 'so you haven't actually got the whole world looking at this. The other piece of good news is that if you do click here,' she moved the mouse until a little white hand appeared over the banner, 'you go through to an as yet uncompleted homepage – which is like the looseleaf cover of a book – it often has some groovy design to get you interested, some blurb to pull you in, and a table of contents.' She double-clicked and the screen cleared to reveal an almost blank page, with several empty boxes marked with identical multi-coloured icons. Almost immediately, a warning box flashed up over the page saying: THIS

PAGE IS NOT YET COMPLETE. SCHEDULED TO OPEN ON THURSDAY 13 NOVEMBER. CLICK HERE TO PROCEED. She did and it disappeared.

'Now at the moment this means that you are reasonably safe because your casual browser won't bother going on with something that they aren't given a taster of first, but by tomorrow this page will be up and running in glorious technicolour.' She paused and looked up to see if he was buying this. 'And video.'

'Video?' At last Alun spoke. 'On a computer?'

'Yeah, look at this.' She moved the mouse to one of the boxes. Immediately a little text box appeared, attached to the cursor arrow. 'See in this text box, this reference ends ".avi"? That means it's a video. Now if we double-click on that,' she did, and the mouse's hourglass appeared, the globe in the top right hand corner whirring round as they went to the next of Nina's ingenious contrivances. 'We get to the video page. As you can see, there's some text explaining what you're about to see.' Cass scanned the text rapidly, 'It's basically an old news-tape of a Lottery winner, a Mrs X, who gave nearly all her winnings to the Labour Party—'

'I remember that!' Alun snapped his fingers. 'It was just before the election – she was one of Frank's constituents. It was fantastic. A great feel-good story.'

'OK, but it says here,' and Cass ran him through the basic details of the Mrs Harrison story, as told to her and faithfully re-typed by Nina over the last couple of days.

'That's just bloody stupid,' Alun said contemptuously. 'Load of old hokum. If she didn't want the publicity, Avalon would never have broken their word – Christ, they reckon under thirty per cent of winners ever take the publicity, so why is she any different? Anyway Frank would never have brought her into the limelight like that. No, it's obvious the stupid old bag changed her mind when the attention got a bit much – tried to back out of it.' He leaned back in his chair, relieved.

Silently, Cass clicked onto the next pages. Alun leaned further and further forward as page after page of evidence was revealed. First, there were scanned reproductions of the correspondence between Boyd-Cooper, Frank and Mrs Harrison – the original letter that Cass had found jammed in the desk which proved that Mrs Harrison had never wanted the publicity of the lottery win, let alone her Labour donation, supplemented by all the various letters which Mrs Harrison had received and sent on to Cass. There were the original clippings of Mr and Mrs Harrison receiving their makeovers, then the photo of them at the Taj Mahal, and the poignant starkness of Alf's wire requests for money from places like Goa and Bombay. The worst was the one from Gwenny herself which attempted a chummy, woman-to-woman tone, trying to 'buck' Mrs H out of her 'post-Lotto blues', implying that all the razzmatazz was to cheer her up and that it would be churlish to deny Frank the chance to show how adored a constituency MP he was that one of his 'people' had given nearly two million pounds to the national coffers; that Alf would have wanted her to do it and that perhaps this way he would see Mrs Harrison on the TV somewhere and know that he could come back to her. It was emotional blackmail at its most honeyed and insidious, and the culmination to a damning portfolio of evidence.

'Go on,' Alun said tightly, when he had read all this. 'Now show me everything.'

So she did. She, Nina and Hallie had painstakingly assembled a log worthy of Philip Marlowe, of all the GB Ltd entries in the diary, as well as a few that Cass knew about on the side, like Alun and Gwenny's aborted trip to Guildford. The clump of papers that Cass had rescued from the Atrium that day when Alun had charged off after their lunch had yielded rich pickings of credit card receipts and hotel check-out printouts. Hallie's sneaky foray at the Cosmopole on Monday had yielded an impressive track record of stays by a Mr and Mrs Blythe – one of which had been paid for on Gwen Blackthorn's credit card.

Alongside this damning dossier Nina had formatted and written a column that was both gossipy and censorious, opening, 'In a tangled mess more reminiscent of Tory excess than the Better Britain of Tony Blair, we bring you the Minister, the Backbencher, His Wife and the Victim – a tale reeking of adulterous sex, ignorant cuckolds, manipulation, political corruption and money, and a great deal of money . . .' and going downhill from there.

'Christ alive.' Alun exhaled when at last he'd seen everything. 'This cannot be happening. This just cannot be happening.'

Cass was silent for a moment, letting it all sink in.

'As I said,' she said softly, 'the good news is that only either very determined people or people who go straight to a certain page like I did by accident, will be able to access this at the moment. I'm guessing that's why the reporters have been hassling you, because they have a whiff and only a whiff, of this. But tomorrow, every single Yahoo user in this country – something in the millions – will be able to see this as bold as brass if they want to.'

'Can we not do owt? Can't we wipe it out or summat?' Alun's Northern accent was getting stronger in his distress. For a moment, Cass's resolve failed her but she just thought back to Wilbur's words of motivation last night and she sat up straighter.

'No, I'm afraid not. But one thing does occur to me.'

There was a gleam of hope in Alun's eyes. 'Yes? What? Anything!'

'When I was working in the Senate, there were rumours flying all over the place about this one Republican Senator having an affair with the wife of a Democrat Senator. Every day, the papers were, like, about to run this total exposé on the two of them, but it never came to anything because it turned out the Democrat wife had just become separated from her husband, and the Republican was a recent widower. So there wasn't anything actually wrong with the set-up – even though everyone knew it had been going on for years – because there were no victims. Even the difference in their politics wasn't enough because she wasn't a political figure herself.'

'Cass, get to the point.'

'Well, listen, it's only a suggestion – and please don't shoot the messenger – but it strikes me that what makes all this stuff,' Cass waved at the screen, 'not just some unpublishable rumour, like the Senator's situation, but into a scandal flashing through cyberspace and beyond – is this Mrs X situation and Frank Blackthorn's dubious links to Avalon. If you and Gwenny were somehow able to disassociate yourself from the Lottery stuff and all the political connotations . . .' Cass didn't dare say any more, without overplaying her hand. 'Of course, I'm not sure how you do that.'

'Hmmm,' Alun chewed speculatively on a fingernail. 'Pass me the phone.'

Now, what was he up to? thought Cass. He was meant to be too shocked to do anything but listen to her. It occurred to her, not for the first time, that Alun hadn't survived twenty-six years of political infighting with just his native charm. In her distraction, as she passed him the phone, her hand pushed the mouse off the desk. She picked it up but must have inadvertently clicked on it because when she sat up again, she was gazing at Nina and Steve's homepage, humorously entitled, this week, THE DEADLINE, THE NOVELIST, THE WIFE AND HER MOTHER in the exact same typeface as the similarly phrased header in Nina's Scandal website.

Cass froze. Without daring to look sidelong at Alun, she crept forward on the mouse and undramatically shut the site down completely.

'Mags? It's me.' He paused. 'For Christ's sake, Mags, pull yourself together. It's Alun.' He glanced quickly at Cass. 'I thought you were cutting down on the, er, handbag accessories after recent events?' He listened for a moment. 'Mags. Mags. Spare me the details. Just tell me what my day looks like tomorrow.' He pulled a piece of paper towards him and started to scribble. Then suddenly he halted. 'Hallie who? Oh Christ, that girl from Bandwick & Parker. I forgot, her secretary called me direct on the mobile to drum into me that I had to go. Right. Cancel everything except that meeting and that initial contact lunch that Neil has set up for me. No harm in that, surely. Dining Room A at one o'clock – and I'm meeting them in Central Lobby. OK. Who's coming? Good, I know Einhorn by sight at least, so I'll be able to spot them.'

Under her desk, Cass clenched her fists. Two out of three wasn't bad, but what about Wilbur's interview?

'What's that? Oldtimers collage? Sounds like a heap of crap. Oh, you promised him, did you? Funny he didn't mention it when I saw him this morning. Crafty bugger. He must have known I'd try to wriggle out of it. Mags, you should know better than to promise anyone anything, even if they are as easy on your eye as Wilbur Coolidge, because you know how I hate to be held by your Irish honesty. OK, OK, keep that in as well, but cut it to ten minutes – at twelve.'

Cass's hands convulsed again. Score!

'No, don't talk to any of these bloody journalists, Mags. And don't swear at them either. Just say I'm on the campaign – no, occupied with ministerial duties. That'll fob them off for a while. And now go home. Have an early night. And try to lay off the juice, sweetheart, just for tonight. I have a feeling that tomorrow's going to be a day none of us are going to forget in a hurry.'

You got that right, thought Cass feverishly.

Alun nursed a pint, his finger going unseeingly around the rim as he considered his options. Was he getting truly paranoid or had even Mike, the landlord of the Marquis, given him a strange look when he'd returned so soon after he'd left with Cass? Perhaps it was because he was hiding down here instead of at his usual billet upstairs. But tonight he couldn't face hanging out with the usual cronies. Nor could he talk to Gwen. His mobile phone battery had died just as he was dialling her, and he didn't dare use the public one in here. Christ knows who might be listening in, in this place, with all its Smith Square types from Conservative Central Office. Before, Alun had often enjoyed the sensation of spying on those Tory Young Turks, but today, it seemed, he was the one being spied on.

He wrestled to get things into perspective. The Internet was much more puff than substance, wasn't it? He had no proof that all these journalists were after him and Gwenny, they could be pursuing him on something completely different. OK, so the whole of the Palace of Westminster seemed to know about him and Gwenny – judging by the likes of Marge's comments – but they were just the little people. Their opinions wouldn't go outside the House.

'Hello again. You and I must have a drinking problem – both back here so soon. Can I join you?'

'Annalisa! Hello, there. Please, sit down. Make an old man happy.'

Alun's spirits rose slightly as he watched Annalisa carefully move all the overcoats, scarves and clobber of the people next door off the banquette so that she could move in next to him, instead of sitting opposite on the stool. Looking at her drink out of her Budweiser bottle, an expression that Tom, Gwen's stepson, was wont to use, sprang to mind. 'She was so cool,' he'd boast after a night's clubbing conquest, 'that her beer bottle had a frosted rim!' This girl, thought Alun with the bleariness of a long day and several long drinks, was so damn hot that she'd be melting the neck of her beer bottle if she wasn't careful.

He watched almost hypnotised as she started removing her layers – fake fur coat, a velvet scarf, then a bumfreezer of a deep gold velvet jacket until she was left in nothing except the infinitisemally small gold velvet mini-skirt and the tiniest little shimmery gold top, the spaghetti straps of which dipped dangerously close to her pert little breasts. This is my reward for this capital punishment of a day, he thought dazedly, it must be.

Then she spoilt it all by putting one gold-painted fingernail on his knee and drawing her finger up his thigh almost speculatively. 'You look tired,' she said coolly. 'I'd get an early night if I were you.'

Alun sighed. Why were the young of today so impatient, he thought sadly, so cack-handed. He had been quite content to sit here with this gorgeous slip of a girl and drink in the reflected glory of her sexiness. He would have been happy to have flirted a little, bought her a few drinks, allowed himself to dream a little of what might have happened if he'd been younger, stronger and less dulled by alcohol. Oh yes, and single. But she had to go straight for the kill, didn't she? It was almost insulting, how she so obviously thought that that was all she had to do to bring him drooling to his knees.

Oh well, he thought resignedly, looking down at the hand now sliding expertly towards his groin, it might have been nice. Gently, he reached down, removed her hand and patted it gently. 'Annalisa, you're a beautiful girl,' he started but she cut him off, using her other hand to lay her index finger across his lips.

'Shush,' she whispered throatily. 'You don't have to pay me compliments. That's my department. This is what I was thinking of doing to you.' In the gloom of the pub, she slid forward on the banquette, swung a curtain of hair to one side and started whispering in his ear, fingers stroking the underside of his palm where she still held his hand captive.

Alun's eyes widened and his lips started to curve. This time he moved her away more firmly and crossed his legs, determined not to show her that she had excited him. 'It all sounds a bit anatomical, to be honest,' he joked, 'but the offer is a very flattering one. Very flattering but – and I don't want to sound like an Ealing Comedy landlady but you are an incorrigible young lady, Annalisa, who should learn to direct her sexual energies at more appropriate targets than pickled old has-beens like me.' He smiled as paternally as he knew how, thinking wistfully of Gwenny's own more beguiling seductions.

But Annalisa's eyes darkened and she pulled back abruptly. 'Not good enough for you, am I then?' Her tone turned from throaty seductress to shrewish ranter, with a matching rise in volume. 'What's wrong with me? You've never been so fussy about House of Commons secretaries before! What's Gwen Blackthorn after all? She may fancy herself nowadays as some political hotshot but she's still a secretary just like me – and you've been shagging her for years and years, haven't you? So why not trade her in for a younger model – I could give ten Gwen Blackthorns a run for their money! What's Gwen Blackthorn got that I haven't got?'

In his paralysed horror at what had suddenly turned from a quiet harmless little flirtation into a fullblown public spectacle, Alun became aware of two particular spectators sitting on stools at the bar, a young couple staring at him and the shouting Annalisa with open curiosity. First, they were facing directly head-on to him, with their backs to the bar, which was strange, and second—

Fuck, thought Alun. One of them had a pad. Lying open on her knee. Into which she was scribbling furiously, then looking back at him and Annalisa. Journalists. Just what he didn't need.

'Top banana! Oh, Tamsin, you are so cool! Yeah, good old Annalisa – quite impressive, isn't she? You've got to hand it to her. Sounds like she went a tad too far. Poor Alun. I hope he sees the funny side of this one day. Yup. OK. Now remember, not a word. And you'll be there at one o'clock tomorrow? Excellent. Allow a bit of extra time for getting through the

X-Ray machines because that's a busy time of day. Allrighty, dudes, catch you later.'

Wilbur watched Cass on the phone, as her still battered-looking face went through the gamut of emotions.

'That was Tamsin and Andy. Trudie, they send their love.'

Her grandmother opened one eye where she was slumbering elegantly in an armchair. 'Fabbidab. All well?'

'All very well,' responded Cass with weary excitement. 'Annalisa went far too far and sang to the rooftops about Gwenny, but, hey, too bad. Alun saw Tamsin and Andy and totally put two and two together about them being journalists. By the way, Hallie and Nina rang earlier. They're going out to some restaurant opening, can you believe it? With Ted. Hey, am I a matchmaker or what? Ted and Hallie. It's just too perfect.'

She smiled and brought a hand up to cover her eyes, wincing slightly as she touched the black eye. 'Oh my God, it's over. Thank God. For today at least. Now we've just got tomorrow to contend with. Getting any energy out of me to do that is going to be like drilling a dry well. I am totally blitzed.' She slumped against the back of the sofa and swung up her long legs in their DMs to rest on Wilbur's lap.

'Remember that you've pretty much done your stuff. Tomorrow is simple by comparison,' Wilbur said softly, beginning to unlace her boots. 'My interview, Andy and Tamsin doing their doorstepping thing. And then the Big One with Hallie. Tomorrow is mostly her gig.'

'Tell me about it. There's no certainty of any of this working unless she steers the right course.' Cass yawned hugely. 'Poor Hallie. I may have had to do all the fiddly running about and chatting up people left, right and centre, but the final responsibility rests on her performance.'

'She'll be great. I get the impression just from Conference and these last few days that she is a real whizzkid at her job.' Dropping Cass's boots to the floor and peeling off her socks, Wilbur began to massage her feet.

'I think you're right. Which is weird because Hal was always the least career-minded of the three of us, yet she's the one who's streets ahead now.' Cass opened her eyes. 'Jeez, you're brave – I had a little fungal research centre going in those boots.'

'Believe me, once you've spent a few hours in an un-airconditioned changing room in a Midwestern summer with fifteen other male ballet dancers, you haven't even taken your nose for a walk in the park,' grinned Wilbur. 'Now shut up and relax. I'm good at this.'

Cass groaned ecstatically and wriggled deeper into the sofa. 'Much as I hate to give you credit for anything, this time you're right. OK, tell me a story about a part of your life I haven't heard about before.'

Wilbur thought for a moment. 'This is terrible. I think you already know my entire life. Jeez, how boring must I be? No, wait a minute, I've thought of something. The first time I ever really fell in love. How about that?'

Cass bit back another mighty yawn and squinted at him suspiciously. 'Is this going to be a trumpet-blowing session?'

He grimaced. 'Definitely not. Probably more like a violin-playing ordeal.'

'OK, try me.' Cass lay back again and closed her eyes. 'Just don't get mad at me if I fall asleep. Rest assured that somewhere in my subconscious I will still be hanging onto your every word.'

'Right,' said Wilbur dryly. 'OK. Once upon a time . . .'

A sleepy eye opened. 'Wilbur . . .'

'Anti-traditionalist to the last, aren't you?' he teased. 'Right. I met this girl, this woman, this goddess. And she reached inside me and rearranged my internal organs every time I so much as looked at her. But she was like a strawberry to a kid with allergies. The most beautiful thing in the world he has ever seen but he knows he would hate the effect that strawberry would have on him if he didn't keep his distance from that beauty, that juice, those pips.' He gently started working on her toes.

'So it was with this girl. Right from the beginning we clashed. In a way, it was inevitable that we would fall for each other but both of us fought tooth and nail against that inevitability. It was like reading a book where you know the ending right from the start and it really pisses you off that the writer isn't trying harder to disguise it, but you can't quite bear to put it down because there are so many things to enchant and alarm you along the way. Then you realise something. Why should the writer tie himself in knots trying to put the obvious end of his book through a labyrinth of blind corners and dead ends just for some fussy need for mystery? Endings in life usually *are* obvious – it's just how much fun and magic you have along the way.

'With this girl, it's never dull and the magic is no sleight of hand illusion. I'm like the writer who's realised that the ending is in sight and that it's up to me and this girl whether we want to go the labyrinthine way, with all its fits and starts but the excitement of not knowing which way is the real way, or do we do the Nike thing and just do it? The important thing is that I'm in love with this girl. For the first time in my life, I'm in a state where either way would work for me, as long as you were by my side. So, one of these days, just let me know how you feel, OK? Because we're wasting precious fun and magic time here, my darling.'

Wilbur smiled down at Cass. She was fast asleep. Had been since about four lines into his story. But her face was curved into a soft smile, so perhaps she was, as she had promised, hanging onto his every word somewhere in her subconscious.

'I think you'll find that "I love you, Cass" would work just as well.' Trudie opened her eyes from the other side of the room, to see Wilbur's shocked face, smiled hugely, and closed them again. 'So. Not such a smoothie, after all.'

Nina sat up to let more hot water into the bath, then lay back, slumping into the bubbles that had backed up again behind her. She had been in here for nearly two hours now. National Prune Week would surely admire her, she thought dispassionately, as she examined the wrinkles in her fingers and toes. Trouble was, she never wanted to get out. It sometimes seemed like she was so busy pretending to everyone else that she had put Jerry right to the back of her mind while Project Yalta was underway, that she almost felt divided into two people. Not the usual division into Nina Kellman and Nina Parvati but some new creations: feisty Nina Strangelove, cunning strategist at the centre of a diabolical political plot, and Nina Crybaby, who spent long hours in the bath, using the running of the taps to cover the sound of her pathetic sobbing.

At least she was beginning to sort out what was going on in her mind. As the red mist that had fogged her brain since Babaji's death began to clear, she started to think, really think, about the cataclysmic events of the previous few weeks. At first, when she'd opened Steve's e-mails and found his proposition, she had leapt at it like a parachutist at a ripcord. His publishers had suggested that he might like to write an anthology of real crime stories from throughout the former Soviet Union. He couldn't bear, Steve had written, to spend a whole six months travelling on his own, with only vodka and the odd Mobster for company, so would Nina consider coming with him? She could use the time to write travel articles but without the pressure of having to get commissions before she left because he'd negotiated a 'partner's' slot into the deal with the publishers, so, as long as she was resigned to sharing the odd hotel room with him, she wouldn't have to pay for much along the way. Nina couldn't think of a better way to shelve all her problems than hiding out in Russia. It was all too perfect. Yet with her usual caution, and knowing that this was not the time to start pumping either Cass or Hallie for the usual advice, Nina had held back from telling him that, yes, she would come.

Now, she wasn't so sure. Running away from her problems had become almost second-nature in the last few months. Could she afford to apply the same logic right down the line? She was mucking about with two lives here: if she went with Steve, that would be it, that would be the end of her marriage. For all her brave words to Cass that day, she still couldn't imagine that she and Jerry really were over. They had been together too long for her to be able to see a real-life future without him.

The telephone rang. Nina prayed that Beth was back from her lacrosse practice, because she knew that Hallie was still at the restaurant with Ted, left there tactfully by Nina, who seemed to spend her entire time these days leaving putative couples to get on with it.

'Hello?'

Yes, thank God, she was. Nina relaxed into her bubbles again.

'Now, look here, Jerry, you don't know me but I am Hallie's landlady and I think I have to take it upon myself to tell you that all these phone calls aren't doing you any good. You're not going to speak to Nina. You're not on her team any more, don't you understand? You're going to have to get it through your thick skull that you're bowled out here, mister, and no amount of barracking is going to get you back into the game—'

Nina couldn't listen to any more, quickly heaving herself out of the bath, trailing a coronation robe of foam across the floor and wrenching the door open.

'Beth! Thanks! I'll take it!'

Beth looked speculatively at Nina's naked body as she reached out, wet-handed, for the cordless phone. 'Well, it's your funeral. The good thing is,' Beth covered the speaker with one square-fingered hand, 'you've lost so much weight since you came here that you'll be able to put him right where you want him when you see him. Those spare tyres have nearly gone. All you need now is a good holiday to beef up your tan and you'll look great, girlie.'

'Er, thanks,' said Nina politely. 'Jerry?'

'Oh, Nina,' said a relieved voice, 'who was *that*?'

Nina closed the bathroom door carefully behind her and climbed back into the bath. 'That was Beth, Hallie's flatmate. She's OK – a slightly acquired taste, that's all. She's actually been kind to me, considering.'

'Nin,' Jerry interrupted, 'I know you'll probably put the phone down on me in a minute, so I'm just going to come out with all my stuff before you get a chance. Look, in a nutshell, I fucked up. We fucked up. But I fucked up hugely that last time I saw you in London. I've been so obsessed with behaving how I think a beleaguered husband *should* behave, that I've forgotten how to be myself. I've cursed myself every day since I pulled that ghastly stunt with the photo of Babaji. It was a lowdown, heel-ish thing to do and I don't expect you to forgive me. Just listen. That's all I ask.'

'Go on,' said Nina guardedly.

'Is that sploshing I hear? You're in the bath, aren't you? Oh,' Jerry's voice suddenly went rough, 'Christ, I would like to be in there with you. No. Shut up, Kellman, and get to the point. The point is that I know now, I really do, that something, well, a lot of things, went wrong. And since this is neither the time nor the medium to go over these issues, I propose that we look forward here. What would you say if I were to tell you that the cottage is on the market, that I've put an offer in for this huge flat in Hammersmith – subject to your approval of course – and that I've even arranged a mortgage? I have to keep on with the job at Kellman's – I actually enjoy it, believe it or not – but I promise, promise, promise, not to turn into some crusty City type. I never turned into a barking Army type, did I? Perhaps it's my destiny to go into these circles and come out again unscathed. To tell you the truth, I was missing London myself. We've got friends here, Nina, and I think we both lost sight of that for a moment: that two people alone do not necessarily a good marriage make. The way I see it, we spent far too much time on our own, stuck out there in the sticks, with not enough to do, after eight years of a relationship which had positively thrived on absences. I think you should take up travel-writing again. Perhaps that way, you'll find yourself again. You always did seem happier when you weren't lodged in one particular sphere: whether it was your mother's awful snobbery, or your father's New Ageism, or even with me, as Mrs Jerry Kellman, meeting the *right sort* in the country. In fact – and I know how you hate nepotism, but you know as well as I do that it's vital in these spheres – I was singing your praises to this chap the other day and his wife is one of the commissioning editors for the new UK Conde Nast Traveller. Apparently, they've taken on some truly terrible writers and she's just beginning to realise this, so this might be exactly the right time to approach them with some ideas. The vital point here is that I'm not trying to pressure you or anything: I'm getting the flat anyway—'

'Jerry! Stop! You're doing my head in!'

There was a deep sigh down the phone. 'I just want you to come back. Sometime. In your own time. I want to see you. I want to start having fun with my wife. Somehow we've missed out on that in the last few months.'

'Well,' Nina took a deep breath. 'You're right. We should see each other. There's too much at stake for us to keep flouncing out on each other. That much I have realised. When do you suggest?' Too late she remembered Project Yalta. 'Although it'll have to be next week now.'

'Now don't start thinking that I am some sort of nutter, rabbit-boiler type,' said Jerry cautiously, 'but I'm actually parked outside your flat. So what about tonight?'

'You're what? Here? In Theberton Street?'

'Listen, I'll go if you're freaked out. Come back at a better time.'

Nina stood up and looked resignedly at herself in the mirror. Damp tendrils of black hair snaked fuzzily across her face and chest. A few vain licks of mascara were now streaked across her face. She had bloodshot eyes from staring so long at the computer screen and the dry skin of someone who's spent too many hours in the bath. Then again, as Beth had so charmingly pointed out, she was looking thinner.

'No,' she said dryly. 'No time like the present, I suppose.'

16

THURSDAY

'What is going on here?'

'Minister, I am merely giving you the opportunity to put your side of this extraordinary story. You are surely aware that there are allegations circulating on the Net about you, Mrs Blackthorn and the recently deceased Mr Frank—'

'Now look here, you jumped-up little Yank, you brought me here under totally false pretences and I will not stand for this. Oldtimers mood piece indeed. How you got past my secretary's vetting process, I will never understand, but I don't have to stay here listening to these trumped-up bits of slander and innuendo.'

Wilbur leant forward in his chair, uncomfortably aware of the electrified silence from his camera crew as they pretended to film all this. 'Minister, if you walk out of here, you'll be admitting your guilt. Within the next few hours, the media are going to be at your throat like a pack of wolves, turning over every last inch of your private life, your professional life, what kind of underpants you wear. That's the reality! Now, don't you want to put the record straight? OK, so maybe you're having an affair with Gwen Blackthorn, so what? You're divorced, she's widowed. Eventually the issue of overlap with her husband will be forgotten. You can even get married. But these Avalon-related allegations are a different

445

ballgame and you know it! Any whisper that either you or she are connected to lottery corruption and you both kiss that by-election goodbye, and you junk your ministerial responsibilities. Two political careers over,' Wilbur snapped his fingers, 'like that. Do you want that? Do you want that? Labour have a week to win that by-election? Is it fair to send them into a by-election with a flawed candidate, when you know perfectly well that with an untainted candidate, even with just a week to go, you could still win?'

Alun stood up and removed his microphone. 'You know, you're right,' he said quietly. 'I just want it all to be over. The whole bloody shooting match. Look do me a favour, Wilbur, son, give me a few hours on this, OK? I promise, you'll be the first to know. But can you scrap all that bellowing you just did? Not that it wasn't great, soul-stirring stuff,' he quipped weakly.

Wilbur nodded and held out his hand. 'I don't have a problem with that. Eric, scrap all that, will you?'

Eric the cameraman nodded bemusedly, knowing perfectly well that there was no tape in the camera anyway.

Alun started to gather together his papers, moving, Wilbur noticed, like an old man. 'Would you think me out of line if I said something to you?' he asked him.

Alun snorted. 'What, worse than all this stuff you've already bombarded me with? No, go on. Hit me with your best shot.'

'I don't know what the truth of all this stuff is, and I know my experience of British politics could be written on a pinhead, but in my opinion, for what it's worth—'

'Wilbur, get to the point,' Alun joked wearily. 'You vain bastard – you're much more incisive when the camera's on you, aren't you?'

'I just don't think you should let someone else's error of political judgement pull you both down.' Wilbur stated baldly. 'The City would lose a fine Minister, through no fault of his own. You know and I know that if Gwen Blackthorn dropped out of the by-election and junked her own political aspirations, this whole storm in a teacup would just leak away undisturbed.'

Alun looked at him quizzically. 'You've never met Gwenny, have you, Wilbur?'

*   *   *

'Alun Blythe's office.'

'Cass, can you speak? It's Wilbur.'

'Yup, sure can, once I've finished this particularly chewy candy one of Alun's constituents just sent him a box of. How did the interview go?'

'Look, we may have a problem – I think Alun's ready to fold, but I don't think he's going to bring Gwen down with him.'

'What? But that's crazy! If he believes our stuff well enough to step out himself, he must believe that it's only a matter of time before she gets toppled herself.'

'I know. I just think he's scared to be the one to tell her to pull out.'

'Christ – and people call *me* a ball-breaker! Well, the only thing we can do is tell Hallie and just hope that she can psych him up into doing it. I'll ring her right now.'

'OK, see you on the roof terrace at three.'

'Yep. Oh, and Wilbur?'

'Yes?'

'Sorry, about falling asleep on you last night.'

'Don't worry, you looked just as beautiful and life was a lot more peaceful! Anyway, your grandmother and I set the world to rights.'

'Yeah, so I heard. You pressed the right buttons there, didn't you, you charming bastard? Got her eating out of your hand bigtime. You are truly unbelievable. Is there anyone you haven't managed to work your magic on?'

'You, apparently,' Wilbur said challengingly, and hung up.

Cass stared at the phone. What did that mean?

For the first time in her life, Hallie discovered what it felt like to have the blood drain from your face, to have your stomach go into freefall and your limbs convulse, and yet still be able to talk normally.

'Engaged?! Gosh! Reuben! That's fantastic! Congratulations!' The words came out of her like bullets, burying themselves bloodily in the corpse that had been Hallie Templeton. 'When?'

'When are we getting married, or when did we get engaged?' Reuben laughed.

Someone was sticking sharp needles into her eyes. 'Both! Either! Gosh! How exciting! Married! Married!'

'Hallie, calm down, you're almost as excited as I am! OK, we're getting married in March because Helen used to be called the Mad March Hare by her father because she used to race around all the time with these enormously long legs and mad eyes.'

Hallie looked down at her own short bowling pins of legs. Mad March Hare. She could almost feel the impact of the machete as she swung it into this Helen's legs.

'And we got engaged last night, so you're one of the first to know!'

'First to know! Wow! Sweetie!' Even to her own buzzing ears Hallie could hear how mad she was beginning to sound. Last night, she had been out with Ted, idly wondering what it would be like to be a political wife. It seemed like another life.

'Yes, she proposed, ironically enough.' Reuben chuckled. 'All this time, I was running so scared of commitment and it turns out that all it needed was for someone else to take the initiative. And the first time she asked, I was so taken aback I said no, but then she walloped me, so I soon changed my mind, heh, heh, heh.'

Looking down, Hallie saw that she had drawn blood on both palms, five little crescents on each hand where her nails had dug in so deep. She held up one hand wonderingly. It looked so incongruous. Ten little smiles of blood, when she could never imagine recapturing the facial muscles necessary for smiling.

'—so I'm really sorry about that but I've obviously raved about you too much and Helen doesn't believe that men and women can be best friends, so she's just insanely jealous. It would be a pretty small wedding, anyway, you won't be missing much – Helen's always wanted just her very closest friends and family at her wedding. I'll be lucky if I'm allowed to invite Josh at this rate . . . Hallie? Are you still there?'

'Still here! But, you know! Busy! Busy! Busy! Gotta go!'

'Hallie, are you all right? You sound completely manic.'

'That's PR, eh? Manic! Gosh! Engaged! Reuben! So exciting!'

'It is, isn't it? Look, we'll have lunch next week when the

brouhaha has died down a bit and I'll tell you all about it. Just, you know, don't ring me, OK? Because Helen will go ballistic. I'll call you and we'll sneak off for a slap-up lunch, eh?'

'Lunch! Yes! Ring me! Byeee!'

Hallie just made it to the loo in time. She was sick five times.

Cass dialled with a shaking hand, candies now pushed to one side.

'Ted? Have you spoken to Hallie today?'

'No, not since last night. Why?'

'She's gone AWOL. Alun's turning up for the final act in just under two hours and Hallie's gone off the fucking air. And of course her fucking space cadet of an assistant hasn't a fucking clue—'

'Cass?'

'Yes?'

'Get a grip, will you? There's no point in everyone losing the plot. Where's Nina?'

'Holding the fort at Theberton Street just in case she shows up there and I've rung the vicar at Holy Trinity Brompton – hang on Ted, there goes the other line,' Cass came back almost immediately. 'It's OK. That was Trudie. She's turned up at St Luke's Avenue – totally out of it. Something about Reuben.'

'Reuben?' Ted's voice sharpened. 'Who's Reuben?'

Cass kicked herself. 'Someone in her family, I think,' she lied weakly. 'I'm not sure. But I'm going round there now. Can you call Wilbur and let him know what's going on. Say he has to make sure that Andy, Tamsin and Paul do their thing.'

'Okey-dokey. And remember, party at my place tonight. No excuses. No matter what the outcome of all this.'

'I'll be there. I'll be wrecked, but I'll be there.'

As soon as Cass put the phone down, she dialled again. 'Annalisa? One more favour! Meet me outside the tube station in five, will you? Look, it's important! Oh, and Annalisa, bring your friend, will you? You know, the one who really gets up my nose? Thanks. You're an angel.'

*   *   *

Trudie opened the door, her normally serene face worried. 'Darling, this is not good. She's a wreck. I've never seen her like this before.'

'If she's how I think she is, she hasn't been like this since we were twelve and that cat of hers was shot at by the next door neighbour's son. Target practice for his air rifle.' Cass kissed her grandmother. 'Boy, am I glad you were in, Granda, I dread to think where she might have gone next.'

They went upstairs and into the kitchen, where they found Hallie in tears, a smashed bottle of milk on the floor, hands bleeding where she was trying to pick up the shards of glass. Cass immediately went over to her, dragged her gently away and pulled her into her arms without a word.

'Fucking thing just dropped out of my hand! Fucking thing just dropped out of my hand! I mean, who still has milk delivered in this day and age? It's fucking insane.'

She wriggled away from Cass, looked up at Trudie's anxious face and continued to sob. 'Stop looking at me like that! Don't worry about me. I'm fine. I'm super fine. Super fine and dandy. I mean, I'm over him, aren't I? I've been saying that to myself every minute of every day of the last year but in the last couple of weeks I even began to believe it.' Her face crumpled even more and she sagged onto the floor. 'Engaged! But he can't be engaged?! I only slept with him two weeks ago. Eleven days ago he begged me to go out with him.' She looked up at them, her face clearing as quickly as a summer shower. 'He actually begged me to go out with him? And do you know what? I said no! I actually said no! Isn't that amazing? Me, Hallie Templeton, who has to beg men to go out with her.'

'Oh Hallie!' cried Trudie. 'That is simply not true!'

'No, it's OK, Trudie. I'm fine about it now. Because the point is that Reuben begged *me*, he really did, I'm not making it up. And I knew that the right thing to do was to say no, because I was over him. I knew that.' Now she looked like a confused child. 'Which is why he can't be getting married to someone else now. He just can't be. It simply doesn't make sense.' She smiled suddenly. 'That's it! I must have heard wrong. He's enraged! Enraged! Well, I would be too – this girl Helen sounds an absolute nightmare.'

Cass laughed out loud.

'That's funny, isn't it? Yes, I can be funny. Reuben says that I am a funny, quick-witted talented little thing.' She started to laugh too, but it soon turned to tears. 'Oh God, oh God, oh God, oh God – God, that's a laugh, no God, no God, no God—'

'OK, Halster,' Cass grasped her gently by the upper arms and tipped Hallie's head back so that she could look into her eyes. 'Time to go.'

'OK,' said Hallie obediently. 'Where?'

'Work. You have to go and work your magic on Alun now.'

'Oh no,' Hallie flipped a careless hand. 'I don't care about that.'

'Well, you should,' said Cass brutally.

'Cass!' cried a scandalised Trudie. 'How could you be so selfish?'

'Trudie, I love and respect you more than anyone else in the world,' Cass said, bundling her out of the kitchen, 'but no-one knows Hallie Templeton better than me or Nina. For once in my stupid blinkered high and mighty "I'm a gender consultant" life, I really know what I'm doing.'

'OK, darling,' said Trudie meekly. 'I'll be next door if you need me.'

Turning back into the room, Cass didn't say a word to Hallie but busied herself getting a small folded screw of paper out of her rucksack, getting out a credit card, tipping out some white powdery chunks onto the glass surface of the table. Ignoring Hallie completely, she concentrated fiercely on mashing the powder smaller and smaller, sometimes pressing down with the flat of the card, sometimes chopping with the sharp side of it. When she was satisfied that it was fine enough she subdivided it into smaller piles and started pushing them into lines with the credit card, sweeping motions to disperse the heaps into neat, straight-edged trails.

'What are you doing?' Hallie asked eventually.

'I'm preparing you some coke,' Cass said evenly.

'Why?'

'Because even though I know that you can do this standing on your head, you don't know it. Because even though I know that you are one of the strongest, loyallest, bravest people I have ever met, you don't know it. Because I know you're going to go back to that office and you're going to kick some serious butt in that way that only you can – with charm and persuasion and intelligence and insight – but you don't know that yet. Because even though I know that you would never, ever let down so many people's efforts, because I know how devastated you would be, you think you're going to go right ahead and let them down. Because you have the self-esteem of a sewer rat and the self-love of a scorpion in a ring of fire and if you're determined to go on being that blinkered and stupid and fucked-up, then I am ten times more determined to kick you up the ass and wake you up to yourself. Because I am sick and fucking tired of seeing you being fucked over by weak-minded assholes who don't have one tiny per cent of your personality, and I'm going to make you see that if it's the last fucking thing I do.'

Cass suddenly sprang forward and dragged Hallie to the mirror. 'You stupid, stupid woman. Just look at yourself. You are bright and beautiful and funny and wise and the best friend Nina and I have ever had and you can't see that.' She thumped her knuckles on Hallie's head. 'Because you're blind to yourself! You see so much good in everyone else, oh yes, every scumbag and toerag of humanity will get a kind word from Hallie Templeton, but when it comes to yourself, you're worse than Torquemada—'

Hallie turned to look at her friend. 'Cass, you're crying.'

'I am fucking not crying.' Cass dashed away her tears with the back of her hand, 'and don't try to change the subject. I'm just so, so, angry I can hardly see straight. I look at you here, dribbling over this Reuben guy, and I can feel my brain wanting to explode out of my skull, I'm so angry with you. Because I want to take trite phrases like "You'll get over him" and "He's not worth it" and I want to brand them with hot scalding irons in four foot letters all over you until maybe the pain you feel then will pop the bungs out of your ears and rip the scales from your eyes and make you see yourself for who you really are. And, and, and—' Cass ran out of breaths and words, leaning against the fridge in exhaustion.

Hallie, calm now, sat down at the kitchen table and looked

dispassionately at the serried rows of cocaine. 'OK,' she said eventually, 'and you think this stuff will – do what? Open my eyes, miraculously change me, something like that?'

'Nope,' admitted Cass. 'The coke's for me – to give me the courage and blarney to say these things to you. But,' she clenched her fists at Hallie, 'you just make me so goddamn angry, I guess I didn't need any artificial assistance. But you can have some if you want: it's nothing dramatic, just kind of gives you the blarney and confidence you sometimes need, allows you take a holiday from yourself for a few hours. Then again, since you've been taking a holiday from yourself for about fifteen years, maybe it's kind of coals to Newcastle.'

'I never knew,' marvelled Hallie.

'There's nothing to know – I don't take it regularly – about once every few months, and I got this stash from Annalisa ten minutes ago.' Cass shrugged. 'No biggie.'

Almost absent-mindedly, Hallie stuck her little finger into the end of one of the lines and stuck her finger into her mouth. 'Eeeeeugh,' she grimaced. 'Like Jif aspirin.'

Cass rolled her eyes. 'You're not meant to—'

'I know. I saw them do it on *This Life* a few weeks ago. Look, Cass, I'll make a deal with you. I'll get Alun out of your hair, if I can—'

'Of course you can'

'And don't think I haven't been listening, because I have. Every word. But for the next few days, I don't want to see you.'

Cass drew back as if she'd been stung.

'Don't react like that – you asked for it,' Hallie accused her. 'I need a few days to wallow, OK? He may not look like much to you, but I have been in love with Reuben Cathcart for every waking minute for nearly two years now, and I'm not just going to snap out of it just like that. I'm not going to have you walking all over me just because you think I'm some bloody project you have to rehabilitate, so you can just sod off and leave me alone for a bit!'

Cass looked at her and smiled.

'Better, Hallie, better already . . .'

Then she ducked, as Hallie threw an apple at her.

*   *   *

'Mr Blythe. Good of you to come in. We've spoken many times on the phone but we only met once, briefly, at Conference. I'm Hallie Templeton.'

'I remember you well,' smiled Alun wearily, stepping into the tiny purple conference room. 'You were being drooled over by Peter Mandelson the last time I saw you.'

Hallie laughed shortly. 'Yes. Perhaps I should have bottled it and then kept it as a memento of my Conference triumph.' She saw him looking at her enquiringly. 'A shuttle bus,' she told him, 'that's all I came up with to save the political day. Nothing more, nothing less. Not quite world peace, is it?'

Alun laughed out loud. 'You're a fraud. You're not in PR. You're too funny.'

Hallie almost wished she could summon up the energy to laugh with him. It was all she could do to keep her smile from slipping like a fried egg off a plate.

'Mr Blythe—'

'I'll walk out if you call me Mr Blythe,' he threatened.

'So how does "sir" grab you?'

He narrowed his eyes at her. 'Someone else said that to me, not so very long ago.'

'I'm sorry. I'm being frivolous. Alun, look, there is no easy way of saying this. As you know, B & P and Millbank appointed me their public relations director for this campaign and they have asked me to get you in here to persuade you to—'

'Drop out. I know. I saw that one coming a mile off. Well, I don't know about Gwenny. I haven't spoken to her. But you are very welcome to my resignation.' He folded his arms obdurately.

'Alun, I'm not the person you tell about that. I'm just a lowly peon. All I am concerned about is this by-election. Polling day is a week from today. We cannot afford to go into this last week with a candidate who is tainted with accusations of corruption and political cover-ups and we can't afford to waste any more time. We must make the changeover swift and sure, for the sake of Labour winning the election.' She looked at him steadily. 'You do agree that it is important that Labour win?'

Alun passed his hand tiredly over his brow. 'To be honest,

lass, I'm not sure I do. I just feel tired by the whole thing. This party isn't the party I joined, and it isn't the party I've served for over twenty years.'

Hallie was beginning to see why Cass had gone so spare on her. This wasn't going to be the walkover they had hoped for. 'So now you're in government – for the first time in nearly two decades, your party is back in government – now you're going to get tired and hopeless and weak and mewling? You total wimp!'

That got his attention. Alun's eyes snapped open and he leant forward angrily. 'How dare you? You can't speak to me like that! You're just a bit of a lass who doesn't know the first thing about politics. Bandwick and Parker? – tyuh! With your fancy-nancy purple walls and your boxy little suit and all your talk of being a "lowly peon". What do you know? In the last twenty-four hours I have been hounded, sneered at, laughed at, fingers pointed at me, set up by scheming tarts. I've had my private life splashed over a million computer screens, total strangers accusing me of being involved with lottery corruption, I've seen my dead best friend's memory blackened, and my girlfriend proven to be a two-faced cow, the media are about to have a field day at my expense – and you wonder why I'm not feeling bright-eyed, and bushy-tailed. Oh, just get back in your box, little girl, you can't dictate what I do or how I feel!'

'But Gwen Blackthorn can, can she?' Hallie asked quietly.

'Now don't you bring—'

'Bring her into it? No, we didn't, did we? We brought you in. Did you never stop to think why, Alun?'

He frowned.

'Why you, eh? When you're really nothing at all to do with the campaign. You're just helping, after all, nothing wrong with that, is there? You're in it of your own free will. As is Gwen Blackthorn. But you're not acting alone, are you? You've been railroaded into the whole thing by someone who is determined beyond anything else to get that seat. So determined, in fact, that had we brought her in instead of you, even if she had been armed with the same information as you, she wouldn't have offered her resignation, would she? She would prefer to go down fighting. She would have stained the whole first year of this administration, jeopardised a valuable Labour heartland and trashed the career of a Minister who is not only talented and well-liked but is one of the few with previous experience in government.'

Hallie leaned forward as well. 'One end result is going to be the same, Alun: Gwen will not be elected Member for Heptonstall. That's as plainly as I can put it. My bosses will have no compunction about letting her fall. Better before an election than after. She's a fighter so she would have no fears about going down in flames of glory. So we're giving you the choice, Alun. You can persuade her to drop out, you know you can: we wouldn't have bothered with this meeting if we didn't think you could do it. You know as well as I do that if she drops out today, the story dies in its tracks, justice has been done for Mrs Harrison and the honour of Frank Blackthorn is left undisturbed. You also know – and I hope you take this as the emotional blackmail it is intended to be – that if you were to resign today, whether Gwen does or not, that's still enough of a hook for news stories to be written and broadcast. Again, speaking plainly – a strange experience for someone trained in PR, let me tell you – the only way everyone comes out of this with the maximum amount of dignity and honour intact, is for Gwen to quietly leave the campaign – but for you, Alun Blythe, trusted local and Grand Old Man of the Party, to stay on – help the new candidate.'

'Ted Austin, I presume.'

Hallie nodded. 'If we can persuade the other short-listees that, with a week to go, Ted is really the only option. He's known locally, respected politically, a successful town councillor, born in the north, and just missed getting elected at the General Election so he has a track record.

'You can think of this as Mandelson donning his Prince of Darkness cape once again,' she went on, 'you can rail against the shadowy ugliness of behind-the-scenes politics, New Labour versus Old Labour – you can choose any label you like. You can bewail the passing of the good old party and the good old party ways. Of course the solution I have suggested suits the Party Executive's purposes – no conflicts, no scandals, our preferred candidate – so the accusation is fair enough. But give yourself the same scrutiny. Don't feel hard done by, and don't feel that Gwen has been hard done by. You slept with another man's wife. She was an adulteress. There's no getting away from that. She's not a criminal, she's undoubtedly a vital, entertaining, intelligent, highly ambitious woman who could still have a future in politics, and I hope she loves you as much as you love her, but I'm just asking you to question whether she would have been the good constituency MP she promises to be. Because the only reason she won't be elected is because she colluded in the humiliation and wrongful treatment of an innocent little old lady and left proof of it for all to see. Is that a worthy champion of your average Heptonstall resident?'

Hallie slumped back in her chair. 'I'm done. I'm sorry if I preached but I'm new to the political side of this game and I'm still foolish enough to care about the underlying reasons and motivations of all this shenanigans.'

Alun brought his gaze back from the middle distance, and almost smiled. Almost. 'You look nearly as tired as I do. I suppose this past day or so has been pretty tough on you as well?'

Hallie closed her eyes for a second. 'Yes,' she said bleakly. 'For different reasons, but, yes, it has.'

Alun was frowning at her again. 'You also remind me of someone. Someone of your age. With the same fire, the same crazy ideals. Someone else still foolish enough to care . . .'

Hallie met his stare warily. 'So what's it to be, Alun? Are you still foolish enough to care?'

To be busted at this stage would be downright representative of her day. She found she no longer cared. Already she was withdrawing into herself, to a place where she could lick her wounds.

Then he shook his head. 'No matter. It's not possible. Surely.' He watched her carefully. 'So, do you know Cass Herbert?'

Had it been a normal day and a normal Hallie, not a strained and distant-looking poor relation, sunk in misery, she would have undoubtedly jumped out of her skin when he said this. As it was, she had to pull herself with difficulty out of her tortured thoughts about Reuben and Helen to respond to him.

'Cass?' she said blankly. 'Cass Herbert? Your researcher? Yes

I know her. I've been in almost daily contact with her through this campaign.'

Her answer seemed to both satisfy and deflate Alun – as if this were his only last defence.

'Yes, of course you would,' he said softly. 'Now, pass me that phone.'

Cass was sitting on the best-kept secret in the Palace of Westminster. It was a roof terrace high above the House of Commons, reached by climbing up beyond the furthest reaches of Arthur's lift, swiping through a security door, and emerging onto a flat paved area between two rows of battlements. To the right was the oyster slickness of the River Thames, to the left the rooftops of Whitehall and the distant green smudges of St James's and Green Park. But, most dramatically of all, was the inbuilt lighting system – dark as it was, even now in the middle of the afternoon, she was bathed in the brilliance of Big Ben's West Face, a cream-cheese moon looming over her only fifty yards away. It was a dramatic sight and made the rooftop experience complete for Cass.

She was sitting alone. Nina and Ted were preparing for their party that night. Andy and Tamsin had long since gone home. Paul hadn't been needed in the end. Annalisa had vetoed the pleasures of sitting outside on a winter's afternoon. Hallie, of course, was at that moment determining the success of the whole plan. Wilbur was on his way. But Cass was content to be on her own for a while – it seemed a long time since she'd had a chance to burrow back into her own head.

Her outburst with Hallie earlier had shocked her as much as it had Hallie, but for different reasons. What had taken Cass's breath away was that she had felt strongly enough about Hallie to provoke that explosion of emotion. When she had rung Annalisa to ask her for the cocaine, she had done so in the conscious knowledge that forcing Hallie to see sense was what she should do, but that she couldn't without the inhibition-stripping effect of a couple of lines of blow.

For over a year now she had been very comfortably locked away in a refrigerator, insulated from the fire and chill of strong emotions. She had remained fixed in the certainty that, when it came down to it, it had been John's intense and frustrated love for her that had killed him, so she had shut herself down to prevent the same happening to her. She wasn't under any illusions: she knew that eventually she would have to come out, but in the meantime she derived a strange comfort from her inability to feel pain or joy, and came in time to refer to it mentally as rather her *invincibility*.

When she had given thought to when and how this cryogenic period would end, she had assumed that it would be a man who would melt her defences. Wilbur had come so close to doing so but it had taken her friendships with Hallie and Nina to get the meltwater flowing. That had surprised her. She thought back to how she had regarded them when she came back from the States: fondly, indulgently, a little condescendingly. Yet this morning's performance had contained none of those soft sloppy words: instead she had been angry, cruel, aching, ready to fight for Hallie tooth and claw. She had thawed, not through joy but through pain.

Now she was waiting to see if she would like feeling vulnerable again. She was waiting to see if she would enjoy being in love. She was waiting—

'Hey, Cass.' Wilbur materialised out of the darkness of the staircase. 'I'm late. I'm sorry. Any news yet?' He sat down beside her on the bench and gently flicked a piece of hair out of her eyes.

Cass caught her breath. Just that one casual gesture had provoked a visceral response deep within her. Forget the refrigerator. Suddenly she had remembered what it was like to feel possessed, bushfired, lost to lust. Irrepressibly, a grin started to spread from ear to ear.

'What are you smiling at?' He couldn't help but smile back at her.

'Nothing. Everything.' She beamed at him. 'No news yet, but Hallie was at least functioning when I left her there.'

'Where is everyone else?'

She explained.

'So we're all alone?' He grinned wickedly at her. 'For about the first time ever. Hmmm, what shall we do?'

She grinned back. 'You know you dropped that provocative little comment earlier about how I was the only one you hadn't managed to work your magic on?'

'Yes?' She heard him take an inward gasp and hold it there. Just a tiny betrayal of his tension but it was enough.

She turned to him and brought his face to hers. When they were a gossamer thickness apart, she stopped. 'Liar,' she breathed. And kissed him.

'Does that mean what I think it means?' he mumbled not a little incoherently into her lips.

Cass threw her head back and laughed her huck, huck, huck laugh. 'Boy, you're a cagey bastard,' she said exasperatedly. 'What do you want, for Chrissakes– a chequered flag?'

'I thought you'd never see the green light,' he growled, leaning over and kissing her properly. 'Oh my good God,' he gasped, 'at last!'

Ten minutes later, things were getting seriously out of hand. Well, into hand – as Cass got to grips with her newly rediscovered sex drive. It was becoming sordid, messy, hysterical and thoroughly exhilarating. Cass had nothing but her coat on while Wilbur was still nominally in his trousers. Both of them were nearly fainting with a combination of cold, pleasure and the realisation of every expectation – when Cass's phone rang.

'Where?' panted Cass. 'Is it?'

Helpless with giggles, they scrabbled around in their clothes until they found the phone.

'H-h-hello?' said a breathless Cass.

'Yes?'

'Yes!' Cass jumped on the table and struck an exultant pose. It was an image that was to be burnt forever into Wilbur's mind's eye, as he lay across the table looking up at her. The woman he loved, clad in nothing but an overcoat and a pair of knee high boots, her naked slimness cast into dramatic chiaroscuro by the light from Big Ben, her arm flung to the sky with fist clenched and her face alight with triumph and sex.

'No!'

'No fucking way!'

'I don't believe it! Wait, I have to tell Wilbur! What? Yes, we're up on the roof. No, no-one else. What do you mean?'

She flashed him an outrageous smile, as he slid his hand right up her thigh. 'Of course we are. What did you think? Love, politics and an outrageous location – talk about an aphrodisiac combination! Yes, we'll come to the party.'

She knelt down and kissed him while she listened. 'Yes, don't worry, we'll come. Just much,' she purred, lying down so that every inch of her length was pressed against his, 'much' she looked up at him wickedly as her hand wandered lazily towards the top of his gaping open jeans, 'later.' And with that she finally pressed END.

'Or maybe sooner!' gasped Wilbur, as her hand found the way back into his trousers.

'Come again?' laughed Cass.

'Gimme a chance!'

Tossing her phone to one side, she narrowed her eyes at him and started to peel off his trousers. Suddenly she laughed again. 'If the founding fathers of Parliament could only see us now! Having sex above the heads of the greatest political minds of the country. What a buzz!'

'How you can say that they're "great" when you've just managed to fool one of the more incisive amongst them is beyond me. Anyway,' Wilbur grumbled, 'shut up, will you?' He sat up and helped her to take off his shoes and socks. 'So we're having sex, are we? Is that a good idea? So soon?' He suddenly sounded nervous.

Cass sat up and kissed him for a long, long minute. 'There,' she said confidently, 'has that convinced you? Of course it isn't a good idea. You'll think I'm a loose woman, sleeping with you on our first real date and you'll have lost the thrill of the chase. You'll abandon me for some worthy Ballet Rambert type and I'll sink into an early grave, with a headstone paid for by a shamefaced Coolidge Clan. We would be crazy to fuck each other immediately. So let's do it! Fuck sensible! Let's have fun.'

Wilbur gathered her into his arms for a bone-crushing hug. 'Love you, even if you talk way too much,' he said gruffly.

Cass wrinkled her nose. 'They have just got to invent a new word, haven't they? But, ditto, you sentimental old fool. Now it's your turn to shut up – we'd better make this good! If we admit to our grandchildren that we made love on the roof of the House of Commons, we need to create something to boast about!'

'Just let me know when I can start boasting!' joked Wilbur weakly.

'Oh!' murmured Cass after a while. 'Now . . . now . . . now . . .'

When now had become later, they curled up together on Wilbur's leather jacket and under Nina's overcoat, totally replete and obnoxiously pleased with themselves.

'So?' murmured Wilbur eventually. 'What did Nina have to say?'

'Oh! I forgot to tell you! It's totally incredible. Hallie has pulled off the most amazing coup. She got Alun to make the call. Gwen Blackthorn has dropped out of the running, citing delayed shock and nervous exhaustion from Frank's death—'

'Ouch,' he winced. 'That's a tad hypocritical, wouldn't you say?'

Cass considered it. 'No, not really,' she said finally. 'I think she genuinely did love Frank, God only knows why, because he was a sexist jerk with a beard, and it probably was a shock when he died. I mean, people can be in love with two people at the same time.'

Wilbur biffed her gently on the chest. 'Try that. You die.'

'Likewise, buster, likewise. No, but the best news is yet to come. They've already announced that Ted is the chosen candidate which must mean that the rest of the shortlist just immediately caved in and – hold onto your hat! – guess who is helping him on his campaign, such as it is in a week.'

'No way!' he gasped.

'Way! The Minister for the City of London himself – Mister Alun Blythe! Come on down! Aw-right, Hallie!'

'That girl is amazing,' Wilbur marvelled. 'What could she have said to him? Truly amazing.'

'Yeah, and one of these days she's going to wake up and realise it!'

17

Hallie looked around with pride. It hardly seemed possible that all this could have been achieved in a week and yet part of it was due to her, Hallie Templeton, Campaign Director, Bandwick & Parker. In a week so busy she hadn't had time to remember to think about Reuben, let alone have time to wallow, as she had insisted to Cass, Hallie had helped to arrange rallies and flatbed trucks decked in red bunting and red-T-shirt-wearing supporters singing ad infinitum, but with passionate vigour, *Things Can Only Get Better*. She had recruited their Forest Mere linedancing teacher to come up for a fundraising barn dance (local party workers, some still disgruntled by Gwen's departure had stood mouths agape, as Ted and Hallie had led the line).

When Ted's candidacy had been announced, they had been swamped by offers of help from younger volunteers chuffed to be enfranchised at last, so they in turn had flooded the Shopping Centre for an entire weekend, turning the normally dour collection of hassled mothers and bored pensioners into a bemused-looking party. Ted had been in his element all week, carried along by the collective high of the campaign, showing a chameleon quality for coming off to his best advantage whether in a working men's club or the local crèche. Hallie had especially laughed here – Ted had not pretended to want to kiss any of the babies but had looked around with such an expression of bemused terror that all the mothers promptly fell in love with him.

Nina had been the real surprise. Calling herself Nina Parvati once more, she had hurled herself into the campaign, designing and writing flyers, canvassing like a whirling dervish, lighting up every group she briefly touched upon, her once-hated difference of colour just a variation on the abundance of shades amongst their workers. Even the old Blackthorn workers, grumbling into their tea and biscuits about newfangled Ted sweeping in at the last moment – even they loved Nina. 'Right nice lass,' was the understated but heartfelt conclusion of all. Ever since the inception of Project Yalta she had seemed somehow lit up, giddy, as if she'd moved out from under a cloud and, much as Hallie had wanted to wallow in her own misery, her sudden happiness had been damnably infectious.

One whose happiness had been clouded temporarily, had been Cass. Going back to St Luke's Avenue with Wilbur after Ted and Nina's party the night of the completion of Project Yalta, they had found Trudie passed out on the kitchen floor. Having taken her to hospital, the consultant had taken them into a private room. 'It would appear,' he had said sternly, 'that this was provoked by the ingestion of cocaine.'

Wilbur and Cass had gaped at each other.

'Are you aware that your grandmother is a drug-user?' he had asked.

'No,' Cass insisted. 'Not at all. No idea.' But she was lying, of course, she had a very good idea.

Sure enough an unrepentant Trudie, when they went to see her the next day, had confessed. 'Well, you'd just left it lying there!' she protested. 'And I suppose it would be a little hypocritical to ask why it was there in the first place, but, you know, I've never tried it, so I thought it might be rather fun.'

'Heap big fun,' Wilbur had commented dryly, 'although, cushy hospital. How much did you have?'

Trudie had looked shifty. 'I'm not sure. Maybe four of those little lines. Maybe five.'

Wilbur and Cass had burst out into horrified laughter.

'Well, I kept thinking that something more dramatic was going to happen than just a fizzing up my nose and a bit of numbness.

You know, darlings, pink elephants and all that jazz. It was all rather disappointing. It was only later that I started to feel a bit peculiar. Then I must have passed out.'

'I think I would have had a stroke if I'd had five lines at once,' Cass had choked. 'Trudie, you were goddamn lucky not to have one yourself.'

'Yes well, moderation gets rather pointless when you're in your seventies – why hold back? And, really, what a lot of fuss,' Trudie had grumbled. 'Policemen, the works. I may have to have some sort of caution. Absurd.'

Trudie's collapse did at least seem to have slowed her down. She was now admitting that working at the Crisis Centre and for the Samaritans for all the hours she could spare, was perhaps not such a sensible course of action for someone in their late seventies. The trouble was, Cass confided to Hallie and Nina, it just left her with time on her hands to interfere in the emotional affairs of those closer to her. Now, whenever she quizzed them about their relationship prospects, Wilbur and Cass got their own back by calling her Truly Medellin.

But they had made it here tonight and Hallie couldn't even bring herself to feel jealous. She and Cass had talked for hours on the telephone over the past few days, breaking Hallie's self-imposed rule of isolation from Cass and Cass had told her all about her emotional fridge period. Hallie was of the opinion that she was now in one of these herself – she couldn't pretend that Reuben was anything less than an agonising bruise, but she was calmer now, more sure of herself. At least, for the moment.

Cass on the other hand could've powered Eastern Europe such was her radiance. It was only a week into their relationship but already there was a relaxed excitement around them that boded well for the future, Hallie mused. She and Wilbur were that rare sort of couple whom their friends wanted to be around – they weren't excluding or joined at the hip, they were just joined by an almost tangible rope of, as Cass had laughingly confessed to Hallie the other night, what they called fun and magic.

'Christ, Hal, who knows what will happen? We're both such emotional cripples, both so unused to trusting any-one else, that neither of us really knows what's going on.

But, hey, we're having fun figuring it out!' she had finished dreamily.

Suddenly, Hallie's reverie was interrupted.

'Hallie! Look, the Sycamores ballot boxes have come in now! Come on, let's go and see how we did!'

Hallie's gaze softened as she turned to face Ted. He wasn't a bombshell, wasn't Ted, but with his anxious eyes and glossy chestnut bob he was certainly dishy enough for her to pretend that she could still flirt. One of these days she would have to confess that she was in the emotional deep-freeze, but in the meantime she could almost imagine that she was having fun as they campaigned side by side and played side by side. So far their main courtship ground had been Sycamore Drive, Sycamore Avenue, Sycamore Hill, Sycamore Straight, Sycamore Road and a dozen different permutations thereof. 'Not one single sycamore,' Hallie had announced in disgust at the end of one day, her hands red raw from pushing flyers through doors, her feet falling off, her knees bruised from nudging closed a thousand garden gates. 'What do you mean?' Ted had laughed. 'They're all Sycamore! Every last bloody street round here!' She had rolled her eyes at him. 'No! Not one single sycamore tree! You'd have thought they'd plant a couple, just as a gesture, but no! Not one!' Now, watching them tip out the square metal boxes and sort them methodically into piles, Hallie began to feel the first warm fingers of excitement about the result.

With a candidate around for one week, no-one could hope for miracles, but within the Austin camp, morale was high. The unprecedented publicity surrounding Ted's arrival had helped enormously – as they had stood outside the polling stations that morning, Hallie had noticed that the other canvassers were often stopped to be asked what the name of their candidate was, whereas most Labour voters seemed to know Ted's name without having to ask. But more than that, it was the sense of excitement provided by them, the Yalta Five, as they called themselves in private, that had infected the whole campaign.

The only ugly moment could have been when Alun saw them all together for the first time. For a moment his careful smile had slipped and they had glimpsed an anger there at what he no doubt considered their meddling. Cass had told Hallie that a couple of nights ago, she had stayed up drinking with him and had come as close to discussing Project Yalta as they were ever likely to.

'Unbelievable nerve,' he had snapped, when she tentatively opened the subject. 'None of you had the faintest idea what you were doing. You played fast and loose with the people of Westminster, none of whom would have had anything to do with it if you'd let them in on your real objective.' He had glared at her. 'I presume you lied to them – made up some cock and bull story about a practical joke – that sort of thing. You corrupted the political process, abused all your real jobs beyond belief – and yes, you are fired – and made a mockery of everything the Labour Party used to stand for.'

Then he paused. 'I can't trivialise the underhandedness of the whole tawdry little scheme. But you, Hallie and Wilbur, at different times, made me realise that you were doing it for the right reasons. You weren't just mucking about. Except for Annalisa – now that was a low trick. And in a funny way, the only way it could have worked – your ingeniously stupid little plan – was in the hands of political babes in the woods like yourselves. Anyone with the remotest understanding of the Houses of Parliament just would not have done all that. The only really clever part was all that computery business. One of these days you must take me through that and show me how you did it.'

'But I thought I was fired,' she had asked innocently.

'You are,' he grumbled, 'Mags would literally knife me if I took you back. But we might have to see if we can't put you to work on, say, a freelance basis – perhaps over at the Ministry. From your point of view, you should always have been there – much more useful for your business.'

Cass, she had confessed later to Hallie, had muttered something noncommittal at this point. Hallie guessed that Cass was finding it a little hard to concentrate on the next stage of the How to Rule the Planet plan, now Wilbur the Meteorite had crashed in.

Only Annalisa had remained as the joker in the pack. They had got one thing right: she wasn't a political player, but when she found out about Cass and Wilbur, she had been so insanely, furiously jealous that she had threatened to go to the press with everything she had – the Brighton orgy, the details of the Plan such as she knew them – saying that she wasn't going to parade her wares just so that Cass could cop off with a jerk like Wilbur. Cass had briefly come down to earth, had taken a deep breath and said that she was off to work the Hallie Treatment on her, judging that no-one had ever cared enough about Annalisa to sit her down and tell her some home truths.

Afterwards, she wouldn't even tell Wilbur what they had talked about but had appeared, pale and worn-out, saying only that she didn't think Annalisa would now be endangering Project Yalta and adding, with a sort of relief, 'Christ, I thought I was fucked up until I talked to that girl. Now all we have to do is scratch together some money to send her on a holiday for a month, because she's blown all her cash, so to speak. Oh,' she smiled wearily, 'and we have to have her round to dinner when she gets back. Introduce her to some *nice* guys.'

'Hallie,' she looked up to see Mark, Mandelson's sidekick, standing there, along with her big boss Kathryn, both of whom had come up for the count, 'a word please.' Roland had been left behind, much to Hallie's glee.

Her heart quailed. If they had found out about Project Yalta then she was signing on the dole on Monday for sure. She followed them into a corner of the school hall where the count was taking place.

'We just wanted to say – job well done,' beamed Mark. 'You have cut your political teeth magnificently. Rest assured that from now on you can name your team.'

'What?' Hallie gasped.

'Roland has, er, decided to pursue other interests,' said Kathryn smiling. 'So you are now my right-hand woman on public affairs.'

'And we will be making a point of retaining your services for various projects, on an ad hoc basis,' Mark had added. Then he had smiled mischievously. 'Although perhaps your definition of ad hoc is rather wider than ours . . . next time we ask for a cheap quiet election campaign, perhaps you won't have to follow quite such a cunning route, eh, Hallie?'

Hallie blushed the sort of blush that would have given them away for sure if Alun had pierced her defences that day.

'And ascribing views to our political masters that are not necessarily accurate – even if well-intentioned – can set dangerous precedents,' he had gone on, 'so next time, perhaps not quite such an all-encompassing use of the party executive "we", Hallie, and definitely no fake librarians and journalists. OK?'

Hallie opened her mouth to ask where they had got their information and closed it again. They would never tell her. 'OK,' she agreed, smiling.

'You can go now,' said Kathryn kindly as she watched Hallie hover. 'I imagine you will be wanting to tell Ted your good news. Ah, just think of the political dynasty you two could create . . .'

'Don't even start,' Hallie had warned her, surprising herself with her boldness. 'Otherwise I'll set the rest of my political hounds on you. And look what happened when we did that last time!'

Once released, she bounded up to Cass and Nina, who were watching the count with a hypnotised intensity.

'Big promotion,' she boasted. 'Big. Huge.'

'How much?' asked Cass, who was still in debt and deeply envious of Hallie's ability to balance her chequebooks.

Hallie looked nonplussed. 'Do you know, I didn't ask!'

'Doh!' laughed Cass.

'You can talk,' Hallie defended herself. 'What's your next Big Plan?'

'Well, you know,' meandered Cass, 'finish—'

'Your dissertation!' chorused the other two.

'That strain, it hath a repeating fall,' misquoted Nina.

'—and, well, live for the moment. That sort of deal.'

'In other words,' sighed Nina, 'go wherever Wilbur's going.' She pretended to whack Cass about the head. 'Girl, have we taught you nothing?!'

'I'm still going to rule the world,' Cass insisted. 'Just not quite . . . yet. I'm bored of being Miss Driven, I might try being Miss Park for a while. Anything wrong with that?'

'Nope,' said the other two. 'Nothing at all.'

'I, on the other hand, know exactly what I'm going to do,' crowed Nina, her dark eyes flashing. 'I have been grown-up for far, far too long. While you lot were flapping through your

Twenties, I had leapt ahead to the Fifties. Well, not any more. I'm off!'

'What do you mean, you're "off"? Off where?'

'Round the world. In lots and lots of days. In as juvenile and backpackery a way as possible. I am going to lie about my age, get my bellybutton pierced, get sold into white slavery in South America, become a gangster's moll in Russia, open up a henna tattoo stall in Sri Lanka—'

'Yeah, yeah, we get the message,' laughed Cass. 'Well, good on you. But what about Jerry? Dare I ask?'

'Yes, you dare, actually,' said Nina. 'We saw each other last week, talked until three in the morning, shagged until seven, and ended up closer than we have been for, well, years.'

'What?' cried the others.

'So how come you're going off travelling?'

'It was a combination of an idea Jerry had, a proposition put to me by Steve – which I refused, but which planted the seed – and the incredibly fucking mature realisation by both of us that a quick-fix solution like a right good bonking, was not going to do it for us. So Jerry is going to let me go off for the first three months, while he sorts out a sabbatical with Kellman's, then I'm going to call him up, say "Pack your bags, boyo," and then he's going to join me for however long he can screw out of the family firm. Then, all being well, we re-discover ourselves and our marriage and the world out there, at the same time as having to slum it to such an extent that we'll be fucking grateful to come home to our lovely new flat in Hammersmith.'

'Sounds like the sort of Mills and Boon fantasy that might work,' marvelled Cass, 'except for the slumming it part. You're too spoilt by the Club Class five-star lifestyle of the travel writer, Nin, I can't see you returning to the student days of backpacking. Then again, maybe it is time you found out just how horrible, smelly, dirty and cockroachy travel can be. What do you reckon, Hallie?'

Hallie's lip quivered. 'I'm not sure actually. As long as you're not going to *find* yourself.'

'How could I? I am an irreparably lost cause.'

'Ho, ho,' said Hallie tremulously. 'It's just that the last couple of months have been such incredibly intense times for the three of us that it seems a shame that we can't reap the whirlwind for a bit. You know, we weren't really friends for many of those years that we thought we were, but now that we are, why suddenly abandon ship?'

'What do you mean – now that we are really friends?' scorned Nina, her nose wrinkled. 'Hallie, I didn't want to say this but you really get on my tits – in fact, that's why I'm going. Sorry, didn't want to tell you, but I can't stand to be in the same hemisphere as you.'

'Fine,' sniffed Hallie. 'Fuck you!'

'Hallie!' chorused the other two, shocked beyond belief.

'You're swearing now?! Cass, it's our pernicious influence, this is terrible.'

'If I knew what pernicious meant, I could confirm or deny it. No,' Hallie was enjoying the effect she had had. 'Still not really swearing. Just on special occasions.'

'And this sure is a special occasion,' smiled Cass. Hallie watched her eyes wander over the crowd, until they found Wilbur. If they could harness the energy between them, she thought admiringly, then the power stations were out of a job.

'Hallie, can I ask a favour?' Ted was back. 'Will you come up on the stage with me. No proposal intended, it's just that the others have all got their partners and agent up there – and I've got neither, except for you – and you're, well, kind of a, sort of a—'

'Hello, point, where are you?' Hallie teased.

'—well, a combination between the two, aren't you? Sort of. Ish.'

'Ted, I'd love to come up there. Watch and learn, girls,' she said over her shoulder, 'impeccable Lady Penelope/Lady Muck impression coming right up.'

Which is how, ten minutes later, Hallie found herself clutching Ted's shaking hand on stage, listening to the counting officer drone to the end of the results. She knew the results, he knew the results, she just prayed that he'd be able to stay conscious for everyone else to find out the results. Honestly, she'd never met such a nervy individual. He made her feel positively strong.

'. . . forty-five thousand three hundred and sixty nine votes.

I hereby declare that Edward Albert Austin is elected Member of Parliament for Heptonstall.'

The room erupted. Beside her, Hallie felt Ted sway. She turned to him, propped her hand under his elbow and said sternly, 'Do not faint! You can't faint! You'd crush me!'

Down in the crowd, Nina and Cass looked at each other.

'Six months,' said Nina.

'Nah, a year,' said Cass conservatively.

'Just try and make it happen while I'm away, would you?' asked Nina. 'If it doesn't work out with Jerry, I definitely could not cope with being a bridesmaid. Not even for Hallie.'

Cass said nothing, but squeezed her friend's hand until Nina yelped. 'Nina,' sighed Cass, 'you cannot go round the world as a hypochondriac. We're going to have to toughen you up before you go.'

'Sounds like you're going to make me into beef jerky!' joked Nina.

The crowd was shushed.

Just as he was always meant to do, Ted stepped up to the microphone, flicked back his hair and started the speech he had written six months before.

'I am proud to have won this election for the people of Heptonstall, for Tony Blair and for the new Labour government,' here his gaze flicked to Hallie, then to the rest of the Yalta Five, and he departed from the script, 'and for the friends without whom I would never have got here.' He flashed them a huge smile and carried on. 'Don't go thinking of me as the Member for Heptonstall. Groucho Marx had it right with that well-known remark, "I don't want to join any club that would have me for a member . . ."'

THE END